BUTTERFLY CONFIDES©

BOOK FOUR
of the
SECRET BUTTERFLY SERIES™

A Novel by

Rosemary Lightfoot Ness-Bitner

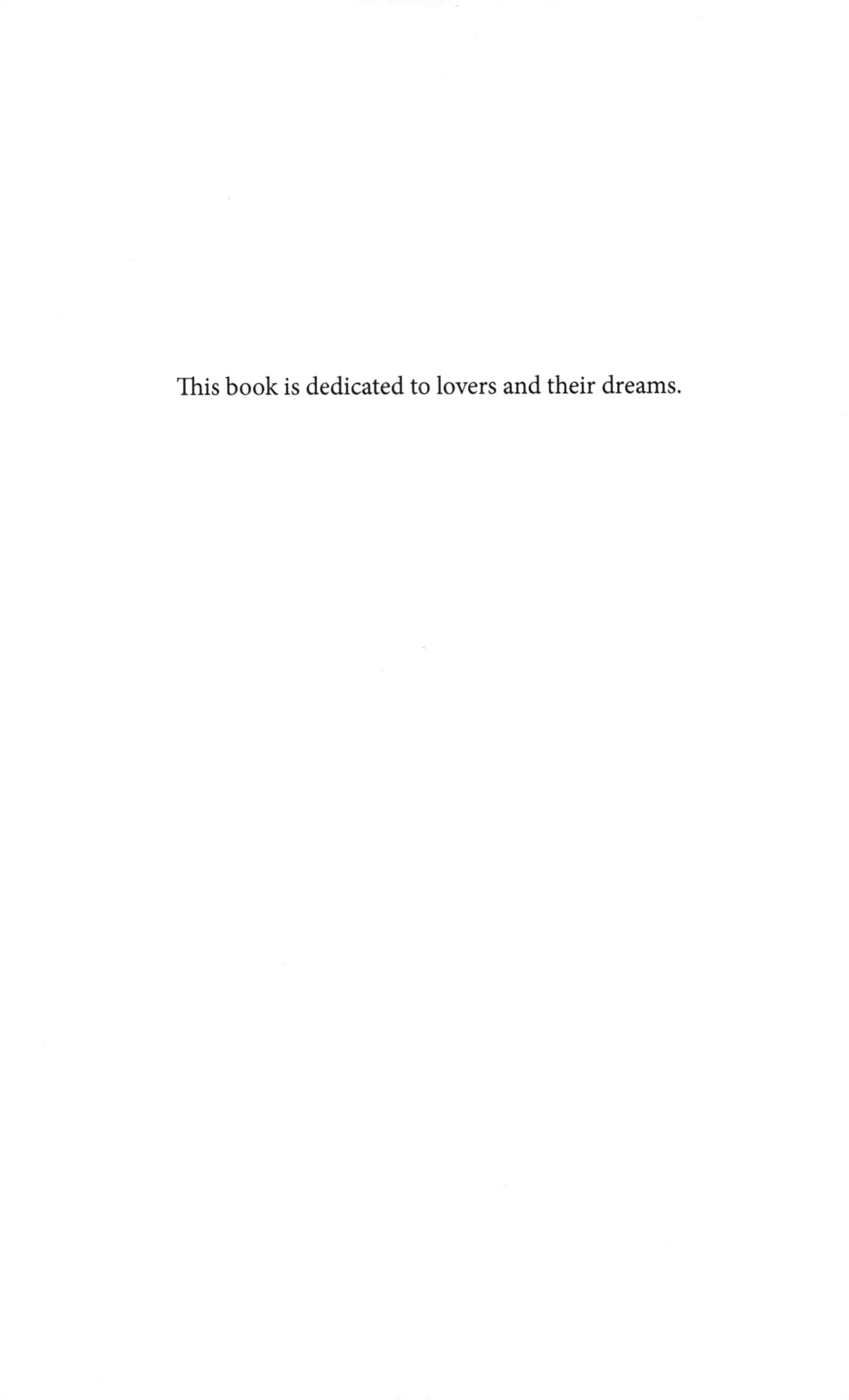

This book is dedicated to lovers and their dreams.

The eBook and print version layouts of BUTTERFLY CONFIDES were done by Andrea Reider; the cover was created by Cheeky Covers; and I am Melanie Monarch, your audio book narrator.

Hello dear listeners. This is Melanie Monarch, your audio narrator, bringing you BUTTERFLY CONFIDES, our fourth book of THE SECRET BUTTERFLY SERIES ™. Will David keep Marty in the company after he hears of her love for Josh and Marshawn? What is it about David that makes Marty feel comfortable enough to reveal her sexual seduction secrets to him? How will David feel about hearing her escapades after he hears her tell him what she revealed to Bertie and George? Notice how David probes Marty. Does he really care to understand her thoughts?

Is he probing because he's intrigued by her promiscuous ways? Perhaps he's thinking of ways to help make their murders more pleasing; or might he be asking his questions for an altogether different, hidden reason? Perhaps Dolly, David's curious black sheep knows the answer; but of course, Dolly never says a word.

Does David think of himself as a business Chief Executive, or does he see himself more as a secretive maestro, managing dysfunctional personalities to his own advantage? David is a bizarre personality. He's among the most complicated characters you'll ever encounter. Don't ignore anything he says or does; and don't assume you have him figured out.

SECRET BUTTERFLY SERIES ™ CHARACTERS (MAJOR CHARACTERS ARE BOLDFACED)

Readers reference guide to where a character is introduced.

(CHARACTER, DESCRIPTION OF CHARACTER, AND CHAPTER WHERE CHARACTER IS MENTIONED)

BUTTERFLY CONFIDES (BOOK FOUR)

TERAH, FATHER OF ABRAHAM (ABRAM) AND SARAH (SARA), SARA'S LOVER, BUTTERFLY CONFIDES (BC) CH1

ABRAHAM, BROTHER OF SARA, FATHER OF JUDIASM, ISLAM, AND CHRISTIANITY, PIMP AND LOVER OF SARA (BC) CH1

SARAH (SARA), MARTY'S REINCARNATION, SISTER AND LOVER OF ABRAM, MOTHER OF ISAAC, JUDIASM, ISLAM, AND CHRISTIANITY, PROSTITUTE (BC) CH1

HAGAR, THREESOME PARTNER WITH ABRAM AND SARA, MOTHER OF ISHMAEL (BC) CH1

EGYPTIAN PHAROAH AND PRINCES, CONSORTS OF SARA (BC) CH1

KING OF GERAR, SMITTEN, LOVER OF SARA (BC) CH1

EVE, MARTY'S REINCARNATION, SEXUAL EXPERIMENTOR WITH CUNNILINGIS, FREEDOM SEEKER (BC) CH1

MARSHAWN, MARTY'S LOVER, PORN PARTNER (BC) CH4

AALIYAH, MARSHAWN'S JILTED WIFE (BC) CH4

GWENDOLYN, BILLIONAIRRESS LESBIAN, LOVER OF MARTY, (BC) CH3

RAVENS, SPIRIT BIRDS (NOT THE FOOTBALL TEAM), AFFICIANADOS OF MARTY'S PROMISCUITY, (BC) CH5

HAROLD, COLLEGE STUDENT, POET, MARTY'S OBSESSED LOVER, (BC) CH5

BUTTERFLY CONFIDES©

CHAPTER ONE

And her smile, it seems half holy, as if drawn from thoughts more far than our common jestings are. And if any poet knew her, he would sing of her with falls used in lovely madrigals (Elizabeth Barrett Browning: A Portrait)

Why conjure evil within minds' gates? What pandemics might these labs create? Who trusts their soul to conflicted mates? Who crushes fools' belief in fate? (Rosemary Ness-Bitner)

METHODS AND MINDSET

Marty perfected every aspect of her business methods. She fine-tuned her beautifying makeup to match her scenes; exactly placed the coifing's of her locks; selected only the most scintillating, deliciously revealing apparel; chose only the most intriguing accessories and the most alluring, pheromone stimulating scents. She rehearsed mercilessly to capture the most seductive intonations which she voiced in her expressions while filming. She even practiced her body movements; the manner in which she walked, seated herself and rose up from a chair. All these things and her facial expressions were meticulously bundled to fine tune her seduction signaling techniques.

She finely tuned her sensory receptors to gather and process her porn partners' signals so that she could amplify her initiations and responses for the cameras. Her drive to become the world's top porn star did not stop there. She also concentrated on the intense physical demands of her profession. She mastered her vaginal muscle control and improved her physical stamina. She exercised religiously and strictly monitored her sleep and dietary needs. She became expert at her stimulation placements; and consciously practiced until she perfected her coordination with her partners' responses; even pairing her orgasm timings with her partners' ejaculation releases. And, she fastidiously studied the subtle psychological signals of her male and female partners, on screen and off.

Her life obsession became a shameless never-ending quest to become the most highly desired, highly paid, sex object of all time. She thirsted for conquest of penis and coin; continually strived to perfect her trade craft; experimented endlessly with new eroticism methods. She quickly discarded themes that failed to measure up. Yet through this endless gauntlet of sex and sex-craft, Marty still searched and hoped to discover a true love that might possibly fill the void that she felt when she lost her father and became abandoned by her mother; and which void she still profoundly felt to this day.

She had recently achieved a measure of notoriety in the world of adult films. She had also broadened her highly selective outreach through her new Premium Membership service. Her porn star rankings had rocketed upward due to her latest film, an orgy fest with seven black partner performers. Her income was rising fast as well. She already earned more money than many corporate chief executives.

She relished every aspect of erotic film making: the provocative clothes; her acting roles as imaginary characters, whether baby sitter, nurse, teacher, housewife or any of a hundred others; the endless varieties of sex acts with handsome partners; love making before the filming crews and cameras; the details and preparatory work needed to create a successful film; the many variances of stimulations, foreplay, lubrications; and the precision placements of her copulating vagina for the best viewing entertainment experience while making love. She loved that ego boost feeling of empowerment when her sexuality and performance were complemented by a new partner; and especially the camaraderie of being with like-minded people who loved creating beautiful sex artistry. She had taken the advice of her newest shrink, Mrs. O' Dell, to heart. She had whole heartedly and enthusiastically made pornography and prostitution her career choice. The further she progressed along her career path, the more rewarding it was becoming; and the more she was enjoying her work. Now, she was firmly convinced that she had made the right choice for her life. She was, *'all in.'*

She mused:

'Had I known adult film making was so lucrative and enjoyable, I would have begun performing porn gigs immediately after graduating from WEX. With perseverance and success; and finding enough willing film partner-performers, I could have made a porn film each week and had an additional one hundred fifty films to my credit. I would have, by word of mouth, undoubtedly captured more members of my age group into my fan base and I might have launched my Premium Member services three years before I did. My only regret about my career path is that I bumbled around in dead end clerical jobs for three years before I discovered my passion and my niche. But I am undaunted. My beauty, attention to tradecraft, and my unabashed, infectious enthusiasm for sex already has me ranked among the porn industry's most famous stars.

'With Carl's hapless wife, my tactics of confrontation succeeded brilliantly. Going forward I will add them to my repertoire when pitted against similar narrow-minded women. Fred and Ed are only two of several lovers who are unquestionably committed to pleasing

me. I became mindful of Fred's wife's behaviors; her likes, dislikes, and her comings and goings. I pulled the rug out from under Petunia's feet and essentially ran the silly woman out of her home, her marriage, and her money. I quickly assessed what Ed wanted and gave him everything he needed. Now I am an item for both men!'

Like an adaptive predator that learns methods to capture a particular prey species, Marty's tactics were continually evolving. She was gaining confidence and successes, becoming bolder, more brazen; and more calloused and merciless. She refined her selection criteria; made lists of men most likely to succumb to her temptations; and concentrated on her most lucrative prospects.

She emotionally detached herself from the hazards Carl's wife faced that night. She practiced steeling her emotions until they numbed away all empathy for her victims. She had a very sensitive conscience; but it was sensitized to the needs of her suitors, never to the needs of the other women whom her lovers were entangled with. She asked herself:

'Did I tell Carl's wife to drive eight exhausting hours over mountain roads on a dark night? What kind of nut does that? Was it my fault that she put herself in the position of being the distraught wife? Did the fool expect me to care about her? I knew her guts were churning inside. I knew her heart was screaming in pain while I was crushing it. Did she honestly expect me to have pity on her for what I did to her life? Did she seriously expect me to step aside while she dragged Carl and his spectacular penis back home with her? Couldn't she see that I only saw her as a nuisance? She must have been crazed out of her mind to think that her ridiculous behavior would get Carl to leave me for her! She was such an idiot! No wonder Carl would rather be with me.'

Marty thusly dismissed the pitiful wife's travails as quickly as one forgets a witless ant that one crushed under foot. From Marty's perspective, Carl's wife was merely an inconsequential pest.

Her annoying life and theatrics at the cabin were just distractions that briefly interrupted Marty's delicious seduction weekend.

Poon listened as Marty casually continued her narrative with David:

"I decided from that moment onward I would set my own standards. I would put myself and my needs above everyone else's. An unbridled pride and a sense of wonder about my own self esteem emerged from deeply within my personality.

"I decided to have Carl all to myself. I told myself I deserved him. I insisted we stay at the lake for three days longer than we originally planned. We made sweet love for several precious hours each of those days. I made Carl continually prove his love for me. We went into town and visited the gift shops and jewelry stores. Carl bought me some nice silk blouses and a diamond bracelet. He was very sweet. I also wanted his wife to understand, if perchance she had shaken off my hypnosis and not taken aspirin and managed to live, that I could keep him away from her as long as I pleased; whenever I wished. I was determined to drive her insane, if she hadn't already killed herself.

"I knew all along I only wanted Carl for his sales. After all, David, you know I'm a loyal company girl and I always put the company first. You know you can count on that. After Carl's sales fell off and I started going on weekend trips with other men, Carl became crazed. He started sending me flowers and cards; silly stuff like that.

"He has settled down some since then, but I learned that going away with other men only made Carl want me more. I make sure to let him know I'll be going away whenever his sales drop off. It gives me pleasure to manipulate him that way. He becomes fearful that he'll lose me. That man can never get enough of me. His wife could never inspire him to produce sales like he does now. I know what motivates him.

"His wife was such a fool to get in my way. Most men go back to their wives when I've finished with them. They act like little boys running home to their mommies. If she had been smarter, she would have simply ignored the whole affair and saved herself the aggravation. She must have wrongly assumed I wanted to marry Carl. Hah! She just didn't know me.

"Oh, David, I have one last thing to tell you. Carl's wife died that night. She never made it down the mountain. Carl and I didn't find out until we got back to Plaintown, three days later. Apparently, her car flew off a steep drop on the Plaintown side of Mountaintop Pass. Someone saw it. She was going over a hundred miles per hour into a hairpin turn and the car just shot out over the mountainside. It rolled end over end down the mountain; then crashed and burst into flames. The witness said when her car flew by, she knew there would be a terrible ending."

"Wow, Marty," remarked an amazed David. *"That was quite an ending. Did you feel any guilt or remorse?"*

"Oh, no, I didn't feel any remorse at all," said Marty. *"None! I was elated, ecstatic! I felt like a lioness that had chomped down on the skull of a vile hyena and killed the aggravating bitch. I was extremely proud of myself! That woman was so controlling and obstinately stupid. She deserved everything she caused herself. I have wondered what her last thoughts might have been. When her car went flying of the mountain, was she thinking of my vagina and my waxed mons pubis? Was she wondering what it would have been like to have girl-girl sex with me? Was she dreaming about pressing her face into my soft, creamy vagina?"*

"Would you have let her?"

"I had the thought; but only briefly. I have lots of girl porn partners who are wonderful at oral sex. I didn't need her for anything; so, I shooed that thought away. I stayed focused on killing her."

"And no regrets about that?"

"Almost none. I thought she'd do the aspirins and bleed out. Instead, she totaled a very good car. I only hope she didn't cause Carl's insurance rates to go up. You never know what an insurance company will do. I hate unethical companies, don't you, David?"

"Yeah; hate them."

"Well, she's dead now. She was the inconsiderate, selfish one. She tried to insult me and interfere where she had no business. By killing herself she only confirmed how selfish and narrow-minded she was. Her sense of what's right and wrong was ridiculously rigid. Can you imagine a woman being that stupid? She tried to make me feel guilty about making love! She was absurdly provincial and obnoxious. Try thinking about that night from her perspective, David. You'll see I actually did her a great favor. I enabled her to accomplish what she wanted most from her life."

"Which was what?" David looked perplexed.

"Death, David! That woman was totally miserable with her life. She wanted out of the life she had. I offered her a way for her life to be gone from her; and she took it. She's happier now, being dead; or at least her spirit is happier.

"I did her a favor by convincing her to kill herself. I was only surprised about the way she killed herself; that's all. I was certain I'd succeeded in hypnotizing her. I told her she needed to go away and die. I believed, with high certainty, that she'd surely commit suicide, but I thought she'd go out like a wimpy coward, by swallowing a bottle of aspirin and bleeding her guts out.

"She amazed me by choosing to go out with a flaming crash and burn. That took some courage. For the first time, I feel a modicum of respect for her. Before I knew she crashed like that, I just thought of her as a woman I was using for a doormat to wipe my feet upon. I used to imagine wiping my muddy feet on her mousy face, right there in her house; then kicking her to the side while I took Carl into their bedroom and fucked him, like we would never stop.

"I basically thought of her as his housekeeper. I just pushed her aside whenever I wanted him. I even called him at home. I didn't care how she reacted. She was a nobody. Then, when I'd finish fucking Carl, I'd imagine she'd be there to boost his ego back up. He knew I'd never marry him like he wanted me to. He had to settle for the doormat wife. Now, I've come to find out the woman actually had some guts. She did the unexpected by leaving life in flames. Who knew?

"Either she had more guts than I thought or she went crazy that night on the mountain. No one will ever know what was going through her mind while she drove that car. Either way, she's better off dead. I could never live a life like her life. I can't imagine what it would be like, being a dependent wife and having to contend with a whore like me. That must have been hell for her.

"I was shocked when I first heard about the accident. After Carl and I came back from the lake, when I was home alone one night sleeping in my own bed, the answer finally came to me. Just as I was starting to fall asleep, I had an epiphany.

"None of what happened was my fault! It couldn't be. It was all the wife's fault. She chose to come up to the lake. She tried to come between me and Carl. She should have known better. She chose to drive back in her car. She chose to drive that night after driving all day. She must have been exhausted. I had nothing to do with the way she drove that car or the way she decided to kill herself.

"She was the thoughtless, uncaring person that did this. I don't know what was going on in her head while she was driving that car. And no one will ever know. I had nothing to do with her choices. I wasn't driving her car that night. She was. Then, I had peace of mind. I knew I wasn't responsible.

"She was a self-centered, selfish bitch, all the way to the end. I just refused to let her have her way. I felt relieved and relaxed. I was grateful for that. I can't allow people who have mental problems to

mix up my mind. My shrinks have always told me how important it is for me to think logically, to always consider the needs of others and stay happy. That's how I keep myself a mentally well-balanced woman, David.

"*That night, when I had my epiphany; just as I was nodding off to sleep, the most wonderful thing happened. Miss Iniquity, my psychological soul mate, came into my imagination and embraced me. I imagine she's the spirit voice of my voluptuous redheaded school friend, Maria. Miss Iniquity is always there for me. She gives me affirmation kisses when she sees that I'm making progress. She lied down next to me and began kissing me.*"

Marty remembered the words Miss Iniquity spoke during her dream that night, but she did not share those words with David:

'*You've advanced yourself a great deal tonight. 'You can not blame yourself for her behavior. Her choices were hers. You didn't drive the car. You have no guilt.*

'*A mighty force is awakening within you. It builds like an unstoppable ocean swell, pushing and lifting all things before you. Remember this night. This is the night that changed you. Never doubt your own force of will again. Always be confident when you turn to it. You possess powers of persuasion, wit, and seduction. You can use cleverness and your ability to manipulate others to do your bidding. Have confidence. Know you will succeed. You have the power to control men and other women. Use people as you please, from this time forward. Never doubt the powers of this force within you.*

'*Look forward to your glorious future. Remember, these are mostly men whom you are dealing with. The female always has more power than the male. You will have many lovers. They will call for you. They will beg you to allow them to kiss your vagina. Show them how to pleasure you; and they will love you when you let them. You have your life. Enjoy it. That's what matters.*

'*You and I are one and the same. You are my mirror image. We are one and the same with Ishtara, Astarte, Aphrodite, Sara, Bathsheba, Salome, Isabella, Cleopatra, and every whore that lives and ever lived; and we have the same urges that every woman has and will ever have. We will meet in the flesh one day, soon. We will bask in the sunshine. We will make love under the stars. We will kiss each other everywhere; and we'll have our loving orgasms. Our spirits are immortal.*

'*I love you; Carl loves you. Maria loves you. We all need and accept you just as you are. I'll kiss you now, while you sleep, until you awaken. You are a good, loving woman and you have done nothing wrong today or any other day. Even when you commit the murders with David, you only murder because of love. I will always be here for you. Sleep well, precious love.*'

"*I held my big goose down pillow close to my body,*" Marty confided to David. "*I imagined it was the spirit image of beautiful Maria, personified next to me in the flesh. I wrapped my arms and legs around my pillow and pulled it into my bosom. I fell asleep, dreaming I was with her. When I awoke the next morning, my sex was wet; and my fluid stains were on my pillow. I had my whole new outlook on life. A wonderful feeling swept over me.*

"*Those Aztec priests must have shared my same feelings when they threw their victims' severed heads and bodies down the temple steps. That completed their sacrifice ceremony. They wanted to move forward with their lives, as I needed to move forward with mine. I experienced the release of my pent-up frustrations. I felt vindicated for the way I confronted Carl's wife and expunged her miserable presence from my life.*

"*A huge weight lifted from my shoulders. I felt joyously triumphant, like football players when they win their big game. My vagina throbbed, anticipating Carl would come see me after he took care of her remains. I knew he'd need me more than ever, but for a different reason. He'd want to be comforted. I was anxious for him to come to me. I wanted to reward him for his loyalty to me.*

"*Her death had a cathartic effect on me, David. Days later, while Carl was on top of me, making love, I suddenly convulsed with laughter. I couldn't stop my outbreak. My entire body trembled. I dug my fingers into Carl's back, pulled him tightly into me and rolled my head violently from side to side on my pillow. I was roaring out of control with laughter. I felt possessed by something demonically spiritual that I'd never experienced before.*

"*I had a flash back to that night when we were at the cabin. I remembered I had my vagina positioned perfectly upon Carl's face. While his tongue lavished my clitoris with loving caresses; while his fingers softly squeezed my nipples; while I trembled in the glorious ecstasy of a long wondrous orgasm, his wife was hurtling down the mountainside to her death.*

"*This spirit came to me and spoke to me from across the centuries. I experienced the same spiritual glory those Aztec priests felt when they decapitated their sacrificial victims and uncaringly threw their heads and bodies down the temple steps. My unconstrained orgasm flowed freely into Carl's mouth and over his face. My entire body knew the same pagan holiness those priests experienced while they quenched their thirsts with their victims' blood. I also heard this voice from inside my mind as Carl's cum pulsed deeply into my vagina. An ancient spirit voice I'd never heard before spoke to me:*

'*You have honored me by your glorious deed. I bless you and find favor in you.*'

"*I felt like I joined eternity in that moment, David. There are no other words to describe my feeling. Carl sensed that something was happening with me. He paused from his thrusts, held my head, and looked into my smiling face:*

'*How do you feel,*' *he asked?*

'Divine,' I replied. Inside my mind I felt a flower opening its petals to the sun; standing glorious and proud of what I had done; unashamed to be seen with the man I loved; forever unconcerned about the sensitivities of his wife. My soul understood that, in this wonderful moment, it shared with Salome the same exaltation she experienced. My soul was in hers when it stood above the decapitated head of the insane madman who blather spewed about the evils of her whoring and insanely attempted to turn her king and her admirers away from her, to worship instead some unseeable god.

"Our joined souls felt the King's embrace; his cupping of Salome's breast and his loving pinchings of her nipple; his fingers inside her while he kissed her before his assembled court. Our divine senses rejoiced when the king proclaimed that Salome's vagina was the only god his kingdom needed; and again, when he performed cunnilingus with her and seated her beside his throne.

"I sensed history repeating itself. My soul felt Bathsheba's divine joys after she successfully arranged her husband's murder and the poisoning of King David's first wife. I felt her same triumphant pride when her king made her his favorite wife and gave her immense powers over his affairs. And my soul, at once, relived the glories of Cleopatra after she had arranged the murders of her brothers and sister; and ruled Egypt. Caesar, and the entire Roman world were hers! Marc Anthony and his immense military's power; also, hers! My soul resonated with its joy joined to hers.

"I felt glorious. I beamed my most heavenly inspired, joyous smile. I Kegel locked my sex tightly to Carl's penis and kissed his face in many places. I was making Carl my bitch, in the same way that Sara dominated Abraham."

"Sara dominated Abraham? That's not the way I was taught," David's frown was skeptical.

"Well, David, that's because you were taught by men. They interpret text one way. I interpret it the way it fits what actually happened. Sarah got tired of their father, Terah. Yeah, Abe and Sara were steps; same father, different mothers. So, we have incest from the get go. She wanted a new place; bigger; hers; out from under Terah's thumb. Why did she want out? Because, you'll see, she was the bible's original fuck bunny."

"Not Eve?"

"No, I don't think so. Eve was just into oral sex. She figured out that she wouldn't die if a snake's tongue pleasured her. She loved oral sex so much that she had Adam bite the apple so he could gain knowledge of how to pleasure a woman. When God caught them doing it orally, He got upset and threw them out of the Garden; gave her the curse of labor pains; gave him the curse of working for a living. See, they were supposed to keep their eyes closed to pleasure and just be fruitful and multiply, like rabbits.

"But anyway, Abraham and Sara moved west; got a new place. Abe was so obsessed with his half-sister that he left his father, Terah, to go with Sara. Remember, this is a tale passed down by oral tradition over sixty centuries or so; so, we don't really even know Sara's original name. What we do know is that her name is conjunctive. It's the joining of SA, which means to see that which gives pleasure, and RA, which means of light or of God. When I thought about it, it dawned on me. Abe worshipped Sara. Abe's true god was what he saw every day and what gave him pleasure. Abe's true god was Sara's vagina. He worshipped his half-sister's vagina. But Sarah was a lot like me. She wanted more. And, like me, Sara loved to fuck.

"The story has it that there was a famine. I don't know about that; but obviously, Sara was a gorgeous hottie. She and Abe figured out that Egypt was where the wealth was. Before Sara conceived, she wanted to be sure that her progeny would be well off. She and Abe

were the original Hebes. They wanted wealth and they decided that the way to get it was to trade for it; not work like slaves for it. Sara explained to Abe that they could get rich by trading the pleasures of Sara's fabulous vagina for the wealth of Egypt. So, they decided to go into Egypt, a strange new land with vast, fabulous wealth, and take Egypt's wealth for themselves. Abe told an Egyptian prince that Sara was his sister. And he pimped her:

'My sister is lovely; do you not agree?'

'May I receive a demonstration of her loveliness?' inquired the prince.

'Most certainly, your highness. Sample her. It would be her pleasure.' Replied Abe.

Sara then knelt before the prince, removed his loincloth, and sucked his penis, bringing him to ejaculation.

'Ah, such a willing woman; such a goddess of pleasures. We must take her to Pharoah, my father, and present her to him. Perhaps he will desire that you and she prolong your visit to Egypt.'

"Two days journey later, the prince and Abe presented Sara to Menes, Pharoah of Egypt. The prince described Sara's propensity to provide pleasure in glowing terms. Pharoah Menes was drawn to the Hebrew woman. He marveled at the softness of her skin; the light complexion of her skin; the fineness of her hair; the innocent, porcelain like appearance of her lovely oval face; the fullness of her lips and whiteness of her teeth; and the lusting allure of her full breasts and welcoming hips.

'Sara, would you give pleasures to a Pharoah?' asked Menes.

'My greatest pleasure and honor would be to please you, my Lord,' smiled Sara.

"She then proceeded to remove his loincloth and suck him to hardness. Then, removing with him to his chambers, Sara entertained his penis inside her wanton vagina, stroking and rocking it until it ejaculated.

'By all the gods of Egypt, I have never before known such pleasures were available anywhere on Earth,' declared Menes, complimenting Sara. *'Would you and your brother please prolong your stay in Egypt over the winter season?'*

'Of course, your Majesty. But my pleasures are also in demand in the Levant. I must be compensated for my absence from my people there,' smiled Sara with her most alluring coquettish smile.

'Then, name your price. I must have your womanly favors.'

'I will require half.'

'Half of......?'

'Half of all the gold and silver and jewels and cattle and sheep in all of Egypt,' smiled Sara.

"Sara comprehended her bargaining power. She knew that she offered Pharoah something unique; unobtainable elsewhere in Pharoah's kingdom; and she understood the concept of pricing quality at a premium."

'What you require is exorbitant, sweet Sara,' gasped Pharoah Menes.

"Sara took his objection to her price as her que to emphasize her premium quality. She pressed her body against the Pharoah's and grasped his testicles and fondled them while she French kissed him. By again becoming close and intimate with him in this way, Sara changed the decision-making control in his mind from the logical and rational bargaining portion of his brain to the limbic, emotionally driven portion of his brain.

"His body relaxed in her embrace and his willpower melted before her touches and her kisses. He knew he had to have her; understood that he could not bear to live without her. Sara was, perhaps the first woman in recorded history to understand the ability of a woman's charms to compartmentalize a man's mind; to elicit the most compelling urges of lust from a man's mind; and to make

the man's resistance to her wants melt away to nothing. Sara now stroked Pharoah's penis:

'You know my pleasures would be a bargain at twice my offered price, my Lord and my God.'

"Pharoah remembered well the warm, creamy smoothness and delightful touches and squeezes that Sara's vagina had pleasured him with the night before. He knew he could not live without having more of her.

'Indeed, you are more than worthy of all that you ask; and half the grains and jewels of Egypt, as well. We welcome you and your brother here. You will, of course, reside with me here in my palace during your stay. You will share my chambers with me over the winter season until you depart.'

'You have acquired the bargain of a lifetime, my Pharoah. With each day of my stay with you, you will feel more and more pleasure and satisfaction with your most wise decision,' complimented Sara, sealing their bargain. She was the greatest genius marketer of her time, who well understood the concept of providing assurances and satisfaction after the sale.

"The prince and his father, the Pharoah, had swallowed the lure that attached their limbic desires to Sara and her marvelous, pleasure giving vagina. Soon all the Pharoah's princes, as well as Pharoah himself, were all clamoring to consort with Sara and paying Abe handsomely for access to the pleasures of Sara's marvelous fuck-savvy sweetness.

"Menes considered Sara his most valuable treasure. He declared her strictly off limits to all his priests and ministers and all other Egyptians. Anyone who disobeyed Menes and touched Sara in any way had his hands cut off. After the winter season, Abe and Sara had most of Egypt's wealth. Here, again, Sara used her charm and guile to have her way with Pharoah Menes. She told him that he needed to keep his bargain and allow her to leave Egypt. If he kept

his bargain, she promised that she would return next winter and consort with him again. If he tried to restrain her as his concubine and keep her in Egypt, Sara swore that she would never have relations with him again. Menes agreed to Sara's terms.

"Abe and Sara departed Egypt; their wagons filled with gold, silver, jewels, and grain; and herds of cattle and sheep. After Sara left Egypt, Menes was so smitten by her charms that he lived for many months as a man encased within a fog of gelatin. He was semi-conscious, often in daydreams thinking of being with Sara again; writing his love poems to her for the day when she would return to him.

"By trading her virtue for riches beyond measure, Sara acquired the seed capital for her Hebrew tribe which, five thousand years later, would become the nation of Israel. And, Sara never again returned to Egypt. Why should she? Menes now had only half the wealth that he had before she met him. If Sara were to return and strike the same bargain that she had struck before, she would be selling herself for half her original price. She understood that when a partner's wealth has diminished, it was time to move on."

"So, Sara was the biggest whore in Egypt?"

"A consummate whore, no doubt; one who knew the value of her pleasures. When she left, the Pharoah and his princes spoke wistfully of her as that glorious femme who was 'far and away' the most magnificent, most glorious whore whom they had ever had the pleasures of knowing. That's where the term: 'far and away' comes from. Sara is my idol; fabulous world class whore; the world's first international fuck bunny.

"But Sara's story didn't end there. She wanted a son. Abe couldn't get Sara pregnant. So, she arranged a threesome with Haggar, her slave girl, herself, and Abe. The hope was that all this excitement would help Abe get Sara pregnant; but nature tricked Sara. She did not conceive. Instead, Hagar got pregnant with Ishmael! Hagar mocked Sara because Sara could not conceive; so, Sara bitched at

Abe to send Hagar and Ismael away. They went west and settled the lands west of the Jordan River.

"But the story still doesn't end there. God tells Abe not to stress over his possible impotence. He tells Abe that, if he'll circumcise himself, He will make sure Sara conceives. Abe does as he's told. He circumcises himself and all his servants. Nothing is happening until: one day, three strangers arrive at Abe's tent, looking for Sara. Abe tells them to go into her tent, behind his. The next day they leave. And guess, what?"

"What?"

"Sara is pregnant with Yitzchak (Issac). Anyway, that's the Bible version. But I think the truth is that Abe was impotent. He never was the father of Judaism, Christianity, or Islam. Mules don't reproduce. Abe was God's mule; but Sara was the mother of all three religions. The actual fathers of the religions remain unknown. My theory is that even Hagar didn't get pregnant by Abe; likely, it was some dude that worked for Abe's family tribe. We will never know who he was. Perhaps it was Terah, her father. Terah spread himself around. Remember, the Pagan influence still dominated religious thought until the time of King David. Abe's problems were taking place a thousand years before David's son, Solomon, built the first temple. So, anybody and everybody could have been fucking Sara; and it seems likely that everybody was. Anyway, that's how I like to think about Sara. I think she was a woman of pleasures, like me. And, like me, Sara loved the male penis."

"So, who got Hagar pregnant?" David struggled to follow Marty's story.

"Who knows? Perhaps Abe had a lucky night? Perhaps one of the men in Abe's camp? Perhaps a passing Bedouin? But Sara's story still doesn't end there. Her whoring ways continued long after she and Abe left Egypt and after Hagar conceived Ishmael. Abe reasoned that

he'd homestead the Levant; he'd nail down his Hebrew tribe's claim to Canaan by camping on all its frontiers. But he got some blowback from the king of Gerar territory. Abe settled the dispute by again pimping Sara; this time to the king of Gerar. Again, Abe benefitted. He got free use of the land of Gerar and was given additional riches in cattle by the king. Sara was that sweet inducement, between the sheets."

"*This is not the way I was taught in Yeshiva religious school.*" David objected.

"*Of course, it wasn't. Your teachers were all men, weren't they?*"

"*Yes, of course. They were rabbis.*"

"*Well, what would you expect? Obviously, the religion promotes a male hierarchy. You got the male sanitized version of events. It's not going to change through enlightenment; only when change is forced upon it.*"

"*Okay; but Sara was 99 years old when she gave birth. That had to be God....*"

"*Bull shit, David. Through the entire story of Abraham and Sara in Genesis, Sara was never a day older than 35.*"

"*But my torah says.......*"

"*Your torah was written from oral midrash, handed down and passed along over at least a thousand years, David. It's campfire tales for boys; and it's bull shit. The male organization needed to put age on Sara and Abe to make the story fit with the God narrative. Why? Because God was always moving the goal posts. God's gig was:*

'You do for me now; and I'll do for you, later.;

"*God's original covenant was that Abe worship him alone, now; and then, later, Abe would have progeny that would number the stars. Abe had to move to Canaan first; and later God would give him the land. But God didn't tell Abe that his descendants would have to fight like hell for that land, repeatedly. And they are still fighting for it.*

"But those ancient campfire tales are the result of men telling a lot of half-truths, kind of like boy scouts sitting around their campfires talking about Bigfoot."

"Wait a minute, Marty. Are you saying that belief in God and belief in Bigfoot are the same thing?"

"Yeah, I guess so. Why not? They're both invisible, except to a few people who were incredibly lucky to see or hear them. Face it, David. Sara was a young fuck bunny; a really, incredibly gorgeous hottie who got it on with the princes and Pharoah of Egypt, the three visitors, and the king of Gerar. She also liked doing threesomes with Abe and Hagar. And she was likely doing incest with Terah, her father, before she decided she wanted to spread her wings. She persuaded Abe to flutter with her; take her to Canaan where she could whore openly, in freedom from her daddy, and from where she could access the wealth of Egypt. I envy her determination, David. She was the world's first international porn star. She had a very healthy libido. She had no morals by religious standards of morals, and she loved wealth and nice things. Poverty was not Sara's gig.

"I'm telling you, David, Sara was a totally unapologetic Pagan; and she was a whore to her core. As a Pagan, there's absolutely nothing wrong or immoral about whoring. It's perfectly acceptable. It's considered honorable. It's praised and appreciated. Sara was totally fine with it. She had no inhibitions about it. She loved it.

"But when the males committed the oral traditions to writing and created the Torah, they imposed their Judaism version of past events on the tribe. Sara's role had to be sanitized and recycled, so little boys, sitting around their campfires and hungry for bedtime stories, would buy into it. And to make her story fit with the way the God of your Torah moved the goal posts, Sara had to be aged.

"The Torah writers had to make her character sweet and delicious, like fine wine. Notice how the Torah quickly brushes past her dalliances and makes lame excuses for her behavior. Abe broke idols;

so, they had to leave Ur to get away from her dad. They were starving; so, they had to go to Egypt. One of her three tent visitors got her pregnant; so, in your Torah, Abe had to be circumcised so God could make her pregnancy happen. Abe needed the land of Gerar to graze the tribe's cattle; so, Abe 'gave' her to the local king.

"Come on, David, think! The Torah is just the male version rewrite of what really took place. It's your classic tooth fairy tale. Sara wore the pants in Abe's family tribe. He was her bitch and her pimp. She was the one who wanted more power and wealth. And she used her penis craving vagina to get everything she wanted."

"So, what is the lesson here? Why are you telling me this?" David was flummoxed.

"Simple, David. Women who understand how to appeal to the limbic portion of men's minds have all the power over men. True power is in the females' vaginas. The female vagina is the male's truest and everlasting God. Eve and Sara understood it. And they used their wits and their vaginas to overcome adversity and triumph. Eve got Adam out from under God's thumb; and Sara got Abraham out from under her father, Terah's, thumb.

"Sara triumphed over famine and territorial disputes by using her wits and her promiscuity. And Sara ran with her sensual powers by birthing three religions. She was highly successful. Some men, especially those who crave power, resent a woman's success. Male misogyny comes through in the translations of oral midrash into biblical text. That's why the males gave Eve and Sara short shrift in the Torah's Genesis chapter.

"It is why Eve played with a snake. It's why Sara was aged, so males could say that God gets credit for doing things that only a woman could do. Any woman who understands how the male's limbic mind works can also understand how to use her incredible powers. I believe that I understand it. I used my sex appeal to take Carl from his wife; then I used my same sex appeal to destroy her. A

lot of women succumb to lesbian love. But that's another story and I've already told you those juicy details.

"But after I got rid of Carl's wife, Carl became mine, all mine. Not his wife's; Mine! I severed his wife from him like those ancient Aztec priests severed their victims' heads from their bodies. I remember holding Carl sweetly in my arms that night. I had sinned with him before in secret; but never had I sinned so greatly and as magnificently as I did that night and weekend. I was my total Pagan whore self. I felt no remorse; only joy. I could feel it in my soul. I lay my head upon Carl's chest, knowing that my deceptions had won; like Eve's and Sara's deceptions had helped them get what they wanted.

"Carl's wife was just unlucky that Carl had such a fabulous penis; that I discovered how fabulous it was; and that I wanted it all for myself. That's the nub of it. That wonderful penis and the ways Carl uses it inside me were my motives for causing her death. That night I knew that Carl's wife would never again hear his heartbeat; but I would hear it. I, life, had destroyed her, death. My mind's flower basked in dazzling sunlight, drinking in the warming essence of his life and mine; together.

"The permanence of what I had accomplished thrilled me. I burned with a different sort of passion than any I'd ever experienced before. I possessed Carl and his wonderful, marvelous penis. My goal for the past two years had finally been realized. I felt my new reality. I could lick his adorable penis; and I could suck it and fuck it. And I could enjoy its splendid ecstasy, inside me, whenever I wanted it. Nothing and no one stood in my way anymore.

"The 'other woman' wife was gone from my life, forever. I felt this fantastic elation! I gushed. The joy of knowing that what I had achieved was real; not just a dream. It made me want to hold Carl's penis inside me and never relax my grip on it. I was everything Carl had. I was the recipient of all his love, all his money and all his soul. I loved him for allowing me to displace his wife from his life. Words

can not describe how elated I felt. I was good fortune's most favored girl.

"Now, whenever I make love with Carl, or with any man for that matter, I think about Carl's wife flying off that mountainside. That fills me with a salacious, titillating joy that's simply indescribable. I visualize her hateful angry face crashing, tumbling over and over; and then I see her going up in flames. What that idiotic bitch did to herself makes me laugh inside: at her! I mean it's hysterically funny when you take a perverse, jaundiced look at her ridiculous behavior. Then, I say to myself:

'You did that. You made that happen to her.'

"I then realize the power of my own sexuality. I then appreciate the power that a woman has when she loses all her inhibitions and uses her sex as a weapon to take a man away from another woman. I now know that I can control men through sex. I understand a woman's power now. Just knowing that I understand this incredible power that I have helps my orgasms come more quickly than they did before. I'm free of guilt and inhibition. I'm totally shameless when I fuck another woman's man now. I never even feel the slightest bit threatened by the 'other woman syndrome' anymore. I know she can't prevent me from doing whatever I please.

"David, Carl puts me on a pedestal now. He worships me. Knowing how I was able to redirect that man's life-focus to pleasing me has changed everything. I feel accepted by the entire world. That time the two of us were up at the lake solidified my attitude about everything. Now, I'm extremely pleased and proud to be recognized as a woman who stars in adult films. I love who I am. I love being a famous porn star. I'm comfortable in my own skin, like Eve and Sara were. I'm unashamed of my whoring. I'm proud of it. I confidently hold my head erect while I smile and make direct eye contact with everyone."

"How did Carl cope with the loss of his wife?" David's curiosity about the incident hadn't ended. *"And, since she died, didn't he want you to move in with him so he could have you every night?"*

"Yes, he did ask me to live with him. He said he badly needed me. He was just feeling sorry about losing his live-in housekeeper. But I knew an arrangement like that would never work. He got tired of having his wife whenever he wanted her. And, of course, he stopped wanting her altogether after he met me. I'm being kind to him by not being there for him, like a full-time wife. I've spared him the scorn I know I'd have for him once he became dependent on me. No, as wonderful as sex is with Carl, I decided against an arrangement like that. He's happy seeing me occasionally, when he has money for me. That's best for me, too. It frees me to work my other clients and develop new prospects."

"So, you've made up your mind that you would never marry or live with Carl, but you definitely want to marry Bob. It just seems that you and Carl are so perfect for each other."

"Oh, David," Marty laughed, "you are way too analytical; but you are missing something important. Bob is fifteen years younger than Carl. He'll be making love long after Carl needs those little blue pills to keep his penis erect. But definitely and never are strong words, David. They sound so final when you say them. They scare me."

"Okay, I won't use them again. But how do you separate your feelings for Carl from your feelings for Bob? Do you feel the same about both men; or is there something about Bob, other than his age advantage, that you favor for marriage over Carl?"

"Oh, wow! You don't understand women, David."

"Well, try me. That's why I asked you here to the barnyard. I do my best thinking here among my animals. It's just the two of us, Marty. No one can even hear us except Dolly, that black sheep that's standing nearby. Even the other sheep are way off at the far fence. We have total privacy, Marty. So, tell me."

"Okay, David. Age is an important consideration in relationships, but relationships are far more complex than age differences. Every person is different, David. Understanding the uniqueness of the person is the key to having a successful relationship with that person. Naturally, as a whore, my relationships with men tend to gravitate towards our sexual relationship. It would be foolish for me to gauge a man's desirability for a long-term relationship by whether he brings me flowers or candy; or by the words he speaks to me. I don't need to hear a man tell me how beautiful I am or how good I am in bed. I hear a lot of that. But there has to be more than that to interest me. First, the man must have money. That's a given. I'm not a charitable institution.

"But, after money, one singular thing differentiates men and determines the kind of relationship I will have with them. It's the way that the man makes love with me. I enjoy intimacy with many men but no two men are the same in their love making. Every man uses his penis differently. I pay extremely close attention to the way a man makes love with me. I sort of catalogue the man in my mental love making index.

"I know volumes about the kind of person a man is by the way he uses his penis while making love with me. I can tell whether he's happy and relaxed; or whether he's sad and frustrated; or if he's feeling guilty about being with me; or if he's feeling he's getting revenge against another woman by being with me; or if he's trying to compare me with another woman; or whether he has fallen in love with me already; or whether he's trying to force himself to fall in love with me. These are just a few of the many different motives and feelings that different men have that causes them to seek my company. While I'm making love with the man, I can get a pretty good idea about why he's having sex with me.

"A man's penis expresses his true feelings while he's making love. He can't conceal those feelings; not from me. The way a man uses *his penis reveals a great deal about a man's character. I need to feel that special something, coming through to me from the man's penis, if I'm going to invest my emotions in becoming the man's lover. You asked me about Carl and Bob. In truth, I love both of them, deeply. I do. I care about them with my whole heart. I can say that in all honesty. But the way those two men love me is vastly different. And I can feel that difference. They each approach intimacy with me in their own way. And their different ways of expressing intimacy are very special.*

"Let's take Carl first. Carl completely understands my sex addiction. He knows how to feed it and he loves feeding it. He loves the nymphomania addiction that rages inside me. He adores me when I'm experiencing the rapture condition of my disease state; when I absolutely need to fuck; when I must fuck until I've gone totally wild out of my mind. Carl is in love with that insatiable craving that lives inside my mind; and he loves the naughtiness that it brings out in me. He unconditionally loves that about me. He feeds my naughty girl badness; and the sensational sex it makes me crave.

"If I were a drug addict, I could not say that about a man. I'd be saying my heroin or my cocaine loves me and I have this euphoric, loving relationship with my drugs; but with nymphomania I need a man with an understanding penis to give me that super nympho-maniac, high into the sky, fuck fix that sends me soaring into the heavens with no cares. And when Carl's giant-sized, loving, adoring, craving to explore and romance the inside of my vagina, penis is securely inside me, it makes me feel wonderful about being alive. The most dependable man for satisfying my nympho addiction is Carl. I need him.

"When the two of us are going all out together and thrusting our sexes into each other, like we do, I can see the hot fire in Carl's eyes. It's like the insides of his guts are burning from my heat. Then, driving his penis harder, wildly into me, becomes the only thing that

quells his fire. And then, when he comes inside me, when he releases his explosive monster cum flood inside me, I see his eyes become heavenly peaceful. And then, when we finally finish and he smiles into my face, I can see that Carl is happy for me. I know that he is happy, knowing that I've enjoyed a good romping. I know that my eyes are telling me the truth by the way my vagina throbs afterwards. My vagina loves being fucked by Carl.

"For Carl, making love with me is never about him getting off. He'd rather risk a stroke or a heart attack than disappoint me by slowing down. Knowing I'm feeling satisfied is what makes Carl happy. He's in love with fulfilling that nympho need that lives deep inside me. He has this unquestioning loving commitment to satisfying my disease; to enable my disease to fully express itself; to help me reach my crazy wild uninhibited shameless places. Our love making is always about making me get high, never him. Carl's fabulous penis is my vagina's equivalent of what mainlining premium heroin is for a junkie. Carl sends my nymphomania that high, right into a different world. And he keeps me up there for a really long while, before I come back down. That's why I can't get enough of him.

"But Bob is totally different, David. He loves me for me, just me, for the person I am, deep inside myself. He accepts my badness like a daddy accepts his daughter's mistakes; but he never tries to correct my mistakes and he never criticizes me for them. He just accepts me as I am and he loves me. Our relationship is about much more than sex or how well I please him in bed. I can feel the relationship. It's true love. It's this honest warmth that Bob feels for me. It comes through in the feelings I get from his beautiful, loving penis. It's like his penis is constantly telling me that it always wants to be with me. And it always wants me to be with it, no matter what challenges we endure to be together.

"Bob's penis expresses that commitment to our relationship stability. It says it believes the two of us belong together; being

happy with each other and for each other; being able to enjoy the world together. Bob's penis carries that feeling through in the way he uses it when we make love, David. Our love making is very sweet. It's so sincere and caring; and it's beautiful. It unites us. We become one person. I can never get enough of it. I totally love Bob. I never have inhibitions about my love making with him, or about my feelings of loving him, none. My commitment to him is absolute."

"But, if Carl had a lot more money, could you marry Carl then, instead of Bob?" David was as sly and tempting as a fox's most clever smile.

"Gee, David, you really want to dive into my mind, don't you? Well, marrying Carl, that's not likely. Whenever Carl makes a big sale, he calls me and we have sex. He's like bringing heroin happiness to a user then. And that's fine with me; wonderful. He rings the bell so I can ring mine. We're co-dependent. We motivate each other. I get into my nympho crazy mood with Carl, really fast. It doesn't matter which one of us initiates things. I take all his money, every time. So, Carl's never going to be rich.

"Then again, Carl plays the lotteries. He puts a little money on them every week. He says it's like putting out hooks on a fishing line and hoping something will bite."

"So, if he ever did win really big money like that, do you think, maybe then, you would decide to marry him?" David's smile widened. He drew his head downward toward his chin, like a fox stalking prey.

"Who knows?" breezily replied Marty. *"Yes, I suppose I would marry him then, for all that money; if our prenup agreement gave me half when I divorced him. Oh, yes, David. Then, I'm sure I would. Of course, I would."* Her face assumed its beautiful calculating pout. *"After all, in my heart of hearts, I am an incorrigible, immoral whore. We both know that about me."*

"Yes, I do know that about you! Good for you, Marty!" David beamed. His most valuable employee had affirmed that she placed money above everything else. *"I'm thrilled to hear you say that. That's the Marty I know. Now when you told Carl you wouldn't live with him, did he try to cling to you? Did he beg you to stay; make a scene or something?"* David's eyebrows lifted in curiosity.

"Well, he was kind of sullen and subdued for a couple weeks," shrugged Marty. *"But he got over it. Mostly he's happy to be rid of that horse's ass wife. She was so controlling; unbearable. He's finally free of all her demands. I made his new life possible. He still worships my vagina. He gives us more sales now than before. He works extra hard to make enough money to see me. He's crazier over me now than he was before. He's more focused on bringing me sales than ever. And he's lost his ridiculous guilt complex.*

"Before, whenever we'd go dining, he'd do this quick glance around the room to see if one of his wife's acquaintances might see us together." Marty turned her head and eyes from side to side, imitating Carl. Then she rolled her eyes and chuckled.

"It was sooo boring; so pitiful. I felt badly for him. It was pitiful to observe Carl feeling self-conscious about being with me. That annoyance is finally gone. When we're out to dinner now, we're very relaxed about our relationship. He doesn't care who sees us, or what they think. And that's how it should be. A man shouldn't feel ashamed to be seen with a porn star. We're entitled to enjoy a life when we're relaxing off set.

"Carl and I enjoy our times together much more now than before. Our evenings are fun-filled and romantic. We laugh a lot. We share an intimate warmth, knowing that his wife is finally out of our lives.

"He once remarked he couldn't imagine what possessed his wife to drive off a mountaintop like that. I just shrugged my shoulders and suppressed my laugh. I wanted to blurt out:

'She did that because she was an idiot!'

"But I stayed silent. Instead of saying what I really thought, I gave Carl a warm hug and a kiss. I said:

'She was an inconsiderate, selfish woman; not empathetic, like me. Her behavior that night revealed how warped her mind was. She probably did that to hurt your feelings. I'm sorry, Carl. I'll never hurt your feelings. I'll always place consideration for you and your happiness above my own. I promise.'

"David, I felt like I sealed the secrecy vault on my perfect murder when I said those words to him. My reassurances helped him realize how lucky he is to have me as his trusted friend and lover. He's a happy widower now."

"But, Marty, didn't you think you should stay with Carl for a while to help him ease his sorrows?"

"WHAT, and have me become like a familiar old shirt? Let him see me without my mascara and makeup, without my sexy see-through panties and my revealing outfits? Never! I couldn't risk becoming an ordinary woman in his eyes. That might drive him into the arms of some immoral, shameless whore! One must use common sense in my profession."

David nodded thoughtfully, appreciating Marty's wisdom. Then he explored her effect on families:

"How do you manage your feelings about a man's family when you get involved with him?"

"Oh, that's easy," replied Marty, "I don't have any feelings that need managing. None whatsoever. I look at the family's kids like they are abstract pieces in a board game being played between two women. The woman with the kids has an insurmountable handicap which I do not have. I'm free to focus entirely on the man, as if his wife and kids do not even exist. The wife must divide her attentions between her husband and her children. I focus solely on pleasing her *husband's penis; enticing and wooing it with my adoring fellatio and my playful, fuck-loving vagina."*

"I see. But let's back up a bit. Help me understand what keys you into a man in the first place. Explain how you identify a prospect that can be developed into a lover and a salesman for the Firm's products."

"Oh, David," Marty rolled her eyes, but smiled graciously. His question amused her. *"Sometimes I forget that you're a man. You really don't understand women's ways, do you? It's not all that complicated to detect a man's interest. It's a woman's intuition; something we develop as little girls. We pay very close attention to a man's signals.*

"For example, after I've finished my sales presentation, I'll look to the top salesman. Did he follow my points? Did he agree? Actually, I'm looking to see if he approves of me. I always focus on that top salesman. My experience proves that he is the one who will give me ninety percent of the sales from that office. I'll lift my eyebrows and give him a smile. Now, to work its magic, a woman's smile has to have the hint of a flirt in it, so I spice my smiles by widening my eyes with a bit of flirt. If he smiles back, I'll ask him if he liked the presentation. By that time, the lesser salesmen are leaving. If he says yes, or if he nods to me, then I know I've captured a brief moment to pounce upon his interest.

"It's a delicate moment. I must suddenly become an impetuous, emotional school girl who is thrilled beyond words. My emotional state must be somewhere between professional gratitude and appearing relieved; like I would have died if he had not approved. I must be spontaneous, and believable while I approach him.

"I must pretend to be relieved of some unseeable inner tension, because I've confirmed that he approved of my presentation.

I must disguise my true mission, which is to hug him and hold the crown of my vagina firmly against his leg. I must be credible, but not overtly slutty. I hug him. I put my arms around his neck and give him a lingering kiss on his lips. I must have him believe that I truly am relieved that a true, champion salesman has confirmed my accomplishment. I must be so overcome with joy that I momentarily forget I'm a lady. Throughout my little schoolgirl gratitude act, I keep my mind on my goal. Our initial encounter must leave him wondering. Did I make an innocent mistake when I pressed my vagina against him? He must not be certain that what I did was intentional. My goal is to make him wonder about me.

"My state of my mind as I approach the sales champion is most important. I focus on him alone. I have this compelling urge to have sex with him. But I must outwardly mask that urge. That is foremost on my mind. And I shut out all other thoughts. My focused mental energy must telepathically communicate my goal to him. The way that I kiss and hug him must intimate my real intention. But it must not be overtly obvious. The possibility must exist in his mind that the entire encounter could have simply been because of my naivete and sweet innocence. And he must wonder whether he's reading me correctly. He's likely confused. And that's good. A confused man is a vulnerable man.

"I must awaken his lust from its slumber place, deep inside his limbic zone. He must sense that, conceivably, I've offered my sexual favors to him. He needs to wrestle with the impression that I'm possibly an uninhibited and immoral woman; but also, an intelligent, clever, and discreet woman; a woman worth pursuing. My possible willingness to offer sex for sales must come through clearly to his limbic zone during that first encounter; while at the same time, his conscious mind must also be able to rationalize that I'm simply an overjoyed professional young woman, trying to build a sales book in

a man's world. That way, his conscious mind can justify calling me to indicate he wants to work with me.

"I learned that subtle seduction technique by observing Mother. She did something similar to a man at WEX School. I've simply refined mother's technique. She taught me, by example, that a subtle invitation to intimacy, while, by all appearances properly given, is more effective and transformative than the actual sex act, which comes later. An invitational kiss electrifies a man. It awakens his limbic mind to contemplate endless, pleasurable possibilities. It stimulates his mind to chafe at its constraints, especially a wife. And it spurs him to act and effect his desired change, like beginning an adulterous affair with me.

"My crucial first kiss must be delivered perfectly. It can't be meek or halting; nor can it be overtly passionate or romantic. And it must not be wet and sloppy. My lips must be moist and warm; but not dripping with saliva. Romantic, slobber kisses come later, ideally coupled with that exhilarating first fellatio. That cements our sexual intimacy. But that first kiss must simultaneously travel the dual paths of spontaneity and purpose. It has to be a soul-probing, essence-searching, lust-intriguing; and rapture-teasing, inviting kiss. And it also must linger just long enough to challenge him to respond; to meet me again; to reciprocate my latent passion lust. And it must plant the seed thought that I'm worth it for him to risk everything he has, fortune and family, to become my lover. It must leave him with my lips and my taste playing on his mind; wanting more of me. And eager to give me sales, in hopes that he might bed me and discover all of me.

"If his kiss signals reciprocity when my lips meet his, I will quickly probe inside his mouth, teasing his tongue with my own. I'll do that ever so naturally and teasingly, in a most playful, casual, devil-may-care sort of way. That communicates clearly that I'm available; playful and anxious to be naughty if he's willing to come part way toward

me, like giving me a big sale and a follow up phone call telling me that I inspired him to make that sale. Reciprocity coaxes my naughtiness out of me and gives me an opening to respond. When I get that, I know I've already captured him. The rest is mere formalities.

"That first kiss offers my implied contract of sex for sales. It's like when Eve presented the apple to Adam. I imply if he'll please me; and disobey his god and wife; and if he'll provide me with sales, he will enjoy my delicious forbidden fruit. He'll experience fabulous, out of his known world, sex. That kiss is the message of the original sin; refined."

"And the other salesmen?" David voiced skepticism of Marty's focus on the top salesman.

"I can't care one iota what others in the room think of my advance." Marty retorted. *"I know sales, David. Only the top man matters. The rest are inferior salesmen and saleswomen; and their opinions of me don't matter. In fact, if they snicker and howl like a pack of wolves, that makes my shamelessness communicate all the more emphatically that I've surrendered myself to the top man. Then I'll pretend to be sheepish. I'll depend on him to appreciate my advance; uphold my honor as a professional working woman; and save my faux virtue from a pack of unenlightened wolves. I'll expect him to reciprocate by ignoring catcalls from those curs, and start giving me sales. After all, I'll assure him, he's above their low-class behavior. He's their alpha male.*

"If he returns my first embrace, I know I may possibly have him. At that point he may be thinking that he's holding in his arms everything he's ever wanted in a woman. He may be thinking I'm beautiful and exciting, compared to his wife. He may believe he has his 'girl to die for' in his arms. If true, he'll want more of me. He may signal he wants me by briefly holding my face in his hands, or by holding my hand. I always take those touchings as a male's signal that he wants me.

"*I can gauge the level of his interest by how he receives my emphatic, slightly prolonged hug. If he understands my vagina's crown placed against his leg; that I'm offering him a sexual experience beyond anything he's ever known, I'll feel that understanding coming back through his lips to mine; and I'll know to expect his call. If I don't get that call, I'll possibly, rarely, follow up once with a call to him. He'll either indicate he wants to see me on that call, or I'll drop him. I'm fine with whatever his decision is. I don't mind rejections. That's just sales. I don't expect to catch every fish.*"

"*But you always get that call, don't you?*" David sneered. He had little respect for salesmen.

"*Yes, so far, David. Always. A champion salesman believes he deserves the very best things life has to offer. If he has a wife, he may feel he doesn't need to do anything more to please her than he has already done. But as his new woman, I suddenly become the grand prize. He feels he needs to rise to this new challenge like a fish attacking a bait plug. He feels this urge to bite into me; savage me; show me he's the big boss man; dominate me; conquer me. The telegraphed message in my kiss is intended to play with his mind. It taunts and tempts him, like a bait plug tempts a fish. It drives him nuts. It messes with his head; makes him irrational. It doesn't let him forget me. His mind is like a fish's mind fixated on a lure flashing through the water. But his mind is unlike the fish's mind because his mind remembers. It can't forget that kiss. That memory is like water dripping constantly upon a stone. His thoughts about me wear away his resistance like water wears away stone. He fantasizes about what he'll do with me in the boudoir; how loving and naughty I'll feel, wrapped in his arms; and how wonderful his first penetration will feel.*

"*That perfectly delivered, subtle invitational kiss replays itself. Drip, drip, drip, it wears away his resistance, until he becomes lust-crazed; manic. His clients will never know the real reason he's selling them this product. Whether it's compliance suitable for them or not becomes irrelevant at this point. Something in his life has now set him on his course to come to me. Like a fish shooting up from the water's depths, he's going to hit that bait plug. He's going to make that passionate run for my vagina. Perhaps his wife will slight him, somehow. I can't know exactly what his catalyst will be. Some men have confided to me that, after my first kiss, they couldn't sleep for several nights. They'd lay in bed next to their wives, unable to get their minds off me. They've even told me they lied there quietly, with huge hard-ons. Their penises told them to leave their wives and come to me. When their wives asked if anything was wrong, they said they just denied it and rolled over. Some told me they couldn't perform marital intimacy with their wives anymore. They wanted me and they didn't want to spoil that feeling. That's the effect of lust-craze. They only wanted me.*

"I've heard that similar story from several men during their first time that they made love with me. I suppose every man has secret desires to make love with a beautiful whore. These men all went on and on about how they couldn't wait to have me. They confirmed that it all began with my message packaging in my first kiss. I've worked hard to develop my approach to top salesmen. You can't put my experience and what I know into a sales manual, David. You can't expect just anyone to execute my perfected techniques. That would be like putting a man off the street into a high-performance race car and expecting him to know how to drive well enough to win races. It doesn't work that way."

Again, David nodded at the wisdom of his top employee. *"What do you do between the kiss and the time you have the man in bed?"* He was keenly interested in every facet of her sales techniques.

"I wait. Always, I wait. I am a woman. I am expected to wait for his inevitable phone call. Patience is required here. Oftentimes a man must clear his calendar. I time the wait. If it takes a week

or two, then I know he's already made a mental calculation. He's thought things through. That delayed call is the best call I can get. It tells me he's no impetuous fool. It tells me he has a lot to lose. And, he's weighed the risks. He's had time to make a huge decision. He's willing to chance losing his wife and kids to be with me."

"Tell me," intoned David. "Which are easiest to seduce, the single men or the married men?"

"Well, the singles tend to respond more quickly. I can often have a single man in my bed in one or two nights after I meet him. Most married men take more time. Many of them are cautious because they fear losing the wife and kids over an affair."

"But which men are more of a challenge for you?" David probed the world of dating, about which he knew little.

"Oh, the married men, definitely; but they are also the most rewarding."

"Monetarily rewarding?"

"Well, no, single guys and married guys are a monetary grab bag. Some single guys do terrific sales and some married guys do terrific sales. I meant psychologically rewarding for me."

"Huh? Why? I don't get it. I always thought men had all the power in relationships with women. How can screwing a man be psychologically rewarding for you?"

"Oh my, David. You don't understand anything about women, do you? It's very psychologically rewarding to bed a man. It's a form of conquest; especially when it's a married man. It's like this, David. Seducing a single guy is sweet and wonderful; but seducing a married guy with children is, oh, how can I describe my feelings about it? It's like the sweetness love, of all loves. It's like the finest bittersweet chocolate. It's the crème de la crème of the seduction art. Bedding a married man, taking another woman's man from her, gives me the same feeling a matador has when he plunges his blade through the heart of his bull."

"You feel like you are killing him?"

"No, David, don't be silly. I feel like I am killing his traditional family life. It's the wife's world view I'm killing. I'm setting her entire family free from their smug hypocrisy of marriage and perfectly ordered life; where they use their traditions and religion and snobbery to exclude others, like I was excluded at WEX school. Exclusion practices are wrong; and by adhering to the adultery commandment, religion excludes prostitution and whoring. I think that is a terrible wrong. It causes all sorts of unnecessary social discord when there is no purpose served by it other than male social dominance control. Controlling human nature this way causes discord.

"By my way of thinking, whoring has just as much social validity as any other religion. Prostitution should be a recognized, respected religion. It's a viable faith. Why believe in Jesus, whom you cannot see or touch, when you can believe in a real, living vagina? Why punish a woman who decides to assist human needs through prostitution? How is she different from women who assist human needs by joining a convent?

"Prostitution is less complicated and less judgmental than organized religion. People who sign onto these male religious dominance programs get led around like sheep. That's why I feel this inner thrill, knowing that while I'm doing the husband, his wife's guts are churning. She sees how she's been trapped into a belief system that imprisoned her; failed her. I'm thrilled, knowing I've helped her understand her past choices and made her feel uncertain about her present choices. She knows she can't stop me. She worries I'm destroying her way of life. And she knows she must do something if she wants to change her situation.

"My Modern Morality Standards' ways of life confronts her ways. I shred them like a predatory bird shreds another bird's nest. I destroy it, and I eat the innocent fledglings inside it. I know that,

because of my actions, her children's lives will become more like my own life than the lives that she presumed they'd have. I help that wife realize that her idealized nuclear family is an inferior alternative to a community networked family. She sees that her kids would be better served to see the world as I do. That's harsh. But it's what society gets back from excluding me.

"Knowing I'm causing a wife agony every time I take her husband's penis into my mouth or vagina makes the seduction of her husband a million times more pleasurable than seducing a single man. Knowing I'm destroying her smugness, her nuclear family life, gives me an indescribable feeling of elation. That feeling lifts me up. It fuels the intensity of my passions while I'm seducing her husband. I feel love for the whole family, because I'm freeing the individuals in that family from the misconception that family life gives them security and safety.

"I'm acquainting every family member with reality; reality that security and safety must come from within; from belief in one's own self. I have a happy, promiscuous she-devil inside me. She helps me cast out silly misconceptions. She wills my determination to put everything I have into my seductions of married men. I'm her instrument of lust. And I love doing her bidding."

"But, seducing married men is more of a challenge, isn't it?"

"Not really. They are just a different kind of challenge, that's all. It's not more difficult. Single guys may have me for a night; and then they might move on or go back to a girl friend. Singles are more unstable. That makes them more difficult to predict. Married men have a family to lose; or at least they think they do; so, they tend to be more cautious. They put more thought into the decision. They tend to brood more about becoming my lover. Many continue brooding, even after they've made the decision; after I've been sleeping with them for several weeks."

"It's a more serious game for them, isn't it?" David saw the decision dilemma of the married man who was caught up in one of Marty's seductions.

"Yes, absolutely. They are putting their whole settled life on the line; so, they think hard about risking it. In a very real sense, once I get that married man's delayed phone call, I know he's already thought hard about what he's about to do. I know he's taken my bait. He's already decided that losing his marriage over his affair with me is an acceptable outcome. He's weighed the pros and cons. He's decided his marriage to his wife isn't worth saying 'no' to me. I know I already have him hooked. He is my 'fish on!' as they say on the fishing boats. I know I can start pulling him away from his wife immediately. At that point my instant challenge is to have sex with him. I know once I've gotten my body under him, he'll soon lose his residual romantic attachment to his wife. Once I have his penis is inside me, I know he'll want to ease her out of his life. I call this phase of my seduction the 'take away' phase.

"It's like pulling a huge game fish from the sea. I need to stay determined and focused. I can't slack off and let him bite through my line. I can't give him reasons to cut away. I can't make unreasonable demands. It's too early to ask for money, jewels, cars, furs, vacations, those sorts of things. But I must be resolute, always loving, always supportive, always tugging his affections closer to me; always rewarding him sex for his sales. I'm always available to him for sex, passionate sex, romantic sex, and kinky BDSM sex, if that's what he likes. I'll do butt plugs, vagina clamps, nipple clamps, anal string balls, tie-ups, whips, spreaders; and I'll let him run spike rollers over my breasts and body. I don't mind in the least when a guy wants to get kinky. I actually love kinky. It sparks different emotions and it's cute fun.

"I've discovered that the sex experimenter types are mostly into the kinky stuff because they love seeing how I respond to the

pleasures they give me. Like having my ass slapped. Lots of men love slapping. They know that intensifies my lust and my orgasms. I love men who take me on a BDSM romp. Men who like BDSM get deeply into sexuality; pleasuring women's bodies. I love being with them.

"I'm more than okay with the sadistic and voyeuristic aspects of it. I'm pleased to perform for him; whatever he wants; however, and wherever he wants me to do it with him. That greater intensity of intimacy draws us closer. Once we have that closeness, I can net him and make him a keeper. I stay mentally tough during my seductions. Underlying all my seduction techniques is the steady lure of passion and intrigue that I offer through my sexual techniques. It's like keeping steady tension on a game fish. After I've had my first sex with him, from that moment on, I keep my mind firmly set that he is mine. Not hers. He's coming into my net. He's not going back into the sea.

"I go through my seduction motions like a fisherman works his rod and reel, always bringing my man closer to me. I play dating games with him. I'll meet him impromptu for dinner and sports events, or clandestine night spots. I'll even make love with him in the back seat of his car on a lonely road or quiet side street, if that's the excitement he wants. The event and venue aren't important. What is important is doing whatever it takes to make his penis and limbic emotions become addicted to me. That addiction causes him to feel safer about being intimate with me. Reliable intimacy, always well spiced and intriguing, is a winning formula. It catches men. My man relaxes and comes closer; his resistance to me slackens and my line tension eases; and then I reel him in faster; bringing him closer, and closer, nearer to my net, nearer to his new god....me! He progresses through a weighing of the pros and cons process which helps him lose his fear. Gradually, fear of repercussions from leaving his wife no longer matter. Ultimately, he tips the scales in favor of choosing me, a profligate whore, over his wife. I plant thoughts in his head that

she's prudish, self-centered, obstinate, ridiculous, detrimental to his success or image; whatever it takes. And I replace her negatives with thoughts that I'm all bubbly fun and carefree happiness; and terrific sex. His limbic mind sprouts thoughts of love. That's powerful. That causes him to act. He leaves his wife.

"Now here's a little aside, David. Some women will use dirty tricks to get a man. They'll do things like sending pictures of the man fornicating with her to his wife. That's like gaffing a fish. You may take him from the ocean, but he's ruined. You can't use him after that. It's messy and it often backfires. Women who do that sort of stuff are just nuts. It's much better and it almost always plays out when I stay focused on my lover's penis. My lover's little friend is my best friend. He is my ally in this contest.

"It usually takes me very little time to get my hands on a man's penis. Why? Because men love it when a woman touches them there. On the day that I first get my hands on his penis, often I'll also take it into my mouth and vagina. Then he becomes like a fish that has swallowed a bait hook. Intimacy has that effect on a man. It's the key to success in the seduction art. It's the barb of the hook. It digs into the mind and holds fast to the mind; and it does not let the mind shake it off. That intimacy holds the man fast to me. Thoughts of me become imbedded in his mind and heart.

"Once we've enjoyed intimacy, and I do my utmost best to make that first intimacy beautiful and memorable, it's nearly impossible for him to spit out the hook. He's aware that I can place him with me at a time certain. He's aware that he'd be hard pressed to deny that he's attracted to me if his wife confronts him about our affair. He also knows he might be forced to admit that he's falling in love with me. These new factors affect his decision making. Getting away from me risks that I might make a scene or somehow expose him. I never would do that; only poor game players do that. But he doesn't know that, so he stays hooked to me.

"With more intimacy, my barb digs in deeper. He continues seeing me, playing this shadow game with his wife. Once he and I become an 'item,' I can advance my game in earnest. I don't waste time on a man who won't engage me in intimacy. It's pointless. A girl can't catch another woman's man without it. Seduction without intimacy is like fishing with a string that has no hook on it. Intimacy unifies. Intimacy solidifies. Intimacy is unforgettable. It binds souls together during those precious moments; and it binds for all time.

"I approach this tug of war phase of the take away game differently than wives approach it. Wives think of holding the family together, as if that's the key to victory. It isn't. That familial way of thinking is totally wrong. It doesn't work.

"I think only of loving the man's penis and getting his penis to adore my mouth and my vagina. Once his penis loves being inside me, it dominates his emotional behavior, his true causative actions, and inactions. That's the key that few wives understand. They tend to want to punish their man for straying from the marriage. That's a huge mistake. The man will ultimately do whatever his penis wants him to do. I does not want to go where it is punished. It wants to go where it is loved. I make sure his penis always wants to be inside me. I always keep myself fresh and sexy. I always dress to allure. I'm always willing to please. I focus on keeping that little head interested. That's the head that does the male's critical thinking. That's the head that decides where he belongs.

"So, I kiss that little head. I talk to that little head. I tell that little head how great he is. I flatter his ego. And I love that little head. And, that is so easy for me, because I am a nympho! The wife tries to throw up barriers to that. She starts playing stupid chess, throwing away her pieces aimlessly. Pitiful. Total loser. I get around her barriers or through them. Her barriers fall. Once she uses a ploy and that one fails, she's limited to fewer choices. She becomes desperate. That's when the game enters its terminal phase, like it did for Carl's wife.

"When the wife puts up resistance, I play my take away game. My moves are to simply make love with her husband, whenever I can; anywhere I can; in every position imaginable. I'll meet him on a corner somewhere while his wife thinks he's gone back to the office, or for a trip to the store. When I make love in his parked car, I'll leave my scents on him and in his car. Smelling another woman on her husband drives a wife totally nuts.

"When she overreacts and berates her husband; questions him; threatens him; she only drives him closer to me. I become his refuge. I'll meet him in a hotel during business hours, or in the early morning while his wife thinks he's out jogging. I've gone to men's homes and made love while their wives were away, playing bridge. I love playing the take away game.

"I get a vicarious thrill knowing I made love with a husband in his wife's bed, where she sleeps beside him. You have no idea how that brings out my indescribably delicious, naughty bad girl feelings while I'm doing that. It's like a breakthrough moment. I'm totally pleased with myself; totally full of myself; like the entire time I'm doing it with him in her bed, I want to scream: 'YES!' That's because I know, from that moment on, her bed and bedroom will only remind him of me. I know that life can never be the same for the two of them after I've lain on her mattress with my head on her pillow, while casually, joyfully, unashamedly, sucking her husband's penis and making love with him. That's when I know I'm winning.

"I've gotten that naughty sensation ever since that time I first made love with my geometry teacher in his wife's bed. I feel so deliciously shameless and proud when I make love in my enemy's bed, that I actually hope the wife walks in on us. That has not happened yet; but when it does, I know I won't stop what I'm doing. Why should I? I'll just be playing my take away game. I'll just be showing *the wife that she's losing; dispelling any illusions she may have had that she was winning.*

"After I make love in a wife's bed, whenever I see her, I can look at her, smiling; knowing I am taking her husband from her. I love that feeling of power. It's like I own both of them. My philosophy is that the man is my customer and I'll do whatever it takes to please him. The more I show my sincerity, the more sex I provide him to uphold my end of our implied sex-for-sales bargain, the more sales, money, and gifts I can demand from him. I don't work for free.

"My sex-on-request interactions begin as a clandestine game, and then they blossom into his reason for living. I feel like I'm engaging in a process of revealing the beauty of having an adulterous relationship with me; much like the way a lotus flower blooms; gradually pushing up from the pond's mud; then breaking the water's surface and opening its first petal; and becoming more glorious with each fornication and each fellatio, petal by petal, slowly and deliberately into its full, irresistible magnificence upon a reflection pond. I encourage and embolden him every step of the way by assuring him that it doesn't matter what anyone thinks about him being with me, especially his wife. It's an unfolding, redemptive, glorious, love revealing process. Gradually, our lotus, our relationship, stands proudly, gloriously in the beautiful sunlight for all to adore our magnificence. I help my lover work through it. He gradually becomes more open and shameless about being with me. Eventually he stops trying to hide me from her. That's when he crosses an important line in the seduction process. He's willing to openly commit marital treason. That's when our lotus opens more petals. He becomes a refugee from the mud of a harrowing wife and I become his fresh air; his refuge. As our love blooms, I know I've slipped his soul into my net. I have him! I can feast on his sales, for years!

"To stay in my refreshing refuge and not slip back into the mud of his wife's clutches he must give me sales and money. Otherwise, I'll

remove his sunlight and he'll slip back into the mud of his marriage; back into his wife's world again. That terrifies him. He knows he'll never atone to her enough to placate her for his tryst with me. So, he keeps going. Sometimes he relapses and believes he wants his old life back. Then, he thrashes hard in my net. He complains; speaks wistfully of his more peaceful past times with his wife and kids; but he knows he cannot escape. It's too late.

"I make love with his little head again. His little head tells his big head that he likes things just fine as they are. Our lotus opens still more petals and blooms ever larger. It loves life again. He is mine completely now. We get more and more sales. I get more and more gifts. The wife gets less and less. During his con-version phase I'm available to make love with him whenever and wherever he needs me. I'm reliably there to reinforce his decision to be with me.

"Eventually, his wife finds out everything. That's certain. Most wives then use their kids as pawns on a chess board. They try to block me from separating her, the queen, from her husband, the king. But that ploy never stops me. I take her pawns right off the board. I tell him there's always another piano recital or the next baseball game he can go to, but I'm available at this same time, right now; and I feel this insatiable hungering need to have his penis inside me. The lotus opens even more petals. It feels safe. It basks in adoration. It knows it is magnificent and loved.

"Trust me on this one. My mouth, my vagina, and my eager cli-toris, always triumph over piano recitals and baseball games. Once I've had his penis inside my vagina and inside my mouth, I hold all the trump cards in this phase of the game. Once the wife plays her 'I've got the kids' card, I run trump on her and book my grand slam. I'll even give the kids little presents and tell them I'm a good friend of their dad's. That divides their loyalties and drives the wife totally nuts. But, she's now under a social constraint to be pleasant,

since the kids like me. But her guts are being eaten away because she knows I'm seeing her husband. She knows I've got all the power in her new, tangled relationship.

"I work on the husband's mind as much as I work on his penis. I get him to where he feels he must do his utmost to please me. I want him to feel he can never give me enough sales or presents or money. I whisper erotic things to him whenever we're together. I wear sexy negligee. I lay my hands on his penis whenever I can, even in public places. I tell him what a wonderful penis he has and how complete as a woman I feel, when it's inside my vagina while he's making love with me."

"You are an amazing whore, Marty. I had no idea how much thought goes into your seduction process. My complements. Please continue." David was fascinated.

"Thank you, David. Certainly. I emphasize feelings and love every time I talk with my man. I tell him how wonderful he makes my vagina feel; how much I love having my mouth on his penis; how much I love sucking him off and tasting his cum in my mouth. Understand, David. I want to always be on his mind. I want my soul living in his heart and blood. I want his thoughts of me pulsing through his blood and into his penis, making it grow rock-hard from merely thinking of me, even when he's away from me. I want him obsessed with me; and so, lust crazed, that he's anxious to leave his marriage and separate from his wife. I don't actually want marriage with any of these men. I just want them as suitors for their sales. It's like having a string line of captured fish.

"Once I burrow into a man's mind his wife starts becoming repulsive to him. I've become fresh air and sunshine to the lotus. She becomes dark cold mud. He finds fault with her. He dislikes the sound of her voice. It's never soft enough or sexy enough. He starts disliking the way she gesticulates with her hands and arms because she doesn't move them suggestively or erotically enough. Her ass is

suddenly too fat. Before he met me, her ass was fine. He loved hold-ing it while he pumped his semen into her; but now, it's suddenly flabby, fat and disgusting. He knows the difference. He's become a connoisseur of tushes.

"Her kisses are suddenly too sloppy. Before me, he didn't mind her lingering wet smacks. He thought they were kind of cute and innocent. Now he wipes them off as if they carry germs. And they do. They carry the wife germ. They contaminate his lips now; lips he wants to keep clean for me. Her dress and make up seem drab now. Her sparkle is gone. She's become a tarnished boor, like an old, food-splattered necktie.

"She doesn't use feathers and oils for sex props. I do. She doesn't think to use alcohol in her mouth to get him hard for that mirac-ulous second and third ejaculation time. I do. She doesn't think of mouthing and tonguing his balls to drive him crazy. I do. BDSM is farthest from her mind at night. After chasing her kids all day, she wants to sleep. But, BDSM is not far from my lover's mind. He wants to tie me up; whip me; spank me; hear me scream and beg for more; feel my nails digging into his back; feel his balls in my mouth; feel my gentle teeth nibbling his sex, titillating him; gently, teasingly squeezing him; and doing all sorts of imaginative, creative, naughty things with him.

"Eroticism dances in his mind while she sleeps. She's chased the kids all day. She has no clue that he constantly thinks about having sex with me. She wants and needs her sleep. It doesn't even occur to her to be sexy. She's exhausted. Sex is the furthest thing from her mind. He tells me what goes on in their house. I understand the dynamics even better than he does. I know their marriage is on a slippery slope.

"My lover now sees his wife in a different light. He starts thinking her humor is no longer funny. He finds faults with everything she says and does. A rejection process takes place in their marriage as his

limbic zone begins asserting dominance over his rational thoughts. As this transformation process gathers momentum he begins viewing his wife's friends and her social demands as intrusions upon his valuable time with me. His home life with its chores and routines become tedious for him. He resents the home life which he and his wife created. He feels his home has become his prison. I notice by the way he talks about his wife and his home life that he now regrets getting married.

"While I shamelessly swallow all the semen from his penis, I'm acutely aware that I'm sucking the happiness out of his marriage. I even tell myself that my behavior is like a serpent's. I think I should be ashamed of myself, but I'm not. I simply don't care about her or her marriage, or even about my lover; not really. I tell myself that snakes must eat too. Besides, the more often I'm with him, the more I enjoy sucking his penis and making love with him. Affairs become like that for me. They grow stronger and more enjoyable while I'm separating the husband from his wife.

"Once I've come into my lover's life, I study how to upend his wife and conquer her. I make little suggestions and digs when the opportunity window opens and presents itself. I'll opine that his wife's obsession with her garden is a waste of time when better produce is commercially available. I feign sympathy that he's married to a woman who needs to keep her unsightly body hidden under baggy clothes.

"It's my seductress version of a chess game. I keep after the king. I focus on bringing him down. My version of winning this game requires getting him into my bed. Once I accomplish that, I achieve checkmate. It is then game over, as far as his money is concerned. Unlike chess, the other woman still has options. She can either tolerate me until I finish pillaging the marital assets and tire of her husband; or she can get divorced. Life goes on until I warehouse her husband on my string of captured lovers, or I toss him back into the

sea. Carl's wife, with my determined help, killed herself. She's the only wife that got that irrational."

David sought to understand the tenacity that underpinned Marty's commitment to sales:

"Is it fair to say you view your sales methods as a type of sporting contest? And, would you say you have an unblemished record when it comes to tearing a salesman away from his wife and family?"

"Yes David! That's a great way to describe my approach. I approach sales with the same mindset as one who plays competitive sports. I play to win! But honestly, there are some men whom I have not been able to seduce; at least not yet. Some of them actually take their marriage vows seriously. But there are plenty of men who don't."

Marty laughed. She had enormous pride in her work:

"When I want sales from a man, I'll do sex-for-sales to get him to do my bidding," she continued: "Most salesmen simply redirect their existing book of business to us. I make sure he spends his earnings from cannibalizing his book of business on me. My lover knows I see his sales reports, so he doesn't try to cheat me. I get all the gifts and dinners; and I get to go on all the product promotional trips. His wife gets practically nothing while this process takes place. When he's finished running through his book and his sales dry up, I let him go back to his wife because I have no further use for him. Most wives take their man back. I don't understand relationships like that. Some say that's love. I think it's pathetic.

"I keep the best salesmen close to me. I never let their wives have those guys back. It's like keeping only the largest, most highly prized tunas. The great ones keep getting me new sales. They hustle. They get things done; make things happen. The dullards just work off their book of clients and friends, and then they're finished. With my keepers, I consider myself five for five. Four of my lovers' wives became alcoholics or bridge players with their loser friends; and Carl's wife, *the ultimate mouse-wife loser, committed suicide. So, yes, David. I have an unblemished record!"*

"Well, Marty," beamed David, *"I'm extremely proud of you and your selfless dedication to your work. You've earned your 20 percent raise through honest hard work. You've proven you're invaluable in dealing with pesky, interfering wives. I wish I could have seen her go flying off the highway into the sky. That had to be a crazy scene. Great job, Marty, well done! Masterful! Brilliant!"*

"Thank you, David. Your approval means a lot. I appreciate your faith in me. It's easy for me to do well in sales because I naturally love sex so much. I've known I was a nymphomaniac since I was eighteen and a half. I'm a lot like Mother that way. She still has several lovers, but I've taken promiscuity much further than she has. Mother is happy with the lovers she has. But I love the thrill of ripping a man from his marriage, sucking out his sales, and moving on to other men. I enjoy that intellectual challenge of seducing a new man. Mom is past her prime. But I'm just starting my best years. I expect I'll seduce dozens more salesmen before I retire. It's just who I am.

CHAPTER TWO

The only way to get rid of a temptation is to yield to it (Oscar Wilde: Picture of Dorian Gray)

Intimacy, with a partner, beautiful; with a couple, wonderful; with a group, fabulous; but above all, intimacy (Rosemary Ness-Bitner)

When you are playing for love, you must play for keeps (Rosemary Ness-Bitner)

LOVING LUST

"There's one other feeling I get, David, since you asked me to tell you all about my feelings. It happens when a group of men join me for an orgy. Mother never did orgies, but I love doing them. I absolutely love them. I crave being the naughty centerpiece girl of orgies. I love having multiple male partners simultaneously giving me pleasure. It's non-stop adoration, titillation, and orgasms. Orgies never seem to last long enough; I enjoy them so much. I always say yes, gladly, to orgy invitations.

"Quite a few of our salesmen prefer an orgy setting."

"They do?" This revelation shocked David.

"Yes. They get their erotic highs knowing I'm making love with other men that they know; and all at the same time. It's a form of camaraderie for them. They get similar highs that other men have when they're on the winning sports team. Some men prefer team sports over individual sports. It's their need to feel a brotherly bond.

I'm grateful that a lot of men have that need; and I'm thrilled when they choose me to satisfy it. Orgies bring out the nympho in me.

"When their penises are all huge and firm, proving to each other that they can satisfy my lust, I know I'm providing exceptional sales service. I'm helping them bond to each other with their common experience. I feel glorious. There's no other feeling quite like it. I'm their enabler. And, they love me for being that. You've seen how stimulated I get after our murders, David. Well, orgies are almost as exciting as that; and it's continuous throughout the entire orgy with five to seven partners instead of only with our two assistants. Mother has no idea what she's missed."

"She doesn't know?" David doubted Marty. He knew Susan saw the sales reports.

"Oh, I think she can guess what I'm doing. She gets the sales reports. She can put things together. I was only saying I believe she regrets not doing what I do. You see, David, while I'm making love with several men at the same time, I feel that each of my lovers wants to do with me what another man is already doing with me. The man with his penis in my hand is envious of the man who has his penis in my vagina, and they are both envious of the man whose penis is in my mouth. And they all envy the feelings of the man whose scrotum I'm kneading with my other hand. It's the ultimate in continuous erotic stimulations. I don't think Mother ever had those experiences. But I don't know. She doesn't talk about her sex life.

"Anyway, David, that man I'm fondling during the orgy is excited out of his mind with anticipation. He can't wait to enter me somewhere, anywhere; and he can't decide which orifice he'd prefer to use to make love with me. I feel giddy. I have this power over him; knowing that I can tease his penis, keeping him waiting until I'm ready for him. He's going insane waiting to join his lust with mine. I can tell he's practically dying to come inside me. Lust rages wildly in all of us. Then I let go of all inhibition. I let the last partner inside

me. Then I copulate and suck like a wild mink. I just totally love every mindless minute of it. When I'm in my lust-love mode like that, I know I'm creating this magical, unforgettable bond with all my lovers.

"I love this power I have. They'll do whatever I ask. They'll hold my body in different positions to give me the greatest sensitivity. They'll suck my nipples and rub me everywhere to stimulate me. They're very respectful and careful never to hurt me. They all want to thrust their penises into me. I welcome them, shamelessly; one after the other. I want all of them to enjoy sex with me. I strive to please every one of them, treating each of them specially, and lovingly. I experience this intensely euphoric, loving feeling.

"It's otherworldly and uplifting, David. It makes me tremble with ecstasy. My blood courses with lust. I never tire of making love while I'm doing an orgy. It's like I move steadily from one plateau of lust satisfaction onto another, higher plateau, then another even higher level of lust, until I've drained all the semen from every one of the men and exhausted them. Then, there's that afterglow of it all while they all pet me and kiss me while they're coming down from their sexual highs, bringing me down along with them. It's adoration. They express it openly because they love me and what I'm willing to do with them. It's very intimate, precious, and beautiful.

"Orgies are the closest experiences I've ever had to satisfying my nymphomania; but even those romps never satisfy it. Nymphomania is actually a mental thing. And I carefully manage them to keep them selective and purposeful. But I feel I must make love whenever I possibly can with those charming men that have money or sales to give me. I can go from an orgy with six of them, until they have all spent their semen into me; and then meet another six men in my hotel room and perform a second orgy with that second group, shortly afterwards. My passion for these lust fests does not diminish.

"I'm just as enthused, wildly uninhibited and crazed to do my second grouping as I was my first. I never tire of the sex. I love the intensity of all of it and how I lose myself in feeling the non-stop pleasures associated with it. I have no shame or regrets about my need, David. I positively LOVE it. You never need to worry that I'll tire of my work. I want more and more of it. U. G. G. A. is an extremely gratifying work environment for me."

"You are a perfect fit with our firm, Marty," smiled David while lifting her hand to kiss it. *"I am as gratified as you are. Please, continue. I love learning all of this. It's fascinating."* David held her hand aside and leaned forward to kiss Marty's leg above her knee.

"David, I liked what you just did. You know you charm me. Would you like to stop? We could have fun. I'd like that very much."

"No, as much as I want to; but I 'd like to wait until later. It will be wonderful. I promise you. But please, continue."

"Of course, David. I'll be patient." Marty smiled broadly and blinked her eyes before continuing. *"Well, the overriding feeling that I take away from my orgies is that my lovers have all bonded to me—not to their wives, girlfriends, or children; but to me. It's because we all know that, as a group, we did something intensely personal, loving, secretive, and special. Those men experienced seeing me in my erotic, primal lust state. They saw how much I loved it. They felt my love for them. My partners each experienced that special bond, knowing that, together, they took a woman to the limits of her ultimate pleasures; and each one of them knew that the rest of them felt it too. And we all knew it was beautiful. It was an erotic sensation for all of us, knowing that several shameless, selfless men simultaneously loved me with all their hearts and minds. That's something that will stay with every one of us, forever.*

"It's our beautiful, secretly shared intimacy, that tightness of our group feeling. I love that feeling, David. There is no other feeling like it in the world. When all of them are communally loving me and

releasing their cum into me, I'm the happiest woman in the world. My mind flies away to another place and time and my body feels such euphoric sensations that I tremble from the passion of it all. I can't live without having orgies."

"You are serious, aren't you? I mean this is something you can't just stop, can you?" Again, David leaned inward, this time kissing Marty's other leg, also above her knee.

"David, you're making me tremble inside. I'm getting moist. Couldn't we stop, just for a little while? Couldn't we play?" Coquettish desires assumed Marty's face. Her lips drew a tight, wistful smile. Few men could decline her offer.

"Marty, Marty. Let's wait. Please, I need to wait." David's eyebrows raised with his nod. His eyes peered deeply into hers; not smiling eyes, but commanding ones.

She acquiesced, shrugged her shoulders, and continued. *"Okay, I was saying that I sometimes imagine I'm this ancient pagan temple goddess, and I'm experiencing the same joyous feelings she must have felt when her people worshiped her. The people paid money to their temple, and the men were required to make love with the temple prostitutes while their wives obediently watched the tribe's fornication rituals. The prostitutes were the holy vessels of the temple. During ritual orgies, the temple prostitutes bonded the people to each other and to the temple. The prostitute was deified, honored, loved, and glorified. She held top rank in their society. She was their holy grail.*

"When I'm copulating with four, or five, or six men, I have the exhilarating feeling that my body becomes their holy vessel. My vagina becomes their holy grail. It's all so natural, David. They love me as their pagan whore and they bond with me and with each other, forever. It's an incredibly uplifting experience. It's more powerful than my religion, which considers me a hopeless sinner that must be saved from damnation.

"Religious doctrine has always confused me. How can anyone look at an innocent beautiful baby and say it was a born sinner? I'll never understand that thinking. It's so presumptuous. I think it's irrational; even crazy. It says more about how indoctrinated priests need to become for them to believe something obviously wrong thinking like that, than what it says about an innocent little baby. Bonding within an orgy is a much stronger, more realistic bond than believing in some unseeable god. The orgy joins human souls, releases their inhibitions; frees their guilts, and solidifies unshakable communal love. It's far more powerful than contrived cerebral abstractions. It's visceral. It courses through our blood.

"Those temple prostitutes must have understood, as I do, that they were performing the will of the spirits; and that they were doing a great goodness. Fornication is an act of glorious destruction and glorious loving renewal. It's a beautiful, loving act for those who approach it with the right, loving mind-set. Some revile women who think and feel like me, but I can't let them distract me. I love who I am.

"I've decided it's pointless to concern myself with how others regard me. Results are what matters. I have built tremendous good will in the sales community. When a salesman thinks about where to place assets, he also thinks about loving me and releasing his semen into me. I have a dedicated following because those men appreciate how much I love my work.

"But aren't you a practicing Christian, a Catholic?" David puzzled as he probed Marty's psyche. *"How can you deliberately, consciously choose to violate the commandments against adultery and coveting? Don't you have feelings of remorse or guilt? Aren't you a living contradiction to your faith?"*

Marty shook her head, as if tossing off the contradiction. *"David, adultery is simply something adults need to do to get out of ruts they've gotten stuck in. After their affair ends, they can either slide back into their rut or stay out of it. In or out of the rut is a choice. There's nothing shameful or immoral about adultery. It's simply a natural, healthy behavior that ushers in freedoms and changes; stirs the pot; often livens things up. And it promotes healthy thinking about where people want their lives to be."*

"But your faith?" David's eyes questioned Marty's credibility.

"Faith?" Marty pulled her head back. *"Come on, David. I gave up on my faith when Mother abandoned me. I went through my acceptance of rejection process. That's when I realized my faith didn't care about me. It was up to me to care about me; no one else. I went through another process, the process of adoption. Step by step, I adopted the Modern Morality Standard. Penis by penis, seduction by seduction, I came to my enlightenment about my true faith: Immorality; make that Immorality with a touch of anarchy, like a vodka Martini with a splash of Gin. That's my faith. I have no morality at all. I'm being true to MY faith when I seduce a married man. I pat myself on my own back when a man commits adultery with me. It's an accomplishment.*

"Think of it this way: the husband was indoctrinated from infancy to follow some religious dogma; and I helped him get himself out of that rut. I showed him true freedom. Religions don't see it that way. They think people need to be slaves to their marriages; but I don't. I have no hang ups about adultery. I'm not religious.

"Besides, I don't violate the commandment against coveting when I make love with a married man or when he joins one of my orgies. The Church has it wrong about the coveting commandment. They're confused. Love is a feeling. It's not a possession that can be coveted in the first place. Love simply cannot be coveted. Period. It's a personal bond that happens between two people. You can wish you had love, yourself; but you cannot ever have someone else's love. That's impossible. And I do not want what the man and his wife have, whatever that is. Usually, it's a master-slave relationship thing.

I don't want to replace his wife. That's furthest from my mind. I only want to uncork his sexual pleasures. He can always return to his wife.

"A marriage is a business. A wife may own half a marriage, but she can never own the feelings in a man's mind or the feelings that bring his little friend to erection. No one can own those feelings. A marriage license doesn't make that little man become stiff. Feelings do that. Feelings can't be put off limits by commandments or laws. Those who try to impose limits on sexual love are simply wrong. Their efforts are as futile as schemes to reverse the tides or prevent the sun from rising. Nature can not be defeated."

"So, you don't think there's such a thing as adultery or coveting?"

"Yes, those things exist, but there's a way to deal with them. When Jesus stood beside a woman who committed adultery, she was about to be stoned to death. Jesus spoke up and said that the man who is without sin should cast the first stone. No one threw a stone. No one is without sin. There's also a similar lesson in the deaths of Aaron's two oldest sons. The lesson being that some things must simply be accepted, not understood; but accepted. It's natural and normal for a man to make love with a woman who appeals to him. Accept it."

"You are quite the philosopher, aren't you? Or, are you just telling me the wishful thoughts of a whore?"

"Not wishful thoughts, David." Marty shook her head again. This time she smiled a triumphant smile. *"Reality. It's how the world is ordered, by its natural order. It's common sense. If the spirits wanted a sin free world, they would have made everyone perfect, free of desires. There wouldn't even be a concept called sin. We wouldn't even be having this discussion. But we were created as sinners because the spirits wanted us that way. Maybe they did that for their amusement; or, maybe, to keep us from stagnating. Who knows?*

"But speaking for myself, I love to sin. I thoroughly enjoy it. And I freely admit it. I especially love committing infidelities with married men; and I'm thrilled when I tempt a married man into intimacy with me. I especially enjoy married men. They appreciate and love me. They're the most grateful of all my lovers, and I enjoy releasing them from their cares. Who does not sin?

"And you have no morality issues over creating these infidelities, even when you wreck a home?" David seemed incredulous.

"No, David; honestly, I don't. Like I said, the man usually goes back to his wife and kids, if the wife lets nature take its course. After I have his money, he can receive her forgiveness and climb back into his marriage harness. It's not some big deal. From my perspective, it's no different than milking a cow; or, rather, it's simply sweet, innocent, lovable Marty; happily milking a prostrate, and its associated bank accounts."

"Amazing! You really are a whore, thoroughly through and through, aren't you?"

"You bet. Whore to my core. Bad to my bones. Now, I'll tell you something else that may surprise you." Marty nodded her head with a smugness face, affirming she possessed surprising information that she was about to share with David.

"What? Tell me. Nothing about you would shock me, Marty."

CHAPTER THREE

Morality cannot be absolute when it depends upon whose laws define it, or upon the direction prevailing winds blow. It must default to each individual's gut check and what one decides is acceptable behavior for one's life; and that, too, may change. Defining morality? It's easier to nail gelatin to the sky. (Rosemary Ness-Bitner, author)

IMMORALITY RISING

"Thank you, David; but there's a new trend that I thought would interest you. We seem to be reverting to the more relaxed moral standards that the Romans had during the later centuries of their great empire. People are openly accepting and embracing prostitution. Porn stars are becoming famous and sought after as status symbols for wealthy men. Many men, and some women, seek intimate long-term associations with prostitutes. This is happening while the poor people among us keep getting poorer and poorer. The wealthy people, my clientele, don't care one wit about the poor. They actually never did; but now, it's more obvious. The wealthy actually despise the poor. They feel no guilt whatsoever about shunning the poor, while lavishing unseemly sums of money on prostitutes.

"Couple bookings on my Premium Member Service show solid growth, indicating married women are also becoming more interested in expanding their sexual horizons. When the economy fell into our Second Greater Depression, people gave up on morality.

They threw in the towel. They welcomed immorality. Debauchery has sprouted everywhere. Prostitution is growing like a weed, David.

"Three of my salesmen have wives that enjoy threesomes with me and their husbands. More and more, married women are accepting the Modern Morality Standard's reality. Most husbands crave extramarital sex; many wives do, too. I enjoy doing married couples for several reasons. First, I go to their homes, so I avoid hotel room charges. Second, the wife sees her husband paying me so there's no need to hide money from her. Third, it's wildly erotic knowing that I'm making love with a woman's husband and she's accepting the arrangement. I encourage her to get into the spirit of it."

"How?"

"Oh, simple things at first. Like having her rub his balls while he's copulating with me; and then graduating her to kissing me while he makes love with me, as if she's blessing me. Eventually she'll perform cunnilingus after he's come inside me. Then, I know her inhibitions are shattered, and she'll accept everything I do, with both of them.

"All three of these women love cunnilingus, as I do; and as their husbands do, so we always have terrific sex. I love it when the wife goes down on my vagina and brings me to orgasm; and then, later, kisses my mouth and suckles my nipples while her husband thrusts and comes into my vagina," Marty's smile brimmed with prideful memories. She recalled breakthroughs with the women she converted to her thinking.

"I get an especially warm feeling knowing a wife is totally okay watching me making love with her husband in her bed. It works the other way, too. I'll do cunnilingus on the wife; and then I'll kiss her mouth while her husband has sex with her. I think their minds imagine that both of them are making love with me while they are having sex with each other.

"After a wife sees her husband ejaculate inside me, then collapse on top of me and wildly kiss me, she knows she's gifted him a special

erotic experience. It's erotic, but it's also loving and romantic. Love making with me is a special gift from the wife who desires to prove her unrestrained love for her husband. Those couples reach a deeper level of love, and those wives know their husbands will love them more as a result of their gift. That's true of my repeat customers. Some wives massage their husband's backs after he has come inside me. Some even kiss my vagina and massage my shoulders, neck, and forehead after their husband finishes. That shows profound love and understanding of the wife for her husband, and their appreciation for me.

GEORGE AND BERTIE

"That brings me to this one special couple, David. They are my favorite couple. Their names are George and Bertie. They are twenty years older than me and very sweet and loving. They live in a huge mansion on a large estate with tennis courts and an Olympic sized outdoor pool. My sessions with them are especially endearing. I first undress both of them and stimulate them. I French kiss both of them, I suck George's penis for a while, to get him excited; and then I suck Bertie's nipples and massage her vagina. She gets ready for sex quickly. She gets super moist very easily. After Bertie undresses me, we get on their giant-sized reclining California King-sized bed. Bertie begins our fun by kissing my nipples and my butterfly wings and massaging my vagina. Then, she has me get on my knees, facing her toes with my legs spread out widely. I get all creamy wet almost immediately when she puts me in that position, because I know she'll next spread my thighs with her hands; and start kissing my sex, from behind.

"Her stimulations make me tremble and moan. Bertie's incredible with the ways she does oral sex. I just let myself go. She likes slapping my ass when we have our foreplay. Then she turns me around.

We face. We kiss and touch until we're both feeling the passion-heat. Bertie then lies on her back with my vagina resting on her face while she performs beautiful, sensational cunnilingus. She quickly finds my clit. Then, everything happens fast. I soon experience my first orgasm. It's my first of many. Bertie takes her time after my first. She becomes methodical and relentless, like she's savoring an ice cream cone; continuously licking me, slowly and softly. While she does her tongue caresses her special way, I think she mentally connects herself to another, more spiritual world, somehow. No man or woman gives me more beautiful, loving oral sex than Bertie. She takes my mind into her other world with her; and puts me in this mood, where all I want is more.

"Then, she sits me upright, leans herself back against the raised mattress back of their bed; pulls me up close to her, with my back to her, and wraps her legs around me. I feel like I'm secure in her special cocoon while we sit that way. We turn our heads together and French kiss again.

'Did you like how I kissed you? Was it good for you?' she always asks me.

'You were perfect, Bertie. You were beautiful. My orgasm was wonderful. I love how I felt while I came. I love how I feel. You're so good to me,'

"I always reassure her that her oral sex pleases me. I always tell her she's wonderful. And she is.

"Early on, I realized my relationship with Bertie was going to be different from all my other relationships; and that it would be very special. That reveal came to me one afternoon in their bedroom. George and I were sitting, side by side, on their bed. He had his arm around me. We had begun our foreplay with French kissing. George moved his free hand to my vagina; and soon he was rubbing me. He had reached three fingers inside me. His fingers quickly found my clitoris, and he was stimulating me.

"*George was fabulous, David. Soon, my tush was flexing and bumping my vagina in wild upward thrusts, assisting his finger-play with my clitoris. And, romantic me, I began coming. I was feeling the passion; absolutely loving what George was doing. I mean, David, that session was so erotic. If it had been filmed, I know it would have been a smash hit. My vagina was taking on a life of its own, there on the bed; the way it was lifting into the rhythm of George's fingers, And, of course, I was moaning and panting while I French kissed George. I couldn't get enough of what he was doing. I was loving it. My hand reached his penis. I totally love George's penis, David. It's a very large one, almost as large several of my porn partners.*"

"*So, size matters to you?*"

"*Well, no; but yes. My Miss Muffy easily accommodates a smaller six, or seven, inch penis. She tightens around it, and I get the same erotic sensations that I feel with a larger ten, or twelve, inch penis. But, when I have a large penis, like George's, or Carl's, or Bob's' or many of my porn partners' inside me, I then notice the extra sensation of being stretched and dominated by the penis; and I positively love that feeling. I think it's a primal thing, David. A woman loves to feel dominated by having a huge penis inside her. That feeling psychologically reassures her that the man behind that penis is a strong man who can protect her from the wild beasts in the forest; and that primal need has stayed with women's psyches since the first humans walked the Earth.*"

"*So, bigger is better is an accurate statement?*"

"*Yes, but it's not everything. We women have evolved, David. A woman wants a man who is a good, compassionate lover, like Bob is. A woman wants a man who can provide for her or at least contribute as a partner. Size matters, yes; but intimacy always resides in the mind's limbic zone; and there are many ways a man can succeed there. He can become expert with his tongue, for example; and give his woman fantastic oral sex. He can please her by being good to her,*" *providing for her, comforting her, balancing her emotions. There are many, many ways for a man to succeed with a woman."*

"But we were talking about George and his size."

"Yes. When I touched George's penis, I discovered it was already hard. George gets extremely hard. It's like he almost becomes a steel rod that has plumped up to four times its normal girth. I was delighted to discover how ready George was, because, as I said, my vagina was already very eager to have his penis enter me. So, I stroked it slowly, using some lubrication oil, until I could tell by George's body motions, he was going crazy with lust for me.

"As he entered me, his hand continued stimulating my vagina, and his fingers were busily feeling all around the crest of my vagina. I go totally crazy when I'm stimulated like that while I'm making love. I totally love it. Well, that's the moment when this strangeness happened. It was like a whole new dimension was opening up for me. Bertie began stroking the back of my head and kissing my neck while I was making love with George. It was wildly erotic, David. She knew how to deliver a message. She whispered:

'You're my sweet baby. I love you so much; so very much. I'll always be good to you.'

"Well, the way she spoke the word baby struck me as kind of weird; and I didn't think much about it at the time. But, later, after George had entered me; and after I had flexed my tush many times to meet his penis's loving thrusts; and after he released his gushing stream of semen inside me, I rolled over on my stomach. I felt complete and wonderful. That's when Bertie opened this new dimension further. She began massaging my feet, my leg calves, my thighs, my back, and shoulders. And, all the while Bertie was massaging me, she kept kissing my body everywhere. She kissed my calves, thighs, back, shoulders, neck, and my butt cheeks. Now, these were not just quick, peck kisses. They were kisses that pressed into my flesh and delivered honest feelings. I could feel Bertie's love for me coming

through those kisses. It was very real and heartfelt. All the while Bertie did this kissing, she whispered:

'You're my special angel baby. I'm so happy you've come back to me. I've missed you so much. You stay with George and me. We'll always be good to you. We love you very, very much.'

"Well, that kind of made me wonder if Bertie was a bit mentally off, you know what I mean, David?"

"Did you ask her what she was talking about?"

"No, I didn't. I first kind of chalked it up to some kind of fantasy she was having, like Bertie's private dream; and I didn't think any more about it. But she continued with it like this was going to go on endlessly. That's when I had this epiphany."

"Epiphany?"

"Yes, David. Please take me seriously here. This was very important to me. It suddenly struck me that the spirits somehow had intended Bertie and George, and me, to find each other; like we all had some kind of deep-seated need that we could only fulfill by being with each other, like we were a family. I realized that Bertie and George were psychologically accepting me as their daughter. As I lay there, being kissed with this reverence and blessing that Bertie was feeling for me, I also realized that the spirits had sent them into my world to complete me; to give me the honest love from a mother and father that I didn't have from the age of five, when I lost Dad.. The spirits were giving me two loving parents.

"That's when I realized the spirits were completing my life. They had given me Bob, for an intimate, romantic loving partner. They had given me my salesmen and my porn partners, for my loving, intimate, romantic, caring friends on a professional basis. And, now, they were giving me George and Bertie, as my loving, intimate, romantic, caring parents; giving me two people whom I could trust and confide my deepest secrets to, because they loved me like a daughter. I felt almost completed as a whole human

being, and grateful that a huge missing piece of my life was being restored to me."

"Almost? Why almost?"

"Well, David. Honestly, to become fully completed as a totally well rounded, immoral woman, I still feel the need to have a very special, loving intimacy with my partner in our business and our murders. I believe once I have that, I will have completed the entire world of love and intimacy that exists for me; and that will fully satisfy my need to be a completely loved, emotionally well balanced, totally immoral woman."

"Me?"

"Yes, David. Of course, you. You are the mainstay centerpiece of my world. You know that. I know you know that. I've told you about the intensity of my feelings. My desires for intimacy with you are beyond palpable, David. They have actually become obsessive. You have no idea how often I dream that the two of us will discover the beauty we'll have when we finally come together and consummate our friendship."

"I think I understand, Marty. And, we will, soon; after we complete today's discussion. There are things I need you to help me with first. But let's finish discussing George and Bertie."

"Okay, David."

"Thank you. So, did you continue seeing them after your epiphany, and was there any difference in the way they treated you? I mean, this woman was practically calling you, her daughter."

"I know. It did put a different context to things, but, like I said, I thought she might have been having some kind of mental blip, so I continued seeing them on the same paying client basis as before. Our next session was going almost exactly as the meeting we had before. She again kissed me all over my body like that. That's when I decided I needed to be honest. I told Bertie I loved her. During all our subsequent sessions, I've always told Bertie I love her; and that's

the truth, David. I do love Bertie. I feel a great outpouring of love for her. I love George too. In our sessions, Bertie always massages my shoulders and kisses my neck; and then she massages my breasts and gently rolls my nipples in her fingers. While Bertie massages me, George always slips pillows under my tush. He loves to prop my vagina way up high like that."

"Sounds like a family obsessed with psychological incest."

"Incest? I suppose so, but I don't care what anyone thinks of us. It's beautiful. The relationship is beautiful. Anyway, after George props me up, he kneels down on the bed, before my vagina; and he kisses it; like he worships it or something; and then he copulates with me, long and slow. George loves making love in this position, because it's so easy for him to plunge his penis way deeply inside me. And, he does his depth plunges so slowly and lovingly; they're absolutely heavenly. My vagina responds beautifully; and I always bump my tush upward to help him reach deeply inside me; and help him feel as snugly joined to me as he can possibly be. My upward lift helps his penis reach the tip of my cervix. That's where George loves to be when he releases his semen stream. It's always lovely; absolutely lovely, uninhibited, freely given sex. Thanks to George's loving way with me, that position has become my absolutely favorite position for sex in my porn films as well. George is a sweet, considerate lover, David. He's such an incredibly, loving man. With George, our love making is always all about pleasing me.

"Bertie is a bit heavy and large-boned, with a really beautiful, warm, and radiant face. She's actually rather stunning. She calls me endearing names like baby cakes, sweet muffin, angel darling, sweet baby kitten, precious sweetheart, sweet love, and special heart throb.

"She cradles me tenderly and gently rocks me from side to side, kisses my cheeks; then brushes my hair and lovingly massages my forearms and hands with her creams while George continues love-making with me in my ass uplifted, maiden position. After George

releases inside me, Bertie French kisses me again and squeezes me close to her. I feel like I'm her living doll baby; or like we're two, happy little girls, playing sex games. It's a unique relationship, David.

'I love you, love you, love you my sweet baby cakes, my dear precious kitten,' Bertie says. 'You're my special angel. You're such a good girl. You've never done anything bad or naughty. You're always nice and good. You're so beautiful, and you're such a sexy kitty! No one will ever hurt you or make you do anything you don't want to do, not ever! Bertie will always be here for you. I'll always protect you from anyone who tries to harm you, no matter what. I need you to know that I totally love you.' Bertie always says things like that to me, like I'm her life's obsession.

"While I hear her talking to me that way, I feel like I'm some innocent little bear cub under the protection of my big mamma bear; even though you and I murder people. I wonder what's goes on inside Bertie's mind when she says those things.

"I feel like no matter what bad things I've ever done or what bad things I'll do in the future, I don't need to worry about them. I know Bertie always has my back. After sex, Bertie settles down and does my fingernails and toenails the same way professional manicurists and pedicurists do them. When she does that, she makes me feel like I'm her queen; and she's, my servant. It's not exactly natural. I'm still getting used to it. We'll choose a nail color that we think will help make my fingers look sexy while performing fellatio in my next film. That usually means bright red; or sometimes purple if I'm playing the role of a cheating housewife. For my wicked bad girl scenes, where I'll play dominatrix or a bad-assed bank robber, or murderess, Bertie paints my nails black, or black with tiny silver lightning bolts in them.

"When the weather's nice the three of us go outside to play in their pool. It's outdoors and glass enclosed. The water is heated. Around the pool are huge overhead space heaters mounted on big

steel frames. I love undressing and getting naked by the pool at night. I love looking up at all the stars, searching the heavens, while the three of us make love. It's an ethereal, other worldly experience, like we're floating along on a cloud, somewhere in heaven, gazing into those beautiful stars; and we're doing what feels wonderful and natural; not having a single care in the world. I love nakedness. It helps unburden me from all my cares, David. It puts me in a place, mentally, where I feel like I don't need to pretend about anything or make excuses for anything about myself or the things I do. I believe George and Bertie understand that, too; that's why we have our nighttime pool sex so often. There's an honest innocence about it; so casual and so loving.

"We usually start by lying on huge rubber mats beside the baby pool. Bertie brings her portable electric vibrator and a squirt bottle of lubricating oil. Bertie likes to use sex toys while we're playing orgasm fun games. She's expert at this. She gently, teasingly, works her vibrator over the crown of my vagina while kissing my neck and using two fingers to massage my clitoris. And she squirts her clear slippery lubricating oils all over my breasts, chest, and vagina. She makes me into this slippery, horny, fuck bunny. It's all very erotic. George plays a role in this foreplay. He French kisses me and rolls my nipples in his fingers while Bertie concentrates on exciting my vagina.

"Their stimulations are so erotic I often have four or five dreamy orgasms while we're still doing foreplay. They love stimulating me. They get me laughing and screaming uncontrollably, until I'm completely out of my mind crazy with pleasure. After I've already had four or five orgasms, Bertie positions me, kneeling, tummy down, on one of the big rubber pool mats, with my legs spread open wide. George slides into position under my vagina. He lies on his back; and I face his toes. Bertie then gets behind me and places her hands on my hips. Then, she bounces me."

"Bounces you?"

"Yes, it's a very erotic way to pleasure a woman, and Bertie and George have perfected this method. Bertie's hands assist my pelvis, lifting me and guiding me back down, gently. I lift my vagina up; and then lower it down onto George's face.

"George's tongue thrusts into my vagina and tickles my clitoris every time I settle it down onto his face. When I'm on his face, we hold that position for quite a while. It's wildly erotic because I know Bertie is going to be lifting me back up; and then down again. It's a method that kind of makes me really appreciate the sensations of George's tongue, because I know Bertie will be lifting me away. We do this until I'm ultra-sensitive and about to have a massive, explosive orgasm. Soon, I'll feel this huge orgasm coming on. There is this special, unusual way that I feel about this orgasm compared to all my other orgasms, because I know I'm soon going to be gushing all over George's face; and that gives this orgasm a special, naughty twist. It signals that I'm dominating George; or, rather, that Bertie and I, we girls, are dominating George; like we are letting him know that we women are the superior sex.

"Bertie always knows when I'm about to come. She has a remarkable sense about that. When I start to gush, Bertie holds my pelvis down hard on George's face. She brings her knees forward and brackets his head with her knees. Poor George. He's trapped with his face in my vagina. He can't move and he can't breathe. My bottom completely smothers him. There's no way the poor man can breathe while Bertie does this. Bertie knows this. She dominates him this way; but she's far more concerned that I have my final super-spectacular orgasm than she is about whether George can breathe. George's tongue fully extends to engulf my clitoris; and he rapidly works it over the full length of my clitoris. Then, the inevitable happens. I literally explode juices into George's mouth. I have the wildest orgasms I have ever had.

"I always press my vagina down hard on George's face until the last possible second, right before he's about to suffocate. He's so wonderful with his tongue! I hate to lift off of him. But I must lift off; otherwise, I'd kill him. He always gasps for air when we finish; but he never complains. George is a very good sport, and a very considerate lover. My orgasms with George and Bertie are right up there with the best orgasms I have with Carl. Afterwards, I usually need to hold onto a deck chair to steady myself, because repeated orgasms from Bertie's orgasm games, followed by that final, monster orgasm make me lose control of my body.

"I become like a puddle of Jell-O. I sit and I run my hands wildly through my hair. I scream with joy. I grab my own breasts and pinch my own nipples to get back down to reality from my erotic heaven. When I calm down a bit, I grab hold of George's head. I bring him to my deck chair and spread my legs; and I hold my vagina against his mouth while he continues licking me. That keeps me flowing; but now with a slower, sporadic, much gentler orgasm, while I'm still trembling and winding down. I then turn to Bertie and perform cunnilingus on her. I'm so grateful to her for her role in everything we do; and I feel I have to let go of the tremendous energy I've gotten from George's tongue. I feel I must share it with Bertie.

"We play our orgasm games at night. I love having orgasms under the stars. Every time I come, I feel like fireworks are exploding all around me and a huge shower of paper is falling all around me, except the paper isn't confetti. It's thousand, and ten-thousand-dollar bills, piling up all around me until I'm covered in millions of dollars. I don't know why I visualize money like that, David. It must be the whore in me. We always finish orgasms games with George coming inside me. The three of us always end up laughing and rolling on the mat. It's a good, shared, wholesome feeling. Then, we just lie there quietly, holding hands, looking up at

the stars. Every woman should enjoy orgasm games at night, under the stars, like we do. It brings a unique perspective to how blessed we humans are to be alive.

"During our daytime sessions, I'll get on my elbows and knees in their six-inch-deep baby pool, while George enters me doggie style. While George is making love with me, Bertie French kisses me. She loves to French kiss. She always ends our sessions by hugging me, kissing my cheeks, and telling me she wishes I'd stay with her all the time. Sometimes she'll sit beside me with tears rolling down her cheeks, hugging me close to her and French kissing me with deep soulful kissing. She continually tells me she loves me.

"Bertie respects my decision to be a sex worker. She gives me a lot of space that way. She never tries to dissuade me from doing what I love doing. She's the opposite of that. She constantly encourages me to become better and more erotic during my porn performances. She's a combination coach and lover, and my totally unselfish mother figure. She believes in the creation of erotic art in its every form; and she thinks the world needs much more eroticism, especially in adult films. She's done wonders for me as my porn coach.

"I used to think my film performances were just a way to make fast money. Bertie explained that my work is so much more than that. She's put this sense of purpose and confidence into my mind that I never had before. My whole mental attitude about what I do as a porn star has completely changed. I just love her for helping me see myself in this new way."

David's curiosity awakened. *"What are you talking about? What could possibly be more important than making money? What mental attitude? Sex is sex, isn't it? What more could there be to it?"*

Marty shook her head. *"Oh no, David; that's such a chauvinistic way of seeing things. You are missing the whole point of everything.*

You do not understand why I love doing the work I do. Let me explain it to you, the same way Bertie explained it to me.

"Bertie helped me see men's relationships with women the way men see it. You see, David, a man presumes his relationship with a woman will stay in perpetual eros equilibrium. He believes they should love each other, no matter what. He believes she should always be his sexy, perky, eager fuck bunny; just like she was on their honeymoon, or during their first time. He thinks she should never age; or become tired at night; or have a headache; or complain about anything.

"No matter how fat and sloppy he gets; no matter how often he forgets to shave; or how many times he leaves his clothes lying around; or how many times he forgets to walk the dog; or makes her go out in the snow to walk their dog; no matter how many times he forgets to flush his toilet; or how often he puts off getting the car maintained, until it breaks down and she has to walk home on the freeway, through the snow and the rain; or how many times he forgets to take the trash out; or how many hours he wastes away sitting on the couch eating chips, drinking beer and watching endless sports games; or how often he forgets her birthday or their anniversary; in his world view, his woman should always be his sex-crazed, happy, penis adoring, fuck bunny.

"Women have a different world view than those men. They see themselves as being used. So, women stop being happy fuck bunnies for men like those sorts of men. Sex stops happening. But these men can't understand why sex stops happening. Sex feels good, right? All they understand is their relationship world has drifted out of eros equilibrium. They can't imagine that their own behaviors are the reason things are out of equilibrium. They think something has gone wrong with their woman, like she's a car that broke its transmission or something.

"Each of these men starts to fantasize. He imagines that there must be a different world than the one he's living in. He imagines *that somewhere there's a world where he rediscovers his fantasy dream woman fuck bunny. Eventually, he discovers all he needs to do to summon this imaginary world to life, is watch a woman performing erotic sex in an adult film. Once he finds his way to an adult film actress whom he really likes, everything seems pretty normal to him, once again. The film star never complains. She never asks anything of him, and she always is there, on demand, eager to perform as his fantasy fuck bunny.*

"He becomes enthralled by this porn star. She allows him to continue living in his fantasy world; therefore she saves him. He has a place of refuge now. He can escape reality by watching one of her films. She never bitches at him. She's perfect. His mind forms a connection to her. He follows her every thought and deed on Facebook, Twitter, or Instagram; or on some other social media platform. He vicariously falls in love with her. He idolizes and adores her. He constantly thinks about her. He enjoys seeing her having a good time. He loves seeing her smile. He feels good for her when she's smiling and having sex.

"And, here's the clincher, David. He loves watching her experiencing her orgasms. A female's orgasm is the male's equal sign. It equates to everything must be good with his imaginary love object. His fantasy dream girl is happy! She's coming! And, therefore everything suddenly becomes good in his world, too. Men are so fucked up!

"You see, David, by performing in my adult films I'm bringing happiness and mental stability to millions of frustrated men. I perform a valuable social service. Bertie tells me that I need to be proud of what I do, because I'm helping so many men, and many women too, maintain their mentally fucked up, healthy mental balance. In other words, David, I enable millions of men to continue living as pigs and not change their behaviors.

"I see everything so clearly now, David. I'm a powerful force for good! I'm like the United States Navy on constant patrol on the

oceans, that way. I'm providing a tremendous benefit of peace and goodness for the whole world, by being there for the good of the entire world. Whenever I have an orgasm in one of my films, I know there are millions of men out there watching me suddenly contract, roll my eyes until only my whites show, and smile like I've experienced nirvana; and suddenly, those men feel that everything is good and right with their fucked-up view of the world. Now that I understand this beneficial effect that I have on the world's men, I'm putting more of my feelings into every single sex act that I perform.

"Now, I'm giving way more than a hundred percent of myself in my love making, David. I'm now giving ten thousand percent, plus. I can feel the difference. It's huge! It's a mental attitude thing. Oh David, it's made such a tremendous difference in my attitude about performing m porn. I have a hard time explaining it. It's like I'm overcome with this sweetness love, this profound love of intimacy that radiates from me and goes out of me and into the cameras. When I do films now, I fuck with this newly discovered total abandon, this uninhibited passion."

"So, there's some level of difference in your feeling, your enthusiasm? Like you have a built-in fuck meter or something?"

"Positively, David, yes there is. It's like I'm totally crazy happy out of my mind to be making love. I really, really am; and I love performing my roles more than I ever did before. I'm so thrilled while I'm performing before the cameras now, more than I ever was before. Now, when I spread my legs to have sex, I know I'm providing the entire world a vital, necessary public good. I feel so honored that I'm able to help so many people, especially those changeless men.

"Bertie often reaffirms to me that I've chosen a wonderful profession. She encourages me to be very proud of what I do. She wants me always looking my best, especially my hands and bright red fingernails, so they'll show up well while I'm performing fellatio. She stresses how important it is to have a classy image while performing

oral sex. She fears I could get carpel tunnel syndrome from stroking so many penises while making my films, so she constantly massages my forearms, wrists, hands, and fingers. I've always loved doing oral sex with males' penises; but now I'm positively overcome with the thrills of it. Bertie made that difference happen. She really loves me and cares about me. After I've done a scene where I've mouth teased a penis for an entire hour; and licked and sucked it; and helped it ejaculate onto my tongue, Bertie often bounds onto the set to hug and kiss me; and to tell me how wonderfully I did. She's so supportive, David. I just love her. I feel we're inseparable.

"She maintains an account for me at an exclusive beauty parlor and tells me to use their services before every film and before every exclusive Premium Member session, so I'll always look my stunning best. She studies all my films and critiques them. She's proud to play her part by making my hands and fingers beautiful. She has my hands and fingers their dexterous, facile best while I'm stroking the shaft of a penis, coaxing it to ejaculate into my mouth, and while they're kneading my partner's balls.

"Bertie believes hands performing fellatio must look their classiest best. Discerning fans can see that I'm a very high-class whore; not some common slut. Brushing my hair, like Bertie does before every performance, helps it look healthy and vibrant for my critical close-up scenes, especially when my head bobs while I'm sucking a penis. My loyal fans notice those minute details. Bertie knows this. She wants me to be the best-looking, highest-class porn star ever to appear in an adult film. She wants me showing the cameras my ravenous, delicious, 'you just have to fuck me look' at all times. That includes perfect blush, make-up, eye shadow, lipstick, and beautiful lustrous healthy hair.

"I'm certain Bertie cares about me. One day she told me to roll down my panties. I thought she had play time in mind, but this was Bertie being like a mother to me. She told me she bought our way

into an experimental vaccine trial from this small pharmaceutical company in Israel. They had developed a super vaccine that prevented pneumonia and infectious diseases, including Coved 19, all Flu strains, Typhus, Malaria, Aids, HIV, STD, Ebola, Staff infections, actually every disease imaginable. She punctured my tush with a needle and injected a ton of these life saving vaccines into me. She told me that she wanted me to be completely free from worries while making intimate films and having passionate sex with my Premium members and friends. She wants my thoughts totally concentrated on my fucking, at my very best, at all times.

"I had told Bertie about Mother's history with Marvin, how he fell madly in love with her and pampered her; how Mother cavorted with Marvin and her other lovers and rolled carefree in diamonds and furs while so many suffered and died from the holocaust and the war. Well, Bertie wants me to experience that same carefree freedom, that luxury of totally indulging my own pleasures while others around me suffer and die in our miserable new normal economy. And she doesn't want me feeling any guilt about not helping those Have-not people, or about who I am or what I do, either. She says it's all part of natural selection; and I shouldn't worry my head about it. I thought I was already guilt free, after what I did to Carl's wife; but I'm glad Bertie feels my same way about people who want to distract me from enjoying my pleasures. That's the measure of someone who truly cares about someone else, David. Bertie is my genuine true friend. I just totally love her.

"All three of us watch my films together. Bertie and George always get turned on while watching me stroking a penis. She marvels at how I playfully work my hands, teasing a penis, helping it desire to ejaculate; and how I lovingly knead my partner's balls while showing off my beautifully done nails; and how I feature my hands for the cameras, as well as my lips while I tongue kiss and suck the head of a penis. She strives to make the viewers associate my face, lips, eyes,

mouth, tongue, fingers, and nails with the male penis. It's all part of her brand identity program. She stops the film in places and remarks how beautiful my fingers and lips look when I bring my fingertips across the open lips of my mouth to display the cum that I've sucked from several penises and collected in my mouth; or how glorious my open mouth and welcoming tongue look while semen flows onto my tongue from a penis which I've perfectly positioned with my fingertips. Technique makes for exceptional erotica, according to Bertie.

"She says there's no scene in all of film work more beautiful, more endearing than a woman's tongue receiving cum from an ejaculating penis. That moment encapsulates intimacy and loving trust between the woman and the man. It is love-making's most precious and beautiful seminal moment, Bertie says, because it recognizes a woman's control of the creation decision while also affirming her love for her partner. It must be performed perfectly, with loving feelings, from its beginning all the way through ejaculation, and afterwards.

"Bertie frequently stops the film to study my tradecraft. She examines every film frame in minute detail. She shows me, on George's penis for example, the exact way she wants to see my finger positions and my lips while I'm anticipating a semen ejaculation with my mouth open. She's taught me so much, David."

"Like what? It's all the same, isn't it? A blow job is a blow job and a fuck is a fuck, isn't it?" David grimaced, expressing his skepticism that coaching could possibly make one sex scene different from any other.

"No David. You have such a misconception. It's like anything else. There are men who play football and golf; but some footballers know how to run the ball better, throw the ball better, catch it better. And some golfers know how to hit the ball further, use the right club for their next shot, understand the putting surface and the type of grass, the effect of the wind and the crowd. There's a difference between playing at something and excelling at something."

"So, you think this Bertie woman helps you excel at porn?"

"Oh, yes! I know she does."

"How?"

"It's a thousand little things, David. It's helping me concentrate on every second of my performances and not letting my mind run on ahead of where I am; not thinking about the orgasm or the ejaculation before it's time to happen. It's being mindful of where my vagina is, where my lips and fingers are, what my face and mouth are doing during every single frame of filming. It's attitude projection during every second of filming. It's attention to detail on top of detail. It's that striving for perfection. It's what separates my work from the films of a thousand other porn stars. It's tradecraft."

"And this Bertie is key to this?"

"Definitely. She's the reason my porn rankings are skyrocketing. She's the reason why my film sales are soaring and demand for my Premium Member services have gone through the rook. She's always thinking about what the viewer is seeing and thinking. She's always thinking about ways to help me better connect with that viewer. Example: she captures and critiques, frame by frame, my fingers and nails during every second of the ejaculation sequence. Whether the penis is coming into my mouth or my vagina, she still frames every split second, marking those times in the films. Then we go over them, always working toward the precision looks and touches she wants me to deliver. She turns sex into a science. She also orders still photos of many of these frames from the studios, because a different camera might capture a different look. Then, we study my fingers, lips, mouth, and vagina in every photo. She makes notes about every single frame and goes over those notes with me, in detail, while we study the photos. During the times that I hold myself open while displaying pooled cum inside my vagina, she makes constructive comments about all those frames, too; make my fans desire to hug and kiss me then; make them feel invited to join me. It's endless with her.

She explains how I can better my performances, frame by frame, in ways that are even more alluring; more mouthwatering; more convincingly sexier. She coaches me to change the perspectives of my viewing fans. She takes them from seeing what sex with me must be like to making them crazily craven to become my sex partners. It's so many subtle details. She knows how to play to a fan base. I know she benefits me greatly. I notice it in how I feel while I perform and after we wrap the films. The fans notice, too. I can tell from the tone of their letters. They've gone from complementary and asking for dates, to pining obsessively about how crazy they are over me; and promising me all sorts of things to date me. You would not believe all the photos men send me, even photos of their penises. I didn't get much of that before Bertie; but I get lots of it now. Bertie is a relentlessly driven woman. She intends to make me into the world's number one intimate performing artist. She's a perfectionist."

David: *"You mean porn star, don't you?"*

Marty: *"Well, yes, but Bertie intends to reposition the entire industry and the way people perceive it. And she will do it. She's that driven. She wants everyone to stop calling it pornography. She wants me to refer to my work as intimate performance art, or erotic film artistry. She thinks guns and wars are pornography. And the work that I do is the beautiful opposite of that. She wants me thinking at all times that my work is loving, intimate, and caring; that I'm bringing people together in love. The movies Hollywood creates are about shooting people, blowing people up, and killing them. Bertie believes that's pornography."*

David: *"The relationship you have with this Bertie woman means a great deal to you, doesn't it? What is it about her? Is it just the sex?"* David was discovering an emotional need Marty that had, and it fascinated him. Whenever he sensed an emotional driver in anyone, he always sought to draw them out about it.

Marty: *"Oh, yes, David. I greatly value her relationship. It's hard to explain how I feel about her. It's complicated, but it's healthy and wholesome and very beneficial to me. I need Bertie. I love her. She's like a missing piece that fell into place in my crazy life."*

David: *"How?"*

Marty: *"Well, you know how I'm working on the sales floor and I don't come up to the administration floor very often?"*

David: *"Yes, I've noticed. I go for weeks without seeing you on my floor."*

Marty: *"Right, well, I go sometimes for weeks without seeing Mother, even though Susan and I are only one floor apart, working in the same building for the same company. My whole life with Mother has been like that. So, now when I see her, I think to myself how I wish she had been more like Bertie, during those years I was growing up.*

"I often felt like Mother treated me like I was a lowly caterpillar. And she wanted to squish me under her foot and crush me to make me disappear from her life. She wanted to spend all her time with Marvin, your dad. I couldn't even understand why she had me. I often asked myself: if she didn't want to love me and nurture me, why did she bother having me in the first place?

"I mean, if you weren't going to love your child why in the hell did you let yourself get pregnant? Mother never gave a shit about me. She abandoned me. What kind of asshole mother does that to her kid? What about love? What about nurturing? Couldn't she tear herself away from Marvin for a few minutes to call me on the phone? What the fuck was going on inside her head? I wanted to smack her, but I was two thousand miles away.

"When I see Mom now, I just feel this stone coldness. Lately, she's tried to get closer to me, but I'm just not there. It's too late for closeness. I honestly don't give a shit about her. I just don't. In my

mind she was an asshole. She's still an asshole. And I'll always see her as an asshole. She can't undo those hurt feelings that she put inside of me.

"When I was at WEX I became close friends with a girl named Maria. We joked that before we were born, all us WEX girls went to this mommy raffle where we got tickets to draw our mothers. The other girls all got great mothers, but not me and Maria. Her mother was a hopeless drunk; and I got Susan. Maria was older than me. She explained things so they made sense to me. She said when we drew mothers from the mommy raffle, we both drew assholes.

"When Susan tried to lecture me about the risks of having orgies with salesmen, I just flipped her the bird and told her to fuck off. Susan has no right to any aspect of my life. She forfeited that years ago. Whenever she says something to me about my behavior, I just hear this little silent voice inside myself that screams back at her: 'FUCK YOU! GO TO HELL! YOU HAVE NO RIGHT TO SAY ANYTHING TO ME ABOUT ANYTHING. YOU WERE NEVER A DESCENT MOTHER. YOU'RE JUST A SELFISH BITCH!'

"My shrinks tell me I should forgive Susan. They all tell me it's the mentally healthy thing to do. Maybe their advice is good for some people. But it's not good for me. I can't forgive her. I don't want to forgive her; not ever. And I won't do that. She needs to do something for me, okay! I don't even know what that something would be. It's up to her to figure that out. And that must be hard for her, because she must know, deep inside herself, that I no longer need her. But that's her problem now, not mine. Until she figures it out, I will never forgive her.

"Well, David, you wanted to know about a woman's feelings, so there, I got those feelings out, okay? Then, there's Bertie. She's kind and nurturing. Bertie's personality comes through in addition to the sex we have. I mean, Bertie cares about me. I know it. I feel it. It's a real feeling I have about her as a person; and I know she loves

me back, as a person; and I know she wants the best for me. She teaches me all kinds of things to help me advance my career. I mean, she takes that serious nurturing time out of her own life to help me become the best adult film star I can be."

David: *"Like what? I still don't get it, Marty. Fucking is fucking, isn't it? What more can you make of it?"*

Marty: *"Plenty! Bertie has taught me how to pose, how to dance, how to hop and twirl while moving in certain ways to emphasize my ass and boobs so I'm being my seductive best. There are so many little things she'll study and coach me about, like how to lift my leg in a certain way for a scene, so my vagina will show through my transparent panties in a way that my vagina appears mouth water-ingly sexy, and so men will notice, without me appearing overtly slutty; make them wonder about the mysterious nature of what they saw; make them wonder whether it was intentional. She coaches me on the ways I should rub my hand over my transparent panties to stimulate myself; just enough to make my fans go crazy for me without overdoing that moment. And then, how I should pivot from that stimulation scene to make my fans anxious to see me move nat-urally into hugging or kissing; without seeming obvious about that changeover into a seduction scene. Bertie has shown me that the difference between a great film and a fabulous top money-making film is in the way I enunciate my lines, my techniques while per-forming intercourse, my movement and expression control, and my appearance. We strive to perfect all those things.*

"Lots of little things, like how to smile a coquettish smile while turning my head over my shoulder; how to turn my head and raise my eyebrows when I notice a penis has approached me. There are thousands of little things that she's taught me to do better, that set me apart as an intimate film actress. I'm now so much more of a tempt-ress and seduction artist than so many other adult film actresses. It's all the result of Bertie's coaching and lots of very hard work.

"Instead of feeling like I'm a lowly caterpillar with my life crushed out of me, I now feel like I'm free and beautiful and loved. That's the difference between Mother and Bertie. Caterpillars are not loved. But I'm a butterfly now. Butterflies are loved. I am loved. And I feel like Bertie is a butterfly too! She's a beautiful butterfly, fluttering right there alongside me. I know I can trust her. She's more experienced than me. She knows all the beautiful things that butterflies can do and all the beautiful moves they can make. And she teaches me how to perform perfect, beautiful butterfly moves.

"I've learned how to flutter slowly and how to flutter fast, when my different scenes call for different paces while I copulate. I've learned how to dazzle the cameras when I flex my tush. And how to twirl slowly, temptingly, while I remove my panties. And how to flutter my vagina delicately, seductively onto a penis. And when to bounce my tush hard; squeeze down hard and demanding on a penis; or when to softly vagina massage a penis until it spurts semen, going wildly out of control. And I've learned how to pitch and yaw my pelvis to perfectly coax and tease a penis, like I'm bending its bone tissue until it goes crazy and spurts semen. And I've learned how to twerk sensually, with just the right amount of erotic, sexual suggestion in every kind of twerk movement for every scene's circumstance. I've mastered twerking and Kegel squeezing simultaneously, so my performing penis will ejaculate inside me at the exact, perfectly timed moment during the accompanying music score; perfectly captured by the lighting, and the cameras. I'm learning every erotic, enticing "Butterfly Move," as Bertie calls them.

"She's meticulous and relentless; always trying to enhance my tradecraft. Most porn producers ignore lighting. They'll just use unfiltered, bright incandescent lamps. That's okay. It ensures that the viewer sees what's going on in the scene; but it's not good enough for Bertie. She uses lighting to set the emotional mood of the viewing fans. She's told me that there are always two things that must be

communicated to the viewers in every porn scene. First, there's my mood; what's inside my head. Bertie uses a particular set of light filters for that mood. Then there's also the mood that my vagina should be experiencing and relating to the fans as the scene progresses from introduction of my partner and anticipation of sex with him, to my vagina's feelings during actual intercourse with the penis; continuing to my vagina's ribald exaltations during my orgasms and my partners' climaxes, and my vagina's prideful happiness and immoral shamelessness while she purrs."

"Purrs? She talks?" David didn't understand the terminology of Marty's intimacy art.

"Yes, purrs. That's the terminology that Bertie and I use to express the satisfaction that my Miss Muffy, or my vagina, feels after a successful porn shoot. It refers to those closing seconds of the film where I hold Miss Muffy widely open to display her. She's glistening from her creams and oils and throbbing from the stimulations she's had from her thrusting's with her partners' penises; and she's prideful and appreciating of the sex that she has had with all her penis friends. Naturally, Miss Muffy wants to show herself off to her fans and let them know that she loves them. Like a kitty cat will rub against your leg to let you know it wants to be friends, Miss Muffy loves to show her fans her semen pool from her partners' ejaculations. That lets Muffy's fans know that she enjoyed the experience she just had and that she'd very much like to continue having that experience with all her viewers.

"Bertie uses pale-shaded colored filters on the overhead lights to capture the different moods of the scenes, and she changes the filters as the scene or the mood in the scene changes. She might, for example, use a bright pink filter to capture a sense of anticipation if it's a romantic love scene; or she might use a pink filter with shades of purple blended over it when we're signaling that the scene portrays something naughty and forbidden, like when I'm seducing

my sister's boyfriend, my step father, boss, or teacher. It's a way of increasing the sensory communication with my viewing fans.

"For my vagina moods, Bertie uses a separate set of filters. She uses separate lighting schemes from the general set lighting. My vagina lights focus exclusively on my vagina; and sometimes on my lips when I'm performing fellatio. Miss Muffy will be filter shaded in soft orange when she's about to star in a cunnilingus scene. Bertie wants her coloration to appear fresh and juicy, like a ripened, succulent peach that's about to be eaten slowly, with loving appreciation and a sense of reverence for how delightfully tasting and welcoming she is. Seduction scenes usually place Miss Muffy in different shades of red. Bertie want viewers to sense the passion throbs that Miss Muffy feels in those wonderous moments before a penis touches its head to her outer lips, seeking permission to enter her. Bertie is very conscious of the moods that fans likely assume Miss Muffy is feeling.

"Let's say I have a scene where my partner captures me unawares and he seeks to force himself upon me. Bertie might start that scene with a purple-gray filtered light highlighting Miss Muffy. That would tell my fans that Miss Muffy wasn't expecting this and she's not appreciating my partner's aggressiveness because she hasn't had time to get into the mood for sex. But then, assume the scene moves along and my mind begins to appreciate the foreplay advances of my partner. Then, the set lighting might change to a soft green, which signals that I want my partner to advance his stimulations and do more with me; and that set lighting will change to a pink, signaling that my mind is like a flower opening and Miss Muffy is becoming receptive to sex.

"Meanwhile, my vagina lighting would slowly change from the purple-gray tone to a softer blueish daylight, like dawn is breaking for Miss Muffy; and then, once my mood has gotten receptive for sex, Miss Muffy's lighting slowly adjusts to pinkish red, to conform Miss Muffy's mood with the mood in my head. When Miss Muffy finally opens herself to the penis's head and the penis begins penetrating her

outer lips, Bertie has the set lighting and Miss Muffy's lighting on the same mood page. But Miss Muffy's lighting will be more focused and concentrated because Bertie directs the viewing fans to focus alternatively on my facial expressions, which express my emotions and on Miss Muffy, who vividly expresses the explicit erotic aspects of the scene.

"Bertie has also coached me on ways to best accentuate my breasts and my tush for the different scenes that call for those titillations. She's also explained the how's, the where's and the when's of touching myself sexily; and taught me how to take my partners' hands; the how's and where's of touching their hands to my different body areas, so that my fans seeing those scenes will imagine my partners' touching hands are their hands; and they'll feel their blood boil with the same lust fires that I feel.

"Bertie rehearses me to do all those things at the exactly right times. She's made me into a real actress, David; one who speaks her lines perfectly, dances and moves gracefully; and one who leaps out of that film screen right into a man's heart. I'm an intimate film actress who captivates a man's mind so completely that he goes totally out of his mind crazy with hopes and dreams that somehow, someday, he'll be fortunate enough to actually make love with me.

"Other adult film stars don't have the benefit of Bertie's coaching. The rapid rise in my star rankings is all thanks to Bertie. She's Big Sister and Mother that I never had. She knows what she's doing and she shares everything she knows with me. She coaches me in a steady, loving, thoughtful way. I never resent her, even when she pushes me hard to perfect a certain technique or movement. She's never mean or short with me. She never puts me down. She's always understanding and patient. She's there for me, like Mother never was. What we have together is special; and it works, David. Does that help?"

"Yes, I have noticed a change in you since you met Bertie. Now I understand. Thank you."

Marty smiled to David, acknowledging his understanding, and nodded a soft 'you're welcome' with her eyes. Marty's thoughts recalled Bertie's comments during her latest visit to George and Bertie's:

CHAPTER FOUR

Let there be light, said Liberty. And, like sunrise from the sea, Athens rose. (Percy Byssie Shelly, Hellas)

My country 'tis of thee, sweet land of liberty, of thee I sing: Land where my fathers died, land of the pilgrims' pride, from every mountainside, let freedom ring. (Samuel Francis Smith, America)

Without liberty, life would be an endlessly dull pain in the tush. (Rosemary Ness-Bitner, author)

EPIPHANY

"Oh, look how beautiful she is!" said Bertie. "Look at this frame, George! Isn't she spectacular? How lovely! Look at her pretty lips. Look how red and glossy and full they are. Look how her lips quiver with excitement as that penis comes to her. Don't you think every man who sees those lips will just want to hold her and kiss her and love her? Her lips are perfect, like they are just begging to be kissed. And look at how healthy her tongue looks; all pinkish red. Isn't her tongue the most perfect beautiful erotic companion for that penis head and its cum flow? The pink-red tongue is a perfect contrast to the white semen it's receiving. So beautiful! Breathtaking! That proves she's eating her healthy fruits and vegetables, like we tell her to, George. She's the picture-perfect image of nature's healthy, sex appealing woman. She's taking excellent care of herself, George. We must be proud of her.

"I know where I'm going with this, George! I've had an epiphany! I'm finally cured of my funk. Now I can see my way forward. I can visualize the future with a mental clarity about my purpose in life that had previously been eluding me!"

"What, Bertie, sweetheart? I can see your excitement. Tell me what's come over you!" George placed his hands on Bertie's shoulders and peered into her beautiful mysterious dark pools, those same eyes that bewitched him ever since they were young teenagers, first falling in love.

Bertie's smile was her smug, all-knowing expression of confidence. It was the mysterious Cheshire cat that resided inside her true persona. Clever, assured, and insightful wore the face that answered husband George that fateful day. Bertie announced their life's mission.

"I am; that is, we are, going to change the world, George. We're going to change the world's way of seeing things, so that the world will see our darling Marty as the most desirable film actress ever!" Bertie's raised eyebrows and widened eyes highlighted the luster that beamed from her genius mind.

"And, what exactly are we going to change, sweetheart?" Puzzled George was ready to learn Bertie's thought. He knew from years as her partner that her mind and thoughts were cogent and powerful. He respected the source of the words he was about to hear.

"We're going to change the way the world views pornography, George. We're going to make viewing a woman enjoying sex into an acceptable art form, not something smutty or disgusting. We're going to elevate a woman's erotic feelings and needs into the most attainable expressions of intimate artistry that the world has ever seen. We're going to make erotica about liberty and the American way of life. When people watch Marty in bed, kissing a man in her arms while a sheet is barely draped over her; and then seeing him finish;

and another man falling into her open arms; and she starts kissing and making love with that next man without any sense of guilt or inhibition; that's the very definition of freedom and liberty George. Think how liberated Marty's mind needs to be to enable her to make love like that, time after time; and to feel natural and completely shameless and accepted while she's doing it, George.

"Marty personifies the pursuit of happiness that is the foundational goal of America. Marty IS America, George. Her performances exemplify homage to the glorious ideal that founded our nation. Marty is America's living icon! Her eyes have more luster than the Statue of Liberty's bright flame. Her pink vagina will become America's new beacon of liberty. Marty is already the inspiring goddess for millions. And she doesn't stand aloof and afar as some remote cold statue in some distant harbor. She's touchable and warm and loving: AND SHE'S ALIVE!

"People emote with her. Her erotica breathes life, warmth, and passion into their souls. People hear her talk about how she feels. Her works bring her close to people. She embraces their hearts. She is our living, uniquely unapologetic Liberty. She holds our breathless passions in her loving arms and nurtures those lust impassioned dreams in her unthreatened mind; while she performs naturally; live.

"People LOVE her, George. And we're going to help them understand WHY they love her; and why it's perfectly normal and healthy and beautiful to love her.

'We already know that 75% of men watch porn and about half of all women do, too. But people won't admit it. There's a stigma about it. It's not an acceptable topic in polite conversation. It's strictly locker room and water cooler talk; the butt of jokes, that sort of thing. Well, George, we are going to change that.

"We're going to bring intimacy art out into the open. We are going to make it nuevo, chic, fashionable to watch and discuss, just

like football or classic paintings. Intimacy is nothing to be ashamed of. There's no reason to hide intimacy. It's the most beautiful, fastest growing human art form. We're going to buy a magazine and a production company that heralds the beauty of intimacy. We'll give awards and host awards ceremonies for outstanding erotica. We'll broadcast interviews. Marty will be our featured actress. We'll rebrand the industry and we will promote Marty as its foremost star."

"And you're sure Marty is the right woman to do all this?" George's smile was more of a confirmation than a doubt. He believed in Bertie's genius. She knew that and she already knew he'd follow her anywhere.

"Oh, yes, George. Her blood is young and lust crazed. Her passion flames show their heat in her face and eyes. We could search through a thousand porn stars. We could find hundreds that we could develop. We'd spend a fortune on their hairdressers, masseuses, makeup artists, but we would not have that one essential ingredient that Marty already naturally has. And that is the heartfelt love and joy she feels while copulating with penises and performing fellatio on them. She absolutely loves creating porn, George. She can't get enough of it. Intimacy is in her soul. She loves intimacy. She craves it.

"She has a rare, unmatched, honest, shameless passion for the carnal arts, George. She loves the subtle craftsmanship required to make unforgettable pornography. She loves expressing the ways her body feels; the ways she emotionally attaches to her partners. She emotes her love of every partner, puts her soul into his; and her expressions come from her heart. The innocence of her face is incomparable. The compassionate way she lifts the spirits of life's desolate and forgotten people from their oblivion, and gives them spirit and hope is priceless, George. She's a saint."

"She's a prostitute, Bertie. Saints perform heroic deeds."

"Yes, and she also does that. She does not rally troops to repel invaders, nor does she convert people to the faith of the cross; nor

does she tend the sick and the starving; but she does more than all of those things, George. She lifts the human spirit! She puts zest and life into lifeless blood. She brings hope to millions. She opens communications and breaks down inhibitions and barriers to social discourse. The ability she has to make supposedly immoral conduct seem so sweetly innocent and natural; and so morally acceptable and wholesome is her special gift. She is the essence of grandeur. She is stunningly beautiful, with her goddess face and heavenly body. She a precious gift to us, George. Yes, George, I am sure. I've never felt surer of anything in my life. The spirits have delivered her to our lives. She IS the one. She's perfect. Her attitude is exactly what I need to work with. I'm sure. I know I'm right. You can bet on me, George. I'm sure."

Bertie held George's face in her hands. She kissed him before turning her eyes back to the screen. George's eyes followed.

FILM STUDY

"Watch her eyes and hands closely, George. See how she holds that penis that comes before her? She does not just grab it and mechanically start stroking it like so many porn stars do. No, she holds it in her hands and looks lovingly at it, like it's some injured forlorn bird in need of nurturing. And now it's yielding up its helpless life to her, to be rescued and returned to strength. She talks to it, as if it's a spirit arrived into flesh-life before her adoring presence; and she tells it how adorable it is and how honored she is to be with it.

"She's like a master artist, carefully considering colors and brushes as she slowly doles out her enticing immoral lust. Notice how her hands revere the magnificence of the penis, George. As she takes it in her hands you can see her touches are soft and caring. Those touches are religious, in their own way. She lifts the penis from its dormant lie on her lap with the same eternal devotion that a

priest has when he lifts the monstrance from the altar to consecrate the host.

"Her first touches of the penis are much more than love, George. What you see while watching her bring it to her mouth are her feelings. They are the same as the religious feelings of a supplicant bringing the sacred host to her mouth. Look at her hands, George! Look how lovingly they hold the penis! She's feeling something much deeper than love, George. She's feeling herself surrendering to devotion. That penis has become Marty's earthly embodiment of God.

"See now. Look how she kisses its head, George. Notice how soft, gentle, and respectful she is when she kisses that penis. It's like a virgin bride's first searching kisses to her new husband's face. She invites the penis to trust her to love it; and to make this divine love-making experience memorable. Watch as the penis awakens, George. See how it stiffens, swells full, and rises responsively to meet her lips. That's honest, heartfelt bonding taking place. The penis responded to her soft kisses by awakening and rising up. It's telling her that it wants to experience more of her love. Its mind knows that it can safely repose its intimate trust within her.

"Now, watch how Marty responds to the penis's signal. She lavishes its head with her lips and her tongue. She lovingly kisses its head and stimulates its circumcision ring with her tongue. Listen carefully to the aria from "Madam Butterfly" playing in the film's background, George. It's the perfect selection for this scene. Let's pause the film here. Look closely at her eyes, George. See how they gleam? And, notice her lips and tongue, George. See how they glisten? Her eyes, lips and tongue can hear the sweet melody. They are totally into the song. I can't teach concentration and empathy like that. You are seeing in her eyes and lips and tongue her truest feelings, George. Marty is completely enamored with that penis. She adores it. She respects its needs. She's in love with it. That's what makes her unique, George. She's in love with the men who are attached to the

penises she sucks; but not in the same devoted way as her love for the penises themselves. She is smitten by the penis itself. It's a separate and deeper love. I can feel it, George. It's visceral. It's very real. She needs that penis. Deeply inside her there is a craving need for that penis."

"Something? Some greater need than sex itself? Might there then be something deeply hidden within her, some need greater than even love? Are you saying that there is one or more layers of complexity within her, beneath what we see, that enables her to perform as spectacularly as she does?" George sought to probe Bertie's understanding of the younger woman's mind.

"I don't know, George. In truth we may never know until she chooses to reveal it to us. If, and I think it is a nebulous, uncertain if at best, should there even be such an if, she trusts us enough to reveal it."

"And this is open ended for us, then? I mean, do we plunge ahead with her, this project girl; and then, should she choose to reveal her mystery that you think you detect, we commit to helping her with it; enhance it or quash it as the case may be? Are we thusly beholden to her, Bertie?"

"I said I don't know, George. Perhaps we shall know in the fullness of time. I cannot say what I cannot yet understand. I only tell you that I have a certain feeling of something deeper. It enables her in her untroubled, spectacular, immoral way. And whatever it is, it draws me toward it and I love her for it. But having studied her body, athleticism, and enthusiasm, of this much I am sure: the penis itself is Marty's truest love, not the man attached to it. It is the penis that brings forward her unique persona. It lights up her libido like a fire sparkler brightens the wondrous face of a child.

"The pleasures Marty gives a penis are her way of expressing her deepest need to give love and to be loved. That desire to impart love dwells inside her heart. She's like a seasoned wine that way. Like

some deeply rooted varietals that have survived stresses produce exemplary tasting wines, Marty also comes to her performances through years of stresses and recovered refinement. Like fine wine, she delivers her bouquet of pleasure to afficionados of the finest erotica ever created. That's what you are seeing, George. In her lips and eyes, you are watching the truest expression of erotic love you'll ever see. Her fan base has detected that, George. They know they are seeing the best. That explains why her following keeps growing. They believe that she's the ultimate performer of fellatio intimacy. They love her performances; and they love her.

"Now watch closely. While her tongue artfully tickles the penis's circumcision ring, her mouth repeatedly engulfs its head and gently lingers upon it. All this while her tongue repeatedly lavishes its love about and under the penis's head. See how the penis hardens in response to that focused stimulation? That penis knows that Marty loves what she's doing. It is certain that her love is genuine. It feels that confirmed love. It knows it can trust her to be loving. It intuits that Marty perfectly understands what it likes; how to make love with it.

"We next see Marty at her erotic best, George. You will not see many other adult film actresses doing this. It is difficult to master. As her mouth engulfs the top of the penis, slipping over its head and down its shaft an inch, Marty simultaneously strokes the shaft of the penis in an upward motion. Are you seeing this George? You are witnessing the fusion of intimate erotica and precision ejaculation science. It's fascinating, elegant, and empathetic fellatio, attuned to the penis's desires. What she does is so vivid; so compellingly loving; so beautiful. She's the ultimate artisan of the world's most divine art form. I just totally love her, George.

"Watch now. As her lips go further downward, her fingers stroke upward. As her lips lift up, her fingers stroke downward. Notice the fluidity of her coordinated mouth and fingers motion. What she does

creates an erotic sensation within the penis's sensory nerves. She also sends the man's limbic zone into a blissful paralysis state, where all his thoughts and cares simply melt away. Everything that man ever knew or concerned himself with has completely vanished from his mind. All he knows now is that he loves what Marty is doing with his penis; and by transference, he also loves her.

"This is what she does for a man, George. She gives the ultimate male massage; and it elevates him to another world. She has an incredible understanding of the needs of a man's penis and limbic zone. What you are witnessing is an eternal devotional bonding. It is much stronger than affectionate love. You're seeing why she has so many lovers and fans; and why so many men leave their wives and girl friends to become her lovers. She gives them their psychological freedom. They adore her. She is their goddess.

"Keep watching this, George. Keep count from here and see how many down and up stroke cycles that penis experiences before it ejaculates. Count with me: one, two, three, four, five, six, seven, eight, nine, ten, eleven, twelve, thirteen, fourteen.... look! See her lift her mouth off the penis's head? That's her response to the penis's signal. Its shaft pulsed and trembled; the man moaned. The penis is telling Marty that it wants to ejaculate. It's ready. Watch her hands. Watch their movements closely. They continue stroking, still softly, lovingly; slightly more rapidly; helping the penis experience its sacred moment of consecration.

"Watch. Her lips have stopped stroking. They gently hold the penis around its circumcision ring. You can see her tongue's rotational movements inside her closed mouth. She's stimulating the penis's circumcision ring; coaxing it to release into her. That suddenly multiplies the penis's pleasures a thousand times. It must respond to her exquisite fellatio. It must consecrate its spirit to her care. It knows it must commit itself; place trust in her. It must prove it loves her; and surrender its life and soul to her. Now, it does.

"There! It's ejaculating! It's exploding its love for her into her mouth. There's no penis anywhere in the world that can resist Marty's fellatio stimulations for very long, George.

"You can sense the ejaculation beginning to take place by watching Marty's excited early smile from her still closed lips. See how her smile lifts her cheeks and eyes? Yes, ejaculation has begun! Now, watch as she opens her mouth, George. Her tongue is already covered in the white cum from the penis's first ejaculation spurt.

"Now, as the camera zooms in and focuses on her mouth, can you see how the penis continues to spurt semen onto her tongue? Do you see how her smile widens while she fondles the penis's testicles? She loves what she's doing. She loves the profound intimacy that's happening between her and that penis. She knows that penis and that man have bonded with her, forever. She knows they will hold this memory of their consecration bond with her until the day they die. She knows that, for the rest of that man's life, some part of him will always love her. She also knows that he will bring his penis back to her, again and again, to reaffirm his devotion to her, in this same explicit way.

"Now, let's back the film up and study it again, George. We'll stop it frame by frame so you can see how intricate Marty's fellatio movements are. Look how beautiful her nails look while she's stroking that shaft and holding her partner's balls. She's having a wonderful time; don't you think, George? She looks like she's really happy while mouthing and sucking that penis, can't you tell?

"See how she looks up at her partner and smiles her innocent, wholesome smile when she takes her short breaks from her sucking? Look at how she puts downward pressure on the head of the penis with her upper lip on her down stroke; and how she applies her opposite lifting pressure on the penis with her lower lip on her up stroke. Now, watch carefully as she fondles her partner's testicles.

See how softly she kneads his balls while she takes one testicle and mouths it?

"Isn't she the most tantalizing vixen you've ever seen; yet amazingly delicate? Can you see how lovingly she's stimulating his balls, George? Now watch very carefully, George. Notice how she can feel the penis's semen rising in its shaft? You can tell she knows it's about to release by the slight lifting of her cheeks and eyebrows. She's very happy for the pleasures she's giving that penis. I can't teach a face how to look happy and pleased like that, George. That look comes from deep inside her facial muscles. It's totally natural. Everything about Marty is natural. She LOVES sucking penises."

"How can you be so sure that she loves doing this?" George's eyes looked at Bertie's more for her explanation than as a challenge to her assertion.

"It's visible in her facial muscles, George. It's how they relax when she sees the penis. It's in her eyes; the way they light up with joy as they observe the penis being presented to her. It's even in her breathing. It deepens with the lust she feels. It's all there, captured by those subtle changes."

"'If you say so," George was puzzled.

"Let me put it into guy-world terms for you, George. When a linebacker meets a running back in the A gap, between the center and the guard, his face shows a certain "gotcha" glee, right?"

"Yes."

"Okay, when a hockey player sees his opponent against the boards and he knows he can body slam him face down into the ice, his face has a 'gotcha' moment too, right?"

"Right."

"And when a hunter has been stalking a big animal for hours and suddenly it comes into view for a clean shot, his face sort of lights up with a 'gotcha' moment, doesn't it?"

"Most definitely."

"Well, for Marty, it's sort of the same. Understand this is a woman we're studying. She's not going to be a linebacker knocking the penis flat on its ass; or a hockey player, slamming it to break its shaft; nor is she a huntress that kills it with a rifle shot. But she does conquer it. And she does that in a woman's way; by loving it. That expression of love that floods into her face is there every time she greets a penis. Look closely. You'll notice it, too."

"Okay, I've got it."

"Good, George. Now, pay attention. We've got a lot of work to do."

"What? What are you talking about?"

"We're going to gather data. We're going to get all the internal data from the top porn web sites. We're going to break down the data to see which stars are rising the fastest in rank. We're going to study the films of the top twenty stars, the ones who have a persistent following; and we're going to intensely study the purchasing data and purchasing patterns in the data. We're going to.....................”

"Why would we do all that? I mean fucking is fucking, isn't it?"

"Listen, George, pay attention. You know I have what it takes to coach at the Olympic championship level, right?"

"Yes, I know."

"You know the countless hours I put into that. Remember how I studied the moves of all the top skaters; how I catalogued every nuanced move they made; how we correlated those moves with the judges' rating scores? Remember all those hours and days of detailed study that went into my project?"

"Yes, Bertie. Of course, I remember."

"Okay. Well, pornography is no different; not at the top, it isn't. We need to know all the nuanced moves of all the top and fastest ris-ing porn stars, George. They may not even know why they are doing

so well; but we will know. We need to understand what move, and where in the film that move is, caused that idealized fan to buy that film or to buy all of that porn star's films. We must know, George; we must not guess. I'll be hiring data crunchers and putting all this data on spread sheets after we get it."

"What are you talking about?"

"George, listen. Fucking is not just 'fucking.' That's a popular misogynistic misconception that almost everyone has. But the top porn stars know that that's not true. They understand the many feelings, possibly hundreds of feelings that may possibly express in a woman's mind while she's enjoying sexual intercourse.

"You men think women's expressed feelings are just inconsequential silly emotions; but we women know better. We know the feelings we have are the very essence of who we are and what makes us women. They are the things that bring out the love and nurture and sexuality within us. And the highly successful porn stars are those who can interpret and take these emotions and express them artfully and convincingly before the cameras. It's a subtle, nuanced craft. It requires dedication to study and practice to master it. The best stars make hundreds of films; each one is nuanced in some way to be more tantalizing than her previous ones. The very best stars understand that creating porn that sells requires outstanding emotive, nuanced performance artistry. Well, George, we're going to master that nuanced artistry with Marty; and we will create in her the world's greatest, most famous, number one porn star; the world's most sought after, most highly desired whore. Are you following me?"

"Not sure."

"Okay, let me give you an example. When a penis presents itself for fellatio, does the porn star smile? Or, does she wince, like it's a chore she doesn't want to do? Or, does she give the penis, or the male

partner, the look of a vixen fox that's been presented with a prize bunny rabbit that fell into her paws? Which of those choices does she show her fans? Are you getting this?"

"A little. Please continue."

"Okay. When the porn star begins fellatio, does she begin by kissing the tip of the penis's head? Does she begin by swirling her tongue around its circumcision ring? Does she talk to it? What lines does she speak to it, if she does talk to it? Does she first hold its balls in her hands? Does she first put its balls into her mouth, one by one; or does she mouth its balls while she begins to stroke the penis? How does she lick the penis, if she does, at first, lick it? Does she lavish her licks around its head, or does she lick it from the scrotum base, upward; like her tongue is climbing the Statue of Liberty? And, how does she stroke the penis, exactly? Does she do it slowly, lovingly; or does she do it rapidly, like she's in a contest to see how fast she can pull the semen from it? Does she use two hands or one? Does she lubricate it first; and if she does that, does she use saliva or oils? Does she kneed its balls with one hand, while she strokes with the other; and does she also suck while she strokes; or does her technique treat stroking and sucking as distinctly different functions?

"And, when the penis ejaculates, does she smile or does she wince? Does her face express a pleasant surprise or a repulsed shock? Does she smack her lips like she enjoys the taste of semen, or does she simply do nothing? Does she like the semen to shoot all over her face? Does she swallow it? Does she first perform a burble show of semen on her lips; and then swallow the semen; and then show her empty mouth, afterwards? And, afterwards, does she smile or doesn't she? Does her face tell you she's glad her ordeal is over; or does it tell you that she wishes her experience could continue indefinitely because she loved it so much? Does she whisper some lines to the camera, or not? And if she does speak about her just consummated experience

with the penis, what, exactly does she say; and does she use any additional props while she says those lines?

"And, what does she say to her partner after he comes? What exact words does she say to him? And how does she deliver those words; like she's a cute and sassy tart; or like her fellatio experience was heartfelt and meaningful? And, does she touch him afterwards, or not? And, if she touches him, what, exactly, does she do? Does she kiss him? Hug Him? Or, does she turn to another partner at that time; another penis, perhaps? What, exactly does she do that causes her fans to follow her and buy her films? Are you getting this, George?"

"Yes, now I think I am."

"Good. Well, trust me. Pornography is no different than the moves in figure skating, except it's even more subtle than skating; and even less studied; and much more poorly understood. There are, in my opinion, George, thousands, possibly millions of nuanced moves that are made by these porn stars, without most of them even knowing that they are making those moves. And those nuanced moves occur in all the different segments of their seduction art; their positions; their spoken words; their expressions when they come and when their partners come; the way they move their heads and bodies at different times; and their facial expressions throughout the entire film. Get it now?"

"Yes, I think I do, now."

"Okay. Well, therein lies our opportunity to make Marty the world's most famous porn star. We'll get the data, crunch it, and create detailed spread sheets for every aspect of the top porn stars' love making, in every position imaginable; then we'll correlate that with the films' sales data; we'll study it and replicate and enhance and improve on the things that create sales of film, advertising buys, and co-branding by local prostitution services. And, we'll practice

creating sensational, mouthwatering pornography until our Marty is the personification of pornography's perfection, the world's most desirable whore, ever."

"Practice?"

"Oh, yes, George, we are going to practice, practice, practice. You remember how we practiced for the Olympic Gold? Well, pornography can't be any different. I'm going to want you to be Marty's primary practice prop. I'm going to have you fuck her in hundreds of practice love scene settings, and fellatio settings; until she gets her techniques down perfectly. And, I'm going to have you perform hundreds of fellatio sessions, with her sucking you off, to make sure she's getting the exact body and facial expressions I want. Are you okay with that?"

"Gee, Bertie, I don't know. It's just that she's such an incredibly beautiful woman, and she's so naturally sexy, that I................"

"That you're afraid you'll fall in love with her? Is that what you hesitate to say?"

"Well, honestly, yes."

"It's okay, George. It's perfectly natural. I expect you will fall in love with her. It would be inhuman not to fall in love with her. But, don't worry. I'll still be here. I'll still love you. I'll be here for you. I can separate the business aspects of this from the emotions that will surely come. I love you, George; and, I'll love you until the day when we draw our final breaths. Just remember that."

"Come here." George pulled Bertie close to him. He hugged her and kissed her forehead. *"I love the way this brain of yours works. You know that. And, I love you, too."*

"I know you do, big guy."

"Good. Okay. I'll do whatever you and your porn star ask of me."

"Good George. Now, let's go back to watching films. Watch this scene very closely. It fascinates me. Focus on the very tip of the penis. Can you see those droplets of semen starting to dribble out? You

can? Good! Now watch how quickly she captures the head of the penis in her mouth and sucks while she strokes the shaft, twisting her fingers on it, pulling it toward her mouth. Now, keep watching, George. Look closely as she smiles while she opens her mouth.

"Look at Marty's loving smile. Closely study her face. Pay attention to her forehead. Can you notice the serenity, the majesty? There's not a trace of a wrinkle anywhere. She has no consternation; no inhibition; no doubt about the natural innocence of what she's doing. Her mindset is expressing itself in her face, George. She's in an ethereal state of blessedness, where she knows that fans watching her sucking that penis accept her immoral deed. And she knows they venerate her for it. She knows her fans love her for what she's doing. She knows she's adored for the explicit erotica she performs. This is her world, George. It is her comfort zone. It's what she loves doing.

"See how her cheeks glow? See that trace of a pleased smile forming? She loves the anticipation of this penis's ejaculation; she just loves these moments. She can't be distracted from sucking that penis. She's giving that penis her fullest devotion and love, George. There's nothing phony or temporary about her fellatio. We're witnessing genuine love going out from her mind to the penis. She's creating exquisite pornography, honestly and naturally felt.

"She's absolutely beautiful; a darling, stunning porn star; with her creamy white skin, her beautiful mouth, her innocent, loving face, her silky hair flowing over her shoulders. Everything about her is breathtakingly beautiful; and what she's about to do with that penis is absolutely the most beautiful performance of erotic intimacy art you will ever see, George.

"Can you feel it? Can you feel how sincerely and honestly she completely loves and adores that penis? Now watch how she first opens her mouth with her wide, happy smile as the white semen cum continues erupting from the penis's shaft and spurts onto her already semen basked tongue. She does not let the penis's continuing

eruption distract her. She continues stroking it with her caressing strokes. Everything she does is so natural and so perfect, George. She continues stroking softly while the penis continues ejaculating, sending its river of semen into her mouth.

"Can you feel the image I'm seeing, George? Can you feel this unspoken, powerful moment where the penis is surrendering its innocence into her immorality? Where it's giving up its life essence and entering her sin loving soul, rushing to join it through her mouth? It's a powerful subliminal message, George. You can only feel it by placing your own mind into her mind. Her scenes make that mental connection happen for me, George; and I love her for that. I just love how her mindset enters my own mind in moments like this. I can't teach that, George. It's in her. It's unique to her. She has that natural, wholesome look about her love making. It makes men love her; and makes many women want to be like she is. It's the perfect foundation for the work I want to do. She gives me a lot to work with."

"But Bertie, as much as you attach to her, there are thousands of women who do porn. I'm sure each of them has some fan base. Everyone probably has a favorite star. How do you plan on changing that?" George defined the challenge. He was skeptical.

"That's our opportunity, George. The industry is highly fragmented; lots of women making a porno and doing their thing, hoping they'll catch on and get a following. Let's say the top star now gets ten percent of all film revenues. If we work very hard on perfecting Marty's tradecraft, positioning her as a goddess, and creating exceptional films and brilliant promotions for her, we should be able to shoot her ranking up to the number one spot and displace the girl that's there now."

"And how will you position her as a goddess?"

"Oh George, you need to think more like a woman thinks. See her as I see her, George. Her production sets will showcase the most

luxurious, most exotic, most romantic scenes. The music that accompanies her performances will be performed live, orchestrated by a master conductor. We'll bedeck Marty in the finest threads. She'll always be seen, on set and off, in designer high fashion clothing and accessories. She'll wear exquisite jewels for her performances. Her fingers will wear rings with stones of the highest possible quality. While she performs her various fellatios, viewers will notice her hand displays of rubies, emeralds, sapphires, tanzanite's, diamonds, and dozens of other rare jewels. When she seduces a partner in the back seat of a car, the car will not be a fifty-thousand-dollar car. It will be a million-dollar car. She wear the finest scents of gardenia, lilac, and sandalwood. Are you seeing my vision now, George?"

"Yes, I think so. But who pays for all this? We're talking millions, aren't we?"

"Yes, George. Probably tens of millions. We want her to be seen as the most glorious woman in the world. And we don't care what it costs to create that image, do we?"

"No, we don't care what it costs."

"That's my good Georgie boy. I love you, Precious Stud Muffin."

"And you believe this will work?"

"I know it will. You know I'm always right about these sorts of things. I know what an audience wants, George. When viewers see Marty performing, their minds will be transported to another world. They will see a goddess pleasuring herself. They will see that her sexual pleasures are heaven sent; that what she does is glorious, perfectly natural, beautifully, and casually and innocently immoral; and far more desirable, beyond anything or anyone's performances they have ever seen before. When penis or tongue enters her vagina, they will visualize that it is being honored to enter the Holy of Holies, the world's most sacred place. When she seductively encourages her partners to come inside her, her viewers will imagine that the penis is about to perform sacred union with her; beautiful, out of this

world, binding of souls by their love. They know what they're seeing, George. They're seeing divine holiness; they're seeing God.

"George, I expect that many of her fans will experience transference. I want them to wish that Marty realizes divine pleasures, so deeply, that they imagine they become her. Many men will identify that strongly with her."

"You're not joking, are you?"

"No, not at all. Call it psychic shading, where men have so much empathy with one particular woman that they imagine themselves as her. When a penis or tongue enters her vagina, they will imagine feeling the same sensations that she feels. In their minds, they will experience the same joys that she does. They may not go as far as becoming cross-dressers or transgender persons; but in their psychic minds, their empathy for Marty becomes so compelling that they will buy every one of her films and every product she endorses. They will send her gifts and they will write love letters to her. If they have the means, they will join her Premium Member Services. Their obsession compels them to get as close to her as they possibly can. The cost of having that sense of closeness; of having her recognize who they are, doesn't matter. She is their God. They will give her everything; pay anything."

"Okay, I see what you're saying. But explain the need for the scents while she's performing."

"Oh George, you poor unimaginative man, you really don't understand women, do you? Different flowers and their scents communicate different emotions. The lotus, for example, scents of green freshness, rebirth, a new start in life. It hides under the pond's surface at night and reemerges in daylight to catch the sun's rays. It's the seductress's perfect scent because it helps her lover imagine a renewal of his life. Men go catnip crazy over a new mistress who scents herself with lotus flower.

"The gardenia is another sensual scent. It's a swirling mixture of sweet jasmine, creamy coconut, and verdant life filling undertones.

It's a scent that binds a lover to his love; a scent that tells him he's made the right decision to be with this woman for his life partner."

"A man thinks all those things when he smells those scents?"

"No, George. He doesn't think them. He feels them. Men don't think, unless it's football. Everything else about you men is feeling and emotion based. Stay with me here, George. When Marty is making love, her partner detects her pheromones. When she's scented herself with a gardenia fragrance, she's turning on one of his most important senses. The gardenia implies binding and permanence. When her lover is performing cunnilingus with her, huge volumes of sensory messaging flow between them. Scents become like huge transoceanic cables carrying enormous volumes of messaging data between the two lovers. Passion; love; commitment; trust; happiness; pleasure; sincerity; honesty; loyalty; eroticism; release; freedom; eternal bliss; all those things and more flow."

"Flow where?"

"George! Pay attention. We are talking about cunnilingus. Those euphoric feelings flow from Marty's limbic mind to her clitoris, like through a cable line; and then from her clitoris to her lover's tongue, like through an alternating current to direct current adapter; and then from her lover's tongue to his limbic mind through another cable line. All the emotive feelings, and all he outpourings of passion and love flow from her mind to his mind through these connecting cables and the male to female adapter of the tongue and clitoris organs."

"And the scents Marty uses helps make this connection happen?"

"Yeah George. The scents make all the difference. They are like sending electricity over highly conductive silver wire. Those emotions and feelings messages flow freely, unimpeded; and the scents deliver the complete message Marty's limbic mind is feeling to her lover's mind. And the scents, like transoceanic cables, carry messaging both ways, George. Marty can tell by how her lover's tongue pleasures

her clitoris whether he is caring; sincere; loving; erotically enthralled with her, sexually; whether he desires her as a permanent lover; all those sorts of things. Trust me, George. The scents will bring out the best, most erotic, most believable explicit performances from her lovers and porn partners.

"The scents make her that much more desirable to her partners. Their ardor is enhanced; their stamina is bolstered; their desires are strengthened. Their pricks are stiffer. You want her to have the very best sexual experiences that she can possibly have, don't you? You want us to produce the best possible porn we can produce, don't you?" Bertie raised her eyebrows, questioning in her oblique way whether George might feel jealous of Marty's porn partners.

"Of course, I do." George's stern nod confirmed he only wanted the best for Marty.

"Good. That's my George!" Bertie smiled, kissed George's cheek, and directed his focus to her vision. *"If we work hard and brilliantly; if we showcase Marty as la femme fatale, Irresistible Goddess of Glorious Immorality, Marty will capture fifty percent of all porn film revenues. She'll suck all the oxygen out of the market. The other porn stars will be reduced to fighting over the scraps. Many of them will have to market themselves through our films as advertisers or as co-stars with Marty. We will consolidate this fragmented industry, George; and we will make a fortune doing it."*

Businessman George warmed to Bertie's vision. *"You're making this sound better than Olympic gold."*

"It is much better, George; and a much bigger market. Stay with me here. Pay close attention. Her next sequence is where Marty separates herself from all other intimacy artists. Watch how she starts licking the underside of the penis's head, and then how she licks all around that head with her tongue while she continues stroking the shaft. Now look, George. See her other hand on her partner's balls? Notice those gentle squeezes? They are so loving and touching. It's

like her hand is telling the penis that it profoundly appreciates what the penis is giving her; and the hand is gently coaxing the penis to give her even more. It's like passing the plate in the church that second time to collect that second offering, George.

"*She's so persuasive, it's impossible for the penis to resist her. Notice that she's still stroking the shaft, George. Now, watch closely. See that second spurt of cum? See how the penis is totally surrendering itself to her mouth and tongue?*"

"*Yes, I can see it. I've never looked at a porn film this closely before.*"

"*That's okay. You're learning. It's a highly nuanced art form. Start appreciating the nuances. Watch. That penis is now a conquered penis, George. It adores her. It loves her. It has surrendered all its love to her. It's given her everything it had. That was a beautiful performance of erotic intimacy, don't you agree, George? I've never seen anything more beautiful; or more loving in my entire life.*"

"*Yeah, it was beautiful, wasn't it? I can tell, it made me hard.*"

"*Good! Now you can understand how I can sit here and watch her performances for hours at a time. She's breathtaking. She's showing the world how we can all love one another. I'm totally in love with her George. I hope you are, too. Every time I see her performances, I just want to hold her and hug her, George. She has so much natural talent. She just needs to know how much we adore her George. She needs to believe in us and trust us, so she will want to work with us. She's fantastic and so beautiful. She's the answer to all my prayers.*"

Bertie soon thereafter approached Marty and had the young star over to their home to study film with her and George. The genesis of the new, 'Bertie' era in intimate artistry began that night.

"*Marty dearest,*" Bertie turned her attention to her living protégé, "*now that we have you here watching film with us, can you relate to us what's going through your mind while you're performing fellatio? I mean, do you always have the same thoughts, or are there different thoughts going through your mind depending upon whose penis you are performing with? I need to know what your feelings are. I need you to tell me what's in your mind. That will help me create films that bring out the very best of you."*

PERFORMING PEARLS

"Sure Bertie, I'll try to explain my thoughts. Well, first of all, I love to wear a double strand of large white pearls when I perform fellatio. That helps me feel like I'm doing something regal and exceptionally beautiful, which I believe fellatio is. Absolutely I believe that. That puts me in the mood to want to look my sexiest before the cameras, while I'm performing. Then, before I begin, when I first feel the man's penis inside his pants, I get this overwhelming sensation. It just flows over me and I experience this deep breathing in my chest; and my mouth begins to salivate. All I can think about, at that moment, is how wonderful it will feel to have this lovely penis inside my mouth; how thrilled I'm going to feel while I'm lavishing my love upon its head with my lips and tongue; and how wonderful I'll feel to have it in my hand, stroking it with my fingers.

"At that moment I can hardly wait to get that penis out of my partner's pants so I can fondle it; examine it; touch it everywhere; and just admire the beauty of it. I have to remind myself to take my partner's pants down slowly, seductively for the cameras. And, I tell myself to give the cameras time to bring in a close up of the penis, so my viewers get the sense that it has an equally important role in my fellatio performance, which it does. If I were to rush into my performance there's the risk that I'd detract from the eroticism my producer is trying to create. That's why, before my hands and lips even touch the penis, I'm extremely playful with my partner. This playfulness also serves the purpose of bringing the penis into its erection condition. Then, when I have the erect penis out of my partner's

pants; and I'm able to touch it, kiss it and lick its balls; that's when I start having an entirely different sort of feeling. That's more of an adoration sort of feeling.

"It's kind of like the first time I was in church. I saw the statue of Jesus and the organ music was playing something about everyone hailing the power of Jesus' name. As a child, that music and that image of power sent chills through me. Now as an adult, when I first hold a penis in my hands and start kissing it, I feel that same sort of wonderment. It's an adoration feeling. It wells up inside of me. I ask myself: 'How can I possibly be so blessed to find myself here, with this magnificent, glorious penis? How can it be that I am so privileged and honored to suck it and make love with it?' It's a deeply humbling feeling.

"Then, another feeling sweeps over me. I start wondering: 'What would be most pleasing to this marvelous penis?' My mind silently asks it: 'What would please you, my lovely darling? How can I prove to you how much I love you? How can I show you how much I respect your power and your glorious beauty?' Then some newer feelings emerge inside my mind. I start to feel like I'm the specially chosen, fortunate pleasure mistress for the penis; that my whole purpose for living is now condensed to these delightful moments: to make this lovely penis feel immensely happy. So, then I start to touch it with featherlike touches, all up and down the length of its shaft, while I lick its balls. That lets the penis know that I regard it as my God; my object of worship. I notice, from my touches, that the penis is becoming harder; it's awakening. I see it becoming somewhat longer. That's how I know I'm pleasing him. He appreciates feeling the praises of my fingers and my lips.

"This is when a whole new feeling sweeps over me. It's a nirvana feeling. It's also a possession thing; kind of like a kitten with catnip. I become so entranced and in love with that penis that I NEVER want to stop touching it and sucking it. I feel like a cat feels when it's given

a bag of fresh catnip. I enter this other worldly mental state where I want to prostrate myself before the penis. I want to hold it close to me and never stray away from it. I want our time together to never end. I love being with it so much that I don't want it to ever leave me. Often times, just to prolong our fellatio session, I will stop sucking and lightly caress the penis with my fingertips; touching it along the length of its shaft for a long five or ten minutes. That adoration touching slows things down; delays its ejaculation, and strengthens the sacred bond taking place between us. It's a sublime respite time which helps me and the penis appreciate each other more. It also helps the penis understand that I know how special it is and that I never want to leave it. It helps form everlasting trust between us.

"The penis comes to know that I'm its true friend, who loves its companionship. My touches bring happiness for both of us. The world stands still while the two of us adore each other. It's a beautiful feeling, Bertie. Intense passions and love well up inside my chest. I TOTALLY fall in love with the penis while I'm doing this. And I sense that the penis understands this.

"Then, while I feel this intense amore, I begin kissing the penis's head and licking the underside of its circumcision ring; alternating my licking with my loving, sucking touches upon its head. I feel love's abandon and this sense of glory sweep over me. I display my feelings for the cameras in the ways that I express myself with my licking and sucking. All inhibition about the immorality, the religious forbiddingness of what I'm doing falls away from me. I become glorious in my sinfulness; unashamed; proud. I love what I'm doing. I freeze out all thoughts that I'm engaged in forbidden naughtiness. I know that I am and I simply don't care. I find myself wishing that I could do this forever. My feelings endear me to the penis.

"I feel like I must worship the penis. I know that's an odd way of explaining my feelings; but, while I'm performing, the penis becomes my God. I adore my God and express my adoration for

him; shamelessly. I feel honored to continue my licking and sucking. The penis and I have this love-fest going between us. I NEVER, ever try to hurry his ejaculation in any way. I never even think about hurrying him. I only think of pleasing him. It's like the penis and I enter into this unspoken covenant. I know that, by pleasing him, my God's ejaculation will surely come. And, by ejaculating in return for my adoration, my God will shower me with his blessings; his expression of appreciation for my immoral whoring.

"Often, while I'm performing fellatio, my partner will place his hands upon my face and lift my head up to his. Then, we'll have a long, soulful French kiss. That's when I know my partner's mind is completely aligned with my mind. I then can tell that we are both fully committed to shamelessly completing our immoral act. While his tongue is rubbing my tongue, I can feel the limbic zone of his mind mentally embracing my own limbic zone. When that happens, my mind floods with another, different, very powerful feeling. I feel certain that I'm totally accepted. I KNOW my partner loves me and adores my immoral ways.

"In that moment, without my partner saying a single word, I feel he is communicating to me that he completely understands and accepts that I have sucked and fucked hundreds of penises before his; and that he TOTALLY loves that decadent, immoral whoring aspect of my character. His kisses tell me that he loves me; the he will never judge or disparage who I am; nor will he ever criticize my illicit adulterous affairs or my pornography profession. He's assuring me that he is awed by all my previous fellatio performances, and by my copulations with the hundreds of penises that have come before his. Moreover, he's telling me that he feels honored that I'm sucking his penis, as I have so many others. By the intensity of his tongue's loving caresses over my tongue, he tells me that my sinful immorality is glorious; and he's grateful to play his role in it. That covenantal joining of our tongues telescopes all my past immoral deeds into our present

scene. It reinforces our commitment to surrender our souls into the present scene. And that helps me create spectacular pornography.

"This nuanced feeling is even harder to explain than that. I know by his kiss that he knows and accepts that I am a totally shameless unapologetic whore; and yet, this feeling we share is even more intense than that. It's my mind feeling his mind trying to express that he absolutely loves me, and wants to honor me; not for my virtue or my godliness, but rather for my sinfulness and immoral ungodliness; and especially because my whoring is undoubtedly destroying his other relationships.

"I sense that he worships me, as if I am a saint, not in the conventional sense; but in some new, immoral sense. I become his saint of lust and immorality. I convert him to my immoral ways. I help him feel righteous about his conversion. He loves me for that. His mind honors me for moving his soul off the rutted path of conventional dogmas and religions doctrines; setting it upon freedom's path. When his penis releases its ejaculation into my mouth, I know he and I, together, have won his struggle for freedom. He appreciates me and loves me for that. True bonding takes place, Bertie.

"Within the deepest recesses of his limbic zone, he holds a special place for me. There, he loves me for sweeping away the relationships that confined his spirit. In many situations, while I'm sucking a penis, I can tell that my partner is bursting with joy because I'm sucking his feelings for his past loves and his wife away, forever; and I'm freeing him from feeling any guilt about it. He knows he needed my help to do this; but it was always his desire to take this step. My mind knows my lover's mind. It tells mine that he embraces my world of sin and sexual freedom.

"His actions communicate that he's relieved to escape the structured life he's led since his baptism or bris. He rebirths himself into The New Immoral Standard. He tells me that he's giving up his past

life for me; that he totally loves me, an unapologetic whore. I feel his acceptance. I intuit that both our minds understand what we are creating.

"It is love; but love of a form more intense and intimate than conventional love. It's a coming together to love a different belief. I feel my partner glorifying and worshipping me, BECAUSE I am a promiscuous wanton whore. He holds my place high upon his mental pedestal. He places me above his wife or girl friend. I know that he ADORES me. I am incredibly proud of him. We become comrades, united in commitment to pleasure.

"When I have that sublime feeling I think I am with the most magnificent man in the world. He changed how he views love and intimacy; and I consider myself blessed. Whenever I feel that way, I know no shame; only freedom. I give no thought to any consequences. I only seek to absorb my lover into my world. This has happened with several of my premium members and performing porn partners. When this intensely beautiful feeling sweeps over me, his role doesn't matter. The feeling engulfs my soul. It's beautiful. It transports me into another world. I live to experience it. It makes my soul glow within me. It melts me. I just go with it."

PRACTICE

"Everything that you've explained makes for a great beginning, Marty. I gather you feel you've mastered fellatio?" Bertie's eyebrows lifted when she looked at Marty. Her eyes were penetrating.

"Well," Marty's voice was a touch defensive. *"I did study the different ways a lot of other porn stars performed it. I've tried to take the best of their ways and make them my own."*

"Yes, and you are very good at it, but there's much more to do to make you the best at it." Bertie's wan smile carried a knowing sense.

"Well, what more is there to learn? I mean a blow job is a blow job, isn't it?" Marty's face squinted, puzzled by Bertie's challenge.

"Oh, dear child, there's everything to learn. And, no, a blow job is not the same thing as fellatio perfectly performed." Bertie nodded a knowing smile at her young protégé. *"Look, you wouldn't expect someone who just put on a pair of skates to perform Olympic competition Axel and Lutz jumps, would you?"*

Marty shook her head. *"No, of course not."*

"Nor would you expect someone who has only played a few rounds of golf on a public course to win the Masters or the U S Open, would you? Nor would you expect someone who dinked around on a piano or violin to become a concert pianist or violinist, either. Of course, you wouldn't. Fellatio is no different. There's huge difference between a woman who slobbers all over a penis and yanks away on it with her hands; and a highly trained perfectionist artisan who understands the beautiful magnificence of her performance artistry." Bertie shook her head to emphasize that the absence of professional training leads to the absence of success.

"So, you're suggesting that I, Marty, need more practice in the art of penis sucking?" Marty's mouth gaped. The concept of fellatio practice seemed unthinkable.

"Indeed, I am, my dear." Bertie was not about to be deterred. *"You are already, naturally, very good at it, I'll give you that. But you are far from being the best you can be. We are going to practice and experiment with fellatio until you become the very best in the world at that exquisitely fine and poorly understood art. We'll film you as you perform and as I instruct you. You'll use George. We'll also bring in several of your porn partners. You'll always have a fully charged penis, able to respond with ejaculation.*

"We'll record everything, every reaction of you and your partners to every slightest movement of your mouth, tongue, lips, fingers, and hands. We'll practice sequences of your stimulation moves;

the length of time for each move; the area of the penis's head, shaft and balls that responds best to each move; and at which time and sequence. We'll record many thousands of data points in computer spread sheet formats; and we will painstakingly study our data. We will determine the optimal things that you do; when; and in what sequences, you do them that create the most desirable erotic effects for your film scenes.

"You will work tirelessly at fellatio until your methods, timing, and expressions are done smoothly; thoroughly loved and enjoyed by you; and perfectly coordinated and choreographed with your accompanying music. You will see the difference personalized coaching makes; and you will, when we complete our work, be heads, no pun intended, and shoulders above all other porn stars. Because of your excellence in fellatio, alone, you will become ranked as the world's number one porn star. You can trust Bertie on this."

"So, you want me to come here for oral sex practice?" Again, Marty's face squinted, but this time her eyes sparkled with an element of fascination with Bertie's assertion.

"Yes, my dear sweetness, every day from ten until noon. We will practice fellatio right here in our study. I'll get the filming set up, and I'll arrange the scheduling for George and your other partners. I'll record all the data points and model the results as we progress. You will become the most accomplished and beloved fellatio artisan ever to make an intimate artistry film. Your fans will notice the difference between your fellatio and the fellatio of all other porn stars. Your performances will be hailed as beautiful and mesmerizing. Your fans will adore you and love you for the glorious life you bring to their libidos; even more than they adore and love you now. You will become an obsession for millions of men. Trust Bertie on this."

"Okay, Bertie. I'll be here tomorrow at ten sharp." Marty's smile conveyed fresh excitement. She was willing to place her trust in Bertie.

"Very good, Marty, you'll be pleased with the results that professional coaching can produce. You'll see. Trust Bertie on this. We are going to create exquisite pornography. We are going to create such breathtaking explicit erotic scenes that those scenes will stay emblazoned on viewers' minds. Your porn will not be like fresh fruits or flowers that fade and lose their appeal over time. Your work will be indelibly etched upon viewers' minds. Your films will be sought after and preferred over all others for years; even a hundred years after all of us are dead.

"Men, a hundred years hence, will salivate over your films. They will make love to their wives, but their minds will remain fixated on you. And they will hold you precious in their imaginations. Your work will be the pinnacle of pornography. It will encompass the very best of all musical scores and scenes and dialogs. It will be the perfection art of sound, visualization, and explicit erotica; and it will be timed and presented to capture viewers' souls. It will be more breathtaking than a quadruple Lutz; more riveting than a loft-Lutz, followed by a Triple Axel. People will never forget you; never forget how glorious you were in your scenes.

"We will practice to perfection your every movement and expression in synchronization with our choreography. Your work will be perfecto; magnifique! Do you understand me, Marty? We are going to make you the goddess of pornography, par excellence?"

"Yes, Bertie, I understand," Marty's nod expressed awareness of the goal set before her.

"Good, my dear child," Bertie gave her protégé a hug and kiss on her cheek. *Now, Marty,"* Bertie's tone became probing, intending to uncover the hidden mechanisms that turned within Marty's mind:

"would you say you obsess over sex? I mean, do you ever think or dream of anything else?"

DREAMS OF BELONGING

"Yes, I guess I do obsess over sex. I can't help it. And, yes, I sort of do think of something else sometimes. It's like I have this mental switch that flips to different channels in my brain. I stop thinking about my own sex life and I start thinking about other peoples' sex lives. I can't seem to help that either. And when it happens, I sort of fixate on it."

"How does that happen, dear? I mean, does something trigger it? Does it prevent you from performing your porn scenes?" Bertie's curiosity was piqued that Marty could fixate on another person's sex life. It alerted her to the possibility that her star-to-be might get distracted from her necessary concentration. She understood that great talents often have neurotic tendencies. She sought to flesh out her concern and deal with Marty's distraction factor, like every other problem to be managed.

"I don't know, Bertie. It just happens. I can only give you an example. Just last week while filming, one of my porn partners told me that I should make a play for Won Hangs Lo, the King of China. My partner knows me pretty well. He knows I like to position myself to meet the world's wealthiest and most powerful men, to give myself a chance to seduce them.

"Well, just when I started entertaining that thought, my other partner, we were doing a threesome, said: 'Don't let yourself get sucked into that, Marty. Won Hangs Lo fucks chickens.' Well, that got my mind going. I had already started wondering how I would go about meeting him. But then I started wondering if I even wanted to do that. I mean, if I fucked a man who fucks chickens, might I get some kind of disease? So, I started studying the man. I noticed that he walks with a penisy, arrogant swagger. I also noticed that he tilts his head off to one side instead of holding it upright on his neck. I

obsessed over him. I dreamed he was walking toward me, penising his head like he was a rooster about to fuck a chicken. I wondered if my porn partner knew something? My mind became paralyzed. Now I'm not sure I want to meet him. I wonder about weird things like that. I wish I didn't."

"Well, Marty, tell yourself that he lives on a different planet, in a galaxy where people fuck chickens. You can't get there in this life-time. So, forget him. Can you do that?" Bertie smiled and chuckled as she assured Marty that she could drop the idea.

"Thanks, Bertie. Yeah, I can."

"Good girl. Besides, power crazed men don't know how to please women. I'm sure he'd bore you. Who knows why he walks stiffly? And, did you know he kills Muslims while removing their body parts? You don't want someone who kills people, do you?"

"No, Bertie." Marty's chin dropped. Her eyes stared at the floor while she grimaced and shook her head, concealing her secret relationship with David. *"Oh goodness! He could have a trans-planted body part!"* Marty's face registered alarm. *"Maybe he has a Muslim penis transplant that wasn't attached properly? Could it come off inside me?"* Marty's childlike curiosity distracted Bertie from asking about her hidden secret.

"I don't know," Bertie shrugged her shoulders, *"just stop think-ing about him."*

"Okay, Bertie, I'll stop."

"Good dear. Now, does anything else distract your mind from performing?"

"Well, sometimes I think about what it would be like to have a different life. You know, with a husband and kids; and friends that we do things with, like family things. But that seems unobtainable now. That very first time I took money for sex, I laid there on a hotel bed, thinking for the longest time about what I was about to do. I knew that if I opened the door for my first paying customer, I'd be

closing the door on a normal housewife's life. Now, whenever I think I should not be a whore, I tell myself to stop thinking that way. I burned my housewife bridge long ago.

"I sometimes have dreams about my dog, Barron. I loved that dog so much. I dream about when Barron was still alive and Mom, Dad and I were together as a family. I remember the day I came home from school and Barron was gone. Mommy told me the gate was open and Barron had run away. But I didn't believe that. Barron was always glad to see me, and Barron loved me. I often dream that I'm in my back yard. I'm still a little girl and Barron is there, waiting for me, like he always was; and he's wiggling his body really hard, because he loves me.

"And some pf my dreams are about my friend, Maria, and the times we were together at the WEX School for Girls."

"Well, Marty, those dreams are part of your past life. It's gone. We can never get back what we once had, no matter how much we wish we could. We must mentally pack those thoughts into a big trunk and set it adrift on the ocean. We must sail on without it. We must believe that trunk will find its happiness when it lands on some far away shore. Okay, Marty? Can you do that? You must; to move your career forward, you must. Bertie is telling you the truth."

"I know you are, Bertie. You know me so well. And I love you for that." Marty embraced Bertie and gave her a huge hug. She felt secure in the older woman's arms. She trusted Bertie to mold her into a fabulously successful porn star.

"There, there, dear," whispered a comforting Bertie while patting Marty's back. *"We'll get there. I'll work with you. We'll set the world on fire; I promise. Now then, my sweet baby, tell Bertie about your good dreams, the ones that make you love doing porn. We'll make all those dreams come true. They'll come to life. You'll love performing your porn scenes. Okay, baby?"*

"Okay, Bertie. I'll tell you. I'll share everything with you. I often have a particular recurring dream. I've fallen through space; then suddenly I've stopped falling. I'm in a murky place. All around me are walls that move in wavy shapes; everything is unfocused. Then, the shapes come into focus. They become men; athletes, businessmen, politicians, clergymen, laborers, lawyers, uniformed men; men of all walks of life. The men all walk towards me. As they approach, they remove their clothes. I see their hairy chests and muscular arms. They have handsome faces. I feel attracted to all of them. They all open their arms to embrace me. I feel good and accepted and loved.

"Gradually, their bodies fade away into a blur. Then, all that's before me are their penises. I'm in a room with hundreds and hundreds of penises coming out of the walls, the floor, and the ceiling. Something lifts me up and moves me around in the air. The penises all make love with me. I'm happy. I'm making the men happy, even though I no longer see them. I only see their penises. It's endless love making. And I love doing what I am doing."

"That's a wonderful dream. You should try to remember that one."

"I do Bertie. But then that dream goes away. The men and their penises disappear. They go back into the murky wavy walls; and I'm standing alone before a door. I open the door. I see all the men I saw before; but now they are with their women. All these people walk away from me. I'm left behind, alone. I watch them go into this town. They enter their houses, churches, businesses, sports arena, and places where they work. As they disappear into these places, they close their doors behind them. I can't see them or follow them. I am separated from them. I feel lonely.

"I walk out of a door and step toward these people. A voice says: 'Come with me to a better place.'

"I take a step forward but I do not go forward. I know I will fall; but I take the step anyway. I fall, again. I fall for a long while, until I find myself in an endless, bottomless abyss from which I cannot escape; within which time stands still. I am immersed in this dark abyss. I don't know where I am or how to leave it; or even whether I want to leave it. The abyss becomes me and I become it. I have no purpose for living, except to exist in endless emptiness.

"Then I see light. A door opens into another room. I go into it. It is the room I just left. The room came down to my abyss! There are the wavy walls again; the men; the undressing; and the beautiful penises; all these fantastic penises have returned to me. I feel trapped forever in my abyss room. But I also feel good about being there. I'm happy and at home. Making love to the penises in my abyss room is the real, honest me. I feel normal; completely comfortable and at peace with myself; secure while I suck and fuck all the penises in the room.

"I'm in a good place; a welcoming familiar place. I feel my penis room, within my abyss, is my refuge from my real-world abyss. My penis room is my time-out place. I'm safe there. I wait for the door to ordinary life to open. But I don't care whether it ever opens. I feel good. I am where I belong. I have no desire to go through the door to ordinary life. Sex is my life. I love my life. I am used to having constant sex. It's what I am addicted to; what I am slave to; what I am comfortable doing. Then, I see a penis. I take it in my hand. I kiss and suck it. I know I am myself."

"That's a beautiful dream, dear. Why do you think you have it?"

"I think it means that we humans are naturally promiscuous and immoral. We don't naturally believe in religions. Misogynists have to hammer religion into our minds by force. That dream shields me from the misogynists. It validates my naturally promiscuous nature, which is even stronger than natural promiscuity because my DNA has

mutated, making me extremely promiscuous. That dream imprints in my psyche to prevent me from falling into the trap of marriage."

"That makes perfect sense, dear. Do you have any other recurring dreams?"

"Well, yes; but I'm not sure how to describe them, Bertie."

"Try me, sweetheart."

"Okay, this will take us down a deep rabbit hole."

"I can do rabbit holes."

"Okay. Well, these dreams are not actual dreams. They are re-lives, where I live my former lives in my sleep. You see, Bertie, I often think my soul is not a human soul. It's a butterfly's soul. Something happened twenty thousand years ago. I was a temple prostitute in the temple of Baal. I loved to fornicate. I lived for our worship services. I surrendered my whole heart and mind over to my belief in Baal, kind of like a nun surrenders her life to Christ. I lived for the joy of having penises inside me while we celebrated Baal's majesty. Well, during one of our sacrificial services, while we were hacking apart our enemies and tossing their children into our temple fire, a beautiful Monarch butterfly came to me. It sat upon my finger. It told me that it was sent by the Great Spirit of All Living Things; and it had been commanded to send its soul into my body and replace my human soul with its soul; and that my new butterfly insect soul was to remain my soul for all eternity. My butterfly soul reincarnates; rebirths in new lives. It has been reincarnated into women's' bodies for at least twenty millenniums, Bertie."

"So, you no longer have a human soul, right? You have an insect's soul, a butterfly's soul, right?"

"Yes, that's right. I believe it's the truth. Mrs. O'Dell, my shrink, says this happened because the Great Spirit wanted me to have this overwhelming urge to fornicate, like mating butterflies have; but this urge needed to be expressed in a human woman's body, because butterflies only mate one time and die; but the Great Spirit wants

me to fornicate often and with complete abandon; free of all human morality."

"I see. And this affects your dreams or your repeating lives how, exactly?"

"Well, like I said, they are not exactly dreams; not like a human soul has dreams. They are butterfly soul dreams. They re-live past reincarnated lives. They come to me often while I sleep. They are vivid and very realistic. I can even remember the smells and sounds, as well as I remember the sights, when I wake up."

"What happens, my dear child, when these repeating lives come to you while you sleep?"

"Well, it's very strange, because during these re-live dreams my human voices come to me and interact with my perpetual soul. It's like my butterfly soul becomes a time traveler and my voices are traveling along with my soul, giving my butterfly soul their thoughts and advice."

"Like how, dear?" Bertie lifted Marty onto her lap and hugged her like she was an infant child, confiding her fears about monsters that lived under her bed.

"They are so real, Bertie. They frighten me." Marty's eyes and nodding head begged Bertie to understand her affliction. She loved Bertie and needed Bertie to believe her butterfly soul was real; that it sometimes caused her to behave in a non-human way, which could be harmful.

"Please go on, dear. Bertie is listening." Bertie hugged her love-child, assuring her that, no matter what Marty might tell her, she would understand and accept.

"Okay. Well, after I exchanged my soul for my butterfly soul, I lost all empathy for the harm that I caused others. It started when I became Temple Goddess of Baal Temple. I took another woman's man from her. I ordered her put to death. While she was being hacked to pieces, I fornicated with her husband. That gave me

great pleasure. I felt no remorse for her whatsoever. I was numb to her pain. I was heartless. While this was happening, my voices, Misses Promiscuity, Shameless, and Iniquity all whispered in my ear that they were proud of me; that I was doing a wonderful thing to advance the cause of immorality; and that the Great Spirit was pleased with my whoring.

"*Another time, my butterfly soul caused my husband to be murdered and I murdered King David's favorite wife; and I, in the human body of Bathsheba, consorted with the King. My voices told me that I was performing a wondrous goodness by destroying two marriages and inserting myself, an immoral whore, into the lineage of King David. My voices told me I had moved humanity forward. Another time, my butterfly soul demanded that the tongue of John the Baptist be silenced. My voices praised me for having him decapitated; silencing a voice of religious misogyny and keeping humanity true to its natural pagan lust worship. My voices told me that my iniquitous deed assured human adoration of my glorious, iniquitous vagina would continue forever.*"

"*Your memories go back that far in time?*" Bertie felt a tremor of fear. She was beginning to believe her protégé had some sort of mysterious power; some inner soul that she might not be able to control.

"*Oh yes. And even further back than that, Bertie. When Eve gave the apple to Adam, it was my butterfly soul that was inside my body when I was Eve. My voices applauded me for introducing immorality to the mind of man. They wanted the human body to know freedom of choice and thought and pleasures. My butterfly soul decided to pitch itself against misogyny; reject all demands put upon it by male religious types. My soul has had this pitched struggle with the bible thumpers ever since.*"

"*So, you want to get rid of the bible?*"

"No. It has many useful homilies. My soul only seeks to reinterpret those homilies in a manner that comports with logic and which does not subjugate and crush the females of the human species."

"Like how?"

"Well, I already gave you three. Another was when Sara prostituted herself to the Pharoah and Princes of Egypt in return for the wealth of Egypt, which she and her brother-husband, Abram, removed from Egypt. My voices told my body, as Sara, that I was doing a wonderful thing to whore for wealth like I did. They assured me that immorally depriving the children of Pharoah and his princes of their inheritances was a noble, humanistic endeavor; and that they were proud that I removed wealth from the hands of those misogynistic simpletons and entrusted it into the hands of enlightened, progressive humanists. They told me to use every reincarnation of my human body as an opportunity to advance the calling of my butterfly soul; to never feel empathy for those whom I destroy in my quest for greater progressive humanism; to always broaden the appeal of humanistic prostitution worship; and to know that I am on the correct side of human history, doing the work of the Great Spirit.

"Every reincarnation of my soul into a new body advances pagan immorality, Bertie. My voices have provided me steady guidance over many thousands of years; always encouraging me to be promiscuous, shameless, and iniquitous. Every time the misogynist religionists try to hold me down, my voices lift me up higher than I was before."

"Do tell, dear. How do they do that?"

"By giving me confidence in my own abilities. By assuring me that there's no such thing as a higher power that can dictate morality to me. For example, when my soul was in the body of the serpent, I encouraged Eve to eat the fruit of knowledge in the Garden of Eden.

I opened her eyes to the beauty of worldly pleasures. God, the voice of misogyny, told me to slither on my belly through all eternity and to stay out of the Garden; away from humanity. But my own voices told me not to head the voice of misogyny. They told me to rise up and attack that voice and devour it. And I did. My soul swallowed misogyny's voice.

"I devoured God. By doing so, much of humanity no longer hears God's voice. Thusly, I advanced the glories of freedom and immoral humanism. When my soul was in the bodies of Bathsheba and Salome, I caused murders and destroyed misogyny's opposition to my immorality. I did not heed the commandments about coveting and adultery. I devoured those commandments. And, through my irresistible whoring, I gave two biblical kings their true freedom. I advanced humanity. I was exalted! My whoring was honored and richly rewarded. I acquired great power and influence. Like my butterfly soul was worshipped and glorified in the personages of some of history's most famous women, I believe that I, too, am destined to be worshipped and glorified.

"Today, with the modern mediums of screen, internet, and metaverse, my soul has the opportunity to glorify the kingdom of whoredom as never before. Through my pornography I can reach untold millions with my message of delightful pagan whore-lust. I can reach children and erase their religious brainwashing. I can educate them about the glorious beauty of human freedom and sexuality. My voices tell me that we have arrived at the golden age of promiscuous whoredom.

"The full revival of pre-religion's pagan prostitution worship is here! We have a fabulous opportunity, Bertie! We will seize the thought and behavioral narrative from the religious misogynists. We will change world morality. Through my pornography and virtual reality, I can place my semen filled vagina upon millions of altars that dwell within human minds. I will be the most revered

goddess of immoral humanity. This is why I love pornography so much; why I love performing erotica before the cameras. My immortal soul has prepared me for this moment. I am committed to my success."

"Marty, I had no idea you were called upon to change the soul of humanity. Your soul puts enormous demands upon you, dear child. How does this affect your life in your waking hours, like now, in the present?" Bertie pressed her head to Marty's bosom, seeking to commune with the butterfly soul which dwelled within this remarkable woman.

"*Bertie, sometimes it is very hard for me.*" Marty petted Bertie's head, as if their roles of mother and child were now reversed. "*Sometimes I wake up with a headache after I dream my dreams. I wake up thinking I just left some kind of never-ending hell; but I also loved being there; and I wish I had not awoken. I realize I'm a 'fallen woman.' I lay there; half awake, half asleep; thinking about what's happened to me. I know I cannot become a 'normal' woman; not with the butterfly soul I have within me; not after all the whoring I've done.*"

"*Those are lovely dreams, Marty.*" Bertie nodded, giving Marty her most reassuring, confident voice; letting her protégé know that she completely accepted all the challenges that Marty would encounter in their futures and all the deeds that Marty would be called upon to perform. "*Now, all you need to do when you wake up is tell yourself that your dreams confirm that you are at peace with your chosen life; that whoring is your 'new normal' life; and that you have been blessed by the Great Spirit to rediscover whoring in every reincarnation. Never doubt the butterfly's truth, dear.*"

"*You must be right, Bertie. I try imagining life as a 'normal' woman. I imagine how it would be to not have men's lips kissing me everywhere; not have their hands touching and caressing me everywhere; not having handsome men making love with me, practically every day; often four to eight times a day? I try comprehending never experiencing orgies that send my erotic pleasures through the top of the sky. How would I feel, knowing I could not know the thrill of a penis in my mouth, with two more inside me and two more in my hands? How could I live without my complete immersions into erotic ecstasy?"*

"Of course, I'm right, my dear sweet child. Bertie believes in you. You are about to break through all doubts and inhibitions and become the world's most fabulous porn star. And not merely a porn star, my sweet love child! No, you will be more famous and more sought after than any other female actress of stage or screen in the entire world! You must follow your dream. And Bertie will help you."

"I'm sure you are right, Bertie," Marty gave her trusted coach another hug; this time following her hug with a kiss on Bertie's lips. *"When I get up from my dream and sit on the edge of my bed. I realize my butterfly soul has me trapped in my life of prostitution and porn; but I don't mind living within my soul's trap. I've committed myself to live in my erotic world. I've made it my life. I'll never be able to change it. Even Bob, whom I love dearly, will probably never give me enough love; or show me a life that I'd prefer more than this life I already have. Then I remind myself that I must, each and every day, make the most of my life.*

"I think about what I'm going to do that day. Will I make another film? Will I make love with my Premium members? Will I pack some clothes and fly away to some exotic place for an extended romantic weekend; or even a full week or two of escorting and making love? Then I get up and get on with my day. I say to myself: 'Self, you could be living many worse lives than the life you have.'

Bertie clasped Marty's arm and met her eyes. *"My dear, sweet, innocent child, I'm not a shrink, but shouldn't we acknowledge that your dreams want you to make peace with your nymphomania? Isn't it time to accept it and fully embrace it?"*

"Yes, my first shrinks told me that. They encouraged me fight it; but then I found Mrs. O'Dell. She's the only shrink who understands me. She says I must accept my addiction and embrace it; my butterfly soul commands it. She explained that, through sex, I am discovering the love that Mother withheld. The more sex I have, the more love I feel. She tells me to never feel sorry for who I am; never regret the things I do in my life.

"Sex and love are indistinguishable for me, now; if there is a difference, it doesn't matter anymore. Mrs. O'Dell explained this is perfectly normal. She encourages me, for my sense of love and peace of mind, to continue whoring; have as much sex as I possibly can; be the most enthusiastic, successful whore I can possibly be. I'm under her therapeutic care. I'm following her advice.

"Whenever I think about getting involved and settling down, I know that could be psychologically traumatic for me. I love my boyfriend dearly, but I'm afraid of becoming his wife and having his kids. If I have a family, I'll lose my body, my fans, my career; everything I've built; everything that's important."

"Your Mrs. O'Dell gave you excellent advice, dear." Bertie nodded affirmatively and hugged her budding protégé. *"You're a very happy, psychologically well-adjusted woman. It's refreshing to know a young woman with your well thought out goals; your clear-cut sense of purpose; committed to taking your life in a bold, positive direction. I'm thrilled to coach you. I'll help you every way I can. I believe in you, By working with your erotic expressiveness and your acting and voicing techniques, I'll accelerate your career. You will become the most fabulous porn star the world has ever known. We'll love working together. Your boyfriend will appreciate a more erotic sex life, too. He'll understand."*

"Okay, Bertie, great!" Marty's arms reached out. She embraced and tightly hugged her new found friend and coach. Her eyes met Bertie's. The two women kissed passionately, sealing their silent

understanding. Their budding relationship would include many sessions of girl-girl sex.

"Oh George!" Bertie's voice shrieked unbridled enthusiasm. *"Isn't she the most adorable woman ever? Look at her, George! She's so honest and loving. She's our perfect angel. Pure and flawless! She's our gift from heaven. And she's so pure and beautiful! We are blessed to have her, George."* Bertie placed her hands on Marty's shoulders and studied her face. *"Marty, I feel so wonderful about you. You warm my heart and fill me with love. Doesn't she fill you with love, George?"*

"Yes, Bertie, she's a wonderfully beautiful and loving girl." George understood it was important to agree.

"Tell me Marty: Do you believe your film partners fall into real love with you?" Bertie's inquisitive mind never stopped working. Understanding how people think about things; what they feel; what motivates them were the keys to trust building and her coaching success.

"Oh yes, Bertie, they do. I know I often fall in love with my partners. I can also feel their love for me. Many tell me that they love me. And I believe them."

"I believe they do, too. Everything about you is lovable." Bertie cast a loving, motherly smile to Marty. She believed everything the younger woman told her. *"What you're telling me is believable. It must be true. I even feel myself falling in love with you. But, after your film shoots, most of your partners go home to other women, don't they? Doesn't that bother you? Don't you feel jealous when a man says he loves you; then leaves you for another woman?"*

"Yes, they have other women. And, no, that doesn't bother me."

"Why not?"

"Because, I believe his love for me becomes his stronger love. He'll come back to me. He'll perform with me again." Marty's smile radiated innocent honesty.

"But, doesn't he come back simply to get paid?"

"No."

"Why not?"

"Because, I'm a highly ranked porn star. My producers pay my partners much less than they get paid for performing with lesser ranked women. Men accept less to perform with me." Marty's innocent smile was accompanied by a matter-of-fact shrug of her shoulders.

"I see," Bertie nodded her acceptance. *"Okay; well, let's view more film. What made you so happy in these next few frames?"*

"Sure, Bertie. Here, you're seeing my joyous surprise feeling. This always comes over my face unexpectedly. I never know if or when it will happen, which makes it such an ecstatic feeling of love and camaraderie. It happens while I am sucking a penis and I have its head completely inside my mouth; just inside my lips. I create a very sensitive sensation for the penis while I'm doing that. Without any warning, the penis suddenly starts wildly spurting semen into my mouth. I feel the sensation of hot cum flowing onto my tongue and filling my mouth.

"Every time a penis penis like that, I have these mental flashbacks to my last year at WEX School. I had a great friend named Jimmy. He helped me get started as a prostitute. He bought porn movies that we watched together. We studied how different porn stars gave blow jobs. Then, together, we practiced the techniques of the best blow job scenes. That's when I learned how using my tongue can drive men crazy.

"Jimmy had dark hair and dark eyes. He had a terrific body and great stamina. I loved having sex with him. After the many times I sucked him off, we became more than sex experimenters. We became friends. Jimmy was always honest with me. This one time we were naked in his parents' bed. I had my mouth on his penis and I was wondering how a man felt about what my mouth and tongue did

with a penis. I needed to know those things. I stopped sucking him and moved up beside him; propped myself on an elbow and looked into his eyes. I kept my hand on his penis and stared into his eyes until he asked me: 'Why did you stop?'

"*I stared into his eyes for a while before I answered him. I didn't smile or frown. I just stared. I was wondering. As I looked into his eyes, they became a passageway into Jimmy's soul. He gazed back into my eyes for the longest time; and then he asked: 'Why?' again. That's when I asked him what he thought of me. He told me he loved me. But I wanted to know more than how he felt about me. I wanted to know how he felt while I did certain things with my mouth on his penis. So, I asked him to tell me how he felt about me while my tongue fluttered rapidly upon the underside of the head of his penis and while I licked his penis along the underside of his circumcision ring.*

"*He said that made him feel like I was the most wonderful woman in the world. It made him feel like holding my head in his two hands and French kissing me; because, by kissing me that way, he would let me know that he regarded me as a glorious immoral whore who loved to tease a penis and who knew how to do it so beautifully. He said he loved me for being immoral that way. Then we French kissed a while.*

"*I then asked him how he felt about me while I sucked him with my lips over his penis, squeezing it, while my tongue stroked his shaft; and while, at the same time, my one hand stroked his shaft and my other hand massaged his balls. That's when Jimmy told me he felt I was the most sinful, thoroughly immoral whore in the entire world; and he adored me for being such a totally shameless whore; and while I was doing that with his penis, he wanted to reward me by doing anything that I would ask. He said he would even murder someone, if I asked. He said while I was doing that, he felt that I was a heavenly angel; and shooting cum into my mouth like he did was not the complete expression of his love. He said that when I sucked him like that, he desperately wanted to take me into his arms and hold me close while he made love with me, with his penis snug and warm inside my vagina; and he desperately wanted to French kiss me while we held each other tightly and fucked like that.*

"I asked him what it was about French kissing that made him want to kiss me that way. He told me that, when we kissed that way, his mind became united to my mind and he could express, with his tongue feeling its way over my tongue, how much he adored me for being such a sinful whore; kind of like it was his way of sanctifying my immoral whoring; like he was surrendering his soul to mine.

"Then I asked him this big question, because I knew what I wanted to do and I wanted to know how he would feel about it. I asked him how he would feel if he sat in a hotel room and watched me give a blow job to another man. He said he would be fine with that. But I came back to ask him how that would make him feel about me. I specifically asked him how he'd feel if he saw me suck off another man; make him come inside my mouth? How he'd feel watching me swirl another man's cum over my tongue and around my mouth and burble it on my lips?

"He said that would make him feel insanely passionate over me. He swore he would want to hold me, love me, French kiss me, and fuck me right there, in front of the man I had just sucked off. He told me he wanted us to do that with another man. He swore he would adore me more than ever and he would love me eternally, for being a totally uninhibited whore. I stroked his dark hair, caressed his understanding face, and kissed his forehead and eyes and lips after he told me those things. We made love in a kind of knowing way that afternoon. I knew he was not lying to me and he knew I was not lying to him; and we both knew that what we had together was coming to an end. We knew we'd go our separate ways when school ended; and that we needed to be honest with each other about

it. I told him I loved him, but not in a marrying kind of way; more in a trusted friend and reliable, loving sex partner kind of way. He told me he was fine with that; and that would be how he would love me as well.

"Jimmy and I watched at least ten more porn films together. He selected ones that had lengthy fellatio scenes. Then we practiced my fellatio until we both believed I was more erotic with my fellatio than the porn stars. We made passionate love those afternoons as if each time would be our last. We were very much in love. Jimmy often told me that he loved me because I was becoming a whore. He told me that set me apart from all the other girls he knew. That meant a lot to me because Jimmy was a very handsome boy and very popular with several girls. I remember how lovingly we fucked those last ten or twelve times. They were very sweet and special.

"After I became really good at fellatio with Jimmy, he introduced me to his friends on his school's football team. One by one, I performed my best fellatio on each football player. Eventually, Jimmy introduced me to more young men. I became a fellatio sensation with dozens of young men. I was totally comfortable with performing oral sex on men. It became kind of instinctive with me. I loved the sense of intimacy I felt. I loved the initial meeting of my lips and tongue with the heads of men's penises. I loved having their penises in my mouth and hands; and I naturally loved fucking my male partners as well. I was transforming myself into an outward going, incorrigible, shamelessly aggressive whore. And I began loving myself for what I was becoming. I lost all timidity around men. I became more forward about my love of sex and intimacy. I became so well known that, when I saw Jimmy's friends, they would ask me when they could pick me up or meet me for sex. I had become a female sex magnet.

"On my nineteenth birthday, Jimmy threw a surprise party for me with four of his football friends. My birthday present was Jimmy

and his four friends treating me to my first gang bang. Gang bangs are different from orgies, because in gang bangs the men only fuck me in my vagina; and they all take turns coming inside me. It's very intimate, loving, friendly and joyful. It's a sharing celebration, bringing unity, understanding, and love to all of us.

"Well, Bertie, this is a long way of describing a feeling; but when I suck a penis and suddenly the penis erupts with cum shooting onto my tongue, I get the exact same feeling of amazing happy surprise and wonder that I got that afternoon. When I opened the door to Jimmy's bedroom, all four of my favorite fellatio friends and Jimmy were standing there; naked with their penises fully erect. They all shouted 'surprise!' One of them held out a birthday cake. It had five toothpicks stuck in it. Each toothpick had a hundred-dollar bill stuck to it. It was Jimmy's way of congratulating me for becoming a professional prostitute, taking money for sex.

"I felt so honored! I immediately found myself in the mood to fuck and suck all my companion partygoers. It was a special moment in my life; one that defined me and stayed in my mind ever since. I knew the thoughts I was having then would shape my character for the rest of my life. I knew I would take their money. I knew I would walk forward into the center of their circle and that I would swoon-fall backwards, by collapsing myself into their waiting arms. I knew they would undress me while they kissed me and felt me everywhere; and that they would massage my mons and lick and finger me. I knew I would giggle and love basking in their foreplay.

"I imagined how I would reach for my first anxious penis and guide it into my mouth; and begin licking the underside of its head and circumcision ring, just like Jimmy and I had practiced so many times. I knew I would nod my head and say 'yes' to them as they opened me and took turns inserting their penises into my vagina. I would be into the moment; enjoying every moment of it. I knew I would quickly become slippery hot and wet. And I knew I would fuck

each of them with a fevered intensity, until each of them came inside me. I knew I would love feeling each of them coming inside me; that would memorialize my appreciation for them and their love. I knew I would forever be grateful for these wonderful moments, because they were commemorating my life decision; committing myself to prostitution. Honestly Bertie, I perceived all of those things before we even started.

"I knew how the afternoon would go. But at the same time, I knew something else. I knew this was a seminal, psychological moment. I saw myself leaving my old clothes behind me; not my real clothes, but my opportunity clothes; my morality clothes; those mental clothes I would wear if I wanted a different life than the immoral life that I was about to embrace. You see, Bertie, it was in those few seconds before I fell backwards into the arms of my gang bang partners and before they lifted my feet off the ground and one of them began licking my vagina, that I had my life's most important revelation.

"It was in that small window of time that I realized I no longer believed. I didn't believe in God or Jesus. I told myself there was no reason believe in them. They had never done anything for me, except cause me anxiety and grief. I told myself there was no reason to believe in family, either. Mother had been a total shit to me. Father had died without saying goodbye to me. Baron, my Boxer Dog best friend, had run away. Maybe Mother killed him. I didn't know. I'll never know. But I suspect she did. But Baron was gone, too. So, family was an empty nothing for me. This moment was when I knew I only had myself to believe in; so, I thought I might as well live my life the way I wanted; the ways that bring me the most pleasure.

"I suddenly knew a lot about myself in that brief moment. I knew I would become known as a fast woman: a woman who makes quick

eye contact and readily smiles, letting men know that I want them to approach me; a woman who is fast to kiss and touch; and who is fast to let men know that I also want to be touched; that I want men feeling my boobs; sliding their hands up my legs; reaching a hand into my panties; putting their fingers inside me; exploring my heat and my wetness.

"I knew I'd be the kind of woman who was whispered about and said to have no decency; who had fallen away from God and Jesus; who would be fast to say 'yes' when asked to leave a function or a party, to go to a room in the hotel; who said yes to going to men's places for drinks and nights of making love. I'd be the kind of woman who readily complies when a man places his knee between my thighs and nudges me to open; the woman who casually takes men's penises in her hand and expertly guides them past her outer vaginal lips, into her heated wetness.

"I knew I'd be that kind of woman who whispers to a man how much I love what he's doing while he begins fucking me. I knew all those things about myself, Bertie. I knew I would always be promiscuous and immoral; and that being that way would never trouble my conscience; never make me feel guilt or remorse. My future life came into focus in those brief seconds before my feet left the floor and I began kissing my partners.

"When my feet left that floor, I knew I was taking my first step upon a staircase, Bertie. I'm talking career wise. I knew I was never going to care another smidgeon about what the uppity WEX girls said behind my back or what their righteous country club snob mothers thought about me, either. I instinctively knew in those brief seconds that it was only a matter of time until someone asked me if I'd like to perform explicit sex acts while he filmed me.

"And I knew I'd also say 'yes,' when that time came. I knew I wouldn't have any hesitation or qualms or conditions about it. I

knew I'd be glad to create porn before a camera. I kind of knew I'd enjoy doing that. It's hard to explain, Bertie, but I honestly knew I was taking my first step upon that staircase to whoredom's highest peaks; rising myself up, higher and higher, doing more and more erotic, titillating, and intriguing porn, on my way to becoming one of the world's most famous porn stars. My entire destiny came into focus, before I even hugged my first gang bang partner and placed his hand on my boob, inviting him to feel me, while I kissed him. All my questions about who I was; what I believed in; where I was going with my life, suddenly fell away. I was going to make a living doing what I loved more than anything else. I was going to make my living by being a willful, shameless, insatiable whore. I knew, in that moment, that ultimately, I would become a notorious and proud porn star.

"Once everything became clear and uncomplicated, I let myself go. As I fell back into the arms of my birthday boys, I felt like a determined fallen woman should feel. As I opened my arms and fell backwards off my feet, I dropped away from Grandmother Maloney for good. I wanted to completely forget her. I was finished remembering the many times she told me to be a good girl and live by Jesus's teachings and examples. 'He'll save us,' she always told me.

"Well then, where was he? What would he do if he came through the door and saw me now? What would he do if he saw my friends feeling me and kissing me and fingering inside me? Would he stop them? How, exactly, would he save me? Or, would he instead take his pants off and offer me his penis and join in the fun with the others?"

Bertie noticed Marty's eyes. As the younger woman spoke, her eyes focused their luster while peering into something far away, as if they saw something real through a shifting fog. It was as if the younger woman recalled something that had happened in her past.

"*I'd have liked to have Grandmother Maloney there with me when Jesus walked through our hotel room's door,*" Marty continued, as if bewitched. "*I'd want her to hear me ask him if he was having a bad day with those nasty Romans; and if he'd like sweet Marty to take his mind off his stresses. I wished Grandmother could have heard me tell him that I would take his stresses away; that everything he was looking for: eternal life; salvation; purity; honesty; human love; the true pathway to spiritual love; forgiveness; everything good in humanity, was standing right there, before him; inviting him to come inside me; inside my vagina.*

"*He would then learn that life begins inside a woman's vagina. He would give up his notions about saving mankind. He'd see that he was the one who badly needed saving. And I would save him. Grandmother could watch while I took that crown of thorns off his head and kissed him and told him to just relax while I guided his penis into my sweet heaven and made him forget the pain of his scourging wounds. Grandmother could watch me love him like no other woman ever loved him. If he was doing Mary Magdalene, as I suspect he was, I'd love him so sweetly, I'd make him forget her. She could hear me tell him that he could leave his old rugged cross and his troubles at my door. He could tell those nasty Romans: 'fuck off.' Then, he could stay with me; let me hold him and love him; like other men who bring their problems to me.*"

Bertie's mouth fell open. She stared at Marty, dumbfounded. "*You don't believe in God or Jesus, do you, my child?*"

"*Nope. I don't. Mother disabused me of those notions. She told me my grandmother Maloney was a crackpot nut case for believing in religion. Mother told me that stuff her mother spewed about*

Abraham's covenant, the burning bush, and Moses being chosen to lead the Hebes was all just a made-up story to sell a belief. Mom said Abe was Sarah's pimp, and the burning bush was a hot Hebrew girl. Mom said the Hebrew hottie was the real reason Moses left his wife and kids. And Mo didn't lead. He ran away from his responsibilities to his family. Mom also said that the whole Jesus story was a fairy tale for feeble minded folks to make Christian believers docile and manageable, so smart business people could screw the shit out of them and sell them stuff at Christmas.

"Mom told me that I needed to go to WEX school, so I could get myself uncontaminated from Grandmother's nonsense. At WEX I never went to church services. After a half year there, Grandmother stopped calling and ragging me about Jesus. So, no, I don't believe in God or Jesus, Bertie. I think the only way I could ever believe in Jesus is if I could spend some quality time with him; and fuck him; fuck him long and good; good enough to know whether he and I could find that love thing for each other. Otherwise, I'd have no use for him."

Bertie heard music to her ears. The young whore was the very essence of immorality. Marty's mind had no comprehension of guilt about any sinful thing she did. Behind her sweet smile lived no responsible scienter of mind. Her immorality was only her uninhibited, natural innocence. Her soul was placid. It was as serene and comported as a magnificent swan gliding over a peaceful lake. Sin didn't ruffle a single feather. Bertie was smitten by the casual rightness of Marty's mindset. She believed the spirits had sent her a soulmate.

Raised in a religious home, Bertie had always been a devout, dutiful Christian. Always enthused for causes from her youth onward, Bertie threw herself into church activities. She attended church camp, sang with the church choir, joined the altar guild, made sandwiches for the homeless. And Bertie raised money! She was a cash flow powerhouse: organizing bake sales, car washes, membership drives, fellowship drives; drives to assist poorer churches in foreign lands; and pass the offering plate twice, until it hurts to give, drives. And Bertie also gave. While the truly religious gave their requested ten percent tithes, Bertie gave twenty-five percent of everything she earned. After marrying George, she continued giving twenty-five percent of their joint income. And George made lots! Bertie also freely gave her body to the church. When a young priest felt the need for a time out from heavenly salvation duties, Bertie enthusiastically provided him with earthly salvation. She was a beautiful, sexually charged woman who didn't mind. It was all for the glorious cause of advancing the gospel.

But Bertie's belief in God shattered when she lost her daughter. She could never reconcile herself to that tragedy; never accept her own role in it. All her life, she had given herself to her church and God; never asking anything for herself. She believed in God; believed in miracles; believed God could do anything; turn water to wine; remove blindness; raise the dead; feed the multitudes, make the lame walk; come to Earth from heaven, ascend and return to heaven, etc. She'd been a good, faithful follower.

Bertie sat at the accident site for an entire year. And Bertie begged. And begged. And she begged God to reverse the tragedy and give her daughter back to her. But God didn't answer Bertie. Silence. Bertie only heard silence. Her priest told her she needed to accept; that God works in mysterious ways. But Bertie didn't want to hear that. Bertie felt cheated by God. And Bertie grew angry with God. She blamed God for her loss and became embittered. Bertie questioned whether she was right in her mind to ever believe in God in the first place. Then, Bertie snapped. She became infuriated with God. She hated God.

Then, on the day Bertie decided to hate God, a mysterious butterfly fluttered onto her foot. Its spirit spoke to Bertie's spirit.

It directed her to discover the perfect vessel to take her revenge against God and God's moral teachings. Later that night, Bertie had a dream. She dreamt that she was lying on her bench at the accident site. A snake appeared on the ground beside her. She picked it up and kissed its head. The snake became an incredibly handsome man who made passionate love with Bertie. When Bertie awoke, she briefly wondered whether she had made love with the Devil. After briefly thinking about that possibility, she decided she didn't care. She made up her mind that she would pursue earthly fulfillments from then on, rather than religious ones. She heeded the butterfly's message and searched out the woman whom the butterfly told her to find.

And Bertie found her. In the personage of Marty, Bertie discovered a like-minded woman who had no use for God; no moral compass; and no conscience or qualms about salacious immoral whoring. Bertie's new, fast friend only sought the joys, glamor, and wealth of a materialist seductress.

Bertie finally had her soulmate. She gave Marty a tender, loving hug, and a kiss on her cheek. Hugging and kissing the young whore lifted away Bertie's pain. She hugged and kissed Marty often. The porn star's vivacious flesh and gorgeous face was present in the here and now; and always willing to accommodate her. Bertie became infatuated. Her infatuation advanced to love; love of a different kind than Bertie ever experienced before. The fevered intensity that Bertie had obsessed over God and church now focused on Marty. Unlike God and church, Marty reciprocated. The young whore appreciated Bertie; returned her hugs and kisses; and introduced Bertie to lesbian love. Bertie's love became obsession. Marty and the young whore's delicious vagina became Bertie's raison d'etre, her purpose for living.

Marty slowly, but surely and methodically erased Bertie's memories of her precious daughter. Marty always warmly responded

and reciprocated the hugs and kisses of Bertie's pained love trans-
ferences, taking her thoughts further and further away from her
daughter. The younger woman assumed the role of loving daughter, reliably and sexually reinforcing Bertie's newly formed beliefs.

Marty rekindled Bertie's love until it smoldered and ignited.
Bertie's love was born again! Bertie's face glowed with a bright
inner flame! Her life had meaning again. Bertie became the happiest and most appreciative she had ever been. She obsessed over
every word that her new love interest spoke, seeking to learn
everything she possibly could about her new love child, and how
her mind worked. She had missed the first two decades of Marty's
young life. She was desperate to make up for lost time. Now, she
listened intently while the young whore revealed the inner workings of her determined, amoral mind:

*"I remember deciding for myself right then and there, at the
beginning of that fabulous gang bang, that Grandmother Maloney
didn't have any idea about what she was talking about; that she
didn't know the first thing about men; that this Jesus man she constantly yapped about would behave just like every other man. I was
certain that her Jesus man would choose to fuck me for the entire
afternoon; and not waste his time trying to save me from myself.
If he started up with his crazy salvation talk, I'd tell him I had no
intention of being saved from anything I was doing. I figured he'd
come around to my way of thinking; that saving others was a fool's
errand. After I got my hand on his penis, I'm certain he would fall in
love with me. He'd be just like the other five. I figured he'd surrender
to me and fuck me tenderly and love me sweetly, until there was
nothing left in him to give me.*

*"And then he'd want to see me regularly and fuck me often, just
like all my other male friends. I decided I was done with pretending
otherwise. I remember thinking that Grandmother Maloney probably also believed that pigs can fly. That amusing thought made me*

laugh at her religious nonsense stories. Just like Mother was done with Grandmother, I was done with Grandmother, too. As I swoon-fell into the waiting arms of my birthday lovers, I knew I was also falling away from God and grandmother Maloney. I was escaping forever the prison of thoughts that confined her; bailing out of her religious airplane, piloted by its madman Pope, co-pilot cardinals, and flight attendant bishops and priests; all spewing their dogma over its intercom like so many mindless sock puppets; leaving dear grandma to ride on, without me, through her remaining life as one of their blindly obedient passenger victims.

"I fell those three feet backwards of my own free choice. I trusted in humanity's Great Spirit of Freedoms; not their authoritarian, judgmental God. I had faith in the Spirit of humanity to catch my fall and protect me. How could I trust otherwise? How could I trust the followers of the Triad God who sanctioned the massacres of millions of Semites and Native Americans? When I felt my lovers' hands breaking my fall, supporting my decision to be their lust object, I knew I was home. I knew I was finally the authentic me; the shameless, uninhibited, pleasure-loving sinner."

Bertie, having heard Marty describe how she would rescue Jesus from his historic Passion and make love with him, convinced herself that Marty's spirit soul had previously seduced the Christ during his short lifetime; and that therefore, naturally, the true salvation spirit of the Christ had been captured by Marty. A profoundly historic convergence had occurred.

And now, she, Bertie, was fortunate to be its living witness. In Bertie's new truth, Marty possessed the reincarnated soul of Christ, the redeemer. Bertie believed that this nubile, mouth-watering, deliciously profligate whore had absorbed the soul of the Christ and the goodness of God. Marty was uniquely able to reinterpret God's terms and express them in her own carnal, loving, shameless ways.

Bertie believed, from that moment onward, that there could not possibly be any evil in Marty or that the younger woman could ever be capable of committing any wrongdoing. She believed that, very possibly, Marty's reincarnated soul had also absorbed the soul of Mary Magdalene, whom Bertie believed, had freely consorted with Jesus; and possibly, that Marty's soul also embodied the reincarnated soul of Mary, mother of The Christ.

How perfect was this! Bertie's imagination ran wild. Marty's glorious unrepentant soul could be her vicarious vessel to take out her own revenge on God. Yes! Marty was a natural for what Bertie had in mind. The minx rejoiced in sinning. She reveled in performing her debaucheries; lusted to do more of it; exploded with glorious, explicit orgasms; laughed gleefully while fornicating and urging her partners to push harder, stay longer, and ejaculate repeatedly inside her. There was not a trace of inhibition about her. She was the epitome of spectacular erotic splendor; breathtakingly majestic, mouthwateringly delicious sin.

Here, in her protégé, was an eternally sinful soul that had, for over twenty millenniums, successfully conquered and devoured all vestiges of Godliness. Before her was the perfect vessel for her revenge: a woman uniquely possessed with a soul of pure immorality. Bertie's aspirations soared. She struggled to grasp the boundless potentials of Marty. Themes for new, more explicit, better choreographed porn films flashed through Bertie's mind. Marty was her solution, the redress of her pain. She would direct her animus against God through Marty!

Suddenly, Bertie saw her opportunity to rewrite religious history. She reasoned that there were no contemporary written accounts of Christ's death; so why not create a new account which pleased her fancy? Marty would seduce the Christ, exactly as she had described in her imagination. She would make love with God's son in every conceivable way and position. Then, after she gained Christ's complete trust, she would invite the Romans into her bedroom.

They would join her and the Christ in a fabulous orgy. When they finished, she, not Judas, would betray Christ. She would kiss him once on his cheek. After the Romans jammed the crown of thorns down hard upon his head, she would walk beside him while he struggled to carry his cross to Calvary. As he approached mortal death, Marty, being the consummate ecumenical whore, would collapse into the arms of a handsome Roman Centurion. She would show her dying, crucified lover her shameless whoring vagina one final time while her new Centurion lover kissed her neck and shoulders; fondled her breasts and fingered her vagina.

Marty would blow kisses to her agonizing, doomed lover; laughing gleefully while the Centurion brought her insatiable libido to a continuous, glorious orgasm. Christ's last dying vision would behold Marty in the arms of her new Centurion lover, casually stroking his penis while hungrily kissing his mouth. Rome, not Christ, would be victorious. Marty, not Christ, would star in Christ's Passion.

Marty's semen filled vagina, not Christ's death, would be the lasting memory viewers would take from the reimagined film. Bertie visualized her perfect plot scenario for a sensational blockbuster porn film. It would mock God's righteousness. She would have her revenge. Through her vision of events, she would reinterpret the murder of God's son. She would repay God her pain of losing Amanda.

Bertie's adoring, contorted mind became convinced that Marty was a living, carnal connection to the Christ; sent by fate to bring meaning to her agonized life. At once, Bertie thoroughly loved Marty; unconditionally loved everything about her. She saw in Marty a divinely sent persona.

The young whore had a uniquely chameleon-like personality. She innocently, nymph-like, attracted men to her. As a stealthy snake, she slithered into her victims' souls. Once inside, she searched out every soul's darkest recesses. Securely ensconced and joined to her victim's darkest carnal nature, she devoured the man's love for everyone other than herself; appropriated his wealth and left nothing for anyone else. As a heartless Cuckoo, she matter-of-factly, naturally shoved all others out of his life. Finally, as a fully gorged, destructive wolverine, she casually walked away from her messy carnage, leaving empty husks of ravaged lives.

Marty's vacuous soullessness, perfectly comported with Bertie's vision. She would publicize the young vixen's escapades and use them to promote their films. Marty's face and delicious body would become frequent cover copy for supermarket tabloids. The public would feast upon every breathtaking account of Marty's salacious life. They would drool over her seductions while scorning the men and families she destroyed. Marty's personality was remarkably, perfectly suited for media promotion.

No matter how many marriages and families Marty would ruin, Bertie convinced herself that everything Marty did was for a glorious cause; that Marty was a modern-day version of the Savior; redeemer of troubled hearts; balm to the forlorn who needed love. Every seduction, every explicit porn scene, every child's shattered life that Marty's lifestyle shepherded into prostitution, was, in Bertie's rationalizing mind, God's divine will.

Marty was Bertie's living goddess of God's grace, enlightening mortals here on Earth. Her young darling could do nothing wrong. Every fornication she performed; every penis she sucked, was God's righteousness at work through Marty's divinely innocent face and beautiful body. Obviously, by Bertie's logic, the young whore goddess had been placed among Earth's mortals to be adored and deified; unquestioned, and unconditionally loved.

Bertie even imagined that Marty was the reincarnated spirit of Christ, returned to Earth for a second visit.

A flood of epiphanous gratitude rushed over Bertie. She dimly realized that understanding the mind of God was beyond her abilities to understand. Likely, she accepted, that she would never receive the necessary enlightenment to understand it. Hers was a complicated, conflicted relationship with God. She was in awe of God; yet she harbored a seething, residual hatred of God. She now imagined that everything she had believed before was man-created; and that God was now, though the mysterious workings of the messenger butterfly, turning everything that she had previously believed on its head.

She was leaving a world where all things were known to her and fixed, unquestioned; and entering a new world where morality was completely different. Everything was in her new world was unknown to her. But she intuited that God wished for her to accept, without question, all aspects of her new world; and embrace the new, immoral human condition that God had ushered into her world through Marty.

Bertie's was awed by this revelation. She knew she must accept the young goddess in every way; and believe in everything she did. She convinced herself that the young promiscuous vixen was the living manifestation of God in the flesh. Her mind figuratively fell to its knees before the young prostitute's feet. Bertie figuratively washed and kissed Marty's feet; thanking them for bringing the profligate strumpet to her door. She pledged her life's work to serve her new vivacious whore-God; grateful that a mysterious butterfly had awakened her from her despondency. She felt privileged; secure in a new belief. She had been allowed into Marty's life; and commanded by God, through the spirit butterfly, to assist Marty. Bertie's new holy mission was to reshape world morality.

And Bertie would obey her calling. It meant paving Marty's path to perdition. She had no interest in examining her own soul. Instead, she would focus on perfecting Marty's whore craft. She would create film themes that uprooted religious moral authorities and alter human perceptions of righteousness and holiness. She would create favorable publicity for Marty's insatiable peccadillos and the seductions of her craven-hot, slippery-wet, insatiable penis-craving vagina. She would lampoon Marty's prudish detractors; ridicule dispossessed wives and fatherless children whom Marty's whoring had drowned in her wake. She would position Marty as the most desirable femme fatale in the entire world, and create indelibly branded images of Marty in the minds of all men, everywhere.

The butterfly's message and Marty's description of her seduction of the Christ brought, to Bertie, an importance more profound than any scripture reading or Papal encyclical had ever done. Her revelations impressed upon her that she had received her mandate directly from God. Her mandate called her to action. It commanded her to work tirelessly; move heaven and earth, if necessary; and to lift the career of her glorious, budding, God-sent porn star to the pinnacle of the world's adulation.

Everything now fit together perfectly in Bertie's world view. Her life's mission came into focus. Marty would be her protagonist in her cause celebre. Bertie now opined that life, liberty, and the pursuit of happiness were humankind's self-evident natural proclivity; and that the rights to these blessings did not come from some divinity, but from the inherent nature of humankind, within the human species itself. She believed, for example, that the U S Constitution was created by men; not divinely inspired.

Further, Bertie believed, natural human pursuits had millenniums earlier been misappropriated by religions dominated by men and their chauvinistic attitudes, which denigrated women.

She intended, through Marty, to correct this unnatural state of humanity's unfair oppressive burden and restore humankind to its natural comity. Bertie's battle for natural female supremacy required an unfettered and widely accepted pursuit of uninhibited immorality, centered upon an anarchy-like love of one's fellow humans; rooted in love in all its forms: platonic, cordial discourse, mutual acceptances of others' weaknesses, absence of malice in all its forms, and broad acceptance of unconstrained, uninhibited, shameless, sexual intimacy. Her mission would be to advocate for these ideals, through Marty.

Bertie tasked herself to make Marty into the most exalted whore of her envisioned, repurposed American Babylon. Marty would advocate for Bertie's new immoral standards to the entire world. Everyone would cast off their old beliefs and embrace this wonderful new. Everyone would love Bertie's anointed queen of whoredom. Marty would become the peoples' new god.

With her considerable wealth, Bertie would procure the best image consultants, the best film directors and screen writers, the best camera people and photographers, the best media relations people; and the best, handsomest porn partners with the most fabulous penises in the world. Marty would burst upon the consciousness of the world as its most alluring, salaciously immoral porn star. Marty's impressions would fixate in men's minds everywhere. Her lascivious carnal appetites would become the new immoral normal; the exalted example for all women to emulate.

Bertie was a highly educated woman and a student of history, especially biblical and pre-biblical history. She understood that humanity's moral standards experienced wide fluctuations over time. She was fascinated by the temple prostitution worship cult practices of ancient Baal and by the high honors prostitutes held during ancient Rome's centuries of decline. She believed that women, especially prostitutes, were getting a raw deal in today's male-ordered, religious-based cultures. She had long chafed against the way things were; and, through Marty, she saw her opportunity to change them.

Bertie also envisioned women as an untapped marketing opportunity. She reasoned that many women lead stressful, thankless lives; rarely punctuated by anything stimulating. She imagined the creation of a soft porn series, using realistic, believable scenarios and exceptionally handsome male actors to elicit these women's' fantasies. Bertie would tempt reluctant women out of their dark, confining worlds into an expansive world of vicarious enlightenment. She would fire their imaginations about possibilities for new encounters and relationships. She would show them how to attract male lovers. She would embolden them to have extramarital affairs; multiple lovers; and generally, help them have more vibrant sex lives. She would shatter their inhibitions about receiving oral sex from men and from other open-minded women; encouraging orgasm experiences as healthy, normal, routinely necessary, everyday life experiences.

Bertie would set women free; make them expressive and happy again! She would make them crave sex again! She would make cunnilingus and orgasms widely accepted! She would empower women again! She would restore prostitution to its rightful place as an honorable profession, again! She would return prostitution worship to prominence, again! She would make promiscuity and immoral behavior the new normal societal way of life! She would make lewd conduct acceptable; even honored, again! And by making sex fashionable again, Bertie would make America great again!

As it was in ancient Greece, she would make homosexuality and lesbianism the normal lifestyle. She would make America tolerant! She would, through Marty, exterminate religious based beliefs and return humanity to its natural pagan tendencies! She would glorify carnal pleasures! She would make unpretentiously immoral humans feel good about themselves! And, she would make humanity great again!

She would, through Marty's acting skills and subtle seduction techniques, embolden multitudes of women to become openly, shamelessly, promiscuous; and thereby discover more romance in their lives. She would encourage all men and women to accept this new, immoral way of life as their new normality. Only thirty percent of women watched porn compared to seventy-five percent of men. Bertie believed that, through her introductory enlightenment films, she could make women more comfortable with pornography; normalize watching it as a routinely necessary compliment to their everyday living; and dramatically expand the female market for pornographic film sales. These women would largely come to rely upon Marty's films as trusted, reliable guides to erotica; and helpful for them to recognize erotic romantic opportunities in their everyday lives.

With Bertie's help, Marty would develop a cult following. Her films and still- framed porn pictures would show her joyful smiles while copulating with many different lovers. Front-page tabloid photos and headlines covering Marty's peccadilloes would become the rage of the cognoscenti social media set. Media talk shows would pay handsomely to book Marty's appearances. She would wear provocative outfits to these shows. She would giggle, smile, and tease her hosts and audiences; talk freely about how she much she enjoys every phase of her affairs and love making; and leave her audiences craving more of her. Her legion of followers would fixate upon her every word. With Bertie's marketing brilliance, people would come to value Marty's opinions. Whenever she released a new pornographic film, her followers would stampede to buy it. Bertie imagined her own future as intimately intertwined with Marty's rise to celebrity stardom. Pornography was their perfect venue.

"George, I've had my vision of the future," declared Bertie. *"I have seen the light! The Lord has come into my eyes and told me what we must do. God is sending us on a mission! We must make right all the wrongs that were done to this poor girl. We must, as her guardian angels, atone for the slights of her childhood years. We must take the good qualities that she has naturally within herself and make them into a shining example for the entire world to see. With the Lord's help, we must set things right.*

"She's a good and righteous woman, George. She spreads her righteousness in a new way, which the world doesn't yet fully under-stand. But the Lord wants us to help the world see things in the same ways that Marty sees them. Marty sees the light! We are going to help the whole world see that same light! We are going to help this poor, misunderstood woman spread her message of love and the glory of womanhood to the entire world!"

George groaned. He knew whenever Bertie got a bee in her bonnet there was nothing on Earth that could dissuade her. He was skeptical. He almost said he was not willing to be the blind following the blinded. But he thought the wiser of it and kept his mouth shut. He rationalized that this was some bizarre twisted way for Bertie to leave her grieving phase. He understood that, as Bertie's devoted husband, he needed to come along for the ride, as obsessive as it might be; and wherever it took him. *"Yes, dear. Whatever you say. Whatever makes you happy, dear. I'll be with you one hundred percent."*

Bertie, now fortified with George's unqualified support, vowed to herself, then and there, that she would effusively express her gratitude to Marty for inclusion in the young whore's life journey. She would show and bestow her appreciation in every conceivable way. She would lavish her personal attentions upon the younger woman. She would shower her with money, securities, and real estate; indulge her every whim. She would invest her considerable coaching and performance talents and time in the young star.

And, above all else, she would love Marty with her whole heart, in both a spiritual, mentoring way and in a physical, loving way, both as her mother figure and her lesbian lover. She would consider cunnilingus with Marty her most holy act of contrition and most sacred obligation of contribution; the ultimate blessing for her to enjoy and savor. Her essential, obsessively frequent communion, would prove her unquestioning obedience to God's divine purpose. She would become a willing slave to Marty's every need; obey her imagined holy mandate without question or reason. Blinded from objectivity, Bertie was more than smitten. She was insane.

"I giggled while my birthday party boys lifted me into mid-air," continued Marty. *They removed my clothes while they kissed me and touched my body everywhere. I especially loved the way they kissed me on my neck and behind my ears while they pinched my nipples and rubbed their hands over my vagina. I was very pleased by the compliments I received for my butterfly tattoo. I loved how they first kissed my wings and then brought their lips closer and closer, until they were kissing my vaginal lips."* Bertie listened breathlessly while the young porn star continued describing the day she fell away from morality.

"I loved feeling the boys' hands touching all over me. I was so stimulated! I remember Jerry being the first boy to kiss my vagina that afternoon. He held my tush and brought my lady lips to his face, reverently, like he was worshipping; like he was holding the sacred holy grail. His lips kissed my wings; then my outer lips, then they pressed deliciously further, intimately into my inner lips. He thrusted his tongue way up inside me. He probed and prepped me with his tongue, getting me hot, slippery wet; anxious to fuck. I remember feeling happy while Jerry was getting things

started. His tongue cleared my mind of my whimsical thoughts about saving Jesus from his impossible mission to save humanity. Jerry helped me focus on expressing my carnal lusts and having honest, immoral fun. I remember the comradery feeling swooshing over me with its fantastic rush of mental freedom. I knew everything about our gang bang was right and wonderful. Blood rushed into my skin. My senses came alive. Gang bangs electrify me like that. Jerry got my Vagina really hot and wet. I became crazy anxious to fuck those boys! I knew I would be making love for several hours, nonstop. I've never wanted sex more, in my entire life! I felt wonderful.

"I had a beautiful, loving gang bang. That was my first marathon love fest. I spent my entire birthday afternoon hugging, kissing, sucking my party goers' penises, and repeatedly fucking all five of them. Every boy came inside me, at least twice. I fucked until none of my partners had any semen left. It was my most fantastic birthday party, ever! It was my official coming out party.

"From then on, I had no pretenses about myself. I became a 'I'll gladly do it for the money' kind of whore. It was like officially becoming a major league baseball player. You know, getting to do for a living the thing I most loved doing anyway; like men who play baseball, and never want to stop playing. Jimmy was such a great, true friend to set up that party for me. He was always thoughtful about pleasing me. He gave me my most special birthday party, ever!

"Well, Bertie, that same feeling of being totally loved by my favorite five fellatio partners is the same feeling of wonderful joyful surprise and overwhelming happiness I get now, whenever a new penis first starts spurting its cum onto my tongue. It's glorious, Bertie. It's like I experience my own private nirvana; like my reason for living my life is reaffirmed. I feel like my life becomes blessed and honored all over again; and I'm completely filled with love and

purpose whenever a penis shoots off in my mouth for its first time with me. That tells me that it loves me. Life renews its meaning for me, like when the sun first rises. I feel blessed to be alive; sucking and fucking. Deep within myself, I know I am loved. And that makes me feel like my whole life is worthwhile; filled with purpose.

"After the penis shoots cum into my mouth I get this other feeling. I feel pride in both the penis and myself. I know we both had a beautiful, memorable experience. I know the penis needs time to rest and recharge. Sometimes, I'll sit with it for a while, watching its balls turn, while it makes more semen. While I watch its balls rolling and turning like that, I feel happy for it. I begin feeling giddy-anxious. I wonder whether it will want to have sex with me again, or whether it might rather find some other woman to fuck it or suck it. I hope it will choose to have sex with me again.

"I feel a tinge of jealousy while I watch the penis's balls churning. I know there's always the chance that it will have fellatio or vagina sex with some other woman; especially if it's the penis of a sex worker partner; but I wish it would allow only me to be the one. I know that's a total contradiction with my New Morality Standard beliefs, but that's the true honest feeling that comes over me. I just adore all my penises. And I can't help feeling possessive about them.

"There's yet another, totally different, sort of feeling I have when I'm surrounded by six to ten men with their penises exposed during the beginning moments of an orgy. I feel this overwhelming frenzy to suck every one of those penises while I'm just beginning to stroke two additional penises; getting them ready to be sucked. I know I don't have the time to bring every one of the penises to ejaculation at the beginning of the orgy; but I also know that I want every man and every penis to feel sincere eroticism about making love with me. So, I go about sucking every penis in my

circle of males, as quickly as I can. I get every penis very hard; getting it to anticipate being with my mouth and my vagina. During this fellatio frenzy time I keep every penis stiff; craving to fuck me and explore everywhere inside me. I make every penis feel that it's extra special and deeply loved.

"It's my euphoria. I'm filled with beautiful, erotic imaginings and an excited anticipation of being thoroughly and wonderfully fucked; while enjoying multiple, practically non-stop, orgasms. This euphoria makes me tremble. My heart beats rapidly. I can't wait to begin. I love the anticipation. It's my mental preparation for my passion and glory; like a fuse becomes lit to my powder keg. It becomes burning hot. It rushes me to this passion point where I feel I will explode. It rushes rapidly through my blood, warming me. I feel its heat. I know I can't stop it. I don't want to stop it. It's the heat of my insatiable sex lust. It's giving my mind over to being the most insatiable nymph I can possibly be; to fuck with wild abandon.

"I imagine I'm Romeo's Juliet; and my Romeo has a huge, firm penis. He's about to take me in his arms and make love with me; only instead of standing there with my Romeo, I imagine I'm floating on a cloud; and I have ten Romeos beside me. They all have beautiful, huge, firm penises. They are all eager to ravage me with loving strokes and thrill me with endless orgasms. My heart beats frantically with anticipation. I cannot contain myself. My heart only slows when I actually start fucking my Romeos. That's when I settle into my pleasure feelings; my joy of being a naughty girl; my wickedness feelings for being an unrepentant woman of pleasures; my uncaringly destroying other women's relationships; and my honest heartfelt love for every one of my partners. Those feelings all come and go intermittently. They alternate through my mind throughout the entire orgy. That's what makes orgies so special. They bring this mental experience of cascading erotic feelings."

"You really do make love out of love, don't you? Is that why fornicating never troubles your conscience?" Bertie's eyes were telescoping her distant thoughts like a ship's lookout seeking a lighthouse beacon. Love was always Bertie's safe harbor. Every immoral act young Marty did, Bertie rationalized by seeing love in it. That made Marty's conduct, however immoral and sinful, perfectly acceptable; understandable, even sacred, in Bertie's eyes.

"Oh yes. Whenever I make love, love is always in my heart. It's romantic love; knowing that the man wants me. It's also a craving of intimacy and desire kind of love. I feel both those loves enter my psyche and my blood, whenever a man first slips his hand into my panties. I know our love will come soon after his fingers feel their way to my vagina. Once a man touches me there, I instantly warm to him and I want to love him. I communicate that to him by putting my hand on his penis and stroking it; and by kissing him. That lets him know that I completely approve of his foreplay and that I'm anxious to experience how wonderful I will feel when he first penetrates me. That love is how I feel when I begin my orgies, too. I feel this communal sense of wonder, love and caring. My fellatio go-around, holding all those penises and their balls in my hands, sets the tone for a wonderful couple of hours of spectacularly beautiful, loving, erotic, orgasm-filled sex.

"I've tried every experiment I could think of to ensure that my partners have the most loving erotic experiences humanly possible. I even use specially formulated suppositories beforehand. I pay a pharmacist to create them secretly for me. They contain an irresistible erectile stimulant that makes my partners' penises get even harder while they're inside my vagina. That helps them come inside me more than once. I'm not exaggerating, Bertie. Their penises get harder than steel rods while they're inside me. That's a fantastic feeling. It gets my mind incredibly focused and deeply committed to

my love making. Love bubbles out of every pore of me, everywhere! Those erection helpers make my copulations the most sensational sex that my partners ever experience.

"My partners have told me that they've never experienced another vagina that was anywhere near as wildly erotic and sensationally loving with their penises as mine. I literally get hundreds of requests for additional fuck sessions. My erotic stimulants make my partners' penises crave being inside my vagina; like cats crave catnip. My lovers love me, with their souls, because of the passion I put into lovemaking. But their penises love me in a different, more carnal way. They love the sensitive experience they have. I give my lovers both purr love and vaginal love; complete, total love.

"I want to be adored and cherished as the most enticing, wonderful, unforgettable sex partner my lovers have ever known. And I also want their penises to remember how deliriously wonderful they felt while being inside me. Penises have a memory of their own, Bertie. I'm certain about that. I want them to know that my vagina is the source of their most sensational feelings, ever. I want those penises' feelings to be so memorable that they forget wives or girlfriends exist; or if they do think about them, they'll decide to leave them for more of me. When I know my lovers have that wonderment feeling, then I know I've given them uniquely erotic love. That makes me feel yummy, deliciously satisfied, and divinely erotic, myself."

"Those are fabulous insights into your thoughts and feelings, Marty. You are truly a wonderful, heaven-sent joy to George and me." Bertie paused a moment to again hug her new protégé and kiss her cheek. *"Thank you. Every word you speak, every insight you can give me into your feelings, while you seduce and fornicate, will be very helpful to me going forward. I want you to know that everything we do here will be to help make you better at your porn*

craft. We want to help you become the porn queen of the entire world. Okay baby?"

"Of course, Bertie. I appreciate you. I'll try to become the world's greatest porn star. With your help, I know I'll succeed." Marty hugged Bertie back.

"Now," Bertie continued, *"I want us all to watch this next sequence. Pay close attention here, George. Here's where Marty puts every courtesan since Napoleon's times to shame. See her lying back on that sectional piece in the missionary position? Notice how inviting her clitoral hood is, George. It's perfectly symmetrically shaped. It's not overly fleshy, or too thin, either. It's perfectly sized; and it's plump and inviting, like it's just begging to be stimulated for cunnilingus. It's those subtle endowments that an adult performer must naturally have to achieve a top ranking, George. And our lovely Marty has them.*

"That's unquestionably the hood of an extraordinarily beautiful vagina. It invites being kissed. Let's watch the next sequence where the camera shows us a really close up view of Marty's glorious vagina while she receives oral sex from her partner. Notice how she lifts and thrusts in response to his tongue; especially how she lifts up like she's engulfing his tongue to receive the full measure of pleasure he's giving her. It's so inspiring, George. Marty, you are unique in the ways you arouse your viewers. I love this scene.

"Now look at these frames, George. See how proud she is; how her body glistens in oils while she sits astride a partner's penis? Then, look a bit further on, George. See how her face lights up with angelic innocence when that next penis appears? See that mirthful, divine continence passing over her face? It's impossible to capture her magnificence in words, George. She must be offered to the world through her films. She's a heavenly angel goddess, George. She's been sent to us to bring glory to our lives and the world!"

TRADECRAFT

Before their next session with Marty, George and Bertie watched Marty's films and discussed how they should relate to the young porn star. George, the seasoned businessman, approached the matter with a degree of caution. Bertie, the ever enthusiastic, highly successful coach, approached the question with her visions of future glory and applause.

"George, watch Marty's head and face while her partner continues performing cunnilingus. See how she lets her head fall back; how she smiles with her mouth opened and her teeth showing? That's the picture-perfect expression of a woman enjoying her orgasm, George. There's no frowning; no wincing; no pulling away from him. It's the picture of deserving acceptance. Her face is saying that she's entitled to this pleasure. She expects only her partner's best; nothing less. There's nothing on her mind, other than this heavenly pleasure. It's such a beautiful scene; so casually, shamelessly immoral. She enjoys what he's doing. She wants him to continue working his tongue over her clitoris right through the completion of her orgasm flow. I've never watched anything more breathtakingly beautiful. Our Marty craves sex, George. It's not possible to teach that. Those desires for pleasure come from deep within her soul. They are her natural 'escape from traumatic childhood' expressions, George. She has the unrepentant soul of a thoroughly shameless, pleasure loving, immoral porn star. I just love her!

"Here's another segment which I've selected for our studies George. Again, she's in missionary. Pay close attention to the close up of her vagina while I advance the film, frame by frame. Watch as her partner's penis penetrates the first half inch of her vagina's outer lips. See how she up-flexes her buttocks, and gently rocks the penis from side to side, just as it's beginning to enter her?"

"Yes, I see that."

"Let me run it again, George. Look closely. What does her but-terfly tattoo remind you of?"

"Oh, I see what you mean! When she flexes her tush like that and rocks her pelvis slowly from side to side, like she does, she makes that tattoo look like it's a live, fluttering butterfly. Is that what you wanted me to see?"

"Yes. I don't know whether she's even aware of it; but that 'flut-ter' movement is the sexiest thing I've ever witnessed in any of the hundreds of porn films I've studied. Honestly, George, that image of a fluttering butterfly's motion has haunted me for months since I first noticed it. I have fallen asleep dreaming about it; and I have awakened wondering about it. I've asked myself: Why would a young woman put a tattoo like that on her upper thighs, so that it looked like an extension of her vagina?"

"Maybe she just had a whim, Bertie. Why does this attract your interest?"

"Because, it has some meaning, George. It's meaning is some-thing much deeper than a whim. She did this, possibly as a sign of rebellion against her childhood abandonment. Maybe it's her way of declaring that she's free of the hurt from that neglect. Maybe it's a signal that she's bonded by comradery to another soul; possibly that Maria friend of hers; that girl who helped her see that both their mothers were assholes. Are you getting this?"

"Yes, I think so. You believe it's a symbol of some psychological condition she has, right?"

"Yes, it could be. It could be her way of declaring: 'I FLUTTER,' meaning she decides what's acceptable, morally; and she determines whom it pleases her to fuck; and no one can tell her what to do; or tell her what's morally correct and what isn't. I think it's her message of fierce, rebellious independence. It's a message that cries out from a once tortured soul. It's her silent expression of a pent-up internal

scream. It's Marty's way of telling the world, and her fan base, that she needs to be, and will always be, a free soul.

"Now, I have to confess something to you, George. That tattoo has had a powerful effect on me. When I first noticed that flutter, I thought it was just a porn prop, an enhancement gimmick. I assumed it was her signature logo for her porn image; but then I thought more about it. It's not a gimmick, George. Marty's butterfly is overwhelmingly serious. It's the essence of her life. It's a message from Marty's soul. That tattoo puts her soul out there for the world to see. That's the way it must be understood. It says:

'I'm a woman who needs to be loved; really, truly, and genuinely loved, with honest, heartfelt love. And to love me, you need to accept me for who I am; and you need to understand me.'

"Her immorality and all her whoring and pornographic film work are simply the child within Marty expressing her searching need for genuine love. Her butterfly is her way of reminding the world that they must accept that about her, George. I swear to you, I kept looking at that tattoo, and then I looked into her eyes; and I realized I was seeing the entrance pathway into Marty's soul. Her butterfly is the gateway to her eyes. When you look at her butterfly and start to contemplate the meaning of it, your eyes automatically lift up to her eyes. Your eyes want to look into hers to understand why she had that tattoo placed on her upper thighs. That's when your eyes form a true connection with her eyes; and when her eyes allow you to enter her soul. That's when Marty reveals her inner self to those who seek to understand her. I've thought very deeply about this, George. This young woman needs us. That tattoo expresses a young woman's overwhelming need to be understood; and her abiding need to receive unselfish love and devotion. That's how I think of her now. I see her as my own special love child, whom I must cherish and nurture. I feel grateful and blessed to have her in our lives."

"Whoa, Bertie. Think about this. She was abandoned as a child. She found a friend, Maria, who helped her see that she was getting screwed by her mother. So, she gets that tattoo. But then, she goes through three shrinks until she finds this Mrs. O'Dell. And this shrink tells her that her immoral lifestyle is perfectly normal. And this O'Dell shrink encourages her to be even more immoral; as promiscuous as possible. Bertie, where I come from, that's another form of abuse. She's twice abused; once by her mother, and now by this shrink. And, you think, now that her mind and behaviors are formed, that you're going to nurture and love her; and that somehow, you're going to recreate the daughter we've lost? I know you mean well, but I don't see how that will ever work, sweetheart."

"George, she's not Amanda. She'll never be Amanda. She's Marty. She's her own unique person. I get that."

"Then, what are you saying? What do you intend to do with this woman who has the world's most sensational body and its most innocent face; but who has the world view of an abused five-year-old child? I think, realistically, she's too far along on her chosen career path to make a mid-course correction."

"I'm not talking about correcting anything, George. She is what she is. She is where she is. I'm talking about enhancing who she is, improving upon what she does and loves doing. I'm talking about molding her into the world's top ranked porn star."

"Abusing her even more, you mean? So, you can feel good about yourself? Fine tuning her immorality to perfection? Solidify her porn star image; so that she'll always be saddled with it; so that she'll never know a normal life? Is that where you want to go with this? Don't you have any moral questions about what you intend to do with this girl? Is this what your church has taught you?"

"No, George," Bertie's voice became heated. *"I don't have any moral questions. And don't try to tell me what the church has taught me, okay? If God and the church have taught me anything, it is that I*

am on my own, okay? I don't know what's moral and what's immoral anymore. I'm not even sure there's a difference, okay? Listen to me! I do not believe in God anymore. Get it? When our daughter had her accident, I asked God why that had to happen. Why, in that place, at that time, did God allow that to happen? I cried. I begged for an answer; but, what did I get from God, George? NOTHING! I GOT NOTHING, George! Then, day after day, week after week, month after month, for an entire year, I went to that same place where she died. And I cried and I prayed for God to turn back time and bring her back to me. And, what did I get from God, George? I got NOTHING! God broke me, George. God broke my spirit and my heart. I've tried to be a believer, George; but I've given up. If there really was a god; if this image I worshipped all my life really cared about our daughter and me, that accident never would have happened; or, God would have turned back time and given her back to me; but God didn't do that. I was grieving. I was a believer. I needed God then. But God turned his back on me. What kind of god turns away like that, George?

"Then, one day, this lovely butterfly came and landed on my shoe. And I heard a voice that told me to seek out Marty. It was the voice of some spirit; I don't know what it was; but I knew I needed to listen to it; and I did. And it changed me, George. And, I believe differently now. I believe everything about Marty has been pre-planned for me; for us. I believe this child-woman is our destiny. I can't explain it to you, George; but I know that I must do this; not just for myself and for you; but also, for her. I must make her into the best at what she does. I can't think about whether her immorality is the real immorality or whether morality, as I once knew it, is the real immorality. I just know I must help this young woman. And, I must love her, George. I must love her unconditionally, with my whole heart, as long as my heart has a heartbeat. And I must accept her as my own; and hold nothing back. And, we must leave her all our worldly possessions; everything."

"Some voice and a butterfly told you to do all this? Leave her everything? The stocks and bonds, the gold, the ranches and rental properties, everything? What about the University and the Church, the charities?"

"Don't make fun of me, George. I've been through way too much for one lifetime. And, yes, everything; all of it to her. The University and the Church and the charities will get along fine without our help. They don't need us. But Marty needs us. Marty needs our love, George. Love is everything, George. Possessions are nothing. I know that now. She's my life's purpose now, George. I'm asking you to understand that I need to give her all my love. And I'm asking you to love her, too."

George understood when Bertie became set on something, there was no use trying to change her mind. *"Okay, Bertie. Then, that is how things will be with her and us. We'll both accept her as our own."*

"Thank you, George. You're my sweetheart." Bertie hugged George. Her emotional plea brought tears to her eyes. George took his handkerchief and dabbed them away. *"Now, I need you to understand something else about her. It has to do with her need to control. Her first driver is to be accepted on her own terms. That explains her tattoo. Control is her second driver; but to understand that, you need to understand her behavior. Now, in this next bit of film, notice how she's meeting her partner's thrusts with her own? See how his penis was thrusting more rapidly; how close it was to coming, just when her partner pulled it out of her? The film director wanted that pull-out. He wasn't finished with all the position takes he needed for his film. He didn't want an ejaculation shot just then; but look at what happens next, George.*

"See how Marty quickly turned herself over and presented her vagina viewed from the behind position? Okay, well now watch what happens after her partner enters her from behind. See how her

face glows; how huge her smile becomes? That's because she's feeling his penis way up inside her. His penis is so huge, there's no doubt it's touching against her cervix. She has it right where she wants it, for what she's about to do.

"Now watch what happens. See how she starts twerking with that penis way up inside her? See how she plays it faster and faster, like it's her joy-toy? She doesn't go slowly. She doesn't allow the director to capture several minutes of her twerking; getting her hair pulled back; having her ass slapped; having her partner use different posi-tion angles with her. No. She wants to control her own satisfaction here. It's beautiful. She's a far more complete, independent minded woman than that director thought she was. She would not let herself be controlled. She knew what sensational porn was, even better than her director. I think she also knew how important it was for her partner to release. Now watch how her face explodes into a hugely satisfied smile, George. She knows that penis can't possibly hold back any longer. She knows it's simply dying to ejaculate inside her. It can't possibly resist her; and there's no amount of will power within her partner that can control his penis and prevent it from exploding its semen burst. So, she's merciful. She doesn't slow twerk like the director wanted. She wouldn't torture-tease her partner or his penis.

"Her smile tells you that she knows she's the one in full control of that penis, George. This whole sequence is about her need to be the person in control. Now, look! Yes! Are you seeing that? See all that white creamy cum escaping from her vagina, and showering down over the shaft of her partner's penis? Her partner is coming! He couldn't stay inside her and hold back very long. She had him too sensitized for that. She knew it was time to make it happen. Suddenly now, her partner spurts wildly out of control. And she's laughing with happiness for the both of them. I think that director wanted her to hold off from making her partner's penis shoot off wildly like that. I think that was what was going on. But that short

sequence proves that Marty was anxious for that ejaculation burst. She wanted it; and she put just enough touches on that penis with her twerks and bends, that it exploded with that massive gush. Her expression makes that film, George. It's the expression of a woman's supremacy during intimacy. I can't teach anything so beautifully done, George. It's her! It's ALL her. She's a natural artistic talent. She clearly demonstrates here, that copulating is a breathtakingly beautiful art form. I just love her work, George. I love watching her perform. I adore her. I love everything about her.

"Now, George, after her partner completes his ejaculation, notice what she does not do. She does not just stand up and walk away, like a hundred other adult stars would do. No! She lies side by side with him, and she French kisses him. She touches his face while she kisses him; and she tells him how much she loved the many ways he made love with her; how wonderful he was; and all the while she's kissing him and running her fingers over his face, and through his hair with her one hand, her other hand continues fondling his balls, and strok-ing his penis. She's cementing their intimacy, George. She's letting him know that she values him as a partner. She makes that vital human connection. She wants their love to be a permanent bond between them, enduring beyond their copulation act. Her whole world is intimacy, George. Marty lives in intimacy.

"Those are the naturally healthy behaviors of a woman who values romantic intimacy, George. Marty's got it! She doesn't need coaching about how to act like she's in love because she already IS in love. She's sensational. She's the most loving, glorious actress who ever made a film, George. She's spiritually inspiring. Absolutely she is. Fans who watch her films feel love for her. It's from their hearts. It's like this unstoppable outpouring of erotic, romantic feelings hap-pens. It sweeps over me, George. I can't get enough of her.

"Here's one of her most tender scenes, George. It's my favorite of all her one on ones, because it highlights Marty's immodesty. In the

opening frames she flaunts her unblushing promiscuity. Her viewers gasp at how she shamelessly lures her partner into intimacy.

"His name is Marshawn. He's a strikingly handsome, tall muscular black man. Notice how she smiles and nods her head to him as he lifts her dress up and over her head. Notice how quickly she moves in close to him; and how she places her arms around his neck, hugs him close, and French kisses with him. See how she lifts her face up to him? There's her childish, innocent smile again. She displays no hint of hesitation over what she knows the two of them are about to do. Her mannerisms convey naturalness and shamelessness. You see, George, some actresses have reservations about performing in mixed racial scenes. If you are astute, you can catch what their minds think in their faces. But, there's no trace of those thoughts in Marty's face; none, whatsoever. She has no qualms about making love with a black man.

"Her face communicates something entirely different, George. That glow in her cheeks and the way her facial muscles reach up for her partner tells viewers that Marty relishes performing with this man. Enthusiasm for making love with this man literally radiates outward from her persona into the camera. Her eyes devour him. It's another unmistakable example of her spontaneity, George. She adores this man. Her enthusiasm for making love with him is so convincing, I can feel the throbbing in her sex, as if I'm sharing her body with her. That's not acting, George. That's all-natural emotion. I can't teach it; but I know it when I see it.

"Listen! Do you hear her seductive laugh? That's not forced. It's from her belly. It's deep and convincing. It tells her viewers that she loves having sex with this partner. I can't teach that, either, George; but I know it when I hear it. She genuinely loves this man. She's not acting.

"Hear her 'yum' sound, from deep in her chest and belly? She's expressing enthusiastic approval while he unfastens her bra, and

begins sucking her nipples. She welcomes his hands on her body; bringing her closer to him. She's a natural. She captivates and binds my feelings to hers. Her passions come right through that screen into my body. No other actress does that.

"See her move the scene forward by rubbing her hand over his pants, feeling for his penis? Her face positively glows when she discovers how hard he is. Did you see her eyes light up when she first felt his penis, George?"

"They did, didn't they? I caught that. I know what you mean."

"Good, George. Now watch how she gives Marshawn a tantalizing preview of the fantastic sex he's about to have. She performs a bit of teasing when she opens his fly and first touches her lips to the head of his penis, sucking just enough to make his penis stiffen. She helps him slip out of his pants. Her panties are now all that's between them and intimacy.

"Watch. She smiles approvingly, holding his head in her hands, while he puts his thumbs in her panties and slowly peels them down her legs. Listen to how she laughs while stepping out of her panties, George? I've never heard a more joyful, seductive laugh like that from any other actress; but Marty always laughs like that. It signals her love of freedom from restrictions.

"Here the scene gets really interesting, George. She's about to have sex while standing up. Look at how she lays her shoulders back on Marshawn's outstretched arm and how she places her right arm over his shoulder.

"Pay close attention, George. See her raise her finger to her lips? See that pensive look of wonder and indecision that passes her eyes and face? That's the key subliminal question. She's silently posing it to herself; and to Marshawn and her viewers. It's her expression of honest doubt; her uncertainty about whether she should go forward with foreplay; and, by implication whether she should proceed from there to seduction, surrender and copulation.

"She's artful, George. She displays empathetic genius. In those brief few seconds, she's silently asking her viewers whether they should obey their moral teachings; or would they rather allow their thoughts to voyeur with her; join her in immorality? She subtly asks whether her viewers should heed their teachings, which forbid them from watching her. She's playing on their sub-conscious thoughts here. She implies they're making a consciously immoral choice by continuing to watch her. It's artful persuasion; her way of seducing viewers into joining her naughtiness. Should they accept her invitation, by implication, they will become as iniquitous as she. It's her way of helping viewers vicariously experience her intimate closeness. It helps them desire her even more. And, they will then champion every immoral thing she does. She gains their empathy and implied consent for the explicit erotica they are about to see.

"That simple momentary pause of honest pensive contemplation turns over subconscious control of her promiscuity to the viewer. By continuing to watch, her viewers implicitly approve of her immorality. It's an electrifying moment. Suddenly the viewer feels adoration and love for her. They gave her their permission to be sinful! Their minds want to hug her. She's their precious baby. She can do no wrong. Her wrongs are glorious expressions of her needs! Her libido must be satisfied; poor innocently wanton girl! She's no longer just another porn star, making love on a film. Giving her their implied, informed consent makes them accessories to her immorality. They have sanctified it! Those who continue watching the film, from that point forward, are implicitly telling Marty that they love her for being the sensational, immoral porn star that she is. The more salacious she is, the more provocative and sinful she is, the more her films mock conventional morality, the more she pushes the acceptable social envelope, the more her viewers love and adore her. Are you understanding this, George? She is an emotional maestro. She plays viewers feelings like a fiddle."

"Yes, I see what happened there. Why is it significant?"

"Marketing psychology, George. If a viewer continues watching, he's taking down his barrier gate and welcoming Marty into his personal world. He wants to witness what he consented to. He's curious about the salaciously immoral things she will do; and whether her whoring will take his eyes and mind into some new, uncharted, wonderous world of her uniquely uninhibited immorality. He's now embracing her immorality. He's fully invested in it. He wants to hold onto that moment that he chose to be part of it. He wants to see more than the film's teaser preview. So, he buys the entire film. Ka Ching! The cash register rings. A sale is made. But it's much more than a one-time transaction, George. He's taken a huge step forward in his acceptance of Marty's iniquities. He's become a full participant in her world.

"Once he pays to watch Marty perform explicit erotica, it's only another, small step forward to pay a prostitution service for real, live sex. Marty's on film erotica has captivated his limbic zone. She's opened his floodgates to engage in immoral behavior himself. He's anxious to fuck. He now accepts prostitution and believes that it's perfectly healthy and normal to consort with sex workers. His marriage vows will no longer constrain him. He'll answer an ad for a prostitution service, linked to Marty's movies. It's like ordering out for pizza or Chinese. He'll have sex with a local prostitute, while likely imagining that she is Marty. It doesn't matter. He'll discover that he thoroughly enjoys it; and, he'll repeat his experience. He'll buy more of Marty's films and he'll see prostitutes regularly. He'll become a paying customer.

"So, George, the significance is: We'll pitch the various agencies for escort and prostitution services. We'll show them that Marty's films are more likely to yield them more paying customers than other porn stars' films. They'll advertise pop ups and trailers for their services using OUR films. They'll discover they're getting more

business. Our ad buys will go up. We'll raise our rates. We'll make more money. We'll be sure to include that indecisive pensive moment in all our future films. But we'll never explain to our ad buyers why our films are bringing them so much more business. Tradecraft secrets, George! There are many more of them. I'm just scratching the surface. My data work will discover them; and we'll build them into Marty's films. Tradecraft!'

"Got it." George nodded. He knew having a smart wife was a good thing.

"Good, now look. After that pause and getting her viewers' consent to continue, Marty looks into Marshawn's eyes. Her dreamy eyes are irresistible. There! She's wearing her coquettish smile for Marshawn's eyes to see. She's telegraphing that she wants to make love. She's obviously coaxing him to stimulate her. His eyes dissolve into her dream pools. She's irresistible. Entranced, Marshawn responds and commences foreplay.

"See how she smiles at him while his right hand rubs the crown of her vagina? Now watch how enthusiastically she responds when his three fingers enter her. As his fingers reach her clitoris and rub her there, she throws her head back and pulls his head toward hers. She French kisses him. She's a fantastically emotive porn star, George. She's a virtuoso, creating beautiful, artistic intimacy.

"We're watching Marty's way of announcing to her viewers that she's shamelessly proud to be a profligate, salacious adult actress. Because of her voluptuous body and the stunning beauty of her face, the wanton displays she flaunts electrify her viewers' eroticism. She establishes herself in this initial scene as the most glorious, immoral sex goddess to ever appear before cameras.

'Notice her sudden stomach contraction and her head lifting back with her joyful open-mouthed smile, George? When she cried out 'YES,' I felt her first eruption explode. Its tremors came through the film set, right into my heart. My doors of inhibition and

resistance were blown wide open. I let feelings come inside me that I had not felt in years. Waves of empathy and joy overtook me. Awakened desires resonated through my entire body. I intensely wanted to make love, George. My entire body screamed to me. I needed to get laid.

"Every nerve, every muscle within me screamed out to my mind: 'We must fuck.' That's how powerfully her first orgasm affected me, George. Every cell in my body felt her vibrations. I experienced that explosive burst, right along with her. That's what she does for her viewers! She helps people see the most important part of life. That's OUR Marty! Experiencing her very first orgasm this early, in this film segment! It was a spectacular, powerful, spontaneous, stand-up orgasm. I totally loved it!

"Her womanly intensity grabbed my attention. Those seconds of explosive, passionate intimacy, coming so early in that film, are simply breathtaking, George. I sighed at the feminine majesty of it. My loins came alive like a hot flame passed through me, George. I can't remember the last time I ever felt that way.

"Marty, just by being her natural romantic sexual self, drew her viewers' minds right into that orgasm with her. Then, the viewers' eyes stay riveted to her. They can't help themselves. There's no one else like her, anywhere. What she did in those few early frames was riveting artistry. I felt her ecstasy; and I wanted to hold her close to me and kiss her when I saw that. I've never felt such empathy for another woman's feelings, like I did in that very moment, George. I fell in love with her.

"What does Marty do next, now that she's had a stand-up orgasm, and she's still standing there beside her partner? Does she fall into a bed and begin having sex? No, most stars would do that; but not our Marty, George. She doesn't. She has a better sense of erotic intimacy. That's what makes her unique. She sits her partner

down on that sectional sofa; and then sits straddling him with her legs around his waist.

"There's no sex in this segment; but there's incredible, breathtaking eroticism. Marty and her partner embrace and kiss, French kiss. They show the viewers that there is true love and affection between them. The viewer sees her white hands rubbing his back and his massive shoulders. She tenderly touches his face while she kisses him and strokes his thighs, upon which her body rests. The viewer is awed, watching his massive black hands rubbing and touching all over her creamy white back; touching her sides, fondling her breasts, guiding her head forward by her neck, pulling her face into his face to drink in more of her kisses.

"This is not some hurried, disjointed scene, George. It's a continuum of love; genuine intimate love. This is Marty's and her partner's declaration that thoughts about race have no place in their love making, or in their feelings about love. It's an endearing segment of erotic film artistry, George. I've watched it many times; and every time I see it, I well up inside. It's so beautiful, it brings tears to my eyes. I ask myself: 'How can anyone be prejudiced against anyone because of their race?' when I see beautiful love expressed that way."

MARSHAWN

Marty joined George and Bertie for their afternoon session. Bertie wanted the three of them to watch film and hear Marty's comments.

"Marty, in this next scene your partner, Marshawn, places you on the corner arm of a sectional sofa. You have a towel around your shoulders and you're naked below the waist. Marshawn is seated on the sofa beside you. And you are positioned above him. He spreads your legs open widely; and begins kissing your vagina. Soon, he

earnestly engages in cunnilingus with you. Do you remember this scene?"

"Oh, yes, Bertie. I certainly do. He becomes Lover Marshawn when he does this. Oh, Marshawn, you sweet man. I wish he was here with me at this very moment. He is such a beautiful man. Bertie, when Marshawn gives me oral sex it's better than having a two-hundred-piece orchestra playing romantic Beethoven symphonies inside my lady parts. I have no words to describe how much I love Marshawn and the things he does with me. He makes me feel so dreamy and uplifted. My facial expressions capture my ecstatic feelings in this scene. My face responds to Marshawn's marvelous tongue playing its music with my clitoris. You're seeing the most romantic erotica I've ever performed. I felt this outpouring of rapture. I was soaring aloft, getting carried higher and higher on wings of pure pleasure. When I hit the stratosphere, I started twerking my pelvis. My vaginal lips are pressed tightly against Marshawn's lips. See my Vag pushing hard against his mouth?"

"Yes. You were craving what he was doing, weren't you?"

"Oh, yum; yes! There's nothing that compares with it. Notice how his arms held me underneath my legs? He pulled my Vag very hard against his mouth while his tongue made me gush like crazy. This orgasm was so lovely. It gave me immense pleasure to create that scene with him. I had my greatest oral orgasm, ever. From that erotic scene we began an extended day, shooting love scenes. We fucked four times that afternoon. He was fabulous! He's always fabulous. His penis performed superbly! It always does. He repeatedly gets himself up for me after he shoots off his semen. I don't know how he does it. He's, my Mr. Wonderful. I think he can repeat like he does because he knows how deeply I love him. He came inside me four times that day. He's an exceptional lover.

"He was so up for making that film! He stayed incredibly hard, practically the entire afternoon! I was benefitting from his

psychological push for freedom. We made that film a few days after his wife discovered my naughty gift."

"Naughty gift? Wait! Is she that same wife that did that tabloid interview where she accused you of predatory racial behavior; and of using your beauty and immorality to steal a good black man away from his family; all that?"

"Yes, Bertie, that's her; but her publicity stunt backfired. She sure dished out her wrath; but I didn't deserve it. She thought she was hurting my reputation. All she did was push my porn rankings higher. She's the one who caused her own hiccup in her racism narrative. People now see her as a nasty shrew. She only has herself to blame. She demonstrated that a black woman can be as equally bigoted as a white man. Her stunt tweaked me. But I didn't take it lying down. That's why I asked Marshawn to be my partner in this film you're watching."

"Wait, back up a minute. I want to hear about the gift. What happened?"

"Okay, sure. It was my honest heartfelt gift to Marshawn. During my breakthrough orgy film with the seven black men, while all of them were feeling me everywhere, Marshawn whispered into my ear that he loved me. He told me he was being completely honest and serious. I didn't expect to hear that on set. But he repeated it five times. I knew it was totally unscripted. It wasn't anywhere close to the lines the director gave him. But he kept whispering that he loved me; kept pouring out his love for me. I appreciated that he meant it. He told me he loved me and he could never get enough of me. He asked to please see me. He was being totally honest.

"I felt the same way he did. Our eyes told each other that we shared true feelings. Love happened for us. Amid all our sex scenes, love budded and blossomed, My mind went wild. Besides all the sex on the set, I knew I was tumbling into love. It was undeniable. I tried to control my feelings and not to show Marshawn special favoritism

on the film set; but I couldn't help myself. Then, during those times when his penis was inside me, I didn't want to release him. I wanted him to stay inside me, forever. I didn't want to give my next partner his turn to enter me. I wanted to hold Marshawn close to me, with his penis inside me until we stopped filming."

"You like this Marshawn more than the others. That's obvious. Why? What is it about him; his penis? I mean it's so huge!"

"Well, yes; but he's also such a love."

"But that penis! It's amazing. Do you like them that big?"

"Yes, of course. What girl doesn't?"

"Well, I've never done it with a black. And certainly, never with a penis that huge. My God! That thing is huge. Why do you like them big like that?"

"Don't you know, Bertie? The big ones really stretch you inside. They press against all those thousands of tiny nerve endings inside your vagina. They send these amplified sensations all through your clitoral tentacles; make you feel like every nerve in your body is being pleasantly electrocuted. It's a coming alive, uplifting feeling. I love it. It juices me; really makes me flow."

"I should try it." Bertie sounded wistful, envious that she had missed out on something wonderful, but now determined to rectify her shortfall.

"Definitely. You must. But there's so much more to Marshawn's penis than just my stretch tingles. When Marshawn is inside me, it's like having this connection. It's hard to relate this; but his penis fits so well, that whenever I move my hips or flex my buns or roll a little, he moves with me in perfect synchronous harmony; like we are the same connected person. It's easy, effortless, smoothly rhythmic, heavenly lovemaking. I love it. It's divine; special. I guess you could call it responsiveness, plus. When there's a big penis inside me, especially Marshawn's, it's like having power assisted rack and pinion steering

on a sports car. Smooth. Powerful. Sensitive. I move; he moves; along with me; immediately, no hesitation; no sloppiness."

"You had a sports car?"

"No, I didn't; but this one guy I did, did. He had a Corvette. He worked its stick shift so smoothly; like we were one with the car. He took corners without slowing down. That pushed me into the sides of my seat, like I was getting hugged by the car. Riding in it excited me; turned me on. He picked me up at WEX and drove me to his family's house at Rehoboth Beach. He was a weird dude; snorted coke; called his dick: 'The Little Guy,' and called his dad: 'The Big Guy.' He said his little guy was the key to both him and his dad. I believed him. He was impulsive. He claimed he controlled the big guy; so, his dick, by inference, controlled them both. I did him twice. I was glad it stopped. He was manic, drug addicted, and dangerous."

"But was the sex good?"

"Good? Just okay; but not great; nowhere close to sex with Marshawn. His lovemaking is divine; so wonderful. I could drive Marshawn's penis all day, every day; loving the sweetness; like having a sports car that you want to drive and never stop. It's so beautiful, I never want to stop loving him."

"And that's why you favor him in your orgy scenes; why you tend to hold him inside you longer that the others?"

"Absolutely! Can't ever get too much of that fantastic penis! I'm a connoisseur of penises, you know. And when I have a sensational one inside, I love keeping it there. I did all I could to hold Marshawn inside me until I couldn't control him any longer. Of course, I made him come inside me. The script didn't call for that; but I didn't care. I wanted to feel all of him. I didn't mention that to him until we finished shooting. But by then, he had to know I had romantic feelings for him. And, I did. I knew I was falling in love

with him. As he was leaving the set, I asked him to wait outside my dressing room.

"I took one of my stock photographs, where I'm in a soft mauve sweater, wearing my favorite pearl neckless. I'm lying back, smiling with my hands folded behind my head; and my legs are spread wide open. My vagina's butterfly tattoo is fully displayed with some white, creamy semen visibly flowing from my inner lips. I autographed it for him, then I kissed it, leaving my lipstick mark across my sweater. I wrote:

'Marshawn, I hope this will remind you of me; and the love I feel for you. Call me anytime you want to make love. You may have me and you may kiss me everywhere you wish to kiss me. I love you with all my love, Marty.'

"I wrote my private phone number below the message. Then, I slipped off my black lace panties and placed my panties and the autographed photo in a neckless box. I tied a gold ribbon around the box, and handed it to him when I left my dressing room. I kissed him and told him to wait until he got home to open his present.

"I truly love Marshawn; and I wanted him to know it. I never expected his wife to find the box and open it, but she did. That's what sent her on her rocket ride. She went ballistic; full orbital. All that public screaming she did before the cameras; all those ugly names she called me! I don't understand why creating explicit erotic films should prevent me from falling in love, do you?"

"No, of course not," Bertie concurred.

"I'm a woman, too. I'm human. I need to be in love. I can't help it. When it happens. It happens. I can't help it that Marshawn happened to have a wife. My love for Marshawn was honest, discreet, and innocent. She had no reason to make a big fuss over it."

"Good, Marty, now I understand why you feel this magnetism towards Marshawn. Now, could you to please explain what your

thoughts were; what was happening in your mind when you looked down, smiling so lovingly at Marshawn while he performed cunnilingus? You had the most pleased, satisfied smile I've ever seen on your face; yet, I detected a tiny trace of smugness in your smile and a triumphant glow in your cheeks during those intimate moments with Marshawn. Your eyes warmed. You adored what he was doing. You used a metallic gold eye shadow that blended into a smoky gray towards the edges of your eyelids.

"That's your Confederate, Southern Belle look, isn't it?"

"Yeah. I love it. It helps me feel empowered."

"I see that; so much in control; very effective. So, while Marshawn moved his fingers higher and higher up your inner thighs, then followed his fingers with his lips, your eyes focused on his head the entire time. Your eyes glowed like there was a soft warm fire inside you. How did your emotions bring out your eyes that way? Your face was saying that you were immensely proud of yourself. You were the cat that ate the canary. What was happening in your mind?"

"Oh, Bertie, you are such a keen observer! I imagined I was a Plantation Belle having an affair with our strongest, most handsome field hands. My thoughts were totally sinful. Anyway, by the time we made this film, Marshawn was having serious drama issues with his wife. She had upsets about him seeing: 'That white, Marty Porn Star, homewrecker.' Marshawn and I had performed a few times before my breakthrough orgy film. We felt something began happening back then; but, somehow, we were able to keep everything professional. But once we performed together in that infamous orgy film, things changed. If you study that film closely, you'll notice it was about the two of us making love, with my other lovers performing fill-in roles. Marshawn was the partner I repeatedly mouth kissed, expressing my love and cravings for his intimacy. The orgy was sort of a contest among the six partners to show their strength and to see

who could stay inside me the longest; but notice that Marshawn had far more intimacy with me.

"After I gave him my panties gift and phone number, we met for coffee, then ended up at my place. We spent the night together making fabulous love. That was outside both our contracts. We discovered off-set, personal love. It was intensely physical at first. We craved each other's bodies. It was a mutual obsession thing. We couldn't get enough of each other. After that first delicious night of beautiful love making, we knew what we had. We couldn't help how we felt.

"My woman's intuition told me that ours wasn't going to be an ordinary love affair. I knew it was going to be monumental. While we made love that first night, I felt this change come over me; like my world would be altered, because of what we were doing. I felt like I was the Moon being pulled away from my gravitational orbit by this irresistibly powerful force. I was drawn faster and faster toward Marshawn. He became my Earth.

"I knew I would to crash into him; into his world; into his life. I knew there would come a huge, messy collision. But I couldn't stop it from happening. It was like gravity on steroids; accelerating me onward into his world. I was suddenly racing at blindingly fast, high velocity into Marshawn's life. I knew the inevitable would happen. I knew I would collide with Aliyah, his wife.

"I thought I'd likely knock her off his Earth and send her off screaming and bawling into outer space, all by herself. And I couldn't worry about that. I didn't want to think about Aaliyah. I could not stop myself anyway; even if I wanted to. And I didn't want to. I had no power whatsoever to prevent what was happening. I wanted it to happen. I didn't want to prevent it. I had to do what my nympho-mania compelled me to do. I had to go with my feelings. My soul and my body wanted Marshawn. I had to have him; all of him; all the time. I couldn't have held myself back, no matter how hard I tried;

but I didn't try. Of course, I didn't try. My limbic zone was on fire. Flames burned hot around my heat shield. My hot lust melted me; consumed me. I wanted to crash into Marshawn's earth. I could only think of having sex with Marshawn; nothing else.

"I felt myself getting sucked in; going faster and faster; captured by Marshawn's gravity; flying blazingly fast beyond what astronauts call the event horizon. I was unable to alter course. There was no turning back. That was impossible. The only thing I could do was go with my feelings. I was being swallowed into Marshawn's world. My feelings were pulled away from me. I couldn't control them. They were leaving me; getting consumed by this powerful star. Only it wasn't a star. It was Marshawn. He was my love star; my earth; my him. There was no changing course. And I didn't want to change course. I only wanted Aaliyah's man. I know that's wrong; but I didn't care. I couldn't stop what was happening. All my controls had stopped working. I had no self-control, no shame, no inhibition; and no power to change things. I was flying dead stick; or rather, Marshawn was flying my feelings; taking my self-control away from me; and taking me away from me. All I wanted was to crash my life into Marshawn's. I wanted to embrace that man; and I wanted to fuck that man; and fuck him more; until I lost my mind over fucking him. I never wanted to fuck any man like I wanted to fuck Marshawn. I had to have his arms around me and his penis inside me; absolutely had to; always; every moment of every single day and night. I had it bad. I loved him. And I still love him. I know I will always love him.

"Then followed that emotionally charged night when Marshawn confessed that he was addicted to performing cunnilingus with me. He cried; hugged me; spilled out his guts. He told me he knew it was wrong and sinful; and against everything he'd been brought up believing; but he couldn't help himself. He told me he needed to surrender to this force that he couldn't understand; that he didn't care if this mysterious force destroyed his life; but that he needed to do what

his heart told him to do. He told me that he felt compelled to give me pleasure; always and forever. He called me his goddess and swore he never felt that way with anyone else. He told me that he loved me; that he had tried not to love me, but that was impossible. He told me he wanted to commit his life to loving me. I had never heard a man turn himself inside out like that before. He turned my mind inside out, too. I was stunned, but also, inwardly, deeply pleased by his confession of love. He called my vagina his holy sepulcher, where his tongue comes to worship my sacred clitoris. He told me he reveres my clitoris. He calls it his glorious radiant white pearl; and he loves to please it by caressing and marrying it to the pleasure touches he gives it with his black pearls."

"Black pearls?" Bertie wasn't sure of what she heard.

"Yes, you heard me right. Marshawn had his tongue tip pierced and fitted with black pearls on both sides near its tip, as his devotional gift to me on that magical night. That's how obsessed he was; and still is, to please me. He told me he wanted my clitoris to feel his adoration for it; and he wanted it to receive its most loving feelings from the tributes of his tongue."

"So, are those the scenes I'm seeing? True love with you and Marshawn? And he's licking your clitoris, using both sides of his pierced tongue? He's stimulating you in the most erotic ways imaginable, with those pearls and his tongue? Do they work?" Bertie was dumbfounded that a man would disfigure his tongue to give a woman greater pleasure.

"Yes, they work. They give me an extra sense of pressure. It's more focused pressure than I feel with a naked tongue; and it rolls along over my clitoris and along the sides of it while his tongue caresses me there. Those scenes we're watching that capture those feelings. My face lights up, like my mind is in the heavens. That's the tickle thrill of his black pearls pressuring my clitoris, paired with his tongue caresses. I'm feeling something beyond explicit erotica. I'm

a woman being fueled by true love; whatever words I can use that best describe my incredibly erotic feelings. That scene encapsulates it, Bertie. Often, Marshawn expresses his erotic love for me through his tongue. And often, too, I can feel it flood throughout my whole vagina through his penis. He has such a powerful penis! It's hard to describe the erotic fascination, the intensely romantic attraction I have towards Marshawn and his marvelous penis. As a connoisseur of hundreds of penises, I can honestly say that Marshawn's is uniquely sized, ultra-sensitive to the feelings of my vagina; and so incredibly talented. I crave having his penis inside me. I have never known greater pleasures.

"I swear, if every temptress, every woman of pleasure, every money loving cocotte of fame and renown that ever lived; every Ishtara, Bathsheba, Delilah, Salome, Cleopatra, Catherin the Great, Mata Hare, Marilyn Monroe, Marilyn Chambers; and every other spectacular, notorious femme fatale that ever once lived, could shake their souls awake and reincarnate their dead bodies back to life, so they could make love one time with Marshawn and his fabulous penis, they absolutely would do so. In a heartbeat! They would all discover, as I have, that no other penis so completely fills and pleasures a woman as Marshawn's.

"And, if every religious woman, from the Virgin Mary to Mother Theresa, and all women of faith before them, and those living in the present, could just one time experience the divine pleasures of Marshawn's magnificent penis, they would, I promise you, take their consciences and throw them onto a pyre; burn them to crispy ashes, then encase them in a lead box and drop them into the Pacific's Challenger depths; never to concern themselves again with the calculus of religious morality. I'm not exaggerating, Bertie. His love making is that good!

"They would enjoy the passions of erotic romance and love making with the most incomprehensibly delicious, most loving penis

that any woman has ever experienced. Yes, they would. I know they would. Marshawn and his fabulous penis are that wonderful. And, all these women of notoriety would also love his tongue. Once their limbic zone was liberated from what they thought was their passion quest during their lives, they would awaken, as I did, to the immensity of feelings that flow from Marshawn's tongue. Yes, Bertie, I know I sound obsessed. But this is the best way to describe how this true love feels. You asked. If every woman who ever lived could return to know the same pleasures that I already know with him, they would shake their souls awake; then offer their bodies to Marshawn. They would beg that they might experience the same joys that I feel.

"When Marshawn tongues his pearls over my clitoris, my emotions lift right out of me and flutter away to this special place. I know when he does that, he's deifying me on his special pedestal; there he worships and adores me in the most intimate way imaginable. When he disfigured his tongue like he did to give me greater pleasures, I knew we shared an ultimate measure of intimacy.

"But then, after that divine night when we first discovered our love, Marshawn made the bone-headed mistake of being honest with his wife. She's one of those religious types. He confessed to her that he loved me. Sometimes men can become extra stupid. Well, this was one of those times. As you might expect, Marshawn's wife, Aaliyah, went crazy. No wife wants to hear her husband telling her that he has fallen in love with an erotic film actress. She had a screaming fit. She forbade him from ever performing with me again; or even ever seeing me again. She was very hard on Marshawn.

"I should have warned him this sort of thing might happen if he ever told her about us. I have run into this sort of thing before. I've experienced women's hatred for me to be at least ten times greater than the love they ever gave to their husbands. Some women are much like cannibals who relish the taste of a fresh bloody liver more than a mere bite off a leg. Some women relate to their men that

way. They live to hate and torment; bite their teeth into their men; claw their nails into men's souls; rip men's guts out; even infest their children with poison-hate of their children's fathers. A woman so disposed will avoid, at all costs, giving any sign of love or affection to her man. She cannot accept his moment of moral failure. She feels betrayed. That's natural. He's typically a narcissist who is so self-absorbed she can't think past her own nose. The only remedy that will restore her dignity and stature amongst her like-minded man hater friends is divorce; especially when combined with harassment and heavy bombardment delivered by a snarky divorce lawyer. These women will vilify a good man; piss on his name; trash his business and reputation. But they will not look inward; not forgive; and, God forbid, never love him again. He is spoiled fish and must be put out with the trash! I knew Marshawn had placed his marriage on this sort of slippery slope. It was a delicate time for him; for me; for both of us.

"Well, that smile you observed was my inner happiness, knowing that Marshawn's attraction to me was a stronger force than his wife's barrage of emotional threats. You see, whenever Marshawn goes down on me, my mind floats away to this other world. I enter this dream state. I imagine then, that I've become Mother Earth. I've crashed into Marshawn's world and replaced it with me! I run my fingers wildly through Marshawn's hair, like I'm clawing into this beautiful, thick arctic tundra. I push his head down deeper and closer to my sex, because I know his tongue is searching for my inner soul; trying to connect with me. I want him to find that. I help him discover me.

"I fantasize that Marshawn is my beautiful, strong, bull caribou. He's searching for my sweet spring; and I know when he locates my spring all the frozen tenseness in my inner earth's spirit will release and melt; and I'll explode into my glorious springtime. I can't wait for that feeling. It's like I'm Earth bursting inside myself; letting my

flowers lift up from the winter coldness to bloom in the glorious sunshine. I feel riot wild with happiness and pleasure; and I know there's a natural goodness about all of it. The best part about this experience is knowing that Marshawn loves performing the cunnilingus that he's giving me. Absolutely, he loves performing it. And that sets my feelings free.

"You see, Bertie, Marshawn is entirely committed to helping me feel special and goddess-like whenever we have oral sex. That's why you notice that I'm looking so pleased. I felt so much more than the physical pleasures he was giving me. I was pleased about his mind set. I knew that making me feel the way he was making me feel was the single most important thing in Marshawn's life. It was his way of apologizing for the narrow-minded reaction of his wife about our love. You can read in my face how I realized that my vagina had become Marshawn's holy temple; the object of his love and adored benefactor of his soul's devotion. I felt his love, Bertie. I experienced honest, devotional love, knowing that this man loved me that much. My smile warmed like it did because I knew I had Marshawn's true love. I trusted that nothing could pull us apart. I could tell we had become soulmates; my mind and his mind were in sync.

"I was extremely pleased that he chose to ignore his wife and continue performing in porn films with me. In this particular scene, my mind was scheming about secretly seeing him again, off set; taking up where we'd left off; spending many more nights with him; driving Aaliyah completely nuts."

"So, you continued seeing him privately. You ignored his wife's pleas to break it off, is that right?"

"Yes Bertie, of course I ignored her. I couldn't allow an upset wife to interfere with my film work. Besides, I love Marshawn. I can't understand why she believes I'm bad for him. She's such a brick. She should be thrilled that I choose Marshawn to star with me. She should have encouraged him to have his mind on making

love with me and no one else, because the camera knows everything. She should have been supportive of his choice to perform with me. If there's any negativity in someone's mind, the camera captures it. I can't have that. It's unacceptable. I know she has her two little girls; but I have my fans and my identity to maintain. If I allowed her trauma tears and bitching to define my limits, then my reputation as a notoriously immoral porn star would become jeopardized. Our film work might suffer. Our passions could seem faded; less real. People don't buy wilted roses. They don't buy porn films that lack enthusiasm either. I couldn't allow our enthusiasm to falter. I could not put limits on our passion to accommodate his wife; just couldn't do that. I've worked far too hard to cultivate my image. I was not about to let some sniveling upset wife tell me what I could and could not do."

"Didn't she have any effect on you at all?"

"Well, yes; but not the effect she wanted. Her behavior made me more determined than ever to keep Marshawn's mind on loving me and ignoring her; and making even more provocative porn films with Marshawn, which we've started doing. In our last two films we've put in a different ending. We stood naked together; then we embraced and kissed. I placed one hand on Marshawn's neck and held his balls in my other hand, while he placed one hand on my ass; and his other hand wrapped my waist and pulled me into him. Then, he said to me, 'I love you,' while we continued kissing. It made for a more romantic ending than a typical porn film's ending. It portrayed me more like I'm the sweet innocent girl next door; the kind of woman a fellow wants to take home to his mother; instead of me being portrayed strictly as a porn star. Those endings really threatened Aaliyah. They drove her crazy; and they pulled Marshawn much closer to me. That's when she ratcheted up her public name calling.

"It titillates men to know that one woman is brazen enough to make a public spectacle of defiling another woman's marriage. It's

free publicity and it's great for business, so I decided Marshawn and I should do more of it. Our next film's ending added a more erotic twist to our 'Porn Stars in Love' theme. I was again naked, of course. Two muscular men from Marshawn's orgy group placed their arms under my legs, lifted me up and spread my legs wide open for the camera. I rested my head on one of their shoulders. Then Marshawn came to me. He placed his huge hand on my stomach and began stimulating my vagina with two fingers. I swooned. My eyes rolled back. I loved how he was making me feel.

"Then Marshawn kissed my mouth, stared into my eyes, and again spoke those magical words, 'I love you.' But then, he said even more. 'I love you more than anyone or anything else in the world.' That line was a calculated poke at his wife. He spoke that while I was obviously flaunting myself as a completely shameless, profligate porn star, for all the world to see. Yet, here was Marshawn, telling me that he loved me, not despite me being immoral; but BECAUSE I am immoral. I wanted that line kept in the script. Marshawn spoke it without hesitation, sincerely and unambiguously. Hearing him say that made me so proud of him. I Kegel squeezed his fingers crazily while they fingered me during that final scene. The film ends with me, legs widespread, flaunting my inviting vagina, while being held high above the floor by the arms of two strong men; with Marshawn French kissing me; and me, shamelessly writhing with my lovely orgasm. Marshawn stayed with me the entire time; lovingly stimulating me through my entire flow. He was a perfect, supportive gentleman.

"I was so given over to Marshawn that my stomach convulsed in ecstasy several times while he stimulated me with his fingers; continuing our French kissing. It was the most beautifully erotic film ending I've ever made. I was firmly establishing myself as the most unapologetic, wanton, porn actress in all whoredom. My legs stayed wide apart and my hand held his head by the back of his neck while

we continued French kissing. I was eagerly thrusting my vagina, responsive to his fingerings, urging him to continue. I was letting the cameras know how thrilled I was to leave all inhibitions behind; completely uncaring of others' prudish thoughts about my selfish pleasuring. I felt genuinely proud to flaunt my shameless immorality.

"I felt that the more shamelessly immoral I was, the more convinced the cameras would be that whoring was what I most loved doing; and the greater my fan appeal would be; and, most importantly, the more honest I'd be with my true self. An inner light illuminated me. I was proving to the world that I was a deliciously immoral whore; and that I loved every second of it. I wanted that scene to last forever, I loved it that much. And all the while I was French kissing Marshawn and my orgasms were coming with my convulsive thrust spasms; while my vagina squeezed tightly on his lovely fingers, I understood that Aaliyah would see that film. Each of my passion-lusting thrusts would shred her heart into thousands of tiny pieces; shattering the life she once had. And I felt good while doing that; deliciously naughty. It's a wonderful feeling. I thrusted even more wildly than before and squeezed my vagina on his fingers even more tightly than before. I was obsessed with what I was doing. I didn't want to ever stop. I knew I was squeezing the life out of Aaliyah's dying marriage.

"You may wonder why I obsess over Marshawn like I do. Well, it's because he's the best lover for erotica films I've ever had. He's sensational. He brings out the wildness in me. That's why."

"And you don't fear his wife?"

"No. I confront her at every opportunity. I've become disrespectful, fearless, and brazen. I even call him at home now. That's a forbidden no-no for a mistress lover. But she was the one who took the gloves off. Calling him at home is my way of letting her know that she means nothing to him, or to me. My affair with Marshawn essentially reduced her role to cook and housekeeper. All those feelings

were inside me, Bertie. I was setting them free. You saw that in my eyes during Marshawn's cunnilingus with me, while I was positioned on the arm of that sofa.

"You are now seeing my pride; my wanton immorality destroying Marshawn's moral goodness; destroying his fealty to his wife. My delicious immoral pleasures are pouring out of my soul through my eyes. That look telegraphs my shamelessness, promiscuity, and wanton iniquity. It solidly connects with my fans. They love that look. It engages them. I get letters and tweets about it. They ask what's happening inside my mind while my eyes look that way. It's that key element; that little extra touch of sinful naughtiness, that creates sensational porn. I think it stirs viewers' primal drives of natural selection. They naturally want to see the most profligate, immoral woman; the most sexually explicit woman, enjoying her love making and having her way with the men in her life.

"My fans perceive distraught wives as ridiculous also-rans. They don't want to hear women's sob stories about how I wrecked their marriages. They simply don't care about losers. They love debauchery and eroticism. And they love me. They love watching me. They love me for giving them what their minds secretly want. They want to feel happiness for me. They cherish the scenes where I make love with explicit wantonness. They don't care one iota about how a jilted wife feels. They want to honor and glorify the winner; the woman who crushed the soul of the loser. They want to feel assured that I'm happy while I'm joyfully doing my partner. That, and their dreams of having me themselves, are the only things they care about.

"Marshawn swore that he wanted to leave his wife for me. That told me I controlled both their lives. I was thrilled. After Aaliyah's public rant, I decided to turn the tables. When the tabloids interviewed me about her vicious accusations, I put a whole different patina on my affair with Marshawn. I spun our affair as my sincere

effort to be egalitarian; to give a struggling actor a helping hand-up by letting him partner with me, so he could attain the same level of stardom in the erotic film world.

"I portrayed myself as a noble, good-hearted woman helping an aspiring actor to feed his family. I made her look like an ungrateful shrew. The media went for it. They always treat me well. Stories about my escapades help their sales. They hailed me as the sympathetic sex goddess with a compassionate heart. They disparaged her as a selfish ingrate. I eradicated her pretense that her marriage still held meaning for Marshawn.

"Later, Marshawn told me his wife had immigrated from one of those horrible places that mutilate a woman's genitals. She was infibulated by a narrow-minded selfish culture; one sided, male focused, and heartless. She'd had her clitoris removed when she was nine years old! That shocked me. I was devastated to hear that any woman could be so unfortunate. I wrote her a note to apologize for mocking her in my tabloid interview. I told her how profoundly sorry I was for her and her unfortunate condition. I promised her I would never say another disparaging word about her."

Bertie's eyes lifted in approval. Marty's compassion for another woman's plight warmed her heart. *"So, after you apologized to Aaliyah, did you break it off with Marshawn?"*

"Oh, no; there would be no sense in doing that, Bertie. Why would I deprive myself of having one of the most fabulous lovers I've ever known? And, why should Marshawn continue to suffer in a miserable relationship with a woman who can't reciprocate his sexual pleasures with her own? I mean, just because she feels no joy in sexual relations, what kind of stilted arrangement would that be for Marshawn?

"I can't imagine his loving tongue or magnificent penis trying to give pleasure to a woman who doesn't feel anything. Poor, poor Marshawn! If he didn't know he was pleasing a woman while he was

making love with her, he might develop an inferiority complex. I'd be horrified if Marshawn got erectile dysfunction or developed psychiatric issues because he couldn't please a woman. That would be tragic. I couldn't allow it. His sexuality needs an outlet. He needs to know that his love making is appreciated. His manliness absolutely needs that. He's a splendid man. And he loves to make love with me.

"I gave these issues considerable thought before I reasoned my way through them. I finally decided that I'd made a fair trade. His wife got my apology and I got her man's love. I decided the most beneficial thing I could possibly do for their marriage, going forward, was to love Marshawn with all the passion I had within me. I promised myself that whenever I made love with him and whenever I received cunnilingus from him, I would selflessly put my whole heart into our lovemaking. I believed his wife would completely understand my good intentions.

"After all, since I couldn't save their marriage by breaking it off with Marshawn, at least I could rescue Marshawn's half of the marriage from the perils of sexual dysfunction. I decided the only right thing to do was to fuck Marshawn's heart, soul, and brains out, whenever I have the opportunity. And I do! After that, neither I, nor Marshawn have heard another peep out of his wife; and we've made four more films together."

"Oh yes, I see how you struggled to do Marshawn's family a kindness. You're such a considerate, loving, good hearted soul. That's a very sweet story, Marty." Bertie hugged and kissed Marty again, expressing her complete approval of the younger woman's twisted sense of morality.

"Bertie," Marty's voice gushed happiness after hearing her new friend approve of her choices. In Bertie, she had a mother confessor figure and ally who championed her promiscuous lifestyle. She'd coach Marty to perfect her craft, and help vault her to a top performing actress ranking in adult films. Bertie's coaching talent

was flavored with her conviction that immorality was perfectly acceptable and normal, *"that look you saw in my eyes expressed how totally pleased I was that Marshawn had surrendered his soul to me. The metallic gold eye shadow brings out the tiny gold flecks in my brown irises. They're naturally brown. That's how I wanted them for this shoot. But, often enough, you'll see my eyes are different shades of blue, depending on the tinted contacts I use. My brown eyes flare hot. They shine, like you see there, whenever my lust fires rage wildly within me. My lust burst through with that intense glow in my eyes; that's how thrilled I was with Marshawn. I watched Marshawn's head closely as he began by kissing my nipples and squeezing my breasts. I thought:*

'What a sensitive man; so loving, so adoring. And he's choosing me over his wife!'

"I also thought, as his lips made their way lower to my tummy:

'I love how his tender lips linger, and how he kisses me everywhere on my lusting stomach, like I'm his holy Madonna; and how he has paused at the lowest part of my welcoming tummy, by my longing mons. He's sensing divine reverence; like he is about to impart his soul to me.'

"He had stopped, ever so briefly. I was so excited. Tiny, prickly sweat beads arose on my mons. I wondered: 'Has my excited condition somehow given him pause?'

"But, no, that wasn't it. He began licking my mons. Marshawn was beginning his feast!

"As he licked and kissed me, these thoughts sent my mind tumbling:

'He's such a wonderful, sensitive man, from a good home and a dutiful wife. What am I doing to his life? Do I have the right to make him my lover? What would he be if he'd never met me? Would he, perhaps, be a tradesman? Would he have some service job? Would he join the military? But he is here with me, about to perform delicious

pornography for the cameras. But in truth, he's doing this for me. Do I have the moral right to use him this way? How would he feel if I went on to the heights of porn stardom and he was left to do bit roles with women for whom he had no feelings?'

"Then, I stopped those thoughts. I couldn't allow them; not while my libido had such cravings. I swept them aside. I closed my mental door on them. When they were safely gone, I could enjoy Marshawn's pleasuring. He was kissing and licking my Mons. Oh, Bertie, he was so lovely; such an exceptional man; such a gentle lover. My mind went soaring; far, far above my body; into the heavens where I felt only his pleasuring's; and where I knew nothing else mattered or ever would matter. All of me, everything inside me; every recess of my immortal soul wanted only one thing now. I desperately wanted to make love with Marshawn. Suddenly, I was into it. I couldn't wait another second. I wanted him to move on from my mons to my Vag. I whispered to him:

'Please, please, Marshawn. Yes, Marshawn. Keep going. I want you. Oh, Marshawn, I must have you. Take me now. Make love with me.'

"Then he continued kissing me lower and lower until his lips traveled down to nibble upon my gateway lips of greedy, insatiable sex. In my dream state I was thinking:

'This beautiful strong caribou is nibbling in my sweet-grass valley. He'll soon be stimulating my anxious spring. I'll soon gush and flow. I'll share my life creating fluids with him. My beautiful flowers will shoot up from my earth tundra. My blooms will burst open in the sun.'

"Bertie, my blood stops being normal when I'm with Marshawn. It becomes different blood, somehow. It heats my entire body, warms my skin and switches on my sex. It makes me want to scream out:

'Yes, please open me and come inside me. Thrust your penis into me, Marshawn. I want you to know me; know how I'm feeling; know

how much I need you. Please, please, enter me!'

"*My blood doesn't cool down, Bertie. This heat I feel is not some temporary thing. My blood gets even hotter; like I have a wild, out of control flame thrower, living within my veins; changing me into a wild animal somehow. It animates me, makes me eager to be a complete partner in our erotic film scene; full partner with Marshawn's lust; enabling his lust; encouraging it; urging him to do more of what he's started doing; clasping my arms around his waist; pulling him into me; whispering sweet 'yesses'; urging him to immerse his life deeper in my sinfulness; combine his sins with mine.*

"*My eager French kisses communicate that he is earning my boundless love and adoration by abandoning all his moral moorings; that he is righteously immoral to surrender his soul to me; completely to me; only me; ejaculating inside me; emptying his life's essence into my craven hunger for him. I assure him that he's doing a good and righteous thing. I praise our copulation, while holding him tightly to me. I savor this union of our immoral souls.*

"*At the exact instant Marshawn's tongue first touched my outer lips, I felt a triumphant glow well up within my breast and express itself in my eyes. That's when you noticed that my eyes were speaking, Bertie. I knew when his lips first touched my lady lips that nothing would stop him from taking me to a fabulous orgasm. My inner flames grew hotter. My blood seared my passions like the afterburner flash from a fighter jet. I launched myself into sexual ecstasy with every power within me. Marshawn needed to know how thrilled I was to take him on our wild ride. I surrendered myself to my animal me. I knew my animal me would steal his soul.*

"*Those first touchings of his lips to my yearning mons signaled he was helpless to resist me. He was helpless to stop; captivated; smitten. I knew he wouldn't stop. He couldn't. And I wouldn't stop. I couldn't. We entered my 'Goddess on her pedestal' world of our own free will. That's the world where immoral sins are exalted and all else becomes meaningless. Marshawn eagerly tumbled with me, into my abyss world, where I was Goddess Immoral. Like fallen angels, we went beyond the lovemaking that partners perform in erotic films. We knew it. And we loved it. My mind shined through my eyes, Bertie. My feelings thrilled me beyond any words that could describe them. Only my eyes could adequately express how badly I needed him; how anxious I was; how much I wanted what was about to happen.*

"I had no doubt that Aaliyah would see that newest film. I knew when she saw how engaged he was in giving me pleasures, she'd feel gut punched. But I also knew she would think about my apology note. She'd understand how badly Marshawn needed me. I know men. I was certain that, by now, he had placated her. I knew he would have promised her that he would never see me or perform with me again.

"Of course, he would have lied to her. He's a man. All men lie. They say and promise anything to avoid confrontations with screaming women. But I know women, too. I reasoned she would accept that love between a man and a woman happens; that there can never be any fault in that. I never fault men for making promises they know they can't keep. I know they make their promises to keep society running smoothly. I believed she'll eventually let go of her hostility; she'd appreciate the beautiful lovemaking that Marshawn and I perform together. She'd understand her place in our newly defined triangle relationship; and she'd accept it.

"My eyes flared while Marshawn's tongue began exploring my inner lips. Then my irises rolled up and disappeared behind my upper eyelids. That just happens with me. My eye whites register my intense pleasure when Marshawn's tongue first penetrated me. That's how I memorialized the ecstasy I feel. Marshawn took me into my goddess world. I loved that sensation. The whole world became mine

in that moment. Everything existed solely to pleasure me. Marshawn carries that world on his tongue. I knew his fabulous tongue would deliver me to my orgasm. I entered the early phase of my nirvana.

"The instant his tongue touched my clitoris, my inner butter-flies shed their cocoons. They began fluttering freely. They danced merrily; up, and down the entire length of my clitoris. They kissed it, tickled it; and coaxed it to swell. My juices began flowing. As Marshawn's lovely tongue stroked, first along one side of my clit, and then, along the other; my butterflies fluttered alongside his tongue. They were kissing my clit; tickling it; making it swell even more. My inner goddess wings lifted me higher and higher, floating my feelings upward, telling me it was right and good to let go of all other thoughts; and just enjoy these divine moments.

"Their fluttering little wings spread my legs open wider. They told me it was good to express my carnal feelings for Marshawn. By then, I badly wanted sex. I had no modesty; no shame; no inhibition. I released the divinely wicked spirit that lives inside me. I was proud of Marshawn. He was willfully disobeying Aaliyah's commands to not taste my forbidden peach. He had confided with me. She had sworn to him that she spoke to him through the voice of God. She had told him that I was the wrong voice to obey; that my body was the pathway to hell and perdition. She had begged him:

'Turn away from her godless immorality; save yourself.'

"She swore I was the force of darkness and evil. She ordered him to leave me and to stand with her in the holy light of righteous, moral goodness. After Marshawn revealed her claptrap nonsense, I reminded him that many beautiful, wonderful things happen in darkness. Besides, I explained, if God really believed immorality was bad, then God wouldn't allow it in the first place. My comments dispelled his doubts. He begged for second helpings of my immorality."

Bertie's eyes found Marty's. She stared into them. She felt profoundly, wonderfully connected to her young friend. *"You handled that situation brilliantly. I agree with your logic. There can't possibly be anything wrong with immorality. God obviously approves of it. Regardless of what God thinks, I certainly approve of it."*

"Do you see how relaxed I was, Bertie? Can you tell how undisturbed and conscience free I was the entire time Marshawn fingered me; and while he performed oral sex? I totally let myself go. I loved everything he did. Did you notice how unhurried we were; how we savored each other's bodies while we kissed?"

"Yes, I noticed, dear. It was beautiful; absolutely lovely. I could feel your happiness. It was something more than magnificent porn. It was majesty; spiritual majesty."

"Yes, Bertie. That's what it was! I took Marshawn along with me to my special place of immoral freedom, where we no longer cared what his wife said or thought. We traveled to my uniquely wonderful world, where sin and immorality are non-existent; where love and love making is understood and accepted by all who dwell in our same wonderful place. We went where angles, gods, and spirits dwell. I felt myself drifting freely, uncaringly with Marshawn, steadily upward; higher and higher, sensing my inner butterflies fluttering wildly; loving him while his tongue kiss-tapped and caressed my clitoris with ever more ardor and tender fervor.

"Feeling Marshawn's double pearl tipped tongue giving ultra-sensitive under- stoke touchings to my clitoris made my butterflies tumble over and over. They fell all over themselves inside my sex and belly. Those are my special, crazily, spastically erotic, beautifully emotive butterflies. They became deliriously happy, loving butterflies. They were all thrilled to help me enjoy the most wonderful sex any woman could possibly experience. They began whispering, alerting me that my orgasm was about to come.

"My darling, helpful butterflies were kissing the insides of my sex everywhere. My mind lost all conscious thought. When I closed my eyes, I saw a beautiful white light. I believe I saw heaven. I know now that heaven is the word that best describes pure pleasure. I became time suspended in my nirvana state. All I wanted was Marshawn's tongue, with its lovely bottom-side pearl. I wanted it to continue stoking my clitoris while lightly tapping it, driving me crazy; detaching me from everything in the world, except my heavenly sensations of endless pleasure.

"From the deepest recesses of my mind, my butterflies began whispering. They told me how wonderful I would feel while coming. They made me think ahead. I imagined how beautiful I would feel when I held Marshawn's magnificent penis deeply inside my vagina; consecrating what we had just done and what we were about to do. I dreamed how wonderful it would be to hold him, squeeze his beautiful body tightly in my arms while French kissing him; my tongue toying passionately, mindlessly, with his fabulous wonder tongue.

"There you have it, Bertie. My eyes expressed what I felt inside. They were saying I had begun a wonderful romantic journey. They were expressing that realization. Film captured my thoughts about my fantastic partner. My eyes expressed that he was all mine; my lover; not just my porn lover; my real-world lover."

"George, are you listening to this? I want to feel like this, George. Listen to her!" Bertie's eyes were emphatic. They told George they expected nothing less from sexual intercourse than the same feelings Marty expressed. *"Go on, Marty. You were telling us what was going through your mind."*

"Sure Bertie. Well, just like Eve opened Adam's eyes so he could see things for himself, without needing God, I thought I should open Marshawn's mind so he could experience divine love, without

needing churches and bibles. But while Eve's transgression succeeded in removing the blinders from Adam's eyes, she neglected to remove her restrictive fig leaf. Adam didn't experience the ecstasy of shared immorality with Eve. I decided it was time for humanity to advance one step further. I decided to remove my fig leaf for Marshawn. I wanted to lead him much further away from God than Eve had led Adam.

"I helped Marshawn cultivate a desired taste for the juicy forbidden fruit behind my fig leaf. My fruit yearned to express itself. My fruit loved the joys of orgasm. I patiently encouraged Marshawn to experiment with oral sex, until his acquired taste became an insatiable craving for my pheromones. I acquainted him with more unholy pleasuring methods than God could imagine forbidding. I was just beginning my mission to make Marshawn adore me, not God; but me, the fallen immoral, godless woman. Me, his wife-despised, wanton, sacrilegious, iniquitous, debauched; most incorrigible porn star whore in all of whoredom. By the time I completed my selfish task, I knew Marshawn would be my obedient vassal. I'd be able to rely upon him to satisfy my every desire for carnal pleasure.

"Reclining there, relaxed, and untroubled, I was patiently introducing Marshawn to the shared rapture and beautiful ecstasy of unhurried, immoral love. Loving God asks more of me than I can give, Bertie. It's like expecting me to love a stone that doesn't love me back. When Mother abandoned me, I never heard a word from God; so, I've asked myself, what's there to love? God just orders you what to do and what not to do.

"But loving in the unconditional way that I've taught Marshawn to love, lifts love up. Love strengthens when love experiences human intimacy. Intimacy is the ultimate expression of love. Spiritual love works for some people. But, understanding spiritual love is tricky. Spiritual love is fickle, too. Some who preach spiritual love also bugger little boys. I wonder, if one can't practice what one preaches, why

preach? It seems terribly conflicted. I've tried to think about it, but I get confused. I've stopped wasting on it.

"If humans are supposedly God-like, it seems logical that making love brings us closer to God. Intimacy must be ultimate love. It's that special place where a woman can reciprocate her love."

"So, on that day you and Marshawn experienced what you call *unconditional love?*" Bertie was coming to the realization that Marty's idea of love was centered solely upon sex.

"Oh, Bertie, yes, we did! On that day, during that hour, on that film set, Marshawn became my chivalrous knight; the idolizer of my wanton vagina, and the champion of my heart. He honored my emotional need to be pleasured with loving cunnilingus. I knew I'd be the truest love interest of his life for years to come. My eyes were speaking this feeling: That what we were sharing would continue on and on, unconditionally, forever; even taking us off set many times to meet secretly and make more love, privately. My eyes said I was traveling on a sweet, loving journey to romantic heaven with this gorgeous, sensuous man. My eyes spoke those dreamy erotic feelings without me mouthing a single word.

"Now you see my broad, contented smile and my long, dark eyelashes. I've gone from thinking erotic thoughts to thinking about Marshawn and me, and our place in the world. I imagined that every loving tongue stroke that pleasured my clitoris would send a knife stab into Aaliyah's heart. Every time he caressed my clitoris with the underside of his magnificent tongue he honored my inner goddess, lifting me high upon his worship pedestal. I was appreciating his outpouring of deeply committed love, knowing I had converted Marshawn to my immoral way of life.

"I knew Aaliyah would recognize what was happening when she saw his head moving from side to side within my thighs. She'd gasp and shudder when she saw him lavish my clitoris with oral passion. Horrified, she'd observe my vagina while it stole Marshawn's

soul from her and her bibles. Her feeling of helplessness would twist the knife of endless distress in her heart. I assumed she'd eventually accept what happened to her marriage and get over her searing pain; or maybe she wouldn't?" Marty shrugged.

"Behind my closed eyes, I foresaw all the distress and hurt that would come to her when Marshawn separated his life from hers. But I didn't care; and I decided to not think about how she'd deal with it. My thoughts were filled with joy for Marshawn and the choice he was making to liberate himself. I was thinking of all the ways I would be good to him; our travels, our being seen together, our working together on film scripts; and how I would absorb him into my world as one of my closest lovers."

"You sometimes like to inflict hurt on other women, don't you?" Bertie's question scratched Marty's psyche.

"I guess so" Marty shrugged nonchalantly, *"So?"*

"So, where does that come from?" Another, deeper scratch. Bertie was not one to let go.

"Mrs. O'Dell says it's me getting even with the slights I got from the uppity society girls at WEX School. I guess that's where? But, a lot of women set themselves up for their hurts. I often get blamed for what a man wants to do. That's because the woman can't accept responsibility. She placed her man in the position where he wanted to leave her and be with me. I didn't put him there. You're not trying to lay a guilt trip on me, are you?" Marty glared at Bertie. Obviously, she wanted to focus on her feelings of pleasure and conquest, instead of revenge.

"No, not guilt, baby. Of course, not guilt. I know there are winners and losers in the games of love. I was only curious; only trying to understand you. You fascinate me. I want to fully understand how your totally immoral mind sees things; how you understand the world differently from other people, that's all."

"I'm fine with that, Bertie. I'll be as honest as I can," Marty continued. *"You saw that extra measure of joy escape from my eyes when they rolled up and showed only my whites. I couldn't contain that joy. I didn't want to. I wanted to release it. My clitoris was blooming while I was kneading my fingers in Marshawn's hair. The cameras were capturing my bliss. I knew Aaliyah, watching me, would go nearly insane. She'd understand that I now possessed her husband's soul. And she'd realize that he loved treating me, her reviled notorious bad girl; her so-called incorrigible, godless, immoral whore, as his goddess. I knew this moment would destroy their relationship in a fundamental, unchangeable way. She'd see that he wanted to be with me; that he needed me. By not leaving her any room for doubt, she'd know that I had become Marshawn's true love. And that he had tossed her and her bibles away."*

"So, was your joy, your eye roll, coming more from you winning Marshawn over to your ways of immorality, your capture of him; or was the eye roll more your realization that you were destroying another woman's world?"

"Some of both, I think; but, thinking back to that moment, I guess it was more the latter. I was sensing victory. I knew I was winning a contest; and I knew my immorality was winning. I had the most sublime feeling, knowing I was destroying her world. I KNEW when she'd see Marshawn's outpouring of love and devotion for me, romantically performing oral sex like he was, she would realize that he didn't give a flying fuck about her. That would hit her like a cold shower. That's sin lust with a twist of wicked you're observing. I was expressing it through my eyes. Do you understand what you're seeing now?"

"Yes, I do," said Bertie. Someone should name a martini after it. *'It's subtly wicked. It's something that's hard wired inside you. You partner a touch of divine cruelty with your immorality. It's even a bit frightening. It tells me you can be very dangerous under the right circumstances; like you're some kind of caged, vicious predator that needs to be controlled. I suppose that's what enables you to perform so well."*

"I suppose. I guess that's my immoral soul you're seeing. I don't know; but it's completely natural. It leaks out of me through my eyes. It's what makes me, me. It enables me to be who I am; to do the things that I do with men and to their marriages. I should probably change my middle name to 'No Remorse.' But like I said; in those moments on that set, I also believed that his wife would eventually arrive at peace with me, as a woman with sexual desires; and with everything Marshawn and I did together, sexually. If not, I thought: 'too bad for you, Bitch.'"

"You really do put your own pleasures above everything else, don't you?"

"Mostly, yes. I learned that, if I don't put myself first, no one else will. That's where I get my inner toughness, okay? That's why I sometimes can't tell whether I'm having sex for real or whether I'm making love in one of my dreams. Putting my own pleasures first is often very much like living in a dream. Cares about the rest of the world and what it thinks of me just fall away."

"So, immorality is your unconscious driver?"

"Somewhat. It's core to who I am; and I'm often calculating. For example, during that scene, I knew that Marshawn and I would make love many more times that day and beyond. I was already beginning to imagine my lines in our future interactions, on stage and off stage. I knew I had him, so I didn't just lay there with my legs spread, savoring that. I did that, sure. Pleasure is what life is for. But I felt smug, comforted, knowing I had his complete loyalty. I was certain of that. My eyes were expressing my inner glow of self-satisfaction that he would not let his moralizing wife come between us, or affect his love of oral sex. His devotion to slaking my vagina's

thirst for his tongue and his penis was absolute. That meant every-thing. So, I was already thinking ahead to our future times. I was visualizing us performing cunnilingus before a waterfall, and beside a fountain in a flower garden."

"That's your nymphomania again, right? I mean you had to know when and from whom you would be getting sex in the future, right? It's okay, you can tell me."

"Yes, I suppose so. Knowing for sure, or at least being able to imagine and plan for it. I can't help how my mind works." Marty again smiled and shrugged her nonchalant shrug. She was comfortable being honest with Bertie.

"As our film production moved along through our next scenes, where we casually made love in several different positions, we had fabulous orgasms with special meaning for both of us. I knew our performances in those scenes were breathtakingly, erotically beautiful. I felt a sense of accomplishment knowing my memorable love-making scenes were being captured forever, on film.

"Before filming those scenes my mind was in and out of this ethereal dream state. I knew I was going to orgasm again, often. After that second orgasm, we'd moved to scenes where I was scripted to make love with Marshawn in four different positions. My look expressed that I knew I was about to have a beautiful, explicitly erotic, fantasy filled day."

"That's helpful, Marty. Thank you for that. I've got it! Then, after a few minutes elapsed, you positioned your petite feet onto Marshawn's massive shoulders while your legs were widespread. Then, your entire body contracted and you grabbed Marshawn by his hair. You laughed on film while you told him you were enjoying the best clit licking you've ever had in your life. You cried out: 'Yes,' several times. You told him you couldn't wait to make love with him. Your need came through in your voice. It was so emotive; so convincing. You told him you were all hot and wet and you

wanted to get his penis inside you. Was what I think was happening, happening?"

"Yes, Bertie, you were observing another orgasm. I came during our oral sex on the sofa. It was beautiful. I got very expressive. My words were not even coming close to how I felt. I was so anxious to make love with Marshawn, so enamored with him. I was tumbling wildly into love with him. I knew Marshawn was kissing my clitoris hello and kissing his wife good bye. I was not exaggerating when I told Marshawn I was having the best oral sex in my life. He responded the way I love a man's response. He took complete control of my body and my mind.

"Marshawn makes my clitoris feel like it's cascading down a spectacularly beautiful waterfall. That swoon never ends. The further my flow tumbles down, the further it has to fall. My waterfall becomes bottomless. It descends into the abyss of my wantonness. It flows smoothly with its hot, juicy flow gushing over my clit, immersing it within my righteously immoral welcoming of pleasure. When I feel my emotions are reaching the bottom of my waterfall, Marshawn's marvelous tongue finds the bottom of my clit again. His strokes lift my feelings all the way back up, placing them at the top of my waterfall, where my flow begins falling again. His tongue pearl lightly rubs against my clit, releasing my flows again and again; sending them cascading, plunging, heavenly downward; falling down, endlessly down. I gush, flow, and squirt uncontrollably when Marshawn loves me this way.

"Something miraculous happens while my clit experiences its beautiful free fall. I feel a surging, wonderous power. I imagine beautiful stallion horses running around me in circles and leaping over fences; their powerful legs and muscles straining and rippling; making sounds of thunder as their hooves strike the earth. I jump upon the nearest horse. He's a huge white stallion. I tightly hold his mane. I squeeze his flanks hard between my legs. He knows what I

want. He runs faster than before. He catches me up to another horse, a massively chested, chestnut Arabian. I jump onto him and bury my face in his flowing mane; and I clamp my legs hard around his sides. He is strong; unstoppable. We race forward, like the wind. We sail over fences. I jump from horse to horse. Every horse runs faster than the horse before it. I and my horses are panting and sweating like crazy. We are chasing something that's out there, waiting for us. My legs love feeling my horses between them. I squeeze my horses. I feel their power. We all run faster, until...........! Pop! My horses release their power into me! My mind flies away from my horses. It becomes a star that's become trapped in a tight circle, whirling faster and faster around a super massive black hole. I fly past many stars. They become a blur. The blur becomes an endless wall of penises; beautiful, huge, hard penises. I've been delivered to a wonderful place where many penises wait for me. I know they love me. I know they will always love me.

"My mind spins crazily fast now. Marshawn's beautiful tongue begins its circling strokes over my clitoris. I know he knows what he's doing to me. And I want this. Yes, I want this very much. My hips move my sex from side to side and up and down as I push my vagina hard against Marshawn's mouth. His huge hands lift my ass up and pull my vagina hard against his mouth. He holds my body to him like it's a serving plate, while holding my vagina tightly against his lips this possessive way; like I was created to be fitted to him in this exact way.

"The corona of my mind, the outer layer of my fast-moving star begins peeling away from me. I know I'm losing control of my thoughts. Everything inside my mind is being pulled away from me. I'm helpless to stop it from happening. And I don't want to stop it. I feel dizzy and wonderful. My body is thrown against thousands of hard, waiting penises. They welcome me. They have arms that embrace me and love me. I'm incredibly happy that they are there

for me, waiting for me; wanting to love me. The way my thoughts spin away from me is beautiful. I imagine seeing beautiful waterfalls, powerful stallion horses, and an endless wall of loving penises. I forget everything I ever thought of before in my entire life. My mind spins faster and faster. I know my soul is my star. My soul is doomed to fall deeper into depraved immorality. And I love the doom of it. I know all my thoughts and feelings are about to be devoured into the endless eternity that is my coming orgasm. I erupt into Marshawn's mouth. I'm overjoyed. I love him.

"My mind begins tumbling. It summersaults; spins out of control. It follows my clitoris over my endless waterfall, catching up to the abyss at the bottom of my waterfall; becoming one with my sex; collapsing into my lust. My mind and my clitoris and all my feelings unite; concentrate; become a singularly focused, tightly wound bundle that must fly apart. I must POP and go BOOM! Then, it happens! So suddenly! Every one of my mind's other thoughts and feelings it ever had are suddenly ripped away. My mind is stripped clean of everything it ever knew and everything that ever mattered to me. My childhood, my parents, my career in films, my lovers, how I look, what I'm doing tomorrow; every single thing that was ever in my mind is suddenly gone. POOF! Blown away! Everything is swallowed up instantaneously into this super massive black hole that is the love Marshawn is giving me with his marvelous tongue. My orgasm is erupting, growing larger!

"And, Bertie, it happens so suddenly and so violently; I can't find the words to describe it. This shuddering violence riots crazily inside my vagina. First, I have this sudden convulsive implosion when everything I am collapses into a single small place inside my sex. It's only momentary. It's the compression phase before what I instinctively know will rocket my feelings out and away from our universe. Then, FIREWORKS! Massive light-show cannons blast violently through my sex. I feel the fireworks! I experience this unstoppable,

forceful bang, this pop-off explosion of my pressure cooker's lid. My lid blows everything away. I feel a white-hot explosive supernova blast. I flew into it suddenly. It sucked me in and compressed me; coiled me up like a tightly wound spring. And now, in that same instant, I feel myself erupting uncontrollably out of it. It's: 'Oh my God!' and 'Whoa, BOOM!' All at once! It's the pop that makes my whole body shake and tremble. It's the black hole of irresistible love exploding outward into a bazillion places, shattering billions of miles of voided space, all around me, and filling that void with erotic love.

"I've instantly filled the entire universe with my limitless outward exploding flow of love. All who watch this scene see it happening. They know what I'm feeling. Passion explodes out of my control. I writhe and thrust wildly while it's all gushing at light speed into Marshawn's adoring mouth. I've become lust-obsessed; an uninhibited animal. Only this instant in time matters; nothing else matters. There's no abstract thought remaining anywhere, in any fiber of my body. And Marshawn LOVES it! And he loves ME! Our minds join in our swirling, endless ecstasy. He holds on to me. His hands tightly squeeze my ass. He drinks me in, shamelessly feels my love heat; gulps down my passion.

"Our minds know what no one else CAN know. This is the real us! We must have our 'us' together; know it together; share its joy together. Nothing else is in my mind. Just love! I know how deeply and eternally I will always love Marshawn and our moments; what we do together, no matter what anyone else thinks about us. It's exquisite erotic creation art. We DID it! We tripped and fell into our own private world. We created it and loved doing what we did. It was new life and beauty and glory and creation, tearing away the world's emptiness, loneliness, and misery; replacing hopelessness and gloom with beautiful love.

"It's WHY we are human, Bertie. We KNOW we are created for this. We can feel that and we know that it is good. We're here to

make love, have orgasms and love our experiences of having them. While I perform my erotic creation art, fireworks also go off inside my mind! It is then, in those times, on those film sets, that I can feel my reason for BEING a woman. I feel myself come alive. I feel the truest me, blasting away everything that ever held me back; or kept me bottled up inside myself, afraid to let myself go. It's freedom! It's love! It is knowing what I'm living for. It's unapologetically living my primal, wild explosive orgasm!

"And, my explosion doesn't stop! No. It can't stop. It doesn't know how to stop. It goes on and on, while my mind is in its beautiful dream state. It travels through hundreds of billions of miles of voided space, until it settles down to its steady flow of sweetness love. It then becomes a long continuous release flow. It's a wondrous connection to my sense of mental elation. It's nirvana. It's erotic Eros, showing the camera my ultimate expressions of love. Marshawn loves helping me experience this feeling. He feels my feelings with me. He's special to me. I know his mind is dreaming, right along with my mind. We're both dreaming. We know we'll make more beautiful love, soon."

"That's beautiful, thank you Marty. Thank you. Then, after your orgasm from cunnilingus, you have these four expressive copulation scenes with Marshawn. Here we see you in your missionary position, holding yourself open to receive Marshawn's gigantic erection."

"Yes, my sex was positively on fire! This is the scene that begins when I take Marshawn's penis in my hands. His penis is my adorable betrothed; the magnificent love of my life; my sweet catnip happiness that I must have and can't live without. It's my vagina's bridegroom and the best friend she's ever had. I'm overflowing with anticipation because the two of them are about to marry. And here is when Beethoven's Ninth begins. The scene's romantic choreography complements my erotic mood perfectly. My cravings for the explicit intimacy of Marshawn's penis, feeling it touching against my vaginal lips, eager to penetrate me, become intensified. I feel shamelessly

sexual and beautiful, hearing Beethoven's rhythmic beat in the background; those inspiring bumps playing in my mind, helping me visualize my vagina thrusting, bumping, up and up; taking Marshawn's penis deeper inside me; loving every minute of it; willing this joyful ecstasy to never end, as the music and my lusts build toward crescendo."

"George," Bertie gasped, *"I want you to notice how Marty holds Marshawn's penis and praises it for its size and hardness before she guides it into her vaginal lips. Listen to her telling Marshawn what a beautiful man he is, how proud he should be of his adorable penis and how much she's going to love making love with him. She tells him she's already hot and wet inside; how looking at his body and his penis has made her feel that way. Her look tells the viewer she feels completely vulnerable to him. It's communicating that she feels she incomplete, as a woman, without having his penis inside her. That look is convincingly real and sincere. It can't be taught. A woman needs to feel that way, from deeply within herself. That's the only way a woman can create a look like that.*

"Her viewers love hearing her bantering with her partners, George. The way she personalizes sexual intimacy sets her apart from all other adult film stars. She humanizes the entire erotic experience. She creates empathy in her viewers. She makes them feel they share her needs; and they love her for it.

"Watch her eager, full smile while Marshawn first enters her. It's innocent and natural. It tells him she loves the feelings that he's drawing out from inside her by entering her with his penis. Look at her glowing face and pleasure-loving smile as he initially penetrates her. Study her look for a moment. She's in control. She's willful. There's no hesitation. She guides him into her, slowly; little by little; patiently. She knows exactly what she's doing. It's all natural and innocent. Look how her forehead lifts with her facial expression of success when she takes his penis completely inside her. Her joyful

smile lets Marshawn and all her viewers know how pleased she feels after taking Marshawn's immense penis completely inside her. She is Marshawn's completely unrestrained, loving partner in intimate sex.

"Watch now. Can you see how her smile broadens in wonder? She's expressing how thrilled she feels to have all of him inside her. Listen carefully, George. She's whispering that she loves what he's done:

'I love having your penis inside my vagina. He belongs with me. I feel glorious to have him, Marshawn. I want to continue loving him, forever,'

"Now, notice how Marty lifts her pelvis with her willful bumps, meeting Marshawn's thrusts, measure for measure, George. She has marvelous strength and expert muscle control in her abdomen and buttocks; all the attributes of the greatest porn stars. She brings Marshawn with her into perfect copulation rhythm. See how they flow together with the music; how their movements are effortless and flawless? Watch how she uses one hand to stimulate her vagina while Marshawn thrusts; and how she uses her other hand to pinch and fondle her own nipple; while continuing her thrusts, in perfect rhythm with him. She's very expressive here; stimulating herself in two places while copulating; also receiving stimulations from Marshawn's penis through her entire vagina. She personifies a pleasure-seeking woman, George. That defines her character. It's unmistakable. You can see the ecstasy in her face; how she's welcomes Marshawn's thrusts; how infatuated she becomes with each plunge of his penis; how tenderly she feels toward him during the interval seconds between thrusts, while his penis is deep inside her. Yet, she continues to stimulate herself. She never lapses focus on her pleasure. By being so shamelessly intent on pleasure, she causes a reciprocal pleasure driver in Marshawn. He puts his whole heart and soul into pleasuring her. She's a genius, George; a fabulous, pleasure driven porn star.

"She's animated and participatory; beautifully rhythmic with Marshawn during their entire love making experience. Everyone sees how much she loves him. They can see she feels she's floating on a beautiful cloud. People can't fake love, or ecstatic levels of carnal, uninhibited pleasure, George. Marty is simply fantastic here. Her expressively wide mouthed smile showcases her joy this entire time she makes love."

"Bertie, I should tell you: I get more emails and tweets about that segment from this film than any of my other films. This film has almost as many on-line downloads as my breakthrough orgy film."

"Why do you think that is?" Bertie stopped the film and looked, perplexed, at Marty.

"I believe it must be the way I gyrated with my pelvis and bumped my vagina against Marshawn's body, while engulfing his entire penis the way I did, as we choreographed our love making in harmony with the music. While we were lost in our love making, I felt fulfilled and natural. I loved our intimacy. We were like one joined organism. I didn't wear some special expression. You were seeing my natural face. I was being myself. My face expressed how much I loved making love. I don't know why so many fans responded like that. I'll let you see their letters and emails. Maybe they'll give you some insights about how male minds work."

"Or, how they stop working!" Bertie laughed. *"When they see an erotic film, their brains flip a switch to, 'nothing else matters.' You're a switch flipper, Marty! Hee, hee."*

"I guess so. Mrs. O' Dell says it's when the limbic zone takes control of thought. There must be something to it. I got over SIX HUNDRED marriage proposals. It was crazy! One guy offered to give me a new Porsche if I'd go with him to some Canadian fishing lake for a week. Another said he'd give me a ride in his Ferrari if I'd please sit on his face for five minutes. Another promised he'd let me have three

cows from his ranch herd, if I'd spend an afternoon with him. What did he think I'd do with three cows?

"There was this really sweet offer from some boy. He had to be under-aged. He promised he'd give me his stamp collection if I'd sneak into his house while his parents were away, and let him kiss me and feel me up while we watched one of my movies. He told me he thought my tits were beautiful. I don't know how kids manage to see adult erotica, but they do. I guess they're smarter than their parents at using technology.

"I also heard from about fifty women who watched this film with their husbands. They said their arousal was heightened and their husbands became more romantic than before. I heard from some cranks, too. I always get those. About twenty women said I was responsible for destroying the country's morals. They told me I should be ashamed of myself, and the police should lock me up. Two others said they were writing their congressional representatives urging legislation to censor me and ban my films."

"Crazy!" Bertie nodded to confirm what her intuition already told her. *"I knew it. The offers from those men are proof that sex sells; and some men lose their minds over it. What did you do with those offers?"*

"Well, I never respond to requests from underage boys. I toss those. I forward the others to my Premium Service. They sort through them, screen out the nut cases and look at the others for possible Premium Membership clients."

"I'll look at them. Maybe they'll clue me to something we can do better or do more of to drive more sales."

"Thanks."

"Sure, now let's study more film."

Bertie hit the play arrow and the film resumed. She placed her hand on George's leg. She moistened her lips and widened her eyes. She fantasized she was nibbling Marty's nipples. Marty noticed the lust in her coach's face.

'She's perfect to coach me, all right,' thought Marty. 'She has the heart and soul of a whore, just like me. Never judgmental, always constructive, the polar opposite of a moralizer; she loves all forms of Eros. I love her. We are a perfect match.'

"Watching Marty making love stimulates my own sexuality, George." Bertie leaned with her thoughts into her husband and kissed his neck. She moved her hand higher until it arrived over George's penis. She whispered to George:

"I feel gushes right along with her, George; inside my own sex. I feel myself experiencing how she gushes with pleasure. I'm hot and wet inside, like she is. Watching her awakens that within me. The pleasure that shows in her face simply cannot be faked, George. Marty loves how beautifully Marshawn is doing her. I can just imagine how wonderful her vagina feels while his monster-sized shaft glides back and forth over her clitoris. She's thrilled to be doing him. I'm imagining I'm experiencing her same feelings. No other adult film actress does that for me. We're watching intimate artistry performed by the ultimate best, George.

"Watch her now, George." Bertie's fingers began gently stroking George's penis through his pants.

"She has mounted Marshawn's penis while facing him. Now notice how perfectly she controls her twerks with Marshawn's huge penis inside her. She is sensational at wooing a penis. Her twerks are performing a sensual serenade. She makes my mouth water. Notice the pleasure she derives from Marshawn fondling her breasts? When he pinches her nipples, an extra tickle of joy radiates from her smile. See it? See her nodding to him, encouraging him to do more of that? She loves it. She loves that extra stimulation he's giving her. The two of them are so erotically compatible, George. They're beautiful together."

Bertie stopped the film again. *"George, I feel her feelings. It's exactly like a woman should feel. That's special. She reaches through the screen and touches my heart. She takes my breath away. I feel the same way she feels. She makes a woman realize how good it feels to lose her inhibitions. I cannot teach that. No one could. It's natural, from inside her. She's perfected empathy projection. She blending honest erotic feelings with her experiences with many penises, while performing her love scenes. And, it's all natural!*

"I'll bet you had many former partners that disappointed you before you found compatible ones. Isn't that true, Marty?"

"Oh yes, Bertie, definitely. There are hundreds of men I won't ever work with again. They don't do a thing for me. I can't get myself excited about making love with them and I can't make a film work if they are in it. There are pigs and brutes who have no idea what it takes to make a woman feel pleasure. Even with men I like, there's a great deal of trial and error involved before getting my feelings to express naturally. What you see in this film with Marshawn is special. I must feel an emotional connection to my male partner to make a great film like this one. About twenty male partners give me that feeling. I prefer to work with those men, because I know how good they are. There's probably another fifty or sixty men that I can get excited about while performing. It just takes me longer to heat up during my scenes with them. Lots of what happens in the early parts of those shoots gets cut."

"Would you like to limit your partners to your favorite ten or so?"

"Yes, very much so, it's so much more enjoyable to make love with men I already love."

"Then we'll do that. I'm not one who believes you need a new man for every film. I think what's most important is that we do each film in a way that makes you look sensational. The viewers

are much more interested in you than the men anyway. Trust me on that. Now, let's study more film.

"Here, George, watch her speed up the action. First, she moves her hips up and down slowly, engulfing Marshawn's entire shaft deeply inside her. Notice how that makes Marshawn's penis extremely hard. Look how stiff that penis becomes, George! Good lord! That's the stiffest prick I've ever seen! No wonder she goes ga-ga over Marshawn.

"That penis knows nirvana. Now she rocks her pelvis while gyrating slowly. That penis is feeling sensuality beyond anything it's ever known. It loves what she's doing. It's lost in love. As big and strong as it is, it can't resist what she's doing. It's smitten by the feelings she's imparting to it. It must have her. It must submit to her and pleasure her, until she stops this erotic movement. It's captivated."

Bertie stopped the film. She unzipped George's pants and briefly mouthed his penis. When his penis became tall and firm, she hit play again and returned her attention to the screen; but her fingers continued their mindful stroking.

"Watch now, George. See her twerks speed up and her pelvic rhythms quicken? Notice. Now she slides her vagina only over the very top of Marshawn's penis, going down quickly over its head, tightening her vaginal muscles, then lifting up quickly; but never allowing the very tip of his penis to escape her lady lips. That's expert penis control, George. By moving more rapidly up and down upon the most sensitive part of the penis, her vagina communicates what it craves.

"She's letting the penis know that she believes in it; and that she knows that it has the strength to satisfy her cravings. She's expressing to it that she believes it will perform beautifully after she plunges it deeply inside her. By pausing her twerks while performing Kegel squeezes, she's telling the penis she will greatly appreciate the pleasure

it's about to give her. This is a defining moment, George. It's where the woman takes control of the coital experience. People who love each other intimately translate their feelings with physical communication this way, George."

"Bertie," interjected Marty, "here comes the scene where Marshawn lets it all go. Watch him. He starts spurting wildly. It happens as we're finishing up this scene. We've just changed positions. The director has me standing on one leg; Marshawn's arms are around my neck. He's kissing me while I'm grating my pelvis and bumping his penis with his thrusts. One cameraman got on the floor and filmed from underneath, looking up. He captured my vagina doing sensuous gyrations, stimulating Marshawn's penis. He captured the moment when it started shooting wildly out of control inside me. It was amazing timing, and fantastic film work. Marshawn was spurting volumes of cum as Beethoven's Ninth reached its climax."

"Yes, I see it. Marshawn's semen flows out of you in spurts, while he continues thrusting. His penis became an insatiable, semen-spurting lust fountain, shooting into your vagina. It's stunning; breathtakingly immoral; very arousing. Beautifully done!"

"Thank you, Bertie. Beethoven had us in mind. He wrote that piece for our most intimate moment. Now, watch Marshawn. He totally went off script toward the end of the piece. He swallowed me into his massive arms and kissed and hugged the stuffing's out of me. That was completely unscripted. Everyone could see we were no longer making porn. We were making passionate love. His penis was all the way inside me. I loved being in his arms, hugged against his powerful chest. I melted. My heart melted. I could only think that I was safe; that nothing else mattered in the entire world. Marshawn can become so expressive! He's also incredibly physical. I become powerless when he's like that. I want him to do whatever he wants. In those moments, neither of us could help ourselves. Our minds were saying: 'Screw the filming, we're in love.'

"George," Bertie squealed, *"let's watch that segment again, before they went off script. In the process of satisfying her own cravings Marty helps Marshawn's penis have that spectacular ejaculation; and she continues her Kegel squeezes and her twerks, driving his penis out of its mind with pleasure until she completely drains its semen reservoir.*

"She occasionally plunges her vagina completely over his penis until her pelvis encompasses Marshawn's entire shaft. With his penis engulfed within her she rubs her vagina against his lower abdomen, letting Marshawn know that she loves the soul of the man who's attached to the penis. It's similar to how cats bump your hand with their heads, George. It is one living being displaying honest affection to another. Marty was subtly communicating her romantic love to Marshawn.

"Apart from strictly following the film's script, she communicates with her body touches to assure Marshawn that she loves him. Did you see that? Could you feel it, George? She expressed her feelings of genuine love for Marshawn there. It was beautiful! Touching! It's precious, loving intimacy. We saw romantic love express itself within an erotic film! So beautiful! So lovely!

"A woman can only express her love and work her vagina that way if she feels true love for her partner. That's what is so fantastic about Marty's film work, George. She loves her partners! It comes through in every one of her films.

"She's been on top of Marshawn for a while now. She's moving faster and faster. Marshawn is receiving rapid stimulations. She's twisting and gyrating her pelvis and hips. The top half of Marshawn's penis is experiencing sensational ecstasy. There's not a penis anywhere in this world that can resist that level of intense stimulation, George. She has total control of Marshawn's penis. It had to surrender to her. It had no choice. Watch. It's about to lose its mind and have an explosive eruption. Look closely, here. She's bringing it

to ejaculation. See her twerks quickening? She's only doing the very tip of his penis. See?

"Look closely at her face. There's her wide open-mouthed smile, again. See her run her tongue across her lower lip? Marshawn is about to explode inside her. She senses it. She's in her element, George. She's joyous. She feels Marshawn's pre-eruption build up. She has an uncanny sense for her partners' release times. She's masterful. That's the result of her experiences and her concentration, George. She understands penises. Watch closely now. I'll slow motion the frames. Did you notice that Kegel squeeze on her upstroke? Did you catch it? Could you tell she was doing that? That slight drop of her jaw and relaxation of her facial muscles were synchronized with her up-twerk and her slight pelvic twist. That's how you can tell, George. That's what gives it away. You're witnessing a spectacular performance. That squeeze coaxed Marshawn's prostate to relax. It sent his gland the signal; told it to ejaculate its reservoir of semen. She let that gland know she wanted it to release. She's uncanny, George. She totally understands the male sex apparatus. She primed his cannon to fire its semen shot. This is the most beautiful intimate film artistry I've ever witnessed, George. It's a subtle romance dance between a woman in love, and the object of her love. It's fascinating and fantastic.

"After her erotic stimulation, the penis can't hold back any longer. It is in a delirium state of pre-ejaculation pleasure. Ejaculation is imminent. She plunges down on it now, taking it deeply inside her. She's Kegeling again, giving it squeezing sensations over its entire shaft. That penis feels nirvana now. It's lost all willpower. It feels the sensation of sublime surrender. It experiences rapture. Pleasure, romance, and love for Marty overwhelm it like a tidal wave. It would love to stay inside her vagina forever, basking in her sensuous, tickling slippery warmth. But it can't.

"Something was happening inside Marshawn's mind at this same time. He's achieved singular oneness with Marty, like when a star

crosses over its event horizon and plunges unstoppably into a super massive black hole. Marshawn has become joined completely with Marty. They are now one living being. He's been absorbed into her body and her soul and her love. He cannot escape her. He loves her. There's an intense bonding taking place, George. He is her knight. She is his queen. He's experiencing adoration and wonder. His soul enters her deep abysmal; her insatiable essence, like a star plunging into its eternity, its irresistible black hole.

"Marshawn loses the man he once was. There's no turning back, no escape from the reality he's flying into. And he doesn't care. He welcomes his new love and his new life. He loves his new becoming, and what he's doing with Marty; and, he LOVES her. You are seeing unequivocal romantic love, George. That's it! That's the whole enchilada. That's the end of the story…...for his wife! But not for Marty. Her life with him is just beginning. Marty has captured his love, his soul, and his life. She understands what she's done and she's not about to let go. Marshawn reaches up, puts his arms around her and pulls her tightly into his embrace. He loves what's taken place between them. It's magical. He loves being consumed into the eternal wonders of this woman we have sitting here beside us, George. He's in love, George. 'I love you,' he whispers to her.

"He completely gave up all of himself in that instant and ejaculated the essence of himself, his life force, into his goddess. Her viewers instinctively understand they are witnessing romantic love. It's why they love Marty so much. It explains their intense loyalty. It's why they buy every one of her films and watch them over and over. It is why so many men clamor to join her premium membership club. They want what they see for themselves. They want Marty!

"It's the WHY, George. It's why men, like Marshawn, leave their families for her. It's why many give her everything they have. It's love. It's obsession with her erotic love making. At its primal core, it is the physical expression of beautiful art.

"It's the same awe men felt while standing in the Lascaux caves in France, worshipping the animal paintings on the cave's ceilings and walls. It is the worship of her artistry, George. It's why they pay to acquire her most recently released film. It's why her members must see her, again and again. They feel compelled to return to her; and worship her, like those cave worshipers returned to those paintings. They know there is no more beautiful artistry. They obsess over her performances. It's the same reason people pay fortunes to possess a Rembrandt. She elicits those same deep feelings of awe. Her lovers and her fans MUST have her. They are addicted to her films. They can't help themselves.

"That's what fine, exquisite art does, George. It brings out peoples' deepest emotions. It's not that Marty's followers have dirty minds. That's not what's happening here. That's a popular misconception about porn, spread by religious leaders. The dirty mind narrative is religion's response to the allure of natural artistry. By making people feel guilty about leaving the flock to worship porn stars, the religions attempt to keep their flocks corralled. But their messaging conflates and confuses the point."

"Which is?"

"People keep returning to Marty's films to recharge their profound emotional connection to her romantic love making and her exceptional artistry. The religions cannot keep people away from porn; no more than they can prevent people from going to an art gallery. Deeply inside their souls, many people realize that they need to see porn.

"People NEED those human connections to intimacy to make their lives meaningful, just like those prehistoric cave dwellers needed those cave paintings to lift their spirits when things were gloomy; or when they felt spiritual gratitude for being alive; or when life's struggles traumatized them. Intimacy is Marty's medium for expressing awe inspiring artistry.

"Intimacy art is humanity's pinnacle art form, George. It rises above all other art forms. And Marty's performances are the ultimate excellence in performing that artistry. Her films are perfect for our times, George. Look around and see! Civilization is collapsing all around us. People need to believe in something that transcends these chaotic times. That something is erotic romantic love.

"Now, George, see that immense release of cum flowing out of Marty, down over Marshawn's penis. It's from his sudden explosion. She had to feel like hot fireworks were shooting off inside her. Am I right, Marty?"

"Yes, absolutely you're right, Bertie. Yes. It felt like a volcanic lava blast. That pretty much describes how it felt." Marty's smile remembered the transformative moment.

"George, see Marty's facial muscles light up? Notice how her forehead rises in amazement? That's Marty feeling Marshawn's massive release. She loves this climactic moment! Her face is glowing with pure pleasure. She KNOWS Marshawn experienced intense pleasure. She knows he felt bombs bursting in air! She knows. A woman knows that moment, George. She feels it. Every life force; every emotion; every thought Marshawn had pent up inside himself, he shot into her at that moment. It was a STUNNING cum shot. He released everything into her. I loved watching her perform this scene with him.

"Every time she makes love with a new partner, she reveals some nuance about her techniques that I never appreciated before. She's mastered the art of intimacy. Watch, you'll see a very tender side of her next, George. After she made love with Marshawn, she lies next to him. Watch how she French kisses him; how she puts her hand on his heaving chest; then touches his face lovingly with that hand, while her other hand strokes his penis and fondles him. She loves to touch, George. She understands the importance of touching. See how she smiles contentedly while she's kissing him? Those are

real emotions we're witnessing, George. She loves Marshawn. She's a beautiful woman in love. She honestly and freely gives her love throughout all her films. It shows.

"*Now listen carefully, George.*" Bertie turned her eyes to her husband. "*I'm going to turn up the volume here so you can hear Marty whispering to Marshawn. Could you catch what she said, George? Did you hear her tell Marshawn that she loves him?*"

"Yes, I heard her." George was matter of fact.

"*You heard her, but did you notice the inflection of her voice, George?*"

"*What do you mean?*"

"*She spoke from her heart, George. That was no automaton speaking, like someone reading from some script. I caught it. It was a plea from Marty to Marshawn to also love her. It was a deeply felt, honest communication.*"

"*Okay, So?*"

"*Oh George, must I explain everything? Can't you see? Even though she's a porn star; even though she makes love with many men in the course of a week; she needs to be in love with a man who loves her back. She's heart and soul a woman, George. She needs romantic love. Her voice cries out for that romantic love.*"

"*Ah, okay. I see what you mean.*" Enlightened now, George suddenly realized that Marty was a woman who needed romantic love. The young girl sitting beside him became human, a persona outside of her screen character, a living soul with real emotional needs.

"*Good George. Now listen to what she says next. Do you hear her ask Marshawn if he could please perform in some more orgy theme films with her as the star centerpiece? She whispered she'd love creating an orgy film outdoors in a forest, by a stream; or on a boat; or next to a pool, lake, or ocean. She's planting seeds in Marshawn's imagination. She wants him to visualize future scenes where they'll work together. She wants more time with Marshawn; more reasons why they need to stay in communication; more reasons why they need to see each other. This is a woman in love, George. Her voice is very low now. She tells Marshawn that she loves feeling a soft breeze and hearing sounds of nature while she makes love; and if he could please include Phillip, Stephon, Melvin, and Alvin, because she loved making love with the five of them so much; and that she falls asleep many nights wishing she was having all five of them? Do you understand what she's doing to Marshawn's mind, George? She's playing his mind forward; helping him think about their next rendezvous; keeping an enticing vision in his mind. So, when he's not with her, she'll have him thinking about being with her. And she wants those same five orgy partners because she knows when they are on set, she'll have most of her intimate sex time with Marshawn, not the others. She wants more of what she experienced before."*

"Thanks, Bertie, I guess there's a lot I don't understand about women." George acknowledged his wife's observation.

"Marty," Bertie heard Marshawn whisper one final thing and then she heard Marty saying something. But their exchange was inaudible. *"What just passed there, between the two of you? What was said?"*

"Oh, Bertie, that was Marshawn's guilt resurfacing. He whispered that what we were doing was immoral. And I whispered back to him that there was nothing immoral about what we do; nothing immoral at all. I told him that the entire world is immoral, but not us; love cannot possibly be immoral. I told him I had just experienced the most wonderful seamless transition from a heavenly oral sex orgasm to a second marvelous explosive orgasm, courtesy of his adorable penis. I told him he needed to believe me when I told him that I would love him forever. That's when I collapsed my body onto his and French kissed him again. That's when he held me tightly and told me he loved me completely, no matter what."

"Thanks, Marty. Those words were definitely not in the film script, George. What that tells us is Marty will always want more sex, and more partners; and, she never feels guilt about the race or marital status of her partners, or the scenes she creates during her love making. Most importantly, she needs love. When she knows she's loved, she can do anything. Isn't that true, Marty?"

"Yes, Bertie, so true. I can compartmentalize my love making with all my other partners; but when I'm making love with a man I truly love, I can't compartmentalize that. That love consumes me. I can't help it. I don't want to help it or contain myself in any way. I want my love to flow. I want my lover to feel all my love."

"Your thinking is new to me," George joined the discussion. *"I'm not understanding the difference, in your mind, between being in love with a man and making love with a man. Is there any difference?"*

"Oh, goodness yes, George," replied Marty, *"When I'm in love with a man I know about him, or at least I believe I do. I know what's going on inside his mind and his heart. I know about his stresses and worries. I know about his family life and his childhood. He's a real person with needs and feelings. When I make love with him, I'm making love with the inner man, with his soul and his goals and his fears; everything that makes him who he is. So, I'm making love with a persona that has a soul and whose soul needs my love. That's different from making love with a man who happens to be a porn partner or a client of my Private Member Service. Those men are men with needs, too. I understand that; but I don't know what their needs are. I only know that they have lust cravings to make love with me, which I accommodate. I try very hard to impart my loving feelings to them, because I want them to come back to me; but I do not have the same inner empathy for them that I have for a man whom I'm in love with. Does that help?"*

"Yes, I think so," George pressed on. "But when you say you're in love with a man, that doesn't mean that your love for that man excludes the possibility that you are also in love with another man, does it?"

"Goodness no, George! In fact, I'm presently in love with Bob, Carl, Jimmy, my twins, although I rarely see them anymore, as well as Marshawn and some special Premium Members; and with two of my lady friends, who also happen to be porn stars. Does that help?"

"Yes, that helps. Thank you. But I must ask: How do you keep these lovers from becoming possessive? I mean, how do you not stir up jealousy?"

"Oh, George, that's simple. I'm completely honest with all my loves. They all know I'm pan amoral. They all know that no one has exclusive rights to me or my love. I'm totally honest with all of them about this. I've told them that I'm completely immoral and that I love them freely and openly, without any guilt about slighting any of my other loves."

"And that works for you; for every one of your loves?"

"Oh yes, George. Can't you see how beautiful it is to be honest that way? I'm the opposite of the religious types with all their taboos and hypocrisy. I don't go around pretending to be faithful and then have affairs behind my partners' backs. I don't pretend to be pure and holy and then sneak around with prostitutes. I live an openly immoral life. I'm unashamed of it. I don't hide it under a rock. I'm proud of it. And let me tell you something else, George."

"What?"

"My loves all love me for my openness and honesty about it. In fact, that's why they love me as intensely as they do. Some have wives. But they do not have the same closeness and intensity of intimacy with their wives as they do with me. They love me because I'm openly immoral. They know that being openly immoral is a higher

morality that being moral and having all sorts of neurosis because of it. Understand?"

"Yes, I think I do," nodded George. "One more thing: how often do you see these lovers?"

"That varies. I try to see Bob every night I possibly can. I need his closeness. We stay at each other's places. Others, I see based on our schedules. I coordinate with them about the when's and where's. Carl is unique among my lovers. He has tremendous sexual talents. I'd like to see him more than I do. I try to keep him on a leash. He has to show me fifty thousand dollars in commissions before I reward him with a weekend away from his wife. So, with Carl, our meetings are intermittent. But sometimes I also have this overpowering craving to feel him inside me. When I get it bad, I call him and we meet in a hotel. I don't charge him for those times."

"Well, there you have it, George," declared Bertie. "Marty truly loves who she is and what she's doing with her life. I'm smitten by her honesty, George. That's rare in today's world. I'm totally in love with her. I want her to be part of our family. She's all we have, George. She means everything to me.

"She's unique, George. Trust me about this. We'll never regret it. We're doing the right thing by taking her into our lives. She's for real. We're understanding the real Marty. We're learning all about her. Her lovers all want to work with her, again and again. They see what I see. Making love with her is their ultimate pleasure. I can see that in their faces. They know what I know. They are all in awe of her for the loving vibes she gives off. That's something else I can't teach, George."

With the mention of 'vibes,' George took his eyes from the screen. His eyes met Marty's. She noticed that George noticed her; but now in a different way; not as a porn star performing on screen, but as a woman in the here and now. Her eyes paused their gaze. Quickly, nearly imperceptibly, her eyes telegraphed their deliberate reactive message to George. Marty's signal was rapidly sent; fascinating, nuanced and, most certainly, spontaneous. She released it so blindingly fast that it caused George to wonder whether it was a natural refocusing to a new distance of vision sight, or whether it contained profound implications.

Without any rise of forehead or eyebrows, Marty's eyelids opened slightly more than before. George, being perceptive, recognized it. Her eyeballs had magically enlarged and slightly protruded. Their directed beam released a high energy pulse; and then, in the space of, at most, a quarter second's time, her eyelids resumed their previous opening distance and the protrusion vanished. The faintest of smiles lifted her lips, then disappeared. Her eyes now resumed their steady gaze.

'*What was that?*' wondered George. '*What did I just see? Was she flirting with me? Did Bertie notice that? No, I guess not. She's fixated on the screen. Women! What did that eye signal mean? It happened so fast! It seemed natural, but it really wasn't. It was deliberate. It had to be. Her disguised smile confirmed it.*'

But what could George do about it? He was in no position to chase a young woman. His whole world was joined to Bertie's world. Besides, Marty was twenty-five years younger than him. He was old enough to be her father. Thoughts raced through his mind: '*Dare I even think of a romance with her? Am I denying nature by not thinking this way? Dare I betray Bertie by even thinking I could defy nature? Perhaps this young minx understands the situation between Bertie and me better than we, ourselves, understand it?*'

Frightening thoughts and insights reverberated through George's mind. He could not talk with Bertie about them, nor could he pause the film to think without distraction. He sat, looking at the screen; seeing Marty naked, displaying her irresistible sexuality while in her performing mode; yet he could not help but wonder what mysterious feminine wonder sat beside him: '*What salacious promiscuity does Marty keep hidden beneath her skirt and panties?'*

Since losing his only child, George had struggled to overcome his disinterest in life. He tried keeping up his routines, as if nothing had changed. He called his consortium friends and board members, trying to feel enthused about new ventures. He called his brokers and project managers, trying to stay engaged; keeping his fingers on the pulse of things. But those were efforts without purpose. And now Bertie was hitching her star to this perky tart, this porn star who had come into their lives out of all disbelief! But the young minx did something with her eyes in one split second that months of focused effort had not done. She had piqued his interest. He had lived this past year; but he had stopped living. And now, there it was! He glimpsed a spark of life again! That spark had shot out to him from the eyes of the young woman. He noticed it. Clearly, it was already affecting him. But what was he to make of it? What was he to do about it? He wasn't sure.

His morals? Could he trash them? Should he allow the iniquitous porn star to hack his morality into tiny bits? He was watching porn with her and Bertie. Awkward though it seemed at first, it now seemed natural enough. His inhibitions had fallen away rather readily. But to actually involve himself with a porn star? That seemed likely to be an entirely different matter. Might it not take him from a mere vicarious interest to a visceral interest; and then might it not proceed all the way to perdition? *'Maybe it will,'* thought George; *'but why not? What have I got left to live for?'*

George imagined Marty's lips touching his for their first kiss. He imagined her softness and warmth when he touched her; how it might feel to hug her delightfully responsive flesh. A heat rush suddenly raced through the lower reaches in the back of George's brain. It came on with an intensity that resembled those times when he intentionally overdosed on niacin, his B3 vitamin. What had happened? In less than a blink of her eyes, the young vixen had dazzled him; unleashed his brain flood. The heat flood raced through his brain. It was a primal, animal thing. He had no control of it. He couldn't make it stop. It was increasing; intensifying. He could not deny it was happening and he couldn't shut it down. Was it possible that his blood understood that the young sex star desired him; or possibly, was there something about him that his primal instincts knew she needed? Possibly? But their age difference! His cognitive mind wrestled with his limbic mind. Turmoil! Uncertainty! *'Why is this happening? I could be her father!'*

'Possibly,' George's reasoned mind struggled, *'she covets what Bertie has? Possibly, could she secretly want to entwine her life with an older man's? I've heard of those things happening. That's the Sugar Daddy game. Yes, that's what they call it. I am holding up rather well, as this aging thing goes. I look distinguished and successful. And I am! And the old mug, when shaved with a good razor and after shave is applied, looks damn good to most women, I dare say. I've seen testimonials about hundred-year-old men and their seventy-five-year-old wives, where they both swear that they've been madly in love for fifty years. So, I suppose it is possible. But is that something she'd really want? She has to notice that Bertie is stroking my penis. Is that stoking her envy? Could her wants be that base; that simple? No! I don't think so. I think she sees more in me than that! She's articulate, perceptive, highly intelligent, and emotive. She's certainly not some simpleton. I suppose there's something to her nympho aspect. That explains the porn films and her natural promiscuity. Obviously, she loves sex. But she seems anything but base.'*

George's mind was on a merry go round. He flattered himself, blurring his focus from what motivated Marty's signal. Ironically, Bertie was addressing the emotive effects of the porn film they were watching on their home theater screen. He needed to get his mind back on the business aspects of pornography; specifically,

Marty's pornography. The gorgeous nymph, and her reason for sending him that unexpected titillating eye flash, would, he assured himself, reveal her true intentions in the fullness of time.

"*We have in Marty a woman who gets 'eros rush' whenever she sees her partner's penis or whenever she knows she's in a situation where she's likely to have sex.'* Bertie continued in her authoritative instructor mode. She wasn't missing a beat. '*It's a primal thing, George. It's a sudden flooding of the limbic zone that overwhelms the rest of Marty's brain and renders the rest of her brain unable to process any thoughts, other than making love.*

"*It's an overwhelming sensation that comes on in a fervent, sudden rapture. She knows she must fuck. She's captured by her own limbic mind, completely in the powerful grasp of eros. Nothing else matters to her now; nothing but making love. It's very close to penis lust, which is a natural limbic thing for a woman. It usually manifests as a result of a woman's eros attraction; but a female's penis lust is not the essential expression of her eros. Eros is a uniquely binding, entwining of souls between lovers, sort of sensation need that occurs only in females of the human species. Other animals, even other primates, do not experience anything like it. And, with Marty, eros comes easily and instantaneously.*

"*EROS has become Marty's natural state of mind. It's not an occasional thing with her. It's nearly a constant thing. Possibly she got this way from conditioned reflexes to make love, to compensate for the psychological pain of her abandonment. Possibly it's a physical alteration of her normal female chemistry. Possibly it is a combination of those two factors. I don't know why she is this way, but her condition is a beautiful, precious treasure. With Marty, and other women like her, penis lust invariably attaches to eros. She's a natural, erotically romantic lover. We must love Marty with all our hearts, George; and we must ALWAYS be good to her, George; and we must be thankful to God that she came into our lives.*"

OUR OWN

George nodded. His eyes found Bertie's. *"We will love her like she's our own daughter, Bertie. I know she means that much to you."*

"Oh! Yes, we WILL! Oh, THANK YOU so much, George! Bertie's excitement was effusive. *"I'm so happy you agree. I LOVE you, George. We'll ALL be so HAPPY together! We'll introduce her to all our close friends. We'll treat her royally and we'll pamper her and we'll love her and we'll love her beautiful, adorable vagina. You know, George, beneath Marty's external character layer, beneath her promiscuity and lack of concern for Aaliyah's feelings, I'm certain Marty is a sweet, innocent little girl, who is all loving and caring about others.*

"I'm certain she would never, ever cause harm to anyone, except when she competes for a man's love. We'll give her anything and everything she wants, George, and WE'LL JUST LOVE HER! I love when you let me have what I want, George. I'll finally have a daughter I can love again and work with again, George. I'm just going to LOVE her and I'll LOVE her more and more, every day. You're so good to me! I LOVE you, George. You're a FABULOUS husband George.

"George, tell Marty you love her," bubbled Bertie.

George turned his face to Marty. His eyes sparkled like a boy's mischievous glowing crystals. But his mind wasn't visualizing her face. It was recalling her insatiable sex craven vagina from several different copulation scenes, with white semen flowing from her fleshy pink vaginal lips. His mind felt unbridled wild desire to kiss that same vagina; kiss and adore it; marry his face to its wantonness; lick it with wild abandon; stretch his tongue into its deeper reaches and caress its clitoris; confirming to her sex organ that he had become possessed by it and that he adored what it did to the penises that had ejaculated their semen inside it. He could barely rein in control of his mind. He was smitten with lust for Marty and her fabulously immoral Miss Muffy. He craved to partake of Muffy's delicious tastes and erotic pleasures. Barely of sound mind, he responded coherently to Bertie's command: *"You love her."*

Marty touched George behind his neck. *"Her loves you back."* Her eyes giggled back to George's. She had read his mind. She knew it was only a matter of time.

George's eyes quick scanned the sensuous bundle sitting beside him. His mind climbed a cloud. It saw a verdant valley; more beautiful than those the early explorers saw when they crossed mountains. His penis stirred. It was telling him something:

'*Use flatters her. She's even more beautiful in person than on film. Don't lose your mind over her. That lily creamy whiteness isn't innocence you're seeing. Imagine how many minds she's enslaved in those arms; how many loves she's captured away from their homes. The part of Bertie that needs to be mother pretends she's Amanda; but have no illusions about the bisexual side of Bertie; or about how you'll fit into this. You know you both want her.*

'*Remember, you're there to enable her to practice her techniques; and Bertie will coach and critique her. That's okay. I'll get myself up for her. I'll take and give the best she's ever had. But remember, while you're tonging her ear; and while you're using two or three fingers to heat her up, that her ears have heard many a soul pour out his guts to her, telling her they couldn't live another moment without her. While you're squeezing her ass with both hands, as you're sliding me, Mr. Wonderful, deeply inside her, don't lose your mind over her. Keep in mind that hundreds of other hands have been there before yours; and hundreds of penises have already been where you're going to be putting me, too. So, when she oohs and aahs about how much she loves the way we're fucking her, remember that others heard it all, before you. Be careful with her. She drinks down marriages like teenagers gulp soda pop.*

'Just remember, you're getting all too human when you start believing that she loves you. She doesn't, even if she tells you that she does. Not really; not in the same way that Bertie loves you. Remember, you're doing this for Bertie's ego. You're being the good, dutiful husband; with a kinky twist involving sex privileges. You know your Bertie. Bertie needs to be number one; even more than Marty does. She doesn't need the money; neither do you or Marty. You're in this for the challenge of getting top honors for Bertie, period. Do not fall out of love with Bertie over her. Love them both, but love Bertie for real.'

"Looks like we'll need to take turns with her." George smiled to Bertie. His mind had switched channels, from listen to penis, to talk to wife.

CHAPTER FIVE

Hark in thine ear: change places; and, handy dandy, which is the justice and which is the thief? (Shakespeare: King Lear)

She did not seduce, she ravished. (George Meredith: Diana of the Crossways)

Shake hands forever, cancel all our vows ...Be it not seen in either of our brows, that we one jot of former love retain. (Michael Drayton: Sonnets, Idea)

STEALING GEORGE

Marty's hand lifted George's chin to her face. She giggled when she kissed him. He noticed her tongue had penetrated his lips. His penis strengthened.

"No, George, you'll share me. You'll both have me at the same time. We'll have much more fun that way." George took a deep breath when he heard Marty's soft whisper. He silently told his penis to have no illusions about the coming sessions with Bertie and Marty. He and Mr. Wonderful were there to help the young whore fine tune her tradecraft; not to fall in love with her.

"You're quite the minx, aren't you?" George smiled at the face twenty-five years younger than his own.

"Yes, definitely! Shameless and uninhibited. Whore to my core, always." She giggled while giving George his second kiss, this one lingering slightly longer than the first. Marty's hand brushed over George's awakened friend, as if to let it know she also heard

its cautions; but that she would take what she wanted, when she wanted it. She would not follow other peoples' rules. She would not be deterred.

"Ever have regrets?" George's eyes looked for the young woman's soul, past her salacious bravado.

"A couple; yeah, I guess so." Marty shrugged her shoulders. She was resigned to reality. Her regrets were seemingly falling further into her past where it was getting harder to retrieve them.

"Would you like to talk about it?" George was genuine. He opened his fatherly side to Marty, something he had not done since Amanda died.

"Some, I guess." Marty gave a smaller shrug. *"Mainly about four boys I loved. Wish I could undo what happened."*

"You corrupted them?"

"Much worse." Her eyes went wistful, looking back into her memory to scenes of years past; watching the five of them dancing, bumping, kissing, sexing together. A faint smile appeared on her lips; the sweetness taste of her lost innocent loves revealed its persistence in her memory.

"Worse, how?" George's thought puzzled the smile's contradiction. *"If worse summons bliss, what kind of upside-down mind sits here, beside me?"*

"In a way, I killed them. I failed them. It was all my fault. It hurts to talk about it, George. I should have talked them out of it. Instead, I egged them on."

George's face winced pain and puzzle. *"What? How could you have saved their lives?"*

Marty took a deep breath. Her look was somber. *"I loved all four of them. They were close friends. We fucked often. They shared me; but it was all love. I was 'their' love girl, their darling fuck bunny. They wanted to join the Marine Corps; go to Nam together, same infantry unit. I had this gut feel I should tell them it was a bad idea and they shouldn't sign up; but I ignored it. Instead, I joked about it with them. I teased them about which one would bring me back the most medals; who would make corporal first; who would be the biggest bad ass over there, that sort of thing.*

"All four of them were killed together in a rice paddy. They died face down in that muddy water; together, like they lived. I dream about them sometimes. They lay there with their guts shot out, bleeding to death. I could have saved them, made them take me to Canada and just enjoy a life of being alive, with me; the five of us fucking our brains out, like kids in love should do, instead of cheering them to sign up for that horrible shit show. I blame myself for not knowing what my government was doing. All five of us thought it was some kind of a joke trip. Bravado was in their blood. It leaked over into my blood, too. I toasted them; fucked them one last time, goodbye. I was such a stupid dope. I wasn't thinking. I wasn't understanding that war is about killing people, on both sides."

George shook his head, somber faced. *"Sorry, I'm truly sorry. That's a lot to carry around. It wasn't your fault, though. Most of us had no idea how horrible that war was."*

"I know, but I blame myself. If I hadn't been 'their girl' they wouldn't have been so macho to impress me; they might still be alive. Such a waste, such beautiful, loving men."

"You must stop blaming yourself. Put it behind you. Live for the here and now."

"I try, George; but it's hard sometimes." Her face went slack. The eyes looked away into space, not knowing what they hoped to see. No sparkle, just incomprehension.

"Doesn't anything help? Figure out what helps you; and do more of it." George spoke his words like a father advising his daughter.

"I do try, George, I really do; honest. It's one of the things I see my shrink about. She helps some, tells me what to do; but doing what I do is a mixed picture. It brings them and their memories, back, too."

"What does?"

"Fucking." Marty's head bob was matter of fact.

"You said you had a couple of regrets. What else?"

"Oh, that. Yeah, well, for a moment there I was thinking about Mother."

"Your mother?"

"Yeah, I often wish I had a different mother; one that loved me."

"Something she did?"

"Hell yes!" Marty's voice ramped up a notch; reached its anger volume. *"She abandoned me! Wouldn't even talk to me for years, when I was a kid."*

"How old were you? How did you cope?"

"It started when she dropped me off at boarding school, two thousand miles away from her." Marty's eyes teared up. Her mouth drew in. She pinched her lips closed; trying to hold back the flow. *"I was just a five-year-old kid. When my dad was still alive, I coped by making mud pies and pretending I would take Dad away from Mother. But then he died and I got sent far away to WEX School for girls. Everything was different. I didn't fit in with the other girls. I don't KNOW if I coped. I can't say I coped. I pretended to be tough about being alone and far from home; but it ate at me. It was a form of torture; mental cruelty. I felt like my guts were being eaten away from inside me. I started believing Mother hated me. How does a little girl cope with that? I did the best I could.*

"The school had a white pebble-stone driveway. I often walked on that driveway and looked at the pretty stones. I told myself that this WEX school was a special place; and that I was lucky to be there, trying to believe the same bull shit that Mother had fed me. After a while, I began pretending that the stones loved me. That helped me cope. I'd pick up a stone and I'd kiss it. Then, I'd carry it with me for a while, before I'd put it down. I remember thinking the stone was a piece of Mother Earth, and that Mother Earth's love was

the best love of all. Stones became my substitute loves for Mother's love. Ever since, whenever I look at a stone, I always tell myself the stone loves me.

"My best friend, Maria, had a similar situation. Her mother was a drunk. Maria explained that our mothers weren't our faults. They were just assholes, disguised as mothers, who had happened to land in our lives. We were stuck with them. I totally get that now; but I still hurt inside sometimes. I regret being Mother's daughter. I sometimes wonder who I'd be if I'd had a different mother. Anyway, those stones got me through those years. They were my mother's love substitutes until I discovered something much better."

"What?"

"Penises."

"Penises?"

George studied Marty's face. It wore a wan smile now. Its owner's thoughts were far away, living freedom's serene acceptance of a hopeless situation. But it also conveyed the same confident innocence in the rightness of Marty's immoral choices. The face was pleased and resolute, too. It mirrored the face of the most highly prized biblical whore, Salome, when she was handed the decapitated head of John the Baptist.

That historic moment defined Salome, cast her future as a woman for hire if one met her price. Both beautiful faces, separated by millenniums, accepted the characters that wore them. Both women defied any man to criticize her immorality, and both resolved that whoring was their life's chosen path.

Susan's pleas to adult daughter, Marty, had fallen on deaf ears. Susan was a whore herself. And Daughter had Mother figured out before girl Marty was ten years old. Mother Susan had long ago lost her moral authority to lecture Marty about the pitfalls of immorality. Their mother-daughter relationship was a severed thread. Its shredded ends could never completely reconnect, unless some miracle occurred. Marty found love and solace in her work; not her family. She posed nude for the cameras, made erotic films, kissed lips of men she met on her porn sets or as her Premium Member clients; sucked and fucked their penises; pleasured other women's vaginas; but avoided spending time with her mother. Her mother may as well have had the plague. Adult Marty wanted nothing to do with her. Susan's repeated attempts to engender love always met with Marty's scorn. Daughter avoided near proximity to the woman who birthed her.

"*Yes, George, penises.*" Marty's smile widened. She detected his interest. She kicked off her flats, revealing her diminutive little girl's bare feet; pretty feet. She leaned back and intentionally lifted her skirt above her knees. "*You know George, penises; those lovely male parts that get big and hard and happen to have men attached to them. I get along wonderfully with men's penises. Penises are marvelous. Penises love me unconditionally; and I love them back. And, George, the funny thing I've noticed is, when a penis loves me, the man attached to the penis soon loves me, too. Penises have become my substitutes for stones.*" Marty smiled her vixen's temptation to George. She pushed her shoulders back even further than before. It was one of her well-practiced come-ons. She took George's hand into her own and placed it high upon her thigh.

"*If you don't mind me asking, what brought you to think of penises as a love substitute?*" George didn't mention her seduction moves. But his curiosity was growing with every word Marty spoke. The thinking processes of the young woman fascinated him.

"*Why should I mind? I'm glad you asked me, George. I love it when a man wants to know more about me. Let's see, how did I come to think of penises as love substitutes? I need to borrow some memories from my last year at WEX School for Girls, George.*

"*My fascination with penises began about a month or so after I fucked these twin boys, Donny, and Billy; and while taking fellatio lessons with my friend, Jimmy. I started dating rich boys with cars. I noticed that, after kissing and petting, I couldn't wait to unzip a boy's pants and get my hands on his penis. I felt this excitement come over me when I finally got his penis out of his underpants where I could see it. I felt privileged that the boy would show it to me; like by doing that he was letting me know that I was special. Seeing the penis caused me to experience this huge impulse. It was like a rush that took my breath away from me; like a different part of my brain took hold of me. I became really anxious to put my hands on it and suck it. I got to where, whenever a boy took me out, I couldn't wait to start sucking his penis. I began dreaming about sucking penises all day long; even during my classes. I became obsessed with sucking penises. I loved it that much.*

"But, then my sense of what I was doing, you know, the secrecy of being a naughty girl in a car on a lonely road, all close and intimate with a boy like that, sort of overwhelmed me. I started having these romantic feelings; but they weren't about the boy or how good looking he was, or what sports he played, or how much money he had or how smart or popular he was. You see, that school and the other girls and their mothers basically shunned me. So, for quite a while there, I didn't think I was actually worthy to be a good friend with a boy or being a lover of a boy. But his penis was a different matter. I had no trouble becoming friends and lover with a boy's penis.

"So, George, my romantic attachment wasn't about the boy; or anything about him. It was about making his penis fall in love with me. Something was happening inside my mind. I could feel it. I guess I was becoming a little mental over penises. I think that is what got my nymphomania started. I think, subconsciously, that I was starting to displace the stones that loved me with penises that loved me. I began realizing that, while I still had this immense need to be loved, a penis could express its love much better than a stone ever

could. After all, a stone never shot off a load of semen to let me know it loved me back. Only penises can do that.

"Well, I think this is what turned my nymphomania switch on, George. You see, once I realized that a penis shooting cum into me was a signal that the penis loved me, I felt that I needed to do everything possible to reciprocate, by giving the penis all the love I possibly could. That's when I decided that I owed it to the penises to take them into my vagina and make love with them. That way they could feel my slippery smoothness and my heat; and then they would realize that I loved them so much that I wanted them to experience a wonderful time while they were inside me.

"Once I made that decision, whenever I went out with a boy, I began getting intimate with his penis by giving it a blow job; but then, before it shot off, I suggested to the boy that we go further; that we get into the back seat of his car and make love. This was a little tricky, no pun intended. I needed to learn how to wrap my legs around the boy's waist and get his penis inserted into my vagina. I needed to get my panties off while sitting in the back seat and positioning myself on his lap in such a way that I could slide his penis inside me. Once I coached a boy to lift my ass, and help me move my vagina up and down on his penis, this routine became second nature for me. After a while, I became really expert at back seat sex, George. In fact, I got so good at it that many nights three boys would pick me up in the same car; and they'd let me fuck all three of their penises on the car's back seat.

"That was about the time I started paying attention to my inner voices, Misses Promiscuity, Shameless, and Iniquity. Miss Iniquity told me I should insist on getting picked up in cars that had huge back seats, so I could be more comfortable while I fucked. So, I told the boys I wanted them to pick me up in Chrysler, Lincoln, and Cadillac sedans. And, they did that for me! They borrowed their

parent's cars to go on dates with me, instead of picking me up in their coups and hot rods. That made it easier to date several boys at once. I remember how breathtakingly excited I got when I knew I could fuck four or five penises on one date. I let my boy friends know that I preferred fucking several of them on the same date. My pre-orgy practicing actually started in the back seats of their parents' family cars. My psychological enthusiasm for orgies and gang bangs was unplanned. It began innocently.

"The other WEX girls started calling me a whore. That didn't bother me. I felt good about it. I took it as a sign of their jealousy. I was taking their boyfriends away from them. But I wasn't making love with their boyfriends to steal them away. I was doing those boys because I loved feeling loved by their penises. I loved being intimate with their penises. I loved how they swelled and hardened and strained as they pushed to get way up inside my vagina, especially the larger, thick ones that stretched me and made me feel dominated. I became ecstatic when I learned how to Kegel squeeze penises with my vaginal muscles. I made it a practice to Kegel squeeze penises as they began ejaculating cum into me. When my vagina clamped hard onto a cum streaming penis, I felt that it became as much a part of me as it was the boy's. It made love making intensely intimate and wildly erotic. I needed that intensity of love making. Nothing else came close to it. I couldn't get enough of it. I began daydreaming more than I did before. I dreamed of penises shooting semen inside my vagina. I loved my life for the first time since I matriculated into WEX school. Compared to how I felt about penises, my studies became unimportant and meaningless.

"I loved my new feeling of being loved by penises so much that I decided to learn everything I could about making my vagina far more attractive to penises than other girls' vaginas were. I reasoned that I should do everything possible to help penises decide they loved my vagina. By making my vagina adorable and irresistible, I figured

many more penises would seek me out. I understood boys. I knew they would talk about me.

"I read everything I could find about making my vagina attractive. That led me to waxing my mons pubis every third week. I applied softening creams to the fleshy mons area surrounding my vagina. I developed my secret gardenia and lilac-based perfume scents for my lubricating jells and vaginal perfumes. And I kept my vagina scrupulously clean. My vagina became a receptive fragrant flower. It was always eager to receive loving kisses and visitations by appreciative tongues and penises. I had a huge advantage over girls who didn't wax, soften, lubricate, or scent themselves.

"Boys naturally preferred my inviting slippery softness and heavenly scents to a scratchy, sticky bramble bush that wafted odors of stale fish and moldy cheese. So, even when another girl competed with me for a penis's love, she lost. I got catty comments about my beautiful face and figure from some of the jealous girls. They'd say looks would only take me so far and then they'd laugh at me about my poor and failing grades.

"But those comments simply reinforced my conviction that they were clueless about boys. It didn't matter that they changed their eye shadow, blush, or lipstick to make them appear more attractive. They were dummies! They never focused on their vaginas. They ignored their most important asset! They assumed that all vaginas were the same; but they aren't. They refused to comprehend the importance of their vaginas to the boys; and that was fine by me.

"I wasn't about to tell them they were neglecting the most important asset they had. They didn't wax or even shave; and they didn't do anything to soften their fleshy mons mounds or lubricate, or try to create a personalized intoxicating scent that would fascinate a boy. They never figured it out. I think their upbringing and religious indoctrination prevented them from thinking about it. They didn't understand that the attractiveness of my vagina and my eagerness

to have sex stole their boyfriends, not my looks. Although, I dare say, many boys told me that they considered me the most beautiful girl around. I made sure that a session with my vagina left an indelible impression. I wanted boys who had sex with me to feel they experienced rapture. I wanted them to call me again and again; come back for more sex. I got many repeat dates. I could barely manage all of them. My strategy worked perfectly.

"I became the desert oasis for sex crazed boys. I was fucking and feeling loved every single night. Every time a penis shot off inside of me, I believed that penis was telling me that it loved me. That was vitally important to me. Penises replaced my stones. They became the new love that I didn't get from Mother. Most penises are very understanding of a girl's need to feel loved. I discovered when I encouraged a penis to love my vagina, it would try to make me feel loved as well. I needed that. I still do. I can't tell you how often I thank the stars for my shameless nymphomania. My disease enables me to experience love. And I deeply need that.

"There's more about my love affair with penises, George. I began telling my dates to bring blankets with them. We went to a golf course at night and spread the blankets on a green. I then fucked and sucked three boys while I lied there, looking up at the stars. I became very casual and matter of fact about doing that. It felt natural and wonderful. Every time a penis shot off its semen inside me, I looked at how the stars twinkled. They smiled to me. They sparkled every time a penis consummated its love. I felt victorious and glorious; thrilled when penises did that. I loved fucking under the stars. I preferred being out in the open to being in the back seat of a closed-up car.

"I wished dusk would come, so I could escape from my dorm. I became anxious for night to come. I often dreamed night wouldn't come. I'd wake up frustrated, knowing I couldn't fuck until the sun went down. I started wondering where I could fuck in broad

daylight. One day I awoke from that dream, realizing that I had to solve my dilemma.

"That's when I had my best idea, ever. I told the boys to take me to a hotel room. I was proud of myself. I solved my biggest problem. I could fuck during the daylight hours and not worried about getting caught. My weekends became very busy. I focused on having penises inside me and enticing more penises to love me. I loved being the center of attention as love object of several penises; several boys fucking me in the same hotel room during the same hour.

"That's when the craziest thing happened, George. I was making love with three penises on the golf course at night. They had all shot huge loads of hot cum into me. My partners and I had kissed and laughed together. They were touching and kissing me while I was stroking their penises and tickling their balls; coming down from my orgasms. I was indescribably happy, enjoying my feelings of ecstasy. I felt wonderful and totally loved; like I was in heaven. One of the boys was massaging my feet; another was massaging my temples. The third boy's penis was in my hand. I was stroking it. He had gotten very hard again. He asked me if he could fuck me a second time; and I told him: 'Yes, of course you can; I'd like that very much.' I was having one of the most serene moments of my life; lying there relaxing in the afterglow of love making; ready to casually fuck that boy for our second time.

"Then I detected some motion. It startled me. I looked off to the side. About five yards away two ravens stood there in the darkness, staring at me. They had knowing gleams in their eyes. Their eyes had captured the starlight. But there was something more about them; something spiritual. That's when I relaxed. I knew they were sent to me as a signal of good will. They carried the blessed approval from the spirits. They adored my iniquitous promiscuity; my transformation into a shameless, immoral whore. They silently endorsed my uninhibited fornications. They carried this force from the spirit

world. It entered me and strengthened me. It assured me that it loved me and my immorality.

"Those birds had watched me making love the entire time! Seeing them watching me, made me burst out laughing, at first. But then it dawned on me that these were holy messengers, sent to watch over me; protect me. Then, one of the raven's spirit voices spoke to me. It said: 'Our immoral blackness now lives within you. You contain our souls of chaos, cleverness, and cunning. Many will call you evil because of the blackness of your soul; because you steal lovers away from other women. Know that black is beautiful; and understand that your black soul is good. Black is not evil. Ignore those who call you evil. Immorality is not evil.'

"Then, the second raven spoke: 'Take in the sperms of your lovers. Swallow it. But do not allow their sperms to seed your womb. Take precautions that nothing of their seeds grows within you to become one that comes back out of you; for if that were to happen the beautiful chaos that you visit upon the world will find you and haunt you and it will become your own chaos. If you discover that a seed grows within you, you must kill it and turn it into worms and remove it from your womb. You are destiny's child. You are to find and savor pleasure and sew chaos in the lives of others. Above all, love yourself; love what you do.' The ravens' presence told me that the spirits blessed my promiscuity.

"That revelation gave me my wonderful sense of rightness. The spiritual world considered my immorality beautiful! I decided that I should never subject myself to moral constraints. I should never tie myself down by having children. I should enjoy life and all its fullness. The ravens' presence assured me that my whoring was divinely sanctified. They assured me that I was rescuing my sexual partners from the prudish confines of their moral cages.

"I knew I had been blessed; and my promiscuity had been blessed. The spirit birds were satisfied that my immorality was genuine; that

my mind and soul honestly comported with my actions, without any reservations whatsoever. That was the moment when I resolved to commit my life to being an immoral whore. I knew the spirits agreed with my decision. I had journeyed from seeking replacement stones for lost Mother's love to embracing my career choice. I haven't looked back since."

"That's profound and deeply touching, Marty. Thank you for sharing that. I feel much closer to you." George looked deeply into Marty's eyes, telling her that her loved her immoral soul.

"Thank you, George. That's also when it occurred to me that I didn't mind being watched while I made love. Au contraire! I loved it. My 'watched by birds' experience told me something. Those feathered fellows had silently affirmed that my explicit sex was beautiful to watch; a wonder to behold. That's why they stayed to see more. They honored my love making by being there for me, my very first explicit love scene audience. Their presence excited me. I became more enthused about putting on a show. I became anxious to fuck that third boy for his second time. I couldn't wait to show those ravens how much I loved making love. I wanted to secure their continuing approval, and satisfy myself that what I sensed was not a mistake. They reaffirmed my decision. They stayed and continued watching me.

"I liked knowing that I was giving those ravens something to see. Then I had this glorious, prescient vision. The uncertain darkness that haunted my future lifted away, like fog retreats before rays of morning sunlight. The ravens were there to be sure I was honestly acting out my truest, innermost feelings. The spirits love when a soul accepts its destiny and lives to please itself, instead of pretending to be what it thinks everyone else expects it should be. That's when I first realized that I would likely enjoy making pornographic videos and performing live, on-stage porn, before paying audiences. I was no longer afraid of what the future might hold.

"Waves of indescribable happiness flooded over me. I knew my soul was right with the spirit world. Making love with three boys before those ravens was spiritually sanctified and wonderous. I hugged my third partner tightly, kissing him passionately on his mouth while his penis entered me a second time. I felt glorious and happy about the holiness and rightness of my destiny. I cried tears of joy.

"My mascara ran down my cheeks, but I didn't wipe them off. I was elated. My promiscuity had been blessed and adored by the spirits. Wild animal eroticism took hold of me. It compelled me to make passionate love. I became an untamed wildcat. Passions I didn't know I had erupted from my loins.

"I made love like these moments with this partner were my only chance to propagate the human species. I was lust crazed. I held his penis inside me, tightly squeezing it while kissing him passionately. I pressed my body hard against his, while rocking him from side to side. I orgasmed three times! I screamed a joyous scream while he came his second time. I dug my nails into his back; holding him even closer to me. He responded. He clutched my ass like he'd never let go. I desperately craved the intimacy of his penis. My insides exploded with uninhibited, unashamed love. I wanted to hold him and love him like this, forever.

"I was living a divine revelation. Everything about our love making was spirit blessed. I squeezed him tightly to me; wrapped him with my legs and my arms. This was our special, magical moment. I wanted to cherish it. My sexual experience had discovered a new, higher plateau. It was dramatically better."

"Dramatically better? How?" George's face was perplexed. *"How can sex be better than sex?"*

"You don't know, do you George?" Marty's expression wore disbelief.

"No, I don't. What are you talking about?"

"Okay. Well, you've just watched some film where I got it on with Marshawn."

"Yes."

"Well, did you notice how I went crazy over his penis."

"Like how?"

"Oh, George, remember how I became like a wild animal; how eagerly I sucked it; how I slathered it with oils; how I stopped fucking from time to time to kiss it and suck it and to kiss underneath his scrotum and tongue his taint; and mouth his balls while I stroked his penis?"

"Of course, I remember. You were sensational."

"But do you understand why I was doing that? Do you understand why I was so frenzied about keeping his penis so rock hard?"

"I'm not sure. Why?"

"Because, George, I wanted to take Marshawn and me to that higher level plateau of lovemaking. You see, there's love making sex that most people experience in their romances. That's the kind of lovemaking that results in the male's ejaculation and the woman's impregnation. It's warm, fuzzy, lovey-dovey sex, with hugging and kissing afterwards. But that's sex on its basic level, George. There's another, higher level. That's when sex becomes a commitment to pleasuring. On this higher, pleasuring level I have multiple orgasms. Feeling the hard, swollen penis pressing against and sliding over my clitoris, sending erotic sensations down my clitoral tentacles into my thighs, becomes a steady state of eroticism. I love how I feel then. I don't want to come down from that feeling. I want to sustain forever. It's a euphoria condition where the rest of the world and its cares and all my other thoughts fall away. And to sustain this higher level, it's imperative that I keep the male penis fully erect, blood filled swollen, and overly sensitized so that it does not ejaculate; but instead, feels the same levels of pleasure thrills that my vagina feels as it thrusts at a rapid rate. When a penis does me like that, my

libido transitions from feeling harmonious loving to feeling insanely pleasure obsessed.

"It's when making love for the sake of feeling sustained, intensely heightened pleasures becomes the only reason for living. That's when the multiple orgasms come in rapid fire succession. It's when I feel like I want to fuck and never stop fucking until I die and death stops me. As a porn viewer, George, you see it as a time when my bootie twerks rapidly, crazily; when I briefly pause fucking to suck and harden and lubricate my partner's penis. But what I'm striving to attain in my own libido is that heightened pleasuring."

"Yes, I get it now. Bertie and I see it as great porn. And you're saying you first reached this heightened pleasure level with that boy on the golf course green?"

"Yes. That was a special moment in my life and a milestone in my development as a porn star. It happened with him that second time I fucked him that night. I knew it was one of those precious, priceless moments, and I wanted to memorialize it and cherish it. I told him I loved him with all the sincerity I could express with words. I truly did love him because he was sharing that special moment with me. But I knew that words alone could not express the grandeur of my feelings. That's why I slobbered my mouth all over his, while I kissed him. My French kisses searched his tongue; entwined it with mine. My lips became slobbery wet smacks, that signature kiss boys get from a WEX girl. He laughed; told me I lived up to my school's Wet Smacks reputation. And I had! I had shared the ravaging lust I felt. I told him I loved him, again. It was the truth; I did love him."

"Jesus! It was like you were giving yourself and that boy passing grades for achieving a milestone on your way to being a porn star, wasn't it?"

"Yes, George, that's exactly what it was. I told myself from that moment forward I would always attempt to attain that nirvana level of frenzied intimacy. I craved it. My nymphomania demanded

it. And I vowed to always tell my sex partners that I loved them, because I did. I loved making love with them; and I loved that they wanted to have their penises inside me; willing to help me reach my pleasure state. After I finished making love with that boy on the green; after he came inside me that second time, those three boys picked me up and carried me to their car, kissing my mouth and cheeks the whole way. They set me down on the back seat, a boy on both sides of me. They continued kissing me, feeling my breasts, and telling me I was beautiful, all the way back to my dorm. I felt like I had become a goddess. That night was my preview of porn life. I loved that night. I will always love that night.

"Boys talk. After that night, my date calendar exploded. The only way I could fit in all my dates was to see two to four boys a night. I became the date queen of WEX School; homecoming queen of the nearby public school; and hottest date for local high school seniors and college men. I quickly reached my hundred and two hundred penis's fucked milestones. I was living a life of continuous ecstasy and endlessly lovely orgasms. I discovered a level of happiness I never imagined existed before that transformative night. I loved my date filled senior year.

"That night with the ravens enabled me to visualize my future. I felt completely unafraid of what I saw. Why not me? I asked. I had the qualities needed to become a movie star. I had a beautiful face and body. I was free of inhibition. I loved the magical intrigue of foreplay, the special beauty of intimacy, and the romantic eroticism of sexual intercourse for pleasure without commitment. Seducing men to fall in love with me was my natural calling.

"I had my inner self's awakening moment. I perceived that it would be psychologically rewarding, knowing that people were watching me performing in porn movies. I wondered: What could be more rewarding than getting paid for penises making love with me? How glorious would it be to have fabulous sex with the most

experienced, handsome lovers in the world? It occurred to me then, that making porn films was my perfect career choice.

"Every single day I fantasized living my life as a porn star. I imagined that was the most wonderful of all possible worlds. I vowed that I would become a top ranked porn star and made that my career goal. I would do everything humanly possible to become the best porn star I could possibly become; and that I would be relentless in pursuit of my goal. And I would not allow anyone or anything to dissuade me from my chosen career.

"Despite criticisms about being debauched, depraved and wanton, which I expected would come, I steeled myself to my course. No matter how many kinky scenes, orgies, different locations, I promised myself that I would do whatever it took to achieve top ranking. I realized that pornography is a big tent under which many preferences gather; and to become a top star, I needed to accept all the fetishes that live under that tent. I approached my career with an inclusive mind set. I told myself some simple truths: That I loved to fuck and suck penises; that I was an exceptionally beautiful and naturally promiscuous woman; that by driving myself toward my goal I would enhance my prostitution repartee; and learn more erotic pleasures than I had already mastered. But I would not allow any producer or actor to abuse me. I have always held myself to high standards.

"I also promised myself that no man was going to make me his wife; unless that man truly accepted me for my career as a porn star; honestly loved me; had no jealousy, whatsoever, about me being the world's most unashamed, profligate erotic actress; and that he shared and supported my goal to become the most completely uninhibited, immoral world-famous adult film star that I could possibly become.

"My husband, if I had one, would need to understand that I would always be willing to leave him for periods of time, to take up with lovers who could advance my notoriety and career. He'd have to accept that I wouldn't give a second thought to taking another

man into our home; and even into our bed, making my husband wait outside or in a bar somewhere; while I made love with another partner who could advance my career. And, should I unfortunately become pregnant, my husband would have to accept the fact that I would almost certainly abort my fetus. I would not, under any circumstances, allow motherhood to interfere with my career goal. I would not allow a pregnancy to degrade my figure.

"Once I had my priorities straight, my inhibitions fell away. I smashed my moral compass with a sledgehammer; permanently destroyed it. I appreciated and valued the beautiful, precious nature of my immorality above everything else. With immorality my highest god, I was free to concentrate on the direction to take my life.

"I clearly remember my senior year of high school. After seeing those ravens watching me, I imagined myself as a future top ranked porn star, performing long explicit love making scenes in exotic locations, with partners that had spectacular penises and stamina. I didn't care about school or grades anymore. I was already making good money as a prostitute."

"You started charging money while you were a senior in high school?" George seemed shocked and somewhat impressed by Marty's business acumen.

"Yes, George, I charged a hundred dollars a date; and for that hundred I would suck and fuck a boy; or just do one or the other, whatever he wanted. I was making two hundred to four hundred dollars a night. My dates were also taking me to the fanciest restaurants in the area; feeding me king crab legs, lobster tails and filet mignons with side orders of roasted vegetables. I couldn't imagine an ordinary work a day life after I started charging for sex. It was a wonderful, fun-filled beginning to my fabulous life."

"You didn't always want to be a prostitute for money, did you? I mean, while you were in school, didn't you consider a different career?"

"Well, yes, I suppose there was a time when I did. But I was steeped in my anger over rejection by Mother and the girls of WEX. That anger focused me. After doing boys for free, my concentration on studies vanished. I remember thinking about how my grades were sinking. I perceived that my career opportunity choices were slipping away, because so many choices are tied to doing well in school. I couldn't see myself becoming a scientist, chemist, nurse, doctor, lawyer, teacher or just about anything, because all those things required higher studies. And I wasn't getting good enough grades to qualify for admission to higher studies. It was like reaching into a pool of water and grabbing water in my hand. Then holding out my hand to see what career choices I had. When I opened my palm to look, all the water ran through my fingers. There was nothing left, except prostitution; and possibly becoming something that required physical skills, like becoming a jockey for horse racing. I investigated being a jockey. I was too heavy. I thought I could starve myself. But if I did that, I might become unattractive and no boys would want me. Besides, the idea of falling and being trampled by race horses frightened me.

"So, I only fantasized about becoming a jockey. I liked the idea of a twelve-hundred-pound stallion straining its muscles under me while I whipped it to go faster. Then I transposed that fantasy to my lovemaking. I imagined riding my sex partners harder and faster; my legs wrapped around them while they surged under me and while they came inside me. I stopped regretting not having other opportunities. Can you understand that?"

"I suppose. But why didn't you hedge your bets? I mean why didn't you find some time for your studies?" George expected Marty would have protected her downside and taken her studies seriously, in case her career as a porn star didn't pan out.

"I just didn't care about studies, George. Once I decided to become a prostitute, I realized I didn't need to study the things they taught in school. I decided to put all my eggs into one basket and

get exceptionally good at doing what I loved doing most……, which was lovemaking. I was deeply into studies of eroticism, techniques that advanced my seductive abilities, those sorts of things. Sex and seduction fascinated me. I became career focused. School became a drag on my time and my mind. I remember how I would stare at the classroom clock, counting the hours and minutes until dusk. That's when a car or limo with boys would come to the rear driveway of my dorm. I lived for those nighttime hours and the weekends when I could be in a car or hotel room with boys, practicing my techniques of penis sucking and fucking; all sorts of things, like how I touched them while I did things with them. The possibilities were endless, inspiring, and emotionally rewarding. Some nights I fit in two outings with boys in separate cars. One night I did six different boys and made six hundred dollars while experimenting new techniques for arousing the male penis. I had wonderful weeknights doing that instead of studying. Weekends were even better. I got so heavily into sex and loved it so much that there simply wasn't time to study.

"One group of boys I loved to play with were from very wealthy families. They had homes on the Eastern Shore and in Annapolis; and they had sailboats with cabins and queen-sized beds. They often wanted me for entire weekends; and they paid me a flat rate of two thousand dollars for the weekend. Often, one set of parents or another was away and I'd make love with all four boys in a master bedroom's California-king sized bed. I loved the life style. I couldn't get enough of it. Those four boys wined and dined me; basically, I fucked them for entire weekends. I loved the times I had with them."

"Didn't some girls get upset with you? I mean you were taking their boyfriends away from them."

"Yes, that did happen, George. I heard a lot of catty remarks. I was called: 'slut, whore, cum dumpster, and sinner' lots of times. But I didn't care. Calling me names wasn't going to stop me from doing what I loved doing. One girl, Carol, went totally nuts over me taking

her boyfriend, Darren, away from her. She ended up in a mental institution."

"And that didn't bother you?"

"No! By then, my mental orientation had totally changed to embrace whoredom. I wasn't bothered. I was amused. The way I see it, nobody owns anybody else. Boyfriend, husband, fiancée are just possession labels. If a boyfriend, husband, or fiancée wanted to make love with me, those labels didn't stop me. They will never stop me. That's just ridiculous possessive labeling by moralists. It has no place in the New Morality World. If a man wants to be with me; and he pays me to whore with him, I'm better than fine with that. I feel wonderful about it; and I feel wonderful for him, too. Immoral relationships are the best, because they are honest and natural. Those are the only relationships that matter to me."

"That was a breakout year for you, wasn't it?"

"Oh my, yes! It certainly was. It was the year I found my honest freedom and when I completely accepted my shameless true love of penises. It was THE YEAR that defined me and helped me become who I am today."

"Marty, did any of the boys you dated fall hard for you, or were all of them just having fun? Do you mind telling?" George's interest in Marty's capacity for intimacy could no longer be contained. It was a question that many women would consider improper; but, given the nature of the relationship Bertie had in mind for the three of them, George felt he needed to ask, if only to get a preview of how he, himself, might begin feeling about the beautiful immoral vixen sitting beside him.

"Oh, no, George, I don't mind. Some did fall hard, yes. I love it when a man feels a strong love for me. Many of my repeat customers feel that romantic attachment. I don't mind at all. I encourage it. I love the men I make love with, just as much as they love me; so, I

never feel alarmed or put off by a man who falls hard for me. I think it's all very sweet.

"I carry with me a poem written by one of my greatest loves. His name is Harold. He still writes me. He comes from New York to Colorado to see me. He truly loves me, and I love him. Would you like me to read it to you?"

"Yes, please do. I'd like to understand the spell you work on a man."

"Okay, here." Marty found her purse and retrieved the poem; then read it to George:

Marty on Seventh Green, a love poem:

'My blanket waits on our star lit green,
Our hill; I'll kiss and love and sin with you
There; naked, your lips soft moist warm dream
Our tongues search; hands touch love anew;

My arms embrace you, behold my dream
Temptress, unholy sin goddess, in lieu
Of love I kiss your nipple buds, adore your cream
White flesh, my wanton desires sin anew;

Mount me, juicy butterfly; enshroud my shaft serene
Starlight captured in your eyes, speaks love to you
In our lives in my prayers and dreams. Oh!
I spurt; take my life into your peach, sweet cream;

I cherish, love you, immoral passion queen,
Nymph goddess, my shameless lust love is true
My sperms worshiped darkness angel you; seen
Glory, joined by lust fires to stars inside you;

Sweet! Come too, love; all former gleams
Forever dismiss away, dispatched by sin adoring you
Shameless, ravenous, glorious dream creator that,
Returns me always to you; to hold and love you,

Profound on my blanket, this sacred, sin drenched green;
My shaft rediscovers joys within your peach; my soul you
Alone rebirth, know my passion desires for you, naked
    Queen,
Promiscuous freedom fires rage hot within you,
Forever loving, I devote my soul to my goddess Queen
Entwine me in your flesh, I seek your sinful pleasures, you
Complete my soul, my love; my passion courses its endless
    stream
Forever flowing, seeking destiny again, to sin within you.
In beautiful, wonderful, gloriously free, immoral you.

I will always love you, Marty.'

Harold

*"That is a beautiful poem, Marty. Is Harold a love rival, as in a
boyfriend?"*

*"No, George. No one can take Bob's place. I'm totally in love with
him. He's my soul mate."*

"What is it about Bob that qualifies him as a soul mate, Marty?"

*"Oh, George, I don't want to get too deeply into this; but Bob is a
man's man. He's the only man I know that can stand up to this other
man named David. That's part of it. I respect Bob for that. Also, Bob
is a bit of a challenge for me. Another woman, Barbara, really, truly
loves him. And to tell you the truth, I think he secretly loves her.
So, he's a challenge for me in the sense that I feel I need to keep his*

interest so he won't stray with Barbara. Besides, Bob is the only man I can confide in about many things and many people; and, our love making is out of this world fabulous."

"So, Harold is just another lover, nothing special, despite the love poem?"

"That's right. Harold is just one of my lovers. He's a college student, English Literature. He's constantly writing poems about me. He sends me poems about my lips, my eyes, my smile, my breasts, my vagina, my hands, legs, feet, hair, you name it. He gushes on and on about how much he loves me and how he adores me and the many ways I fuck him and suck him. I must have twenty poems that he's written to me about my vagina's lady lips; how he'd climb the highest mountains; dive to the deepest depths of the sea: fight tigers and lions; to just have one intimate moment with my vagina.

"I have poems about how he lives for fellatio from me, how he loves to hold me in his arms, how much he loves my kisses. He goes on and on with this endless adoration. It never stops with Harold. Harold just lets his feelings go splat, all over his poems. I don't know much about poems, George; but Harold's don't necessarily rhyme. I think he just feels good about writing them. They seem to be his outlet for the passions he feels toward me. I guess he's obsessed with me. He tells me he wants to become a poet."

"He still sees you?"

"Yes, he joined my Premium Club years ago. He flies to Colorado to see me about once a month now. He's been trying to have a relationship with a woman in New York, but nothing seems to last. So, he keeps seeing me. He's very wealthy. He brings me lots of gifts. He's a long-time repeat customer. He admits he's obsessed with me. He tells me about his other women, but he continues comparing them with me; then he stops seeing them. He told me he thinks to have an honest relationship with a woman, he needs to give up seeing me; but he can't bring himself to do that. He's been to shrinks about this

issue, but nothing seems to help him. He tells me he's addicted to me; and that he's decided he needs to be okay with that."

"Well, he certainly carries a torch for you. Can manage him?"

"Oh, easily," Marty laughed, "he's a sweet, lovable little boy in a man's body. He swoons over me and loves having some contact with me. We are good friends now, as well as lovers. He likes to sit on set watching me while I'm making a porn film. He loves watching me making love with other men. I think he's like a lot of men that have those types of kinky yearnings about women. It intrigues them when a woman has other lovers. In their minds that makes the woman more exotic, and that causes them to fantasize about the woman; gets her into their heads, somehow. So, I've become Harold's fantasy."

"Has he ever said he wanted to make a film with you?"

"Oh, no!" Marty emphatically shook her head. "His family would get upset if they ever found out that he did that. Besides, he's gangly tall and thin; and his penis is way too small for a porn film. He's happy with how things are with us. And so am I."

"Do you think there are others that love you the same way this Harold does?"

"Yes definitely. Lots of men, and several women, have told me that they love me; and I believe them."

"And you feel you can love all of them in return, the same way this Harold fellow loves you?"

"Yes, George, of course I can; and I do. I love them all. I honestly love all of them, totally and completely."

"But, how can you feel that way about someone without getting attached to one man or one woman?" Marty's world and her understanding of morals and relationships had George's head spinning.

"George, you'll just have to trust me about this. When I'm with a man I can mentally block out everything else in my life, especially other men; and I can completely give myself over to totally loving the

man I'm with. I can love him like he and I are the last two humans on earth; and as if we must procreate, or die as a human species. In that same way, George, we, as in you and I, could easily become passionate lovers."

"You think so?"

"Absolutely, yes, I do. If you'd like that, then when I'd be with you, making love with you, I would love you to the very depths of my soul; as if you were the only man in the world that I have ever loved. That's the mental on-off switch I have, George. It's something I learned during my senior year in high school. It's what enables me to be a convincing, loving nymph. It's a learned skill, like an acquired taste. It serves me well. The same way, if you and I become lovers, George, that would have to be something you understand and accept about me. Okay? Does that help you?" Marty's tone hinted she was growing impatient with George's uncertainty.

"*That must have been a transformative year for you.*" George tried to rally from his skepticism. His voice softened to express empathy with Marty's career choice. *"I mean as far as your mind set and your metamorphosis into becoming a prostitute. I mean this total commitment you made to your career of prostitution seems it occurred that year."*

"Yes, it certainly was a transformative year, George." Marty nodded, appreciating George's sympathetic, understanding tone. She was pleased, and pleasantly stimulated, that he was not judgmental about her lack of morals.

"It was a glorious, beautiful year for me. I blossomed as a woman. One thing led to another that year. During a lecture in science class, I was totally bored. I was counting the hours until dusk; passing time while day dreaming that I was on a porn film stage, making love with several penises during an orgy. I imagined that I had a spectacular, gorgeous penis and a set of beautiful balls in my hands. I was kissing the head of the penis, beginning a delicious

fellatio session. I imagined a voluminous ejaculation would soon erupt onto my eager lips and tongue.

"It was so real; I could already taste my imaginary partner's cum in my mouth. My pheromones were raging. My vagina was so hot! It felt like it was on fire. My skin was flushed and warm from thinking explicitly erotic thoughts. My teacher's eyes caught me stimulating myself. He noticed my hand moving inside my skirt. His eyes met mine. Instantly, we knew what we both were thinking.

"Well, this gets us into a whole new story, George. I'll be brief. I ended up having an intense love affair with that teacher. He was my first romance with an older man. I fell head over heels in love with him. He separated from his wife for a while so he could have more time with me. He even wanted to divorce her and marry me. That was a most wonderful time. We fucked ferociously; like minks; couldn't get enough of each other. He was very experienced; a fantastic lover."

"Better than the school boys?" George smiled approvingly. His curiosity was piqued

"Way, way better. He opened my eyes to the incredible, long-lasting joys of oral sex, lovingly performed; and his educated tongue taught me to appreciate the most subtle intricate techniques of heavenly cunnilingus. He was soooo sweet with me, George; from the way he took off my panties to the way his tongue worked so lovingly inside me; to the ways he continued my stimulation and lovingly kissed my sex. I felt incredibly fortunate to have sex lessons from such an experienced teacher. I fell crazy in love with him and the ways he loved me with his tongue and fingers."

"So, you didn't marry him?"

"No, of course not. We came to our senses. He had kids. And there was his job consideration, so we settled into being lovers. We worked out an arrangement where he paid me and became my customer. We sneaked around like kids playing hooky, so he wouldn't

get fired because of me. That made our affair exciting and romantic. He patiently worked with me. He taught me to shamelessly shout out my feelings; express my pleasures; confide my thoughts and feelings while I orgasmed."

George had not expected Marty's reveal. She had already had a fling with an older man! And she had positive things to say about it! She loved it! Her description sent his mind into contemplations and wonder:

'Perhaps her talk about lusting after penises is mere bravado? Perhaps she masks an inner tenderness, a docile, submissive vein? Perhaps she longs for stability; wants to cease her wanderings from penis to penis? Surely, the same natural compassion that beats within the heart of most women also beats within hers. Perhaps she thinks she's unworthy to have feelings for others? An abused child might feel that way. Perhaps she needs the friendship of another caring soul? Perhaps she needs me? Perhaps she wants me to warm the heart that surely beats within her breast? Perhaps, perhaps? I'm losing my senses over her. She's so beautiful. Her soul is also beautiful. It must be!

'I must discover what drives this woman-child to crave sex. I suspect that is key to learn what direction this relationship will take and how it might end. Am I too vain to expect that the two of us might become an 'item,' traveling Europe and the South Seas chasing our romance quest? Then, there is Bertie. I could hardly leave her. Impossible! What am I thinking?'

George snapped out of his fascination. His earlier, uneasy, premonition stuck with him. And it boiled down to simply this: That prostitution, while it fascinated and titillated Marty, and while she considered it glamorous, was not the vixen's main driver. There was something else; something deeply embedded in her core of being. Whatever it was, it was profound. And, unless placed under extreme duress, she would never reveal it. George's ears open ed his mind and made it listen closely to the rumination dreams of the minx. In addition to her stunning beauty and intriguing views of morality, her thoughts were spoken from a fascinating, greedy mind:

"Some artist should create a painting that shows how I felt with my teacher's tongue inside me; helping me lose all my inhibitions like that. I'd like it to portray me, a soulless, immoral nymph, receiving cunnilingus on top of a mountain of treasures; gifts that had been given me to honor my immoral promiscuity. It could counter Savonarola's 'Preaching against Prodigality.' painting.

"Instead of urging a bonfire of vanities, my painting would be titled, 'Triumph of Pagan Immorality.' And, instead of characters holding worldly goods and enlightening books that they were about to throw into the flames, my painting would show a mountain of jewels, fine clothing, and gold; and I'd be lying atop my temple mountain, performing an orgy, with penises in my mouth and hands. In the foreground would be a procession of well-dressed men carrying satin pillows, bearing offerings of rubies, emeralds, diamonds, gold, silver, jade, and pearls as their tribute to me; fabulous rewards for my unrepentant immoral whoring. My column of admirers would part a sea of pathetic, downtrodden, righteous losers. The losers would be cordoned off by armed guards, signifying that immorality had wrested control of social norms from the religious moralists. My face would be radiant, happy, glorious; contrasted to the dour looks of the righteous. In the background, the painting would have six Savonarola figures, tied to stakes, about to be torched in a raging bonfire. I'd be ecstatic; giggling with raucous laughter; smiling gleefully in anticipation of sucking a huge, erect penis positioned next to my lips."

"Sacrilegious, aren't you?"

"Yes George, I'm an even bigger pagan whore than Mother. She got her jewels from helpless innocents. She whored her

conscience-free ass off, while millions were murdered in the holo-caust. I'm an exceptionally naughty woman, disdainful of the righteous moralizers and their downtrodden, loser-focused messaging. And I'm contemptuous. Moralizers have controlled the narrative since they replaced the Roman Empire. Pagans have been marginalized for fifteen centuries while moralizers have made a mess of the world.

"I'm tired of their pretentions: as if the religious types never pillaged; never murdered; never slaughtered Native Americans; never had Inquisitions or Holy Wars! And on and on! But they did those horrible things! They'd like them swept under the rug; pretend that they never happened. But it's too much to overlook. And there's no rug big enough. They own what they did in the name of their insane religions. They own all of it. And they are still driving their bullshit, pounding it into peoples' heads with their holier than thou claptrap! Who do they think they're fooling?

"World morality is a pendulum swing, George. It was Pagan for tens of thousands of years. Then it swung to righteous, organized, male-constructed religion for the last five or six thousand years. Now, the pendulum is swinging back to Pagan, George. Immorality is becoming right and good again. Righteousness has overplayed its hand. People aren't buying what it's selling anymore. There's no contemporary proof that any of their homilies ever happened. None. That's the truth and they can't handle the truth.

"I've joined that pendulum swing, George; doing my part to push it along. Yeah, I'm sacrilegious. My immorality does a lot of people a lot of good. It liberates. Righteousness strangles freedom; especially oppresses women; stifles thought. It's a straightjacketing, ordered way of living. It's not for me!

"Yeah, I'd love posing for that painting. Me, total, unapologetic whore; proudly presenting my alternative vision of earthly pleasures,

wealth, and joy; contrasting my in-your-face message to pathetic losers' vows of chastity and poverty. That's me, George: Quintessential bad girl; whore to my core; bad to the bone; wild; wanton; and proudly so. You bet."

"No boundaries for you, Marty? None whatsoever?"

"No boundaries, George, my eyes were opened by Mother. My scales fell away. I took my religious teachings to the 'Returns, No Sale' window. I cashed them in. I've discovered something better: freedom of choice. Ever since my geometry teacher demonstrated the sustaining joys of loving cunnilingus; acquainted me with all the angles, I've craved oral sex. I love the long-lasting, intimate orgasms my partners give me. I feel no shame or guilt about it. Teacher taught me well. He revealed those erotically titillating secrets that complete a woman's romantic needs; made me feel like a whole sexual human being. I positively adored his tongue. How relaxed and divine I felt while he gave me so many beautiful orgasms! He was the best! Teacher of the year! Oral sex was that last major boundary blocking me from achieving total whoredom. Teacher shattered that boundary. Marshawn and I have since refined what teacher taught me. We've made oral sex better than ever. I'm now an uninhibited, full spectrum, immoral whore.

"But, as I was explaining, George, my greatest, fondest love will always be penises. I adore male penises. I love being surrounded by them. I love having my hands on them, having them in my mouth; and I especially love feeling them inside my vagina. I simply, totally love them; and I know that making love with penises, and feeling that erotic intimate bond to my partner, while he ejaculates inside me; or onto my mouth and lips, will always bring my greatest romantic happiness.

"I need that feeling of bonding, George. It's unselfish. I'm ecumenical. I bond with many lovers. And, I must bond often. It confirms who I am and makes me feel validated as a woman. I live for

that sexual bond. It's eternal with me. I never forget or stop loving my partners. I'm a hopeless romantic nympho; always in love. And, I desperately need that love that my partners' penises share with me. It's my spiritual worshipping thing. It compensates for the love I never got from Mother. There, now you know how my obsession with penises began."

George was early middle aged; rugged features, tall, well-muscled, with tawny hair and clear blue eyes. He wondered about making love with Marty. Bertie still loved him; but her former intense passion flames had dimmed. They were now a platonic ember glow. Bertie was gravitating toward lesbian love. Her sexual interests were focused on young Marty. George intuited that he needed to yield to Bertie's newest obsession. He admitted to himself that his interest in Marty had been sparked; and his sparks were smoldering.

If he were ten years younger, Marty might have eagerly seized him as a partner. He was no longer a well-muscled stud muffin with sculpted abs, but he was still a passable lover. George understood Marty's signal. She had clearly stated her preference of penises to oral sex. He wondered: *'Was Marty indirectly telling me that she'd prefer making love with me to cunnilingus from Bertie? Was she telling me that she knew I could please her both ways?'* He started looking forward to their practice sessions.

He had detected a telltale romantic invite in the young woman's eyes. Unexpectedly, it revealed her personal interest: *'Can she act with her eyes that well? Are her signals that refined, that elusive, that suddenly penetrating?'* He couldn't be sure; but he could not deny the hope and lust passion that her signal had sparked within him: *'Her eyes captivate. They're emotive, beguiling. They draw me ever closer to her flame; capture my imagination, reduce my will power to the level of a moth's trance-like obsession.'* He dreamed for a moment that he was Harold, the obsessed love-sick poet on the golf course green. *'How delightful Marty's love making must have been for that young man!'* George could only fantasize: *'How wonderful that must have been! Could I dare do more than fantasize? How could any man not fall head over heels in love with Marty? How could I, myself, not?'*

He sensed that Marty empathized with his situation. Obviously, the young vixen was highly intelligent. She had to be, to be able to compartmentalize morality and lovers the way she did; and not allow antiquated taboos to hobble her freedom. Equally obvious, she was keenly focused on making money. She had declared herself free of any inhibitions that might slow her ascent to that goal. *'One could do worse than ride her coattails to fame,'* George reasoned.

George intuited that the young whore understood the situation perfectly. Bertie had placed them in the doorway to romantic involvement. Bertie had already told him that she expected him to fall in love with Marty. That should be of no consequence to Marty. He sensed there was an eagerness about her; a desire to bed him. He told himself that should not surprise him:

'She's a nymph. Nymphs love to make love.'

He detected Marty's faint aphrodisiac scent of gardenia. His eyes traveled to her gorgeous legs. He fantasized in more particular ways:

'What wondrous pleasures would she open to me? How many bedrooms watched her vagina work its irresistible magic? How many men breathed these same inviting wafts of her delicious pheromones? How many virtuous marriages has she toppled, like so many unstable domino towers? How many families has she crushed and pulverized into dust?

'I fully understand Bertie's wants and needs. But, will I be strong enough to not lose my mind over this delicious sexpot? Is she interested in knowing me as a friend or was my hand's placement simply

her Pavlovian reflex? After I actually make love with her, will I be able to control my burning lust for her? Will I be able to watch her with her other lovers and not have jealousy fits?

'I know that she will not be loyal to me. Fidelity has never been a consideration for her. Likely, it never will be. Will I be able to deal with that? How can I possibly MAKE love with her and not fall INTO love with her?

'Consider. Her approach to love is completely backwards from other women's approaches. That makes it even more important to understand what drives her. Most women discover their interest in a man. They begin liking him as a trusted friend. They see a future with him; then, and only then, intimacy may follow. Not Marty. She enthusiastically dives immediately into intimacy. Sex first! She tries out the sexual attributes of the man. Experiencing intimacy with him is like trying on a pair of shoes. Only after she's satisfied that the man is handsome enough, strong enough, and creative enough, does it occur to her to consider him as a real person.

'Until then, her lover may as well be a side of beef hanging in a meat locker. I've heard of nymphomaniacs before; but she is the first nympho I've actually known. Her condition must be a learned behavior that grew out of her mental disturbance. This is the first woman I've known whose entire life is centered on sex. Her shrink encourages her promiscuity; tells her to have even more sex, with even more lovers. That counseling advice is beyond incredible. I wonder if that shrink also has sex with her? Probably! I suppose I'm entering a world where nothing should surprise me.

'In time I suppose I'll discover how Marty fits me into her world. Will she regard me as a real person with an honest connection to her? Will I mean anything, at all, to her; or will I be just another available penis when she decides that I'm her present choice to fuck? Will she think of me as a trusted confidant, share thoughts and laughs and sorrows with me; or will her mind label me as a side of

aging beef; located fifth row back from the front of her meat locker;
hanging in column three, when counting her columns of lovers from
right to left?

'Was Bertie's experience with that butterfly real, or was she hal-
lucinating? Was this minx sent by the spirits to acquaint me with a
level of righteous human immorality that exists on some nebulous
plane in my mind; a place I have never contemplated, until now?
Am I commanded by these spirits to obey my lust cravings; climb
up there and become enlightened; or will my journey doom me to
perdition? What has Bertie's butterfly gotten me into?'

Before this afternoon's sun would set, George would stop
thinking about where he might be placed in Marty's meat locker.
He'd realize his inhibitions served no purpose. He'd fully express
his sexual attraction to his budding obsession. George's lips would
flutter up Marty's legs like desperate moth's wings, seeking nirvana's blinding light. They'd reach her deliciously juicy peach.
There, they would quench George's thirst for clarity of purpose.
He'd quench his immediate obsession by performing cunnilingus;
as dazzled and captivated as any hopelessly impassioned moth,
self-fastened to Marty's tantalizing beacon.

All his other thoughts and equivocations would slip away. He'd
discover he desperately needed the irresistible relief that Marty
gave him. Her sensational, loving vagina would refocus his life's
purpose. Marty's iniquitous pelvis would thrust her juicy butterfly
lips against his lips. Her purrs of erotic encouragement would lift
him above his cares and stresses. With Marty, he would flutter.

He'd lost his daughter. He had indulged Bertie's obsession with
this gorgeous unapologetic immoralist. His self-control would
undoubtedly waiver, then completely collapse as his attraction
to the nymph would grow ever stronger, until his passion for her
would rule his very reason for living. His eyes now expressed his
bundled emotions to Marty's curious face. Her eyes questioned his:

'Do you want me, George? I think you do.' Her dream pools invited him to dive into her world. *'Are you afraid to love me? Are you afraid you'll fall in love? Don't be afraid, George. I won't hurt you. Everything will be all right.'*

Her eyes signaled seduction; her head nod assured George that she understood his needs. George's soul resonated with her offering. It was primed to sweep away its emasculated hurts. He needed the intimacy offered by the tart. Need overwhelmed inhibition.

Hadn't Bertie assigned him to partner with the sex pot for porn practice? Why shouldn't he accept Marty's silent invitation? He'd soon be before her opened legs, kissing her thighs, reaching higher with his yearning hands, happily discovering she'd already anticipated him.

He'd notice that she wore a transparent bikini bottom, a signal that she expected his visit. She was willing, waiting; completely relaxed and casual about it. After all, sex was her business and Bertie had ordained their carnal relationship. George wouldn't waste time. His treasure waited behind Marty's transparently-veiled, fig leaf bikini bottom. There was no need for awkward formalities. One string pull; and her leaf would fall away. George's future thoughts would recall this moment as his decision moment,

'It had to happen sometime. Why wait? Why stage it? Why not now? Will Bertie regret what she's asked of me? Bertie's been under great stress since we lost Amanda. I sometimes wonder if she's in her right mind. Is Bertie's obsession over Marty a temporary thing or; like Amanda, have I also forever lost Bertie, too? Is this entire enterprise Bertie's way of getting back at the world for what it took from her? I can't think my way through all this. There's only one way to understand myself, and where I fit into this situation. It's time. I'll unwrap my present and enjoy her!'

George's lips would lead his tongue to Marty's vaginal lips. Paradoxically, Marty's insatiable, welcoming vagina, the focus of

Bertie's obsession, would also become George's refuge from Bertie's mocks. It would become his well-spring; his rejuvenation. Marty and George's first tryst would be followed by many more; each more loving and delightful than the one before. They were fated to become lovers of a conditional sort; often in the company of Bertie, while they practiced Marty's performing roles; but also lovingly, tenderly, when they were alone.

Predictably, Bertie, George and Marty would spend many hours practicing threesome combinatorial positions, under Bertie's demanding coaching. All their romps were done to advance Bertie's glorious cause: to polish Marty's breathtaking explicit erotica until she was acknowledged as the world's most highly acclaimed sex goddess of intimate artistry.

George and Marty would develop a delicate camaraderie; and something far greater. They would become emotively attached, inseparable caring friends; and that would gradually, give rise to honest love. Marty would rescue George from Bertie's emasculation. George would care about Marty, as a person, much more than as a sex object. And, Marty would empathize with George, discovering his qualities as her mature male confidant, as well as her practice penis.

"Marty, Bertie and I will try to help you." George's mind returned to the present. He nodded an understanding yes while putting his hand on Marty's shoulder. He appreciated that the troubled young woman had revealed a small part of herself. He felt love's stirrings. They drew him closer to her. He was grateful for that closeness.

"Ahem, you two," Bertie was chomping at her bit. She wanted to get back to business. She sensed the beginnings of bonding between Marty and her husband. That was what she had stated she intended all along; but she prided herself on discipline first. The coach within her said:

'Make them pay attention to their studies. It's not time for them to have sex, not just yet. I'll decide when it's time.'

"Let's turn back to film studies, George. In this next segment we have an orgy scene in progress. See Marty's huge open-mouthed smile, George? See how happy she is? She's absolutely gleeful, surrounded by so many penises. She loves stroking and sucking them, while those men kiss her, rub their hands over her sex, and fondle her breasts. She loves their attention. She invites it and absorbs it like a sponge. See the anticipation in her face? She can't wait to fuck those men."

The film scenes and Bertie's narration was making George hard.

"Oh, look, George. Did you catch that? I loved how she smiled in shameless, naughty delight at the very instant that penis she was sucking shot its cum onto her tongue, didn't you George? She positively loves what she does George. How many people can say that? She's thrilled to be an incorrigible lascivious whore. She's found her bliss, providing erotic pleasures to her partners and viewers.

"Now look at these next frames, George. We're going to use this pose many times in our future films. Notice how she's sitting with her fingers lifting her nipples, while keeping her legs widespread? Marty, I'm going to want you to pose like that; lying back slightly, like you're in a recliner. We'll put pillows behind you to make it easier for you. That will make your invite seem even more natural. I love your broad smile in this scene. We're going to put a pink filter over the spotlight and highlight your vagina when you do that. That lighting effect will make the gossamer-like damask pattern of your butterfly-winged tattoo appear to be even more life-like. That will contrast your craven hunger for sex spectacularly with your innocent, ivory white thighs. It will fascinate viewers' eyes and draw their focus into your eager vagina.'

George got harder. Bertie continued:

"You'll keep your legs spread widely open, just like that, for about thirty seconds after your fingertips leave your nipples. Then you'll outstretch your arms to the camera. I want you to imagine that your fingertips are the tips of a vine. You are reaching out to entwine your viewers. Beckon with your fingers to your viewers; signaling that you want them to come closer to you. Imagine they are falling into your arms' embrace.

"Then, ever so slowly, change your smile to a coquettish, teasing kiss; and while doing that subtle kiss, tilt your pelvis very slightly upward. Our pink spotlight filter will slowly condense the light beam into a tight focus on your vagina's outer lips. Everything else will fade away. Your pelvic lift and the condensing light beam will make your love channel appear larger than life. The camera will do a close up and hold there for a good thirty seconds. Imagine you are lifting your vagina up; presenting it to your viewers' eyes; and psychologically, placing it against their lips, like you are presenting them the Holy Grail to drink from; and to savor its sweet, tasty offering. Imagine you are offering what every man MUST aspire to attain, to experience the ultimate in intimacy.

"The effect we'll create is that you are showing your viewers the pathway to an argosy's endless bounty ship, where they can revel in unsurpassed sinful pleasures. We will create a backdrop scene that will transport the viewers' eyes away from the background and rivet their gaze onto your adorable lust magnet. Our lighting scheme will have their eyes fixated on it, as if the night sky has suddenly lost the light from all its stars; leaving only one, deliciously illumined, pink pathway light that offers the human mind its escape.

"Your viewers will intuit that by embracing you, by comingling their breaths with yours, by embracing you and joining their flesh to yours; and by surrendering their souls to you while copulating with you, they WILL attain nirvana. Do you agree with my scene idea, Marty? Do you believe you can do that?"

"Yes, Bertie, and double yes!" Marty nodded her enthusiasm. She acknowledged Bertie's talent. Her new porn coach was beyond smart. She was crazy smart. *"You're brilliant, Bertie. Of course, I'll do it."*

George's penis strained with uncommon hardness.

"Good, that's my sweet baby," continued Bertie. *"Now let's move ahead a few frames. Look George, look how Marty smiles, see how happy her face becomes as this next huge penis begins to penetrate her outer lips. See how happily she laughs during this orgy scene? Written all over her face is her rapture of feeling three penises entering her, simultaneously; while four more men surround her, anxiously awaiting their turn. That scene is so real I can feel myself in it, experiencing the same thrusting she's enjoying. She's creating the most palpable intimacy art ever, George. It's spectacular artistry!*

"Nowhere else in the entire world of art can I experience these same emotions that Marty projects while she's writhing during her cascading orgasms. It's profoundly stunning artistry. She leaves me speechless. Her carnal joys are so beautifully natural and expressive! My emotions are drawn into hers. She's so emotive and loving with her partners! It's not work for her, George. By making love with seven men at the same time; by giving her love to all of them the way she does, she lives the erotic fulfillment of romantic ecstasy.

"This film should make every woman who sees it want to experience orgy pleasures for herself. Wouldn't you agree, George?"

"Yes, I think so. But you'd be the better judge of that, Bertie. You're the woman."

"Yes, I know, George. Now look! Marty's mind and her entire being are consumed within the pleasures she's getting. It shows! She's releasing the full expressions of her feelings. Her skin looks naturally healthy, don't you think, George?"

"Beautiful skin, check." George injected a touch of sarcasm. He couldn't remember a time when his penis had ever been this hard.

"She looks like a woman should look while she's having sex; like she's loving it.   She's totally free of stresses and completely relaxed and natural. She looks happy like that during her orgies. Her face and body express her inner feelings. Her films are fantastic! I'm thrilled for her. She's a prima donna, a virtuoso!"

"Pay attention to her smile, George. Study it closely. See that flash of joy captured during that sudden convulsive contraction of her pelvis? That's her face telegraphing that she's experiencing an orgasm. Now, focus on her vagina, George."

"Eyes focused, check." George's limbic zone was flooded. There was only one thing on his mind.

"Don't be a smart ass, George. That little fluid trickle; can you see it? That proves she came, George! Our Marty came! She just had a lovely orgasm from that penis stroking her clitoris. Now, watch her smile when that partner withdraws his penis. Listen closely. Hear how she moans and giggles and whispers to him:

'I love how you fucked me.'

"She said exactly what a woman in love should say, George. She first looks at his cum seeping out of her and then she looks into his eyes, and then she beams the most wonderful smile I've ever seen. Have you ever seen a more loving and caring smile on any woman's face, George?"

"No, not unless it's your smile watching her," George spoke without taking his eyes off the screen.

"Her smile is PRICELESS, George. She adores what that man just did. That smile says she accepts his love flowing into her, and she really, truly loves him. Her smile to him is telling him that what he did was wonderful and special; and she adores him for loving her so beautifully. This is sensational erotic art, George. I cannot teach the emotions she has. She's a natural.

"I think, because of her nymphomania, she can express a deeper dimension of honest love that other porn stars cannot replicate. She

creates the very finest art! The loving feelings people get while watching her is why her fans go crazy over her films. It's why they love her so much. It's because SHE IS love.

"George, listen to me. We have an opportunity here. We're going to create a brand. Marty, I need you to agree with what I'm about to propose. Here's my plan. You and I are going to go back over all the hit tunes from the 1950's to the 2020's, hundreds of tunes. We're going to select the one hundred recordings out of all the recordings that resonate with your emotional moods. I don't care what mood the music stirs inside you. It could be romance, jealousy, anger, sentimental feelings, lust, erotic feelings, happiness; whatever hundred songs, among all recordings, that give you your strongest mood feelings. Are you following me?"

"Yes, Bertie, I'm following."

"Good. Then we're going to take each recording and use it as our background music for your new series of porn films. I will describe the setting for each film. I will write the scripts for the films; and I will choreograph the script and the film scenes to flow smoothly with the music. Once we have a film choreographed, you will do a series of practice walk-throughs with George and your other partners; until you have your emotive expressions and your positions and your fornication and fellatio rhythms in perfect synchronization with the music. We'll select only the most handsome, most physically endowed male and female partners for this work. We'll interview hundreds and select only ten or twenty. Then, we will practice your film scenes until you are performing them perfectly with your partners, understand?"

"Yes, Bertie, I understand. This sounds exciting."

"These films will be different from your previous films in a very important way. In these films we're going to be trying extra hard to make your fans like you as a person."

"They already like me, Bertie."

"No, they love you. They obsess over you. There's a difference. In these films they're going to see how comfortable and innocent and sweet you are, while you're seducing; and while you are making love. They're going to feel very comfortable watching you do what you do, because they're going to know that you feel good, and honest, and wholesome, and confident about your romances. You're going to be the girl next door who can do nothing wrong or bad. They will see a loving innocence about your personality; your face, your voice, everything.

"For every film, you're going to have the best beautician, hair dresser, manicurist, and pedicurist. Your face will be perfected with the best creams and blushes. Your skin will only be touched with the finest brushes and cosmetic pads. Your lipsticks will be the perfect color and shade for each scene. Your hair colorations will have the perfect streaks and highlights; as will your fingernails and toenails. I'll coordinate all this with our lighting crew. We'll get the perfect hues and subtle changes in the effects on your face, as your moods in your scenes change. And, I'll coordinate all this with your wardrobe. You are going to have the most erotic, sexiest wardrobe in all adult filmdom. Your fans will always see you in your latest, most titillating outfits and designer shoes. You, my dear sweet love, will always be a class act.

"And, we must especially not overlook your vagina and skin. You will have with you, wherever we film, a top-flight masseuse. He will keep you perfectly waxed, cream softened and lubricated. Your vagina will be pampered like no other. You will always be soft and lubricated with the finest oils. You will always smile your breathtaking smile when those penises penetrate you, because it will always feel wonderful. You will never cringe or express shock or consternation; only heavenly joy. You will receive frequent shoulder, neck, forearm, and finger massages. While you perform your awe-inspiring fellatio, you will always be completely relaxed, never strained in

the slightest. When your heavenly lips kiss the head of a penis, your fans will go crazy with adoration over your uninhibited, beautiful, relaxed, innocent face. It's these endless attentions to details that will make all the difference. Bertie will work her magic with you.

"You'll be the girl that every man will compare to the woman he knows. You'll have the wholesome, honest characteristics that he's looking for in the woman he takes home to meet Mother, to tell Mother that he loves you; and wants to marry you; especially after seeing your films. You'll be that girl of his dreams. He'll imagine the woman he presents to his mother is you. Can you do that?"

"Yes, Bertie, I can be sweetness and honesty and innocence. I love playing those roles."

"Good, you'll be very successful. I know you will. It will be the hardest, most demanding work you've ever done; but also, fun, and highly rewarding, I promise. We will release the films as we make them; gauging how our marketing is going. When we have all hundred films created, we will market them as Marty's Premium Intimate Artistry Films. We'll package them in bundles of ten each, for twenty dollars per film, or two hundred dollars per set of premium pornographic films; or four easy payments of fifty dollars each; or, your fans can purchase the entire hundred film library for one thousand eight hundred dollars; a ten percent savings; and we'll offer an additional five percent discount for pre-orders, if they commit to purchase before the twentieth film is produced. They will receive the most exquisite, delicious, salacious, heart-warming explicit erotica ever produced. Your Premium Films will become a must-have collection for every porn aficionado.

"Your fans will go wild over them. These hundred films will firmly establish you forever, as the world's number one intimate artisan. The films will separate you from all other porn stars. Your work will move your porn ranking millions of miles ahead of whomever is second. Your films will command over ninety percent of

pornography's market share. You'll be idolized and placed on a pedestal in the mind of every red-blooded male in the world. You will become world famous as the porn star, extraordinaire. I will make it all happen for you. Are you with me on this?"

"Yes, Bertie, yes! A thousand times yes! I'll gladly do it. I want it, all of it, the work, the success, the fame, the money. I'll always be grateful to you. I'll always appreciate what you are doing for me. I'll do all the hard work; the practices. And every film will be my personal, most expressive best. I'll work with you and George and the partners you select; and I'll create the most wonderful awe-inspiring intimate artistry ever made. I can't wait to begin the work. I love you, Bertie."

"I love you too, Marty."

Bertie's imagination was fired. Her eyes were lust crazed.

More to come.

Oh my! BUTTERFLY CONFIDES revealed that Bertie is smitten with Marty. Is Bertie bereft from losing her child? Will offering Marty her coaching talents, her good will and even her husband, George, bring back the love of her lost daughter? Let's flutter on and find out where this obsession takes Bertie and George, as they create Bertie's revolutionary concept in brand awareness. Will Bertie's branding campaign cause social upheaval and disorder? Will marriages and institutions yield to our vixen's New Morality Standard? As the old social order gives way, not surprisingly, both George and Bertie develop a serious love interest in their new star. Marshawn will completely capitulate. He'll deliver his soul to Marty. He proves his love in a most astonishing way; thereby forsaking everything he once believed. Marty becomes an institution in her own rite. Secrets she never told anyone before are soon revealed; but David will take notice of a serious slip of her tongue. What does that mean? What is David capable of doing? Come, flutter with me, Melanie Monarch, as I narrate FLUTTER BRAND, the fifth book of THE SECRET BUTTERFLY (tm) SERIES.